KATHLEEN EAGLE

Fire and Rain

AVON BOOKS  NEW YORK

FIRE AND RAIN is an original publication of Avon Books. This work has never before appeared in book form. This work is a novel. Any similarity to actual persons or events is purely coincidental.

AVON BOOKS
A division of
The Hearst Corporation
1350 Avenue of the Americas
New York, New York 10019

Copyright © 1994 by Kathleen Eagle
Front cover art by Hiroko
Inside cover author photograph by Robert Knutson
Published by arrangement with the author
Library of Congress Catalog Card Number: 93-91646
ISBN: 0-380-77168-3

First Avon Books Printing: January 1994

AVON TRADEMARK REG. U.S. PAT. OFF. AND IN OTHER COUNTRIES, MARCA REGISTRADA, HECHO EN U.S.A.

Printed in the U.S.A.

RA   10   9   8   7   6   5   4   3   2   1

For Clyde, who gave me Eagle's wings

Prologue

Minneapolis, 1971

Cecily Metcalf closed her eyes and pressed the antique glass doorknob into her palm. With an almost imperceptible turn of the wrist she created in her mind a soft *click*, then a *creeeak*, and then the smell of stagnant attic air.

"Cecily, come look at this clock."

Quickly she set the doorknob back on the table beside its twin and glanced askance, as though she'd been on the verge of doing something illegal rather than just plain silly. Her mother's voice had a way of sweeping her musings aside, momentarily at least. Resenting the intrusion, she usually ignored the first summons, and her mother's interest often disappeared before meriting a second call. But that was because her mother's brain was a high-speed calculator, while Cecily's was a silver screen.

At the other end of the North Star Hotel's largest meeting room the auctioneer for the Twiss-Varner estate sale called for bids on lot number twenty. Cecily heard only snatches of the description of one of the brooches in the jewelry collection as she headed in her mother's direction, stopping to examine any old thing that caught her eye. She'd half hoped to find an inexpensive chair or a lamp to add character to her room at school, but this was not that kind of auction. The items for sale were no longer furnishings, but collectibles, or even investments.

Cecily never bought much anyway. Buying, acquiring, possessing—these were Mother's passions. Ever since Cecily could remember, she had been dragged along, or she had tagged along when Mother went antiquing. Cecily loved to touch. "Hands Off" warnings, whether printed or muttered absently by her ever-rummaging mother, had been wasted on her when she was a child. She had learned to love the feel of the worn corners of old things and to imagine old people once young, old times once new.

The polished planes of a brass lamp base warmed to Cecily's caress. Turn-of-the-century, she judged. Mother wouldn't be interested in it, but it felt well-used, like something people had come home to over the years, depending on it to be there, reaching for it in the dark. Darkness, even across countless years, was still the same.

"Mostly junk," Lorna Metcalf decided, turning her nose up at the lamp. "That's junk. I wish they'd get to that anniversary clock. It has a lovely, resonant chime."

Mother's assessment was never an opinion. It was fact. She knew her antiques. She knew dollar values right down to the penny. Cecily listened to the *ting-ting-ting* announcing the hour, and she nodded. It was a cold sound, befitting Mother's imperious taste.

Cecily moved away, drawn to a hundred-year-old brocade settee. She fondled the rose that was carved into the wood trim on the arched backrest, and she imagined a time when the piece was new. She pictured a young man draping his arm over the carved rose, sprawling restlessly when no one was looking. He was waiting to take his lady for a buggy ride. Cecily rubbed her thumb over the grooves in the wood as she imagined his thumb absently doing the same thing in the same spot a century ago. Maybe he was her age then— nineteen, nearly twenty. Maybe he was thinking about marrying the young woman upstairs—the one who was fussing with a curl that wouldn't behave in her otherwise perfect upsweep. The man would have been impatient to get on with it. The buggy ride. The wedding. Their life together.

And he would be dead now.

"Oh, this is a nice piece, but it'll go too high," Lorna said as she stooped to examine the tufted seat closely. "You can tell it's been stored for years. Carefully, too. Not much fading, no holes." With a practiced hand she tested the spring in the upholstery. "Horsehair. It'll go high."

Cecily nodded dutifully. She wasn't interested in buying the piece, but it was her mother's custom to disclose her wisdom routinely, just in case anyone besides Cecily was listening. Lorna knew full well that her practical information was lost on her daughter, who tuned it out along with the mutterings of browsers and the auctioneer's staid pronouncement that another old treasure had found new ownership.

Moving along the line of tables, Cecily found a petit-point dresser set. She examined the hairbrush, hoping in vain to discover the color of the original owner's hair. She gripped the handle and imagined putting the natural bristles to use on hair as long as her own. She wondered if the brush had ever been packed in the old steamer trunk the auctioneer had shoved aside to make room for the more elegant offerings.

The trunk beckoned, drawing Cecily closer. Hardly aware of her surroundings at all now, she knelt beside it and touched the desiccated leather. Oddly, it warmed her hand. She tested the hammered tin cornices and the brass fittings, which felt as though they had been sitting in the sun. With a forefinger she traced the keyhole, and it expelled a suggestive breath into the lungs of her imagination. This trunk had taken a trip once. A marvelous journey that had changed someone's life.

Between sales now, the auctioneer noticed her interest. Cecily felt his attention before she raised her chin and met his eyes. The look he gave her seemed to pose a threat, and she wasn't sure why.

"The trunk is locked, and there is no key." The rotund auctioneer stared at her as he made the announcement, seemingly out of the blue. With a pudgy hand sporting three chunky gold rings, he signaled to an assistant. "We're about to auction off a mystery here. That trunk is probably full of memories. The heirs chose not to break the lock. We're told it was a long-standing taboo."

"It's probably full of mildew," Lorna muttered.

Cecily turned, surprised by her mother's hostile tone. Another threat. She wondered at her own sudden inclination to defend this trunk as though it were a living thing about to be hoisted to the auction block.

"They know what's in it," said a woman who was seated near the platform in one of the chairs occupied by the more serious buyers. "Who'd sell it without checking for valuables first?" She glanced at Lorna. "I think you're right. Mildew and mouse droppings. What I heard from one of the Varners was that a Twiss ancestor owned it. A girl who went out to the Dakotas and got swallowed up by all that empty prairie." She illustrated with a wave of the hand. "Just disappeared."

Two assistants delivered the trunk center stage.

"Who'll bid five hundred?"

There was no response.

"So how did they get the trunk back?" Lorna whispered to the woman.

"Apparently her father returned to Minnesota. He was an Indian agent out there, back before the Black Hills gold rush and all that."

Lorna spared her daughter a pointed glance, then asked the obvious follow-up question. "Was the girl killed by Indians or something?"

"Probably." The woman shrugged. "*Disappeared* is what they said. Out there in the Dakota Badlands."

"Four hundred dollars," the auctioneer demanded, flashing his rings as he waved an index finger toward the crowd. "Do I hear four hundred?"

Still there was no response. Cecily felt a strange tension in her shoulders. The air around her seemed to grow thick and heavy, as though a storm were gathering right there in the hotel meeting room. There was something about that trunk, something that called to her, something that connected with her plans.

She, too, would be leaving for the Dakotas soon, no matter what her mother said. And she, too, was headed for an Indian reservation and a summer program she had read about and applied for without consulting her parents. So what if there was no pay involved? She had her own savings, and she had her scholarship. She was old enough to make her own decisions, her own plans. What she needed was a change of scene, just for one summer.

"Who'll give me two hundred dollars?"

The trunk absorbed Cecily's romantic fancy. It had taken a trip to the Dakotas with someone who had also made her own plans. She imagined it being loaded onto a train while a young woman hiked her long skirt above the top of one high-buttoned shoe and climbed aboard the passenger car. A young woman headed for Indian territory . . .

The auctioneer suddenly became vexed, as though the lack of bids were a personal affront. "Ladies and gentlemen, this is an intriguing piece of family history. This trunk has not been opened in who knows how many years."

"One hundred."

"Did I hear a hundred?"

Cecily lifted her hand shoulder height and nodded. Her face got hot in the light of the attention she'd just drawn to herself, but the trunk's strange magnetism held her fast.

"What are you doing?" Lorna hissed. "You're not going to *buy* that thing just because . . ."

Cecily pressed her lips together, but she was unable to suppress her smile when the auctioneer pointed her way and pronounced, "Sold."

She was awash in a sense of sudden and unexpected triumph, as though she'd just come up with the right answer without even hearing what the question was.

"Oh, *Cecily.*" The admonishment came complete with a disgusted-mother sigh. "Just because you heard the word *Indian.*"

"I'm just curious, Mother." Cecily flashed a self-satisfied smile. "I have a feeling about this trunk. I think it wants me." She waggled her eyebrows as she claimed the bidder's number from her mother's hand.

"*Wants* you," Lorna scoffed.

"Haven't you ever bid on a hunch?"

"I've never wasted a bid on a piece of junk. Nor would I waste a whole summer languishing out there in God's country when I could have a good summer job in an air-conditioned department store." Lorna dismissed the "intriguing piece of history" with one last scornful look. "If nothing else, I hope it gets you off this Indian kick."

The auctioneer signaled for the trunk to be placed at the disposal of its new owner, whom he spared a grateful glance. "Let us know what you find inside. Now the next item . . ."

"Look, Mother, here comes your clock."

"The next item," the auctioneer repeated for Lorna's benefit, "has kept time accurately, constantly, day after day, season after season, for over a hundred years . . ."

Part I

The land is parched and burning
Going and looking about me
A narrow strip of green I see.

The light glow of the evening
Comes, as the quail, flying slowly
And it settles on the young.
—PIMA SONG

Chapter 1

Wyoming Territory, Late Spring 1871

There was no station, no platform, not even a name. It was just a place on the boundless, spring-green plain where the Union Pacific train stopped to take on water and occasionally put off a passenger or two. But nobody would ever get off there unless somebody happened to be expecting him.

First to disembark were two soldiers, bound for Fort Laramie. One after the other their feet hit the dry brown hardpan, then they nearly tripped over each other as they turned, hands lifted like supplicants to the passenger car door. The young lady behind them had no patience for their assistance, but she uttered a "Thank you, gentlemen" as she hopped nimbly past them and mentally embraced the open spaces at last. Priscilla Twiss was bound for adventure.

"Dear girl, we have waited hours!"

The bellowing voice was music. Priscilla had seen his rubicund face through the window, and she'd waved, then lost sight of him as the train shuddered to a halt. He was shorter and wider than the other men gathered beside the tracks, but, as always, he let no one stand in his way. His arm shot past the gallant sergeant like a shepherd's crook, plucking his daughter from the small flock of men.

She sank into his plump, spongy embrace, forgetting

herself briefly with the kind of delighted squeal that befit a girl less than half her age. But she had not seen him in almost a year, and even though he'd been generous with his letters, no man's company pleased Priscilla more.

It was their customary hard, quick hug, too soon over. Her father patted her shoulder awkwardly as he cleared his throat. "Young soldier Erikssen there will claim your luggage."

"That one is mine," she told the tall, dusty corporal who had accompanied Indian agent Charles Twiss to meet the train. The corporal watched as the freight was unloaded, furtively eyeing her all the while for her signal. "The leather-bound trunk. It was perfectly free of dents when I left Minneapolis. Be careful with it." She flashed her doting father the kind of smile any other woman her age might have turned on the hardy and handsome young Erikssen. "It was a gift from Aunt Margaret."

The slighted soldier loaded the trunk into Twiss's buckboard, then stood ready for a second notice.

"You managed with a single trunk?" Charles tugged at the front of his vest, adjusting it over his paunchy midsection. "Your mother would have brought half a dozen, at least."

"For a summer?" Priscilla tucked her hand in the crook of her father's elbow. Bits of information about her mother were always fondly squirreled away in her head in the hope that someday she might put the pieces together and have a whole person to remember. "Ah, but then would my mother have agreed to fill your list of special requests? Your cigars, your tin of sweets, your—"

Charles Twiss's aging eyes suddenly brightened boyishly. "You found the French mints?"

"*And* the books you wanted, along with a few other surprises." She squeezed her father's arm and patted the sleeve of his black frock coat. "Two new novels, Father. One written by a woman."

"That should provide some entertainment out here in the desert. I hope you had room for some clothes."

"Of course." She pointed to a box that had been unloaded from the train and glanced at the corporal, whose face expressed his readiness to do her bidding. "Yes, that crate. That's the goodie box. Thank you."

Clothes were not so important. What *was* important was that after much pleading her father had given his permission for her to spend the summer with him, that she had finally arrived, that she had brought some of his favorite amenities, and that now they would have time to talk over every curiosity that entered her mind, as they had since she was a child. Elated, Priscilla squeezed again, reassuring herself as she assured him, "I have all I need in my trunk and room to spare for the things I collect while I'm here."

Charles laughed merrily. "And what would you propose to collect out here, dear girl? Sod?"

"Perhaps. I might press some wildflowers, among other things."

"Flowers are among the things you'll sorely miss. And trees."

"Then I must discover what grows in their place."

"Thistles and cockleburrs."

"I can't believe that, Father." She turned her back on the puffing train and stretched her arm toward the distant meeting of the yellow-green hills and blue horizon. "And I can hardly believe I'm actually here. I've been watching through the window mile after mile, and I've seen that it's true. That sky goes on forever."

"So do the snakes. Rattlesnakes. Laid end to end, I expect they would reach the moon," he declared as he signaled the corporal to stand by.

"You won't discourage me, so don't bother to try. Had you denied your permission, I would have come anyway this time. 'Go where no one else will go and do what no one else will do.' That's my new motto."

"Of course, we both know it's hardly original," Twiss said absently as he glanced at the last piece of cargo that had been unloaded. "The founder of that female seminary you've set your sights on said it first."

"Mary Lyon, yes. One more year at Saint Catherine's, and then I intend to make my application. That box isn't mine," she added. "Your article in the *North American Review* made no mention of snakes or thistles."

"No, but my next one will. I must make it perfectly clear that this land is inhospitable. The hordes of immigrants with their plows and prospectors with their pickaxes . . ." He scowled impatiently at the red car, but the door stood empty. The unloading was done. "I was expecting a shipment of ladies' clothing to arrive in your company."

Priscilla shifted her glance to the waiting buckboard. The leather-bound humped lid was all that was visible of her trunk. "I wouldn't call it a shipment."

"From the Mission Board. They promised . . ." His scowl deepened. "I can't seem to get anything I need out here. Anything I send for, *anything* anyone promises to provide, be it the church or the government"— he flapped his arms against his sides like an exasperated penguin—"is waylaid or withheld or just plain stolen."

"I wasn't," Priscilla said, smiling. "And no one told me about any ladies' clothing."

"How can I function here as Indian agent unless I have goods and services to provide?" It wasn't a question he meant for her to answer, or even to understand. She soon would, of course, because he would go on sputtering until his frustrations with bureaucratic ignorance were vented. Then he would wax more philosophical, and therein she would find her father's answers. They were answers she would respectfully consider, certainly, once she saw for herself what the problems were.

"I simply asked them to round up a few dresses and whatnot, box them up, and put them on the train with you," Charles explained, patting her hand by way of dismissing an oversight she'd had no part in. "I have a notion that we can convert the women to our ways first, and the men will follow." He smiled admiringly at his daughter. "What choice would they have? What choice does any poor, foolish male have when the women in his life set their hearts on a course? We give them their way."

"It wasn't easy getting mine this time," she said as he handed her up to the buckboard seat.

"You fellows may put your gear in the wagon and climb aboard," Charles told the sergeant and his traveling companion. "Plenty of room, plenty of room."

The two soldiers sat in the rear, using Priscilla's baggage as a backrest, while the young corporal mounted his sorrel gelding and rode out ahead of the wagon. It would take two long days to reach Fort Laramie, which was still several miles from Twiss's agency. The railroad, completed two years before, had brought the frontier within easy reach of the civilized world—the world for which the Sioux were not ready. Not as far as Charles Twiss was concerned. But getting them ready, according to his own writings and heartfelt espousals, was his job.

The train's huffing and groaning faded into the distance as the buckboard rumbled over the wagon ruts. Amid the tall grass and a huge canopy of sky, the song of grasshoppers and the tweedle of ground-nesters replaced the noise of the smoking interloper. Suddenly the only connection between the world of shops and houses and the rugged land that surrounded her was empty railroad track. Priscilla had never felt so utterly small.

The wind seemed like a living presence rather than a force of nature. It toyed teasingly with her hair, working small strands free from the pins and from her firmly anchored velvet hat. She tucked her generous skirt tightly around her thighs, shoving the bulk of the fabric between the wagon's seat and her own for cushion, and she tingled with trepidation as she soaked up the astonishing sensations of vastness.

"What were you about to say about the immigrants, Father? Something about the inhospitable land and the plows and pickaxes."

"Only that they must stay on the road that skirts Indian land. The Holy Road, the Sioux call it. The Bozeman Trail. They must continue on their way West, as the treaty promised. This is no place for land-hungry farmers."

"It isn't?" She lifted her hand to shade her eyes as she glanced at the reins in her father's gloved hands, feeling safe in his charge. "But you say that the Indians must become farmers." It took a moment to file mentally through the many writings she knew almost by heart. "In your treatise on—"

"They will. Given time, they will learn to farm. But we must have time to turn them from the primitive to the productive." He turned to her, suddenly excited by the prospect of being able to share with her, face to face, some piece of what he'd experienced since he had accepted the appointment a year ago. "They are like children. I am Father Agent, you see, and they are very much like children. They must be trained. They must be *re*trained, broken of their old habits and taught—"

"It's their old habits that interest me." Here was the difference between them, she acknowledged privately when he gave her that challenging look of his. Her chosen field versus his. It was a friendly difference and one they had often discussed, taking their pleasure in the debate, even though *his* theories, finally, were never debatable. "I think we naturalists must learn about them before you missionaries civilize them completely, Father."

"Then you'd better be a very quick study, my dear. You haven't much time. The Laramie Treaty guaranteed that the army would protect the reserve from white encroachment, but the army is quite simply here to protect the railroad." He goaded the team along with a flick of the reins. "You haven't much time to observe them in their 'natural state,' my dear budding naturalist, because your father is making a good deal of progress with them, thank the Lord. The army would as soon see us fail."

"They want war?"

"They've had war with Red Cloud. It was not successful, just as I said it would not be."

"Often and eloquently," Priscilla recalled dutifully. No one could deny that her father was a humanitarian. Under President Grant, political sway in Indian Affairs was shifting away from the War Department as more men like Charles Twiss received appointments as Indian agents. "The Quaker agents" they were called because many of them were missionaries or, like her father, Christian men of letters who had taken up the challenge of Indian reform.

"There are those in the War Department who believe

that the complete extermination of these people is the most expedient way to deal with the Indian problem," he continued. "Extermination and war are not the same thing."

"No," Priscilla agreed. "Indeed not." She'd heard it all before, and she believed it heartily. But at the moment she was more interested in the sea of grass that rolled in every direction as far as the eye could see. "It is a desolate country, but so beautiful in its desolation."

"When you return to civilization, you must speak of the desolation, but never the beauty, dear girl," he admonished. She responded with a quizzical look, and he sighed. "The immigrants only complicate matters."

It was called the Red Cloud Agency, named for the Oglala Sioux leader whose people were assigned to its care and supervision. But Priscilla saw it as her father's agency. He was the man in charge. He took pride in showing her the improvements he had made, assuring her that upon his arrival he had found the place in a shambles. The buildings were few. Except for the log house that served as residence and agency office, they were poorly constructed of rough lumber, and the repairs that had been made stood out on them like bandages. But the facility was at least in working order now, Charles said. The sawmill and the shingle machine had been repaired, and permanent houses could be built as soon as more tools arrived.

Red Cloud and his people were willing to pitch their camps close to the agency, which Charles deemed a good start toward the fixed settlement of an ancient nomadic people. He was pleased with the way many of the younger men had taken an interest in using the blacksmith's forge. He wasn't much of a laborer himself, he admitted, but he was certain that honest physical labor would turn his charges into good American citizens.

Priscilla, too, was proud of her father's accomplishments, especially since they were a little out of his league. But the fact that her scholarly father would doff his hat and roll up his sleeves was all the more proof of his devotion to the Indian cause. There would be no half measures on her part, either. She was the scholar her father had raised her to be, and her interests ran parallel to his. Charles Twiss was determined to mold the Indian into a new man. Priscilla was eager to learn everything she could about the classic Indian before her father transformed him.

During her first few days she merely observed the comings and goings while she busied herself putting her father's living quarters aright. Her father met with two or three men each day, most of them leather-faced elders, who wore their graying hair in braids, their wool blankets hitched around their waists, and who came to the agency for a smoke and a cup of coffee. Few words were exchanged, but the men seemed comfortable in her father's presence, and he in theirs. After an hour or so the Indians usually left with a swatch of calico or a bag of dried fruit from the agency storehouse.

If they noticed her, they paid her little mind, so she went about her business, turning the little pantry off the kitchen into a room of her own. She made a yellow curtain for the window and put one of the small rag rugs she'd braided on the plank floor. There was room for the small bed with the rope mattress and feather tick, and her new trunk served as her chest of drawers.

"There, you see," her father said when he looked in on her progress. "That's what a woman does. That's what she *is*. The homemaker." He patted her cheek, and she wondered just what theory of his she had inadvertently given credence. "The maker of a permanent hearth and home. The woman is the key," he said as he wandered off again.

All she really wanted was a place to keep a few things. She had a project in mind, and all she needed was a desk, a few tools, and a key of her own. A key to gain access. A little nerve, perhaps. On the way to the agency she had seen the village from a distance, the smoke rising from the tipis, the horses grazing on the hillside. The Indians were there. Not just the old men, but younger ones, too. Women and children—whole families lived there. All she had to do was walk in and introduce herself.

But she busied herself in her father's house instead. She found a little table and a ladderback chair, and she commandeered an oil lamp from her father's room. He didn't need two. Pen and ink and journal were placed squarely in the center of the table. Now she had her own frontier study, and she was ready to begin her task. It was only a matter of determining the best way to approach it.

Captain Timothy Harmon was a fine military gentleman whose pleasure rides from Fort Laramie to the agency had become more frequent since Priscilla had moved in. He was at least ten years her senior, and his demeanor toward her tended to be more paternal than her own father's, which made for proper, if prosaic, drawing room conversation.

"Would you care for more port, Captain?" Priscilla offered. At his nod, she poured a second glass from the cut-glass decanter she remembered adding to her father's packing crate well over a year ago. She had given it to him for Christmas, and it was one of the many small things she'd slipped into his bags so that he'd have a scrap of home, a bit of comfort, a remembrance of his only off-spring.

"One of Father's requirements in granting me permission to come was that I bring a supply of his favorite cure for the lumbago." She slid her father a coy smile as she handed a glass of wine to the stocky, fair-haired captain. "Of course, he doesn't have lumbago."

"And I don't intend to get it. This is not a cure," Twiss acknowledged as his daughter served him a glass. "It's a prevention."

"President Grant's 'Quaker agents' have a penchant for spirits, then?" Harmon asked.

"That's just an expression," Priscilla quipped lightly. "We're not Quakers."

"But your father is still a missionary at heart."

"Among other things. Have you read his latest treatise on Americanizing the Indian in the *North American Review?*"

"I believe I've heard him recite it verbatim."

Twiss seated himself in his favorite cane-back rocker.

"The army doubts the so-called Quaker agent's ability to get the job done."

"I do respect you personally, sir. Your ideas amuse me, certainly." With a smile the captain raised his glass in mock deference, sipped, then expounded to impress Priscilla. "In the end, the job will be done by soldiers, as it must be when the interests of the Union are threatened."

"*That* war is over, I believe."

"You must have some memories of the Sioux massacre in '62, which was certainly a war against the good people of Minnesota, present company included."

"A botched bit of Indian policy, that," Charles pointed out. "If we want them to come to us for rations, we must supply them with rations. Otherwise, we can expect an uprising. It is that simple."

But the reference to the incident that always seemed to follow any mention of the word *Sioux* had arrested Priscilla's attention. "I was quite young," she said, remembering the tales that had trailed off into hushed whisperings, lest the children be haunted by nightmares. She had understood only that there was more, and it was much worse. Her own father, who was not in the habit of keeping secrets from her, had told her in worried tones that she was not to worry. "It started in Redwood Falls, some distance from where we lived," she told Harmon. "But, of course, it affected everyone."

"You must have been terrified." He took a step closer, as though he had some notion of protecting her. She avoided his eyes but glimpsed his brass buttons and his red sash cinched over dark blue.

"I remember the hangings. I didn't attend, of course, but I remember the newspaper accounts of the thirty-eight Sioux who were hanged, and later two chiefs." She had read them many times over and studied the photographs when her father wasn't looking, trying to imagine what it would feel like to be jerked by the neck at the end of such a thick rope.

"Over three hundred were sentenced," the captain recalled. "Which would hardly have paid for the deaths of over four hundred settlers, even if they'd strung up the whole bloody lot." He eyed Twiss. "A meddling missionary persuaded President Lincoln to commute most of those sentences. One of your 'Friends of the Indian' brethren, sir?"

"An Episcopal bishop, actually. Henry Whipple." Charles rested his head against the chair's high back and rocked backward once, then forward again. The chair creaked softly. "Good man, Henry. Compassionate man. As I said, there will be no such carnage here. We have a treaty."

"Not a good one."

Twiss dismissed the objection with a tilting of his glass. "Good enough for now. Red Cloud's people are content to collect their rations, do a little hunting, a little trading. Eventually we shall have them planting crops and sending their children to school. The Great Sioux Reserve is only a prelude. It is a place to start. The army's job is to keep the settlers and the prospectors out of the territory while we do the work that must be done."

Priscilla swept her black bombazine skirt to one side and took a seat on the bench near the desk, which was the most massive piece of furniture in the room. "You must read my father's earlier treatise on educating the primitive man, Captain. The only civilized policy for civilizing the Indian is to show him new ways."

"Kill the Indian, save the man," Harmon echoed as he shadowed her, ostensibly to examine the books on the shelf above the bench.

"Father certainly did not coin that phrase."

"No, but he embraces that philosophy. I have enjoyed your father's wit and his taste in cigars. He is the only man I know who had the foresight to cart a whole library to this godforsaken desert."

"You know mostly soldiers, I take it."

"Soldiers read." He touched the spine of a book consideringly, then smiled and seated himself beside her. "Some of them. Some of my men read in German, some Swedish, some Gaelic. Some not at all, of course, but you'd be surprised how many literate men hop off the boat and enlist in the army."

"To fight Indians."

"To make their way west. The Indians won't be here much longer, Miss Twiss. Your father espouses an interesting philosophy, but all points are moot. I'm here to protect the railroad, not the Great Sioux Reserve. He knows that."

A sardonic chuckle was Twiss's only confirmation as he rocked and sipped his port with eyes closed, as though he were savoring a cherished pleasure.

"Still, I enjoy our debates. I pay him frequent calls. Over the course of your stay, you will see me often. I hope that meets with your approval."

"My father does not wish to *kill* the Indian," Priscilla insisted, neither his hope nor her approval uppermost in her mind. "He would never kill anyone."

"There are many ways to kill, Miss Twiss. I deal in the literal sense, the one that brings death to the body. That is the cleanest, purest sense of the word." The captain studied the bits of sediment in the dark red wine still left in his glass, adding quietly, "And it is probably the least painful."

"My father truly would save the man." She glanced at the dear man in the rocker, whose chin had sunk into the folds of his vest.

"Would he, now?" Harmon quirked an eyebrow as he spoke instructively. "I am a soldier, Miss Twiss. If your father told me that tomorrow I must become a farmer, I would say, 'Over my dead body.' I would tell him that he would have to kill both the soldier and the man. And my father was a farmer, so the concept is not foreign to me. But your father would not save *this* man by putting a plow in his hand."

"You're saying it's better to kill them."

"I am saying that soon there will be no more Indians. They will fight, because that is their nature," he told her with a shrug. "And we will kill them."

Priscilla believed none of it. She decided that the captain's *we* was really a very small word.

Chapter 2

Journal Entry, June 7, 1871

    I am living on the Holy Road.

    That is the Indians' name for the trail that so many families are following to Oregon. One wonders what the Indians must think as they watch the wagons pass. It must appear to them as some kind of pilgrimage. The Red Cloud Agency (which is really Father's agency) is situated near the wide, lazy Platte, and I daresay the stream of travelers moves faster than the river. Fort Laramie is almost a day's journey by wagon. Father hopes to maintain a separate presence from the army in the minds of the Indians. It is the agent's job to dispense supplies and annuities from the government and to try to keep the peace between the white traders and the Indians. This is not an easy job, and Father says it would be best if the traders would simply stay away.

    The Indians come to Father with their complaints—mostly about the supplies, which are late (as usual, Father says). He is particularly distressed because some of the wild bands from up north have come to the agency, and he wants to gain their trust. He calls Red Cloud's people his "friendlies." They make their camps close to the agency or the fort, and they do not wander, except to hunt. Father says this is the first step in civilizing them. There are other bands of Western Sioux who refuse to be so cooperative.

I have met Red Cloud and two of his children. He is a dignified man and quite imposing. He wields a good deal of power. When the government proposed to move the agency to the Missouri River not long ago, Red Cloud refused to budge, and so here it stands. This is not good farmland, and Father is frustrated in his efforts, meager though they be, to initiate tilling and planting. I remind him that he's no farmer himself, but he insists that his Indians must grow a crop sooner or later. For now, though, we must feed them, for the buffalo, their staple for everything, are growing scarce. I have yet to see one, and Father says that the railroad has hired professional hunters to kill them, and so they are driven north. Father says that the farm must succeed the buffalo hunt, but I should like to witness one before that happens.

At first Father insisted that I must not visit the camps without him, but he has given up on that dictum since he has his own business to attend to. I have mine, and a summer is not much time in which to accomplish all that I hope to do. I intend to learn enough of the language so that I can make sense of my observations. (I shall have a wonderful treatise in the making, and if I can persuade Father to allow me to attend school back East, think what a fine showing I shall make!) I intend to earn the trust of these people also, and I've made a start with the children. That's how I got over my own inopportune shyness the first time I ventured into the camp alone. I took some stick candy and made friends with a group of young girls. I think I'm somewhat of a curiosity for them. Yesterday my new little friends included me in a game of Button-Button, which they played with plum pits. I managed to lose a hair comb, which I did not realize I had wagered.

If the supplies arrive today as Father hopes, he says there will be feasting, dancing, and horse racing, more games and gambling. Favorite pastimes of the Sioux, he says, which I'm to observe politely. Of their savage customs, he feels that gambling must be among the first to go by the wayside. Father is tolerant of drink, but he has always opposed gambling. I didn't tell him about the hair comb.

Whirlwind Rider labored alone over the blacksmith anvil, left behind by two of his cousins who said they had done enough for this day. He stood in the shade of the overhang that was attached to the side of the barn, but the fire in the forge blazed hotter than the midday sun, and sweat ran over his bare chest like rivulets of rain. His cousins might come back to the blacksmith lodge tomorrow, but Whirlwind Rider would not. Whatever iron points he would make would be made this day, for he would not be loafing around this place much longer.

Whirlwind Rider had told his mother plainly that he would not spend the summer at the agency waiting for the easy meat to come. He was a man of two villages, truly, but the way of the Minneconjou, his mother's people, agreed with him well these days. Takes The Gun, his Oglala father, had been killed in a raid for Crow horses when Whirlwind Rider was just a boy, and his mother was now married to Two Bear Claw, his father's brother. With uncles and cousins in both camps, Whirlwind Rider moved freely between one and the other. There was always a place to make his bed, always food for him in the cooking pot.

But more and more Two Bear Claw was content with the beef the agent supplied. More and more Whirlwind Rider hunted with the Minneconjou and wintered with them also. After the supplies came, his Oglala cousins promised purification and a hunt, but there would be no purification without a fast. It amused Whirlwind Rider to hear them say, "After the supplies come." Little Wolf, his fat-cheeked cousin, was the one who did not want to be away when the supplies came lest all the sugar be gone when he returned.

Whirlwind Rider had come to visit his relations, not to waste the summer waiting for agency rations. If they came soon, then he would join in the celebration, and he would easily beat LaPointe's challenge—his red roan horse against his brother-in-law's grain-fed pony, two heats out of three. But if not, Whirlwind Rider would leave his Oglala family to their waiting. Today he forged arrowheads. Tomorrow he would begin fastening the iron points to fletched shafts. Soon he would be making meat the old way.

It was the best use he'd found for the trader's iron skillet and for the blacksmith's forge. LaPointe had told him once that he had a knack for smithing. Whirlwind Rider had laughed and pointed out that having a talent for fixing iron shoes to the hooves of a good, swift horse was like being skilled at scaring off game. But Whirlwind Rider never scoffed once he'd found a use for something.

It was a task that made a man's eyes burn with sweat, but it was worth the effort. He liked the resounding *clang* the mallet made against the butt of the chisel as he cut his points from the hot iron. A horsefly buzzed around his slick shoulders. Unwilling to be distracted, he chased it away with the twitch of a muscle each time it tried to light. When the iron cooled, he turned to thrust it back into the forge. It was then that he noticed the woman standing in the shop roof's short shadow, quietly watching him.

She was pale—even more so than Agent Twiss—and as slender as a river willow. Adequate for a tree, but surely not for a woman, he thought as he met her gaze.

So, the white men do have women. He had heard they were carried in the tented wagons that followed the Holy Road, stopping over at the fort but never at the agency. Like his Minneconjou relations, he had avoided the wagons and the road itself. The promise had been made, and even though not everyone agreed with the Laramie Treaty, few Lakota people wished to tamper with the wagons as long as they kept to their trail and took their seed and their sicknesses with them.

But here was a white woman at the agency, making no secret about watching him, and when he caught her at it, she did not turn away. If their women were as bold as this, Whirlwind Rider thought, how was it that the white men had not killed each other off already? Such a woman would cause nothing but gossip among the Lakota. Her eyes were remarkably large and as blue as the high lakes of Paha Sapa, the sacred Black Hills to the north. Glass eyes, he thought. Like the trade beads his mother favored.

He exchanged his cool stare for her bold one. It was rude on both parts, but it stirred the blood in the way of counting coups with a swift strike and then turning, waiting, taunting an enemy still within range. There was a kind of bravery in her boldness, too. He saw no fear in her eyes. No aversion. Only curiosity and more than a little admiration, a look that would not have registered so plainly in a Lakota woman's eyes, but he recognized it. A man past his nineteenth winter who had not already received such looks from women, albeit more discreetly, was a poor excuse for a man.

He would be a poor excuse yet if he dropped the scrap of iron, as he nearly did when the woman, still staring into his eyes, suddenly smiled. She neglected to properly shield her mouth behind her hand, and her eyes flashed like water rippling in the sun.

"You don't, by chance, speak English, do you?" she asked.

Whirlwind Rider was astonished. He didn't recognize all the words, but he understood the question. He could have tested out the English he'd learned from LaPointe, but he neither flinched nor spoke. What kind of a woman would not only stare and smile, but speak first as well? He hoped she was not a troublemaker. The thought surprised him, but he hoped those pretty eyes had not been wasted on a woman without virtue. He pivoted slightly, easing the iron toward the fire, but he took his time about turning away.

"I'll let you get back to your work, then," she said. "I was just curious."

He understood the word *work*. White men were always working, according to LaPointe, and Agent Twiss said that the Lakota must *work*, too. And now this woman had said it. The notion didn't fit with what the agent had Whirlwind Rider's Oglala relations doing these days, loafing around and waiting for supplies. Neither did it fit with this woman, pale and soft as she looked. A smile flashed in her eyes as she backed away. It was the kind of a smile that might make a man do foolish things. A *white* man, of course.

Whirlwind Rider jerked his hand back from the hot iron. The skillet thumped to the ground, and the heat rushed from his hand to his face.

"Oh, my."

Inadvertently he retreated a step in response to her abrupt advance, compounding his humiliation.

"Did you . . ." The only threat in her voice was its tenderness. "Is it very bad?"

Bad, he knew. It was bad to be caught unaware, bad for a man to be clumsy in the presence of a woman, even a white one. Mentally he disowned the stinging hand. It deserved to suffer. But he wasn't sure what to do about the woman except to meet her staring eyes and stand his ground until she had the decency to go away.

She moved closer still. He refused to flinch when she suddenly reached out, but her target was the bucket on the bench just behind him. "Here, may I help with some . . ." She stepped back again, sloshing the bucket's contents as she held it out to him. "Cool water helps."

Water, he realized. A sensible suggestion, but one born of pity. Worse, she thought to take credit for causing his injury. To show her how little damage had been done, he retrieved the skillet with his burned hand, ignoring the pain.

"Very well, then." With a quick shrug she set the bucket on the ground and backed away. "I hope it won't blister too badly."

He put the skillet aside as soon as she was out of sight. When the sound of her mincing footsteps had faded completely, he thrust his hand into the water, more angry with himself than with anything she had done. A woman's sympathy sounded soft in any language. A boy might go yearning after it, but a man knew how to tighten his grip on himself and revel in his own hardness.

Chapter 3

Priscilla dared not ask anyone about the young man at the forge, but surreptitiously she did watch for him when she visited the camp. Once the novelty of her presence had worn off, most of the Indians who lived there paid her little mind as they went about their business. She was delighted when a young Indian woman approached her with a gift—a piece of fried bread dough—and a greeting in English.

The woman's name was Sarah, and she was the wife of half-breed interpreter Henry LaPointe. Her more than passable English was Priscilla's godsend. She decided to begin her study by observing the primitive woman's daily routine, which had been changing ever since the first white traders offered to exchange glass beads for animal skins. With the rations and the tools the agency had begun to provide, there were even more adaptations, clever combinations of the old with the new.

For several days Priscilla followed Sarah about, watching her cook, watching her gather wood and water, watching her tend groups of children, which might or might not include her own. Priscilla made sketches and notes that eventually became journal entries, penned in the shadowy lamplight of her room.

She had written about the man working in the shade of the blacksmith shed, his brown body slick with the sweat of his labor. The fact that he was mangling the iron skillet was worthy of note, particularly since she'd seen some of the women using skillets in their cooking fires right alongside their buffalo paunch boiling pots. She wondered what the young man's mother—or possibly his wife—had said when she couldn't find her cooking pan.

The fact that the look in the man's eyes had made her heartbeat suddenly surge like a steam engine was not noted in her journal. But as she worded her description of his fine buckskin leggings and moccasins, she remembered that the absence of a shirt had made more of an impression.

The unmentionable details were somehow the most memorable. The impossible length of his sleek torso, for example, the imposing breadth of his shoulders, the squareness of his jaw, and his dark eyes telling her he knew exactly what he was about. No matter that he was handily using the white man's tools to destroy a useful piece of equipment. There was nothing about the man at the forge that spoke of any need for advice or assistance from anyone.

It was an outrageous observation, Priscilla realized. Her father would dismiss it outright with indisputable logic. The man was a savage. Like the child who could recite his letters, he had been tutored in a skill, but he would continue to be a savage until he took plow in hand, and then, ah, *then,* her father would say, his skill would have a purpose.

The young man's eyes spoke otherwise. In them she saw his curiosity about her, and beyond that there was a certain male confidence, a knowledge of her beyond what she knew of herself.

Something he *thought* he knew, she amended. What could any man know of her beyond what she permitted him to know? Captain Harmon, with all his spit and polish, had never looked at her that way.

Not that he didn't admire her. He often uttered the inane sort of comments men seemed wont to make about the notions that might appropriately reside in her "pretty head." It wasn't the flirtation that bothered her. It was the stiff-

necked way he went about it. That and the way he was always fussing with his waxy yellow mustache. He knew as
much as he cared to know about her, which was nothing
of any real importance. He enjoyed lecturing, but he had
no interest in discussion, and none of his posturing was
half as exciting as the enigmatic look in the dark eyes of
the man at the blacksmith's forge.

The supplies arrived at last. The people stood in line
outside the storehouse door, and Agent Twiss did his best
to keep track of who came to claim the annuities. One of
his tasks was to try to count these people, to record accurately their names and their band affiliations. He was making some headway with Red Cloud's people, but he knew
that there were people from the hostile bands claiming rations also. Hostile or friendly, they all looked alike. It was
difficult to keep track of them. His policy was to be generous as a means of luring "the wild ones" into the fold.
Let them taste the rations. Let them enjoy their cousins'
feast. He and his daughter would be their guests, and their
trust would continue to build.

Priscilla was interested in building trust, too, and she
was beginning to enjoy as much success as her father was
having. On the day after the rations were dispensed the
two went to the camp early, but Priscilla left her father to
sit and smoke with the old men while she went in search
of Sarah. As she made her way among the concentric circles of tipis, several children greeted her with joyous chatter and universal gestures that said, "Welcome! Come join
us for some fun."

She met Sarah at the door of her tipi. Her older boy,
Pierre, came barreling out behind his mother. She spoke to
him in Sioux as he scampered away with an excited bunch
of six- or seven-year-olds, all dressed in moccasins and
breechclouts and jostling for the chance to lead the way.
"The young men are racing their horses," Sarah explained.

The little boys' enthusiasm was contagious. "May we
watch?" Priscilla asked. "Is the track close by?"

"Beyond the hill." Sarah pointed, a teasing smile danc-

necked way he went about it. That and the way he was always fussing with his waxy yellow mustache. He knew as
much as he cared to know about her, which was nothing
of any real importance. He enjoyed lecturing, but he had
no interest in discussion, and none of his posturing was
half as exciting as the enigmatic look in the dark eyes of
the man at the blacksmith's forge.

The supplies arrived at last. The people stood in line
outside the storehouse door, and Agent Twiss did his best
to keep track of who came to claim the annuities. One of
his tasks was to try to count these people, to record accurately their names and their band affiliations. He was making some headway with Red Cloud's people, but he knew
that there were people from the hostile bands claiming rations also. Hostile or friendly, they all looked alike. It was
difficult to keep track of them. His policy was to be generous as a means of luring "the wild ones" into the fold.
Let them taste the rations. Let them enjoy their cousins'
feast. He and his daughter would be their guests, and their
trust would continue to build.

Priscilla was interested in building trust, too, and she
was beginning to enjoy as much success as her father was
having. On the day after the rations were dispensed the
two went to the camp early, but Priscilla left her father to
sit and smoke with the old men while she went in search
of Sarah. As she made her way among the concentric circles of tipis, several children greeted her with joyous chatter and universal gestures that said, "Welcome! Come join
us for some fun."

She met Sarah at the door of her tipi. Her older boy,
Pierre, came barreling out behind his mother. She spoke to
him in Sioux as he scampered away with an excited bunch
of six- or seven-year-olds, all dressed in moccasins and
breechclouts and jostling for the chance to lead the way.
"The young men are racing their horses," Sarah explained.

The little boys' enthusiasm was contagious. "May we
watch?" Priscilla asked. "Is the track close by?"

"Beyond the hill." Sarah pointed, a teasing smile danc-

of his labor. The fact that he was mangling the iron skillet was worthy of note, particularly since she'd seen some of the women using skillets in their cooking fires right alongside their buffalo paunch boiling pots. She wondered what the young man's mother—or possibly his wife—had said when she couldn't find her cooking pan.

The fact that the look in the man's eyes had made her heartbeat suddenly surge like a steam engine was not noted in her journal. But as she worded her description of his fine buckskin leggings and moccasins, she remembered that the absence of a shirt had made more of an impression.

The unmentionable details were somehow the most memorable. The impossible length of his sleek torso, for example, the imposing breadth of his shoulders, the squareness of his jaw, and his dark eyes telling her he knew exactly what he was about. No matter that he was handily using the white man's tools to destroy a useful piece of equipment. There was nothing about the man at the forge that spoke of any need for advice or assistance from anyone.

It was an outrageous observation, Priscilla realized. Her father would dismiss it outright with indisputable logic. The man was a savage. Like the child who could recite his letters, he had been tutored in a skill, but he would continue to be a savage until he took plow in hand, and then, ah, *then,* her father would say, his skill would have a purpose.

The young man's eyes spoke otherwise. In them she saw his curiosity about her, and beyond that there was a certain male confidence, a knowledge of her beyond what she knew of herself.

Something he *thought* he knew, she amended. What could any man know of her beyond what she permitted him to know? Captain Harmon, with all his spit and polish, had never looked at her that way.

Not that he didn't admire her. He often uttered the inane sort of comments men seemed wont to make about the notions that might appropriately reside in her "pretty head." It wasn't the flirtation that bothered her. It was the stiff-

triumph as he rode past with the fluid grace of one who might have been born on the back of a horse.

Then she realized that she was the only one clapping and that Sarah was giving her a strange look. Her hands froze mid-clap, and her silly smile melted like beeswax. "I love horse races." She clasped her hands behind her back. With any luck the sudden flush in her cheeks might actually be mistaken for a rash.

"Your father tells us not to gamble." Sarah nodded toward a group of men who were exchanging markers. "This is what I was telling you before. You must be prepared to make bets. It is part of the game."

"Every game?"

Sarah's impish smile offered a challenge, and Priscilla chanced a parting glance at the winning rider, who had dismounted and joined his friends. "My father and I agree to disagree on occasion. I see nothing wrong with risking a little something. It makes life far more interesting in the long run."

It felt good to share a rebellious boast with a friend. Her school chums would have been shocked by the notion of disagreeing with their fathers, especially about something as improper as gambling. Sarah was a little older, a little wiser, perhaps, at least about some things. But unlike her own Aunt Margaret, who had never married and knew absolutely nothing about men, Sarah was not too old to have fun. There were times when Priscilla actually found it difficult to think of Sarah as the primitive woman she knew her to be.

Sarah waved to a group of girls who had been tending her younger son while they watched the race. They plucked themselves off the ground and scampered over, the tallest one bouncing little Joseph LaPointe on her slim hip. "He has outgrown his cradleboard," Sarah said as she took the chubby babe in her arms and cheerfully dismissed the girls. "But he still needs his mother."

They retreated to a shady buffalo berry thicket, where Sarah put bare-bottomed little Joseph to breast. Both women watched him go to work. They smiled wistfully in the way of all women, as though the child were per-ing in her eyes. "Is it the horses or the young men my friend wishes to see?"

"Your friend wishes to take part in all the festivities." Her feet were already on their way, but Sarah's were deliberately dragging. Priscilla had to take the woman by the hand.

"I have more berries to grind," she said. But Priscilla saw that this was a game and she tugged at her friend's arm. Sarah play-groaned. "They're only men. Young warriors showing off, no more." She shrugged. "Not important."

"I'm not interested in men. I'm interested in games." Now that they were on their way up the grassy slope, she dropped Sarah's hand and took a few swipes at her hair, adjusting one of the pins to anchor a stray lock. "What do the women do? Do we get to race horses, too?"

"There are games for us, but you must be prepared to . . ." Sarah had to quicken her step to keep up. "I cannot think how to say it."

"Run?"

The two women skipped and jogged, laughing as they reached the crest of the hill. On the flat below they saw the men, most of them stripped to their moccasins and breechclouts, just like the boys. Some cavorted on horseback. Others were seated in the shade of a lone spreading scrub oak, watching the race between a roan and a stocking-footed sorrel.

"That's my husband, Henry, riding the horse with white feet," Sarah said. She shook her head, clucking in her cheek as the other rider leaned down close to his mount's neck and sailed past the two men who stood as markers for the finish line. A chorus of yelps and cheers greeted the winner as he circled his horse and came trotting back toward the spectators. His long black hair fluttered loose behind him like a victory banner.

He looked straight at her. The connection produced a mental *click* and a tingling sensation that spread over her. It was the man at the forge. She'd not seen him smile before, but he did now, and she did what came most naturally. She returned his smile and giddily applauded his

forming some delightful feat. Priscilla felt a sympathetic tug on her own breast, and she quickly pulled her knees up to her chest and clasped her arms about them.

"Your husband rode well," she told Sarah. "He was very close at the end."

"But my brother won. He always wins."

"That was your brother?" The question was out before Priscilla had a chance to temper her astonishment. Sarah nodded, smiling in a way that made Priscilla squirm a little. "Well, I've seen him before, but only once."

"After this celebration he will be gone again. He chooses the camp of our Minneconjou relations. He comes to visit our mother, but I think also to take Henry's horse."

"In the race? Your husband wagered his horse?"

"Since he was a small boy my brother always has the fastest horse. He races with Henry, he wins Henry's horse." She patted her son's little bottom and smiled, remembering. "Then my brother takes this one from my arms, sits him upon the horse he has won, and says, 'This pony will carry you far, *tonśka,* but it will be a slow journey.' He calls him his nephew in the special way a man speaks of his sister's sons. And Henry promises to win next time."

"They are friends, then, your brother and your husband?"

"Yes. Brother-friends, even before I became Henry's wife."

Distracted by a ladybug coasting above his mother's head, Joseph released her nipple with a loud smack and scrambled off her lap. Sarah laughed as she steadied him on his feet. "How many steps today, little one? Are you ready to run?"

The ladybug landed on the droopy bloom of a nodding thistle. Touching her fingertip to a spiky purple petal, Priscilla retrieved the tiny beetle for Joseph's closer inspection. "What is his name?" she wondered as the baby extended one tentative finger toward hers.

"My brother is Whirlwind Rider. Already he is one of the Tokala, the Kit Fox Society. He is a lance bearer. He has proven himself by counting coups and taking many horses, so he may take a wife soon."

"Has he someone in mind?" She was just curious. "A new sister for you?"

"I don't think so. He does not behave like a man who has a woman on his mind." Sarah shifted her legs from one side to the other and tucked her heels under her hip as she confided, "His thoughts are his own, that one. One day I think he will offer for someone, and we will say '*Mahn!* So he has been looking for *this* woman.'"

One of the wild ones, Priscilla thought. The "hostiles" her father spoke of who refused to make their camps close to the agency. But he was there now, visiting relatives as any civilized man might do on occasion, and what she had seen in his eyes—the look that had haunted her since the first time she saw him—was not hostility. Heated and potent as it was, it held no malice. If it be wildness, then wildness was a quality worthy of closer study, for it did not offend her the way one might expect it to.

She maneuvered the ladybug from her slender finger to Joseph's stubby one and smiled when he turned to offer the prize to his mother. "And that's how it's done?" she asked, for research purposes only. "A man simply offers marriage to the woman of his choice?"

"He courts her first. Then he offers gifts to her family. Then her family asks her if she wants this man. If she does, they accept his gifts, and there is a marriage." Sarah caught Joseph mid-stumble, and the three of them watched the ladybug fly away. Sarah glanced at Priscilla. "How is it done among the whites? Not the same?"

"Custom has it that the woman should have a dowry— gifts or property to bring to the marriage. Then all of her property becomes her husband's."

"Even her lodge?" Clearly this was unthinkable.

"The house is his. She takes care of it, of course, but the man owns . . . everything."

"Owns everything," Sarah repeated slowly, as though trying to imagine what it truly meant. "It's a strange way to be."

* * *

Priscilla did not see Whirlwind Rider again that day. She joined in the feast, sampling fried breads and soups and spit-roasted meat. In a camp of at least two hundred lodges, maybe more, the face of one man might easily be missed, Priscilla reasoned, and she was too busy to keep close watch. When she joined the women in a game of Knocking the Ball, which was played in teams using long shinny sticks, she wished for less cumbersome clothing. It was a big field, and it was awkward to chase the leather ball from one goal to another with petticoats swirling around the ankles. Secretly she hoped that if she were going to run into Whirlwind Rider again, this would not be the time.

Her hope became actuality, and she had to shake off a vague and foolish feeling of disappointment. By the time her father was ready to go home she had half a mind to ask Sarah what had happened to her elusive brother. Just casually, she told herself. But, of course, she didn't ask.

After a good night's sleep, she was the sensible scholar once again. The celebration had given rise to marathon journaling. She added a whole page to her vocabulary list, and when Captain Harmon paid his next visit, she was fully prepared, just for fun, to play the devil's advocate against both men. She served them their port. Smiling prettily, she took her seat on the bench and waited patiently for one of them to take a step into the province she was schooling herself to claim as her own.

"We must reach the women," Charles said, unwittingly planting his foot in her square. Priscilla smiled slowly. "We speak of training and educating the men, but if we can stimulate the natural female proclivity for permanent homes, the women will discourage this nomadic bent. I'm sure of it, by God. What woman would not chose to be mistress of a house firmly fixed to a plot of land? The Sioux women are treated like beasts of burden, hauling their dwellings from campsite to campsite."

"The lodge belongs to the woman," Priscilla said. "The lodge and all its contents, save the man's personal effects. It is an interesting concept, I think."

"This is what you've learned?"

"Well, surely you knew this, Father. As for the burdens, I've not heard Sarah complain. She's very strong for a woman. She can carry twice as much water in one trip as I can."

"How would you . . ." It was a rare moment when she managed to surprise him. "Priscilla, *you?*"

"I find that it's easier to describe the tasks in my journal if I try some of them myself."

"Don't you think you're carrying this little project of yours a bit too far, Miss Twiss?" Harmon uncrossed his legs and leaned forward. "Getting involved with them in a personal way seems rather . . ." The ladderback chair creaked beneath him as he fidgeted. "Unbecoming, I would say."

Her father laughed. "You don't know my Pris, young man. 'Unbecoming,' you say? She sets the standard by which 'becoming' might be measured. Hauling water in those buffalo bladders, indeed. I wish I had been there to see it. I doubt she spilled a drop."

"I appreciate your confidence, Father."

"Red Cloud has recently expressed to me the same sentiment. I've been invited to attend the summer gathering of the seven council fires. The Sun Dance will be performed." He leaned back in his rocking chair, quite self-satisfied. "I believe that means that I have earned their trust."

Priscilla could hardly believe her good fortune. The Sun Dance! "Oh, Father, you must take me with you."

"I cannot very well leave you behind, dear girl."

"You cannot mean to watch that grisly ritual, sir, and *certainly* you cannot expose a lady to such—"

"I don't know what to expect, and that's the beauty of it. But, of course, Priscilla will be excused if the proceedings become too—"

"You know what they do, don't you? They mutilate themselves in a way that would shock the devil himself."

"Have you seen it for yourself, Captain?" Priscilla asked.

"Certainly not, nor do I have any desire to do so. But if you insist upon accepting this barbarous invitation, then

I shall insist upon accompanying you." Harmon looked at Priscilla. "For your protection."

"Do you have anything to wear, Captain?" The startled look in his eyes made her snicker. "I've never seen you dressed in anything but a uniform."

"The Sioux get nervous when soldiers get too close to their beloved hills," Twiss put in. "I'm told they take offense at the sight of brass buttons."

"That may be so, but I've led several patrols into the Powder River country just to let them see these buttons flash in the sun, along with my saber." Harmon squared his shoulders as he set his glass on the lamp table. "They respect a show of force, sir. In the final analysis, I believe that force is all they respect."

"I doubt that, Captain." Twiss sipped his wine before elaborating. "I think they respect me. They respect the authority I derive directly from the President through my appointment as his agent to them. Red Cloud has been to Washington, Captain. He understands the President's power."

"The President is my commander-in-chief as well."

Priscilla sprang to her feet. "Oh, will you two stop posturing. I can't think that we need a military escort when we've been invited by Red Cloud himself."

"There are those among the hostiles who regard Red Cloud as a traitor," Harmon said. "I don't care how welcome you are in *his* camp, you cannot say the same for the northern bands."

"Spotted Tail ripped all the brass buttons off the army surplus hats and coats in the last clothing annuity he received. The uniform is an affront, and I don't want a patrol trailing us." Twiss calmly waved the captain's concerns aside. "I know you mean well, my boy, but like as not, your show of force would get us killed." He smiled reassuringly for his daughter. "These people hold me in high regard, and we have Red Cloud's personal guarantee."

Chapter 4

Priscilla hated riding in her father's buckboard, but it was the only way he would make the journey. He insisted that this was the best way to transport "a load of gifts, a proper lady, and a corpulent old man." It was a good thing the trail left by the huge Sioux camp was easy to follow, for they were far more adept at covering ground than were Charles Twiss and his lumbering buckboard. They traveled in a northeasterly direction, deep into the land of the Teton Sioux and ever closer to their precious Black Hills.

Once she had set aside her impatience, Priscilla enjoyed having her father all to herself. The wilderness had not reduced his girth, but it had taken a few years off his age. Priscilla could not remember a time when his preference for a comfortable chair close to the hearth and a glass of port had not prevailed over an invitation to take a stroll outdoors. But at night when they made their camp he marveled like a schoolboy at the prairie's star-studded black velvet canopy.

By day, while the two-hitch team labored steadily in their traces, Charles talked hour after hour about his plans for his "red children," about the changes he planned for them and the extraordinary citizens they would one day become as a result of his efforts. Their ways were interesting, yes, but no longer viable. Oh, he had such visions. He had lobbied and lectured and published, and now he had the authority to demonstrate the legitimacy of his ideas.

The lectures were not as much fun as the campfires. Priscilla listened with one ear while she kept the other one attuned to tall grasses stirred by the wind and to the double-note song of the meadowlark. Her thoughts skipped ahead, imagining—when and if they *ever* reached their destination—what the next few days would be like. She had asked Sarah many questions about the Sun Dance, the apex of a Sioux summer, but as often as not the answer was "It's hard to explain," or "This you must see." She knew they had already missed some of the ritual preparation. Sarah had warned her that there was much she would not see; the dancers prepared themselves, with the help of the holy men, in the privacy of the ceremonial lodge. But the Sun Dance was a rite for the whole Sioux Nation, for the life of the people, and everyone participated in some way.

She wished she could make the horses go faster. Off in the distance a dark, imposing silhouette suddenly seemed to rise up from the prairie and touch the sky. If those were "hills" she couldn't imagine how grand real mountains must be. And if those were the Black Hills, she and her father were almost there. Oh, she hoped they wouldn't miss the actual ceremony. This was a rare opportunity. Her description of the Sun Dance would be the highlight of her study.

When they saw the pony herds grazing on the hillsides, they knew they were close. Under the summer-bright afternoon sun the lead team topped the last rise. Priscilla gripped the seat to keep from popping out of it prematurely. She felt as though her birthday or Christmas morning were waiting for her just over the hill.

At last they saw the camp. Dotting the bottomland of the White River, stretched across the flat, and tucked under the oaks and pines were more tipis than she had imagined ever seeing at once, and among them, beneath the curls of gray campfire smoke that sketched the sky, there was considerable activity. A group of children splashed in the river's shallow waters. Near the edge of camp a pair of dogs scrapped over some morsel until an old woman sent them whimpering into the bushes with the whack of a stick. Favored horses cropped the grass around their pickets.

And there was singing. The closer they came, the more distinct was the sound, which came from the center of the camp. The steady, muffled beat of a drum kept time for plaintive male voices. Priscilla couldn't see the singers, but their songs seemed to surround a circular arbor, thatched with fresh boughs, which must have been the dance lodge Sarah had told her about. It was the centerpiece of the roughly circular camp. Everything was round, Sarah had explained. In the middle of the arbor stood a towering forked pole—the *wakan* tree—selected, "captured," and erected during the ritual preparations.

She'd already missed so much! Either the dancing had not started, or it was all over. She was so glad she had a friend who would explain it all. Since the camp was arranged by clans and by seniority, Sarah had been able to tell Priscilla exactly how to find her lodge.

She accompanied her father to pay respects to Red Cloud, who invited them, as his guests, to make their camp near his. Her father was more interested in being seen than in seeing, but Priscilla intended to observe *everything*. She couldn't pitch their little army tent fast enough. She was eager to find Sarah and to learn what she'd missed and what was yet to come.

Sarah was glad to see her. The pageantry of bringing in the ceremonial tree was over. This was a quiet time. While those who had pledged themselves were purifying themselves in the sweat lodge, there was time to make final preparations for the feast that would follow the dance. Another pair of hands would make the cherry-picking go faster.

Priscilla's hands were less adept at the job than Sarah's, but the pouches were filling. While the voices of young children were ever-present and always buoyant in the Lakota camp, an unusually subdued mood pervaded. The wailing songs of phantom singers prevailed over the drum's steady cadence. The men who would be pierced, Priscilla assumed, were contemplating their ordeal. She wondered where they were and who they were and whether they feared the piercing, even a little. She knew she would.

"Is your brother here, Sarah?"

"My brother?" Sarah smiled innocently as she dropped a handful of small wild cherries into the rawhide collecting pouch.

"Whirlwind Rider. Isn't that his name?"

"Yes." Sarah's eyes sparkled knowingly. "And he is here, camped with our mother's relations."

"Your mother's relations." Avoiding her friend's teasing eyes, Priscilla ducked under a leafy branch and reached for a cluster of ripe berries. "Let's see if I have this straight, now. Your father's side of the family are Red Cloud's people."

"They are Oglala. Say this."

"Oglala," Priscilla repeated. "And your mother's band is the Min . . . Min-ne . . ."

"Minneconjou." With one hand Sarah held her pouch open for Priscilla's pickings. With the other she pulled a piece of prairie gama grass from her belt. "I have found this for you. I am past needing it, but I give it to you for a . . . a sign."

"A sign?" She accepted the stem and inspected it, wondering what more it could be than a piece of grass. She rubbed the stalk between her thumb and forefinger, twirling the spindly sprouts at the top like a child's stick puppet.

Sarah touched one of the feather-shaped heads of grain. "Four on one stalk is rare. It means love will come to you."

"Love?" The weed scorched the pads of her fingers like a tiny hot poker. Impulsively Priscilla tried to give it back. "Not to me."

"Why not to you? Do you have these things as turned around as they say?"

"What things?"

"What is between a man and a woman." Sarah pushed Priscilla's hand into the valley between her breasts, settling the four heads of grain into the soft folds in her white blouse. "So many white men come here without women, and they stay in the forts . . ." Sarah's long, shiny braids bobbed against her breast as she shook her head. "I have heard people talk of this strange thing. Some say, maybe the white women drive the men away."

Priscilla laughed. "Some of the recruits may be running, all right, but I don't think we women are the cause." She considered the grass stem again, giving it another twirl. "No, I expect to be married one day, but for now I have other plans. There is so much I want to see and do first. So many things to learn."

"You will keep that?"

"Of course." Priscilla slipped the stalk carefully into her skirt pocket. "It's a gift as well as a lesson."

"Yes, I believe it will be so."

It was the drum, she would later say. Its strong steady beat became one with her, or she with it, and she was drawn into the heart of the ceremony. There were seven dancers who had made vows, and Whirlwind Rider was among them. Priscilla recognized him through the red-earth paint striped with black that covered his upper body, and beneath the wreath of twisted silver-green sage he wore low over his forehead. She knew him by the proud way he carried himself, and by something else—some intangible inclination that drew her, like the persistent throbbing of the drum.

Sarah had given her sage to wear in her hair. She'd explained that the people would surround those who had pledged themselves, and there would be dancing until sunup, when the pledge-makers would greet the light of day and make their sacrifice. She taught her the women's demure dance step, bouncing at the knee, rising, moving the feet almost imperceptibly, barely an inch at a time, while the men stomped the grass and postured like ground-nesters, seeking and searching. The drum became a community heartbeat, and the night passed in a frenzy of dancing and song.

Priscilla forgot about studying or analyzing. Becoming a physical part of something so elemental as a heartbeat de-

fied scientific scrutiny. She ignored the disapproving look
she saw on her father's face. He kept himself apart, a
watcher on the periphery and, oddly, a stranger to her now,
for she was dancing. The motion consumed her. It was as
natural as breathing.

Before dawn everything stopped, and the seven who had
pledged themselves left the dance lodge. "We must offer
gifts now, as my brother's relations," Sarah said. She withdrew a handful of tiny bundles from her pouch. *"Kinnikinnik,"* she said. "Tobacco."

Priscilla questioned nothing. It felt good to be included
this way, knowing that she shared both the exhilaration
and the weariness she saw in her friend's eyes. She helped
distribute the tobacco offerings around the perimeter of the
dance lodge, placing them with the gifts offered by the
other dancers' relatives.

At dawn's first light the seven entered the circle once
again, accompanied by the pipe bearer, who offered
prayers and burned grass that gave off a sweet-smelling
smoke. The sun rose from the flat side of the horizon,
dressing the hills to the west in a rosy mantle, as the dancers circled the center pole. Their song seemed to drive the
night's shadows from the horizon.

Mesmerized, Priscilla whispered, "What are they saying?"

"They are singing, 'Wakan Tanka, Grandfather, be mer-
ciful to me. I do this that my people may live,' " Sarah
replied, and then softly she chanted in English, " 'The buffalo is coming, they say. The power of the buffalo is
coming; it is upon us now.' "

Whirlwind Rider's voice became louder and more plaintive as he stepped up to the tree and grasped it with both
hands. Suddenly several men seized him and flung him to
the ground. Priscilla stiffened with surprise, but Sarah laid
an admonishing hand on her arm. "They will pierce him
now. If you would uphold him in this, do not turn away."

She did not. She stood with those who formed the circle
of witnesses, supporters, and prayer-givers. Steadfastly she
watched the men pinch the skin high on his left breast and
drive a skewer through it, and she felt the pain in her own

breast as surely as she had felt the tug of Sarah's nursing child. They pierced him with a second skewer on the right side, and she clutched herself as if to stem the flow of blood.

The men stood him up as roughly as they had thrown him to the ground. He leaned back on the rawhide rope that connected the top of the tree to the pegs in his chest, and he danced. Priscilla was only vaguely aware of the piercing of the other six, each according to the terms of his vow. From the moment Whirlwind Rider began his ordeal, he became her central focus. When the beat of the drum urged a communal rhythm, it was for him that Priscilla danced.

Somewhere in the periphery she heard her father's voice, urging her to come away now. For the first time in her life she ignored his summons. Those around her must have closed him out, sent him away. Now there was only Whirlwind Rider and the blood that streamed down his chest and the clear, bright sound of his song.

When his throat went raw, he blew on his eagle bone whistle. The shrill sound pierced Priscilla's heart. He danced gazing at the sun, and she danced, willing him strength. At the moment when she felt his weakening pulse seek hers out, she was there for him. His face was streaked with sweat and red-clay dye. He looked past the others and struggled to focus on her. She lifted her chin, and he did the same. She squared her shoulders, and he did the same, tugging against the thongs that pulled his skin away from his body. Instinctively she thumped her fist over her heart, keeping time with the drum's quickening cadence. *Dance on, dance on,* a voice in her head sang out to him, and he lifted his gaze once again to the sun, nearing its zenith.

He stumbled, staggered a little, and Priscilla felt Sarah's hand on her arm once again. "You have become his helper," she said. "Sing for him, and he will feel the strength return to his legs."

Priscilla imitated the voices around her. Whirlwind Rider regained his equilibrium, but the music of his bone whistle had gone dry.

"Can't they have any water?" Priscilla whispered desperately.

"There is this that you may do for him." Sarah produced a sprig of wild mint from the pouch on her belt. She tickled the corner of Priscilla's mouth with the leaves. "Soften it in your own mouth, then put it in his. But you must not touch him, and you must not allow him to touch you."

She chewed the leaves as Sarah instructed, releasing the minty flavor while she waited for him to dance closer. Then she darted into the inner circle, took the mint from her mouth, and offered it up to him. He parted his lips, and the bone whistle tumbled to the end of the thong around his neck. His body was smeared with blood, paint, and sweat. Every aspect of his demeanor betrayed the strain of containing his pain even as he taunted it, as though it were his demon in chains.

But none of that frightened her. She offered solace, from her eyes to his, and moisture, from her mouth to his. He leaned toward her as he took the mint between his teeth, and she longed to offer her arm or her shoulder for his support. But she backed away slowly. He tipped his chin up and chewed savagely on the mint, then gave a mighty tug on the line that tethered him, ripping free of the left peg. Blood flowed anew as he went down on one knee.

Priscilla reached out reflexively, but Sarah was behind her, pulling her back into the crowd. Whirlwind Rider jerked his shoulders and tore his right side free. "Thank God," Priscilla breathed, while the people around her cried, *"Hi ye!"*

When it was finished, the dancers were given the pipe to smoke in the presence of the people. Then they were taken back to the purification lodge, while the people celebrated.

She was not about to ask after him again, so she kept watch. She was subtle about it. Groups of men caught her attention but never turned her head. She would know his voice, she thought. If she saw him from the back, she would know him by the way he moved. It was not an attraction, this thing she felt. It was only that she had been so moved by the power of the dance, so frightened by it,

yet so completely spellbound. And it had come to her
through him. Through his experience and the rapture of his
pain. She needed to see him, simply to assure herself that
he was, indeed, a mere man. Then she could proceed to
describe the event with the proper objectivity.

When he was ready, he sought her out. He knew she
had asked about him even before he had left the agency
camp, for his sister had told him so. And then she had
come to witness the sacred spectacle. He had felt her presence. At the moment when his strength had begun to fail
him, she had drawn his eyes to hers, and she had restored
his stamina.

Undoubtedly his sister, Two Star Woman, whom the
white priest had named Sarah, had prompted the blue-eyed
woman to ease his thirst as a woman might do if she cared
for a man. He had not asked for anyone to aid him in the
customary way, for when he had gone to the hill to cry for
a vision, his spirit helper had told him there would be no
need for an assistant. But when delirium had threatened to
overcome him before it was time, he had searched among
the faces of his people, and his eyes had met hers. He had
found strength in an unexpected place.

She was standing near a family of cottonwood trees by
the river, and she was waiting for him. He knew her expectancy, even if she did not. He felt it reach out to him
as he strode toward her, holding his trade blanket close
about his shoulders. The *pejuta wicaśa* had dressed his
wounds with healing herbs, and the pain had lessened, but
he had sensed that she could see it lingering in him even
though he kept all trace of it from his face and carried
himself with dignity. She was a strange woman, to stare so
conspicuously.

He knew little English. His brother-friend, LaPointe,
had given him some words, although not as many as his
sister had learned. As he drew close to the woman, he cast
about in his mind for something to say to her. He wanted
to ask her whether she meant to tempt him as she did
whenever she met his gaze with hers. He wanted to ask
her why her yellow-brown hair was bound up in a knot
and how she came to have such slight shoulders. But he

could say none of those things. He used what words he had.

"I know you."

"Yes. We have . . ." She made the motion of hammering, and he recalled his own surprise when she had come to stand before him in the shadows without making any sound. "At the blacksmith shop. You . . ." She held her hand out to him and touched the crotch of her thumb. "Did you burn yourself?"

He remembered dropping the skillet like a foolish boy, but because her eyes did not mock him, he stuck his hand out, palm up, so that she could see he'd done no damage.

"Ah, that's good," she said. "You are Whirlwind Rider? Sarah told me."

With a nod he acknowledged both his name and his sister's, then solicited hers with a gesture.

"Priscilla."

"Priscilla." He made a fist and thumped his breast gently to remind her of what she had done during the dance. Her cheeks turned pink as the twilight sky.

"It was the drumbeat," she said softly, and she made the motion of beating the drum. "I found it compelling. It made my heart . . ."

He understood when she laid her hand over her breast. In the heat of such a moment the drumbeat took possession of the human heart.

"It made my heart feel good," she said. Absently she fingered a heart-shaped locket that was pinned to her dress.

"Good," he agreed. He knew the word and, yes, this was good.

"My heart felt good, even though . . ." Her hand went out to him, hesitantly approaching his chest. She did not touch him, but he saw that she wanted to. "Is it very painful?" she asked shyly. He eyed the pale hand hovering close to his blanket. "Does it hurt you now?"

None of the words was familiar to him, but her eyes were full of compassion. He shook his head, denying pain as a strong man must. Tenderness lingered in her eyes. Even as he reminded himself that a Lakota woman would know better than to behave this way, he opened his blanket and displayed his bloody gashes. In a short time they would become scars, badges of honor, but for now they were raw and unprotected parts of him, and they were private. He shared them only because she had given him strength, thereby sharing in his ordeal.

"It will heal," she said softly, laying her fingertips against his breastbone. He felt healing in her touch, even though the word meant nothing to him. "You must keep it clean. But I'm sure you know . . ."

She drew her hand away and stepped back, suddenly ill-at-ease, speaking quickly. "Was it all right when I . . ." She bent close to the ground and searched through the grass as she continued to talk. "Sarah told me what to do. Your mouth must have been terribly dry. I wanted to give you some water, but Sarah said . . ."

He wasn't sure what she was saying, but in her strange agitation she was reaching toward a plant whose prickly stem would sting her. He stayed her hand. She looked up at him, then back at the ground. "Oh," she said softly, like a field mouse who had tripped on his moccasin. "Nettle. I was . . . I was looking for mint."

He drew her to her feet again, then plucked a harmless piece of curly-leaf switch grass and chewed on the stem to show her that he understood.

"I hope it was all right for me to do that."

"Pilamaye," he said, thanking her. He touched the wet stem to her lips, then his own. "Help find . . ." Struggling to recall the word LaPointe had taught him, he pointed to the river. "Water?"

"Good, yes. Water." She nodded vigorously, and he thought her quick smile was almost as enchanting as it was indiscreet. "You were thirsty."

"Thirs-ty," he repeated, and he wondered what more she might offer him.

"Of course, you would be." She lifted her small shoulders, which he took to be a gesture of helplessness. As she spoke, he strove to catch a familiar word. "I don't know how much of this you'll understand. I don't know how much of it *I* understand, but . . ." Her hand went to her chest, her fingers splayed over her locket and the small blue buttons that marched up the center of her body from her waist to her chin. She was thinking of the piercing, he supposed, but he was thinking of the way her dress molded to her breasts and the way he knew buttons worked.

"It was a beautiful thing. Not the blood, of course, but . . ." Her hand closed into a small fist. "Yes, the blood. That, too. What you did was a beautiful thing."

"Beautiful thing." He knew that word, and to prove it he gestured broadly toward the sky and the colors of the sunset. "Beautiful."

"Yes, that *is* beautiful. The sky"—her voice was high-pitched, childlike, full of wonder—"is beautiful."

"The sky is beautiful."

"Good!" She clapped her hands, but softly and only twice. Not wildly the way she had after he'd beaten LaPointe in the horse race. "Your English is wonderful, just wonderful."

He nodded. "Good. *Wašté.*"

"*Wašté,*" she repeated.

Again he nodded, smiling this time. "Beautiful." He touched her shoulder and, with a quick jerk of his chin, directed her to consider the courting couple who stood on the bluff above them. But the man would not be observed. He opened his blanket, held it above his head, and created a little tent, just for the two of them.

"*Wičáša,*" Whirlwind Rider said, pointing to the man, then to himself. "*Wínyan.*" He gave her a nod.

"*Wičáša,*" Priscilla echoed, glancing up at the moccasins that were toe-to-toe beneath the edge of the courtship blanket. "*Wičáša* must mean man."

"*Wičáša,* man." Again Whirlwind Rider touched her shoulder. "*Wínyan . . .*" When he had her full attention, he smiled. "Beautiful."

"*Wínyan* is woman," Priscilla corrected, but there was a pretty twinkle in her eyes. She knew full well that he understood what he had said.

He nodded, and a light danced in his eyes, too. "*Wínyan* is woman."

Chapter 5

It was the beginning of a friendship that evolved secretly under the summer sun. Whirlwind Rider's English improved dramatically under Priscilla's tutelage, an accomplishment she assumed would please her father. Eventually she would tell him—perhaps in a letter, after she returned to Minnesota. It was not her habit to keep secrets from her father, but this one, well . . . this one changed a few of her habits.

The time she'd spent in the Sun Dance camp seemed fanciful, breath-stealing, and mind-misting when she thought back on it. It was like leaving the real world for a time. Back at the agency, she meant to reclaim her observer's role. She had only the summer. After that, she belonged in school, and Whirlwind Rider belonged with his cousins to the north, the wild ones who preferred to roam the plains and hunt for buffalo. They, too, had only the summer.

But Whirlwind Rider was free to come and go as he pleased, and it pleased him to come and go often. Their first meeting after the Sun Dance had not occurred by her design. He had followed her on her way back from a visit to the camp. She was properly attired with riding gloves and hair neatly pinned under a small black velvet hat. He wore little more than a breechclout, a beautiful bronze tan, and hair free to fly like a black banner in the wind. Few words were spoken as they rode a short distance alone together, but the bold-shy looks and suggestive smiles they exchanged were the same in any language. By the time he'd wheeled his beautiful red roan and rode away, her heart was fluttering crazily. The next day they'd met the same way. He'd brought her a gift of dried meat because she had managed to convey to him that she was curious about buffalo. They had walked along the river, sharing the chewy jerky, which he'd called *papa*, and traded words, English for Lakota.

Soon Priscilla found herself waking up each morning wondering whether she would see him. Each day was colored with a new aura of anticipation. Sometimes several long days would pass without a meeting, and Sarah might mention that her brother had left the camp to join a hunt. There was always the chance that he would decide not to come back. But there was also that chance that he would return any day. Unable to predict his whims or his ways, Priscilla only became more intrigued.

Some days she was beset by a visionary itch that compelled her to take a walk along the riverbank, where the water and the rustling cottonwoods might temper a sultry afternoon—the place he knew she was likely to choose at the time of day he knew she favored. There if she found grass pressed into soggy soil in the shape of a horse's hoof, she knew she had only to wait and wonder how close he was and when he would show himself. And how. He liked to catch her off-guard, which was easy to do when she was absorbed in her sketching.

She had just watched a young red fox leap straight up into the air and pounce on a gopher, and she wanted to get it down, get it just right. But her ears were alert. She heard a twig snap behind her.

"Were you looking for me?" she asked innocently without turning around. She knew she was expected to jump right out of her high-top shoes and look as startled as the animal she'd just sketched. It pleased her to continue her work on the gopher's stripes without the slightest hitch.

"Are you a deer?" He sounded a little brusque, but she knew he was only feeling cheated of the start he meant to give her. He picketed his horse a few feet away and came to sit beside her in the pale green-yellow grass. "I hunt only for deer today."

"This time of day?" She tipped her head back, squinted one eye, and closed the other. The sun had just slipped beyond high noon.

He laughed then, but he refused to grant her total triumph. "*You* come finding *me*. You follow my tracks."

"Tracks that even a woman might follow, left by a lance bearer of the Tokala."

Not that he looked the part at the moment. He wore no hairbone breastplate, no feathers, no kit-fox fur around his shoulders. Once, during the ceremonies following the Sun Dance, she had seen him dressed in full regalia and carrying the curved bow lance that represented his position. Later she had been unable to describe him in her journal without gushing like a girl who had just watched her soldier boy march past in the Fourth of July parade.

Even now, dressed in unadorned tan buckskins, he cut a handsome figure in a fashion she had considered a curiosity not long ago. He wore his straight hair long and loose, but for one narrow braid that hung near his left cheek. It was as attractive to her now as the smile that touched his eyes. "I think this must be a hunter's trap," she said.

"If I trap you, I keep you." He lifted a warning finger, which he then laid against the corner of her smile. "This is a woman's trap, for play. A man's trap is no game. You must take care for these things, *wigopa.*"

His warning slid past her. With one of the gestures that had become part of their way of speaking with each other, she questioned the meaning of the word he'd used.

"It is only a way of speaking." Smiling, self-satisfied, he stretched his long legs out in the grass and leaned back on his elbows. "I call you a woman whose face pleases me."

"Pretty?" The word came out unexpectedly, with an incredulous spin. Avoiding his eyes, which were probably laughing at her, she insisted quietly, "Does it mean you think I'm pretty?" He was too slow to answer, and she was too quick to air another thought. "Does it mean ... Does it have anything to do with *waŝicun?*"

"*Waŝicun* is white *man*. You are ..." He studied her for a moment. She knew she was blushing under his scrutiny, but there was no help for it. "I call you *wiġopa*. A woman with pleasing ..." He shrugged dismissively. "A woman who pleases me. Not white or Lakota. Just woman." Again he took inventory of her, head to foot, and he smiled, as though he'd just thought of a private joke. "I should call you *ciyotanka.*"

"*Ciyotanka?*" she repeated carefully.

Mischief danced in his eyes as he arranged his hands before his mouth and fingered imaginary stops.

"Flute? You should call me *flute?*"

"You are ..." He drew a straight line in the air.

"Shaped like a stick, I suppose. How flattering."

"Your voice comes to my ear, pleasing me." He sat up, crossed his legs, and braced his elbows on his knees. "In the night when I go to my blankets, you are not there. I hear a flute, someone playing it in the dark. But my ear tells me, 'The voice of Priscilla comes again.'" He smiled in the knowledge that he'd charmed her speechless. "It is a pleasing voice sometimes."

"Oh," she said, all innocence at first, but that wouldn't do. She summoned a touch of the coquettishness she held in short supply. "Oh, my, a poet." It was a word he didn't recognize, a compliment she didn't care to explain. She paid him a less personal one in its stead. "Your English improves faster than my Lakota. You are a quick student." She touched the blunt end of her drawing pencil to her temple. "Very smart."

"A man learns the words he needs," he said, still with that cagey light playing in his eyes. "*Tanke*—you call Sarah, my ..."

"Your sister."

"My sister makes these English words with me also. She laughs. She says, 'What new friend do you have, *misunka?*'"

"Brother?" she guessed. He held his hand at shoulder level. "Her *little* brother."

"Not little," he said indignantly. "She is born, then I am born."

"Younger. You are her *younger* brother."

He put his hand on top of her head, flattening her hair. "Little one."

"Oh, not so little." Ducking out from under his hand, she grabbed his wrist and pressed the heel of her palm to his. Her long, slender fingers were no match for his, and her skin looked like white paper next to his sturdy tan boot-leather hide. She sighed, as though she'd lost a point. "Smaller than yours, but still . . ."

She released his wrist, but he reversed positions and claimed hers, preserving the contact as he rubbed his palm up and down, fitting first the base of his knuckles, then the heel of his hand into the hollow of hers. "Smaller than mine," he said.

His rock-hard strength gave her a delicious sense of delicacy. She felt a quick stab of regret when he let her go.

"You have brother?"

"No brother. No sisters." Out of a sudden need for something to hold on to, she flattened her hands against the front and back covers of her journal. "No mother, either. My mother died when I was"—she glanced at him as she cradled the book in her arms— "just a baby. Baby?"

"Cinca," he offered. "Baby."

"My Aunt Margaret raised me. My mother's older sister."

He nodded. "The sister of your mother took you. The brother of my father is my father. *Ate.* "

"You mean Two Bear Claw." His relationships were complicated, but she wanted to keep them straight in her mind. She was learning about Lakota kinship through his family and what he would tell her of his past. "Your mother married him after your father died," she recalled.

"From the day I am born, Two Bear Claw is my father. Always. The sister of my mother is also my mother." He gestured. "Like you."

"But not always. With my people it is not always that way. I have a very small family. No *tiośpaye,* no large family like yours. In our household just my father, Aunt Margaret, and me."

Understanding spawned a sadness in his eyes, as if he now saw her as someone totally impoverished. She was shaken by the notion that he should pity her for her lack of family, and she added hastily, "My mother's younger brother just got married, so I may have cousins yet on the Varner side. And I have many friends. *Kola.* Many, many *kola.* School friends, and soon I shall attend a new school, where there will be more friends. We shall become like sisters."

"I have heard of this school." He made the word sound diseased. His eyes narrowed, and she felt as though the ground between them had suddenly caved in. "They take the children away. Your father speaks to Red Cloud of this."

"My father wants the Lakota children to learn to read books, and to write." She opened her journal to a random page and pointed to the neat lines of writing. "Make words on paper, this way."

"I know of this talk on paper. I know of the treaty Red Cloud made with the soldiers." He glanced at her work, then away. "He is not the old Red Cloud."

"The changes the treaty brings will be good. Red Cloud knows this. He trusts my father."

"The Minneconjou and the Hunkpapa are calling them 'loaf-around-the-fort people.' My uncle and my cousins, Red Cloud's people."

"Are you calling them that, too?"

He gazed at the river. The ripples were like knife blades, catching the glint of the sun, and on the far side a magpie chattered. No one would think to ask the bird to speak any differently or learn to "make words on paper." Anyone could see that the magpie had her territory. Anyone could understand her warning. The black-winged intruder circling above her would have to go elsewhere.

"I am coming here to speak English. I have other uncles. Other cousins. Not loaf-around-the-fort people. They have no English. I learn this for them."

"You learn quickly." Her compliment did not seem to

impress him, but the playful shadows cast by the rustling cottonwoods softened the severe angles of his face. "You keep coming back only for this? No other reason?"

Still he watched the river. Something told her she should leave well enough alone, but something else, something deeper, would not be still until it had a word of concession. "You go off and hunt, you come back, you go again." *Tell me why.* "You *do* come back each time."

He turned to her, finally, with a fierce demand that burst the bonds of his own discretion and challenged hers. "Go with me, *wigopa.*"

"Go with you?" The suggestion was so surprising that she imagined the unimaginable—a man and a woman on horseback arriving in a mystical place where water rushed cool and clear among the deep green pines and dark hills arched in the distance to touch the clouds. Regrettably, the image was as short-lived as Eden.

Apparently he knew it, too. The notion was absurdly sweet, but just a game. To save face, he made light of it. He inclined his chin, indicating the bluff across the river. "Not too far. Just over that hill and the next one. I will hunt in English, for you to make in this book."

"Just for the book, hmm?"

Ŏhan, for my friend's book." He sighed dramatically and shook his head. "But it will ruin me. My brother the buffalo will think me a fool to hunt for show."

"I saw some wild buffalo on the way back from the Sun Dance. I would like to see how you . . ." It was as hard to sustain as it was to resist the thought of going with him, of following him deep into Indian country without her father's—what? Protection? Approval? Knowledge?

He was watching her face, as though the workings of her mind were visible. She hoped they were not. A mental picture of her father reined in all wild notions and inveigled her to come up with a sensible one. She offered it brightly. "You could go to school, Whirlwind Rider. You could learn to read, and then I would write to you. Letters from school. From my school to your school."

"I want no school." He laughed. "You would make

writing for me? Woman, you must make meat. No man can fill his belly with paper."

He was right. It was hard to imagine him cooped up in a classroom. But she was right, too. It would be good for him. She wasn't sure how the two rights might be reconciled, but she didn't feel like worrying about that now.

She felt more like imagining Eden again. "You would show me how to make meat?"

"My sister shows you."

"Well—" She thought about the time she had helped Sarah chase a pair of sneaky camp dogs away from her meat-drying racks. "She only showed me part of it. Not the first few steps. Not . . ." Not the things he might show her if they rode beyond those two hills. "Not how the hide is cut away."

"I will make you a fleshing blade for this."

"Would you cut up my skillet, then?"

"Skillet?" She described it with her hands. "Ah, that day," he said, nodding. "You stared at me that day."

"I didn't mean to stare, and I didn't understand—"

He waved the explanation away, for he had heard it before. Another difference between them. She did not think she was as bold as *he* thought she was, and they were both able to laugh about it now. He reached into his buckskin shirt and drew out an arrow-shaped amulet that was suspended on a thong around his neck. "I would make your blade from this."

"Flint," she said as she examined the fine-chipped edges of the opaque reddish-brown stone. "We call this flint. You can make me a knife from this?"

"For making meat. Fine blade." He took her journal from her hands and opened it to the sketch of the fox. "You make this for me."

"You cannot fill your belly with my pictures," she teased.

"Make this on my—" He pulled a fistful of buckskin away from his chest.

"Shirt," she said, and his imitation of the word was muffled as he whisked his shirt over his head, the fringe swishing softly as he handed it to her.

She had no business looking at his magnificent bronze chest. He had no business baring it before her, but there was a magnetism between them that outpulled the constraints of impropriety. Wordlessly they struck a bargain to liberate each other, to uncover, to admire. "You have healed," she said.

She reached out to touch his puckered scars, but he intercepted her, held her hand, held her gaze.

"I am a Lakota man."

"I know." And he was not at all what she'd expected. "I am not a Lakota woman. I am . . ." *Not the same woman I used to be, but still a white woman.*

"I know you." They were the same words he'd said the first time he'd spoken to her, but the claim held more meaning now. He pressed her hand against his breast, palm over his heart, fingertips touching his scar, the sign of his sacrifice. He stroked her fingers and smiled. *Wiǧopa."*

A woman who pleases me.

Priscilla whispered the word to herself that night when she put her journal away in her steamer trunk. Before she stowed Whirlwind Rider's buckskin shirt beneath the petticoats she hadn't worn in months, she held it up for one more look at her preliminary sketch. Her fox would please him, too, once she applied the vegetable dyes Sarah had helped her make.

She held the shirt up to her own shoulders and entertained a fleeting thought of trying it on. She would be lost in it, the way she sometimes felt when she looked into his dark eyes or when she had to listen especially close because his deep voice could be so quiet sometimes. She had discovered that she could not get enough of learning about the customs of his people, and now it seemed she could not get enough of learning about him, of absorbing his every nuance like a thirsty sponge. Perhaps it was only because summer days were passing quickly, and her time was so short.

But then, so was his, she realized, and that of his people, unless her father . . . maybe *even if* her father had his way.

Their meetings became more frequent. Often he had something to show her—a special vantage point from which to observe a raptor's nest, or a place where the spring water tasted especially sweet. Once he brought her a newspaper that his cousin Little Wolf had taken from a trader's wagon. Little Wolf had thought the drawings of Indians pillaging a settler's cabin were funny. The clothing and the weapons were all wrong, and the faces were outlandishly distorted. But Whirlwind Rider was not amused by the drawings, and he wanted Priscilla to tell him what the words said. The words *heathen* and *savage* were difficult to explain. No matter how she phrased her explanations, he only stared at her in disbelief.

"The man who made this picture," he said, tapping his finger against the paper. "Did he see this thing?"

"I suspect not."

"Why does he lie this way?"

She was afraid to give him the answer that came to mind. *He lies to stir up trouble. He lies to breed hatred.* She opened her journal and showed him her drawing of Sarah and baby Joseph. "Do you see any lies in this picture?" she asked.

He shook his head. "That is the way my sister cares for her little ones." He pointed to the beadwork depicted on the yoke of Sarah's dress. "This is her finest dress. She takes LaPointe for her husband in this dress."

"Her wedding dress?" He nodded, taking her word, repeating it, committing it to memory. "I've written about what I've seen here and about some of the things you've shown me," she said, and she pointed to her picture. "I see this way because of—"

"You have eyes."

"Maybe it's good that I stare sometimes." She waited for a smile, but still he was not amused. "Maybe someone will print my pictures. Maybe I can write something for—"

"Write?" He crumpled the newspaper in his fist and held it in front of her face. "Go to school," he recited. "Write and read. Read what, Priscilla Twiss? What do you have us read? These lies?"

"If you read a lie, you can challenge it by writing truth."

"I will challenge," he promised, laying his hand on the hilt of the knife that was strapped to his waist. "These are paper lies to go with paper promises."

It was more complicated than that, Priscilla wanted to say. Complicated beyond his capacity to understand or hers to explain. Her father could be trusted to deal in the delicate balance of truth and hyperbole and to see that all would turn out for the best.

For her own part, she told no lies. When she told her father that she was going to ride along the river or that she was going to visit Sarah, it was always true. He never asked about Whirlwind Rider. She, of course, gave him no reason to.

"I see that you have followed my tracks," he would always say when she found him waiting for her. He was not always in the same place, but tracking him was like searching for a birthday gift that had been hidden for one special person to find.

"As usual, your trail was easy to follow," she called out as she urged her chestnut mare over the grassy edge of the bluff. "Sarah gave me your message." The steep, narrow path had been created over countless years by countless creatures making their way to the river. Priscilla had to lean forward for balance, which was tricky in a sidesaddle.

"A man makes a trail for a woman to follow by leaving his tracks in another woman's ear." He motioned to her. "Come down. I have tracks for your ear."

"A gentleman helps a lady dismount."

"I have no mind for your gentleman's games this day. A woman has legs and arms." She tipped her head to one side and gave him a hint of a smile, waiting until he laughed and put his hand on her waist. "Come, then, little *unśica* one. Use mine."

"I am not pathetic. This is simply a show of courtesy," she insisted as she braced her hands on his shoulders. "Of respect."

"I come to speak with you. I hear your words. That is respect." He lifted her easily and lowered her until her feet touched the ground. He was as pleased as she was with the excuse to grumble and tease and show off his strength. "If there are one-leggeds among the whites, you must give them this saddle. You have two legs." Pointedly he eyed her gray skirt and the toes of her black boots. "I do not see them, but I think there are two."

"This is the way a woman should ride."

"It is no way to ride." He picketed her horse, then interrupted his roan's grazing. "No, I think you must try a new way," he insisted as he straightened the fringed blanket on his horse's back. "Come here, Priscilla."

She was indignant. "I can't get up there without a step, and where will I put my foot if there's no stirrup?"

"Use my arms. I will be your gentleman this day." He lifted a supplicating hand. "Come."

"That's the wrong side."

"Not for an Indian pony."

She stared at the horse's withers for a moment and wondered what Aunt Margaret might say, what her classmates, past and future, might think. When she stepped closer he lifted her so high that she had only to throw her left leg over the animal's back. She was fussing with her skirt when he vaulted over the horse's rump and slid up close behind her.

"It feels strange to put my legs all the way around his back like this." *Strange* was not quite the word to describe everything she felt with Whirlwind Rider's breath in her ear and his body pressed against her back.

He chuckled as he slipped his arm around her and took the reins. "Strange for you, little maiden, but good for him."

"Why should he care?"

"He wants this much here" —with his knuckles he touched her left thigh, then her right— "this much here. Now he can move . . ." He sliced an imaginary path with the side of his hand, indicating a straight line. "Now he carries us both with ease."

"I could argue that my horse carries me just as easily when I ride sidesaddle, but you probably know better. You can ride like the wind. I've seen you. You're the best horseman I know." He tucked his knees behind hers and tapped the horse's side with a moccasined heel. At a brisk walk they moved from shade to sun. "The best rider," Priscilla said. "Which must be why you are named Rider."

"I am *Whirlwind* Rider. Wamniomni Akanyanka."

She repeated his name in Lakota, then turned to him for approval. The small rolled brim on her hat bumped his nose. "Oh, Rider, I'm sorry." With a quick jerk she unpinned the little hat and took it off. "Sometimes the sun makes me—"

"I have news to tell you," he said impatiently.

"I'm listening." She stared ahead at the lazy curve in the river, half wishing she could see his face, half relieved that she had her back to him. He would tell her now that he was not coming back anymore.

"There will be more talks at the agency soon. I am to be the eyes and ears of my cousins."

She took a deep breath, closed her eyes, and exhaled slowly. Progress she thought, and her tutoring had been a factor. "You're going to serve as a translator?"

"LaPointe will do that. I am not so quick."

"You are very quick. You amaze me, in fact. I've never known anyone who learned—"

"Only with you. You help me understand. I listen to white men speak. When they talk fast, some words—" He shook his head, and his gesture indicated that the words escaped him.

"That happens to me, too, when I visit the village. But I think I understand a great deal of what is being said. More, I think, than some people realize. Isn't it fun when they think you don't understand?"

"Sometimes." He did not share her excitement. His charge was too weighty. "I must know what they say. Every word."

"You are to be the eyes and ears of your cousins," she repeated slowly, and then she realized which cousins. "The hostiles."

"The Minneconjou. The Hunkpapa. The Oglala who follow Crazy Horse now. They will know what is said at these talks."

"You can trust my father. He wants what's best for your people. The treaty gives you land and plenty of food and clothing, and soon there will be schools and farms and churches. It will be just like . . ."

"Some of these words mean nothing to me, *wigopa*. It is like fast talk."

"I would like to take you back to Minnesota with me, so I could show you." Aunt Margaret's two-story house overlooking the Mississippi River would be the place to start. "Except that you might not"—moreover, Aunt Margaret might not—"like the way . . . it might take some getting used to. Things are different there."

He ignored the suggestion completely. "How is it now with legs on two sides?"

She had ridden astride before, of course, but not bareback. It was a bit more of a stretch, and the warm body between her legs coupled with the one at her back were more than a bit unsettling. "It isn't that I can't manage it," she said, "but I don't think a woman is made to sit the horse in this manner."

He chuckled close to her ear as he reversed the horse's direction. He understood most of her words, and the rest he could guess, but she knew much less than she thought she did, especially about women and what they were made for. He had no interest in seeing her land or the inside of her schools, but he wondered about the teaching she had had. What was the sense of learning so much about reading and writing and so little about the nature of life?

"The soldier fort is strange," he mused. "Too many men without women. LaPointe tells me the soldiers come for protection. What do they protect? Where are their villages and their families?"

"Some of them probably have no families. But they protect more than . . ." She thought for a moment. "They protect their fellow countrymen and all of their villages and all of the—"

"Why must they come *here* to protect those things? A hunter travels far to find meat. A warrior rides to raid for ponies. Not to stay." It was a curiosity often discussed among the Tokala when they shared a pipe and the warmth of a fire. It was his *aḱicita* that bore the responsibility to protect the most vulnerable members of the village—the women and children and old ones. A man gave his protection with the strength of his body and with his presence in time of trouble. "Why must soldiers come here to protect villages far from here?"

Her answer came hesitantly. "There's the road to Oregon. The people on that road need protection."

"This I understand. But the soldiers do not follow. I am a Tokala, a warrior and a lance bearer. When the people strike camp, the *aḱicita* will take the road to protect them. It is not so with the soldiers. They protect the road, not the people. The Holy Road." He gestured toward the west and added disgustedly, "And the Iron Road."

"The railroad. That's how I got here." She glanced up at him as if she hoped he would concede its usefulness on that point, but he did not.

"How many roads will they make? The soldiers do not raid for ponies. They do not hunt for food. What do they want?"

"Land," she admitted. "But not yours. The treaty protects your land, and the government has sent my father here to see to it. And to teach you some new ways."

"I teach you a new way to sit on a horse. Does your father know a better way?"

"He prefers to ride in a carriage, actually, but he knows some other things. He knows how to grow food."

"The Mandan grow food." He pointed to the north. "Now the Mandan are dead from sickness and hunger. And now your father would give us their tools." The traders understood better what the Lakota people needed. "The soldiers have the tools we want."

"Guns, you mean. My father will not let the soldiers make war on the Lakota, if only they will not make—"

He had heard this promise before, but he would not hear it from her lips. She knew nothing of making war. "The treaty says we must not hunt in the Powder River country."

"I know you hunt there anyway." She presented him

with her profile, the knowing sparkle of one eye, one side of her smile. "I won't tell anyone that."

"Not even your father?"

"Not even my father." She rolled her eyes skyward. *"Especially* not my father."

"I think he must know." They were back where they started in the cottonwood grove. The mare lifted her head briefly as they approached, then went back to the business of cropping the grass around the stake that tethered her to the ground. Whirlwind Rider pushed back a little, then sprang effortlessly to the ground. "There will be fighting," he told her as he looped his rein loosely in a low bush. The roan tossed his head and stripped off a mouthful of the small green leaves.

Whirlwind Rider patted the horse's sleek neck, then raked his fingers through the black mane. "I see white men shoot many buffalo and make no meat. The hunt is hard for us now. The Red Cloud people sit in their lodges and wait for the agency rations, like boys who watch their snares, hoping the rabbit will come." He looked up at Priscilla. "We are not rabbit-eaters. A man must hunt for food when the children hunger."

"You can grow food." She gave him a tight smile.

"Like the Mandan."

He reached up to help her dismount, and she put her hands on his shoulders as though it were routine. "Yes, like the Mandan," she said blithely.

"Like the Arikara people, who make their lodges of earth. Now they scout for the soldiers. Such that have few horses must beat up the ground with their hoes and be farmers."

Sandwiched between Whirlwind Rider and his roan, she was dwarfed by them both. She had to tip her head way back to look up at him, making her long, pale throat appear especially delicate and vulnerable.

He took half a step back. "It is a poor excuse for a man who would beat his mother."

"Mother Earth," she reflected as she drew her chin down a notch and stepped to the side.

He followed suit, smiling, keeping her boxed in.

"We call it ... that is, we say Mother Earth, too, but these words are not to be taken—" She fluttered like a trapped fledgling, casting about for a word, an explanation of the kind of thinking he did not care to understand, and a little more space. "We don't mean that earth ... that we are truly *born* of ... We only *say* mother."

"You say many things." He had only let her flutter away so far. She clutched her little hat in both hands now and stood her ground. It was what he liked most about her— the way she met him head-on, made a show of being sure of herself even when she was not. "I believe what your eyes tell me. I know when your woman's eyes see a man and find him pleasing."

"I see a man who has come far, so very far." There was no pretense now. She laid her hand on his arm, and in her touch he felt no hesitancy, no inclination to draw back. "You have an important job. To be present at the talks, Rider. Such an honor!"

"Have I been given a new name, then?" He took her slight shoulders in his hands. "We must make a naming ceremony."

"It's just a name between friends," she said as he leaned gradually closer to her. He heard the catch in her breath, and when he finally touched his forehead to hers, she closed her eyes and whispered, "Because I think ..." He rolled his forehead from side to side, letting his nose lightly, briefly touch hers. He felt the velvet hat graze his belly as it slipped from her fingers and fell to the ground. Above his hipbone he felt her fingertips fleetingly touch, then skip away.

"I think we are friends," she said, her voice as vaporous as the hiss of a dying fire. Ah, he realized he had her poised on the precipice now, and she had made the decision not to fly.

"This ceremony has no words, *wiǧopa.*"

"No words?"

She wanted to touch him, but she didn't want to interrupt or interfere. His approach seemed so transitory, like a cat making friends with her, learning her contours and textures, face to face. Be still, she told herself. Be cautious.

The tip of his nose traveled softly over her temple. She felt his warm breath and warmer skin, and she wished that his lips would touch hers, just once, just for a moment.

"I have no blanket here," he whispered into the upswept hair, some of it damp, some of it wispy, some of it coming undone.

"Blanket?"

"No courting robe to hold around us."

"Are you courting me?"

He touched his chin to the bridge of her nose and passed it slowly over her eyebrow. "I am learning you."

"Teaching me?"

"No." He lifted his head and looked into her eyes. "Learning you. There is much to learn, and there are many ways."

"I know how quick you are to learn." She wondered if he knew how to kiss and if she knew enough about it to teach him if he didn't. The silly, crazy thought had her smiling at him like a wanton. "I suspect you know a great deal about . . . all these different ways."

"I can teach as quick as I can learn." He chuckled when her face went hot and rosy. "You are a strange woman," he said with a wry smile. "Bold with your eyes and your words. You ask many things. Would you have me answer all these things?"

"I would have you tell me . . ."

"I would need more words than you can teach me. But I can tell you with no words."

"Words are safer." It was a reminder to herself. "You've never threatened me, but sometimes I'm afraid." He let her go, and she felt bereft as she watched him turn away. "Because my father keeps talking about hostiles and friendlies," she said quickly. "And Captain Harmon says that the hostiles want to fight."

The addendum brought his attention back. In his eyes a fleeting question was followed hard upon by a look that was markedly male and seemed to challenge her in some way. "That's what hostile means," she explained in a tone that was markedly female, gently instructive. "Ready to fight."

"In my heart I am a hostile, then. I am not one of your father's loaf-about friendlies. You are wise to fear my touch."

"No, I'm not . . ." She moved toward him, her skirt swishing in the grass. "Sometimes I'm afraid of my own—" They stared at each other. *Her own what?* "Sometimes I forget that . . . that I am not a Lakota woman."

"You are a woman." The pronouncement made her tingle from head to foot as his insolent gaze washed over her. He stepped close, touched her cheek with the back of his hand. "You have a woman's skin, a woman's voice." He put the tip of one finger to the corner of her eye. "The eyes of a woman, the look a woman gives a man."

"I don't mean to be—" She closed her eyes and shook her head. *Flirtatious? Yes, she did. Sometimes she did.*

"Who is Captain Harmon?"

Her eyes flew open. "No one." But she saw his doubt, and she confessed, "A soldier. One of their leaders, I suppose. In his heart he is hostile, too."

"Wašicun," he said, as though he were making an accusation. "He is a white man."

"Yes." Turning away, she snatched a triangular leaf from a drooping cottonwood branch. "And I suppose there is a difference between being a hostile and being—"

"A white man." He stood close behind her. "Does he court you in the white man's way?"

"He might think that's what he's doing, but he has not expressed . . . has never asked or suggested . . ."

"Do you want him?"

"No!" she bellowed as she whirled to face him. She was almost as amused as she was appalled by the notion, and she managed to toss off a quick laugh. "Heavens, no. Tim Harmon? He's of no real interest to me. He thinks he knows everything about everything, like most men, and he has no interest in what I have to say about . . ."

She was talking too fast and furiously, and Whirlwind Rider looked as though he didn't know quite what to make of her protest. "He has a mustache," she blurted out, as if, finally, that might explain everything. He scowled, with a gesture demanding an account of this thing. "Hair—" she

touched above her lip, as though probing for some—
"here, like so. And he always pulls at it and makes faces."

She pulled her mouth and chin into a long moue that
soon had him laughing. It was a deep, delightful, muscle-
relaxing sound, this laugh of his, and it was contagious.
She sank to her knees in the grass, her gray skirt billowing
around her like a mushroom. He followed suit, and they
laughed and mugged and tugged at each other's imaginary
mustaches. He dropped back in the grass, and so did she,
their shoulders only inches apart.

When the laughter faded, they lay there quietly and
watched a fat white cloud drift between two treetops.

"Red Cloud and his close relations—those who are
called the Bad Face people—are friendly for your father,"
he told her while they both still watched the sky. He shifted his arm until their hands touched, edge to edge on a bed
of prairie cordgrass. "I am friendly for you."

"It was good," she mused, and she turned her head,
seeking his eyes. Close-up blades of grass blocked her
view, so she propped herself up on her elbow and reached
over to touch his square chin. He tucked his arm beneath
his head and answered her touch with a smile. "Learning
your face this way was good," she said.

But it was as risky as it was engaging, because she was
still a white woman, and he was still a Lakota man.

Chapter 6

When she cared enough to persist, Priscilla usually got her way. Her doting father's attempts to dissuade routinely left her an opening. "It won't be very interesting," he warned time and again about the negotiations he was to host with the Sioux. "Sometimes these things go on and on, with a lot of smoking and not much discussion."

"I'll be a mouse in the corner," Priscilla promised. A mouse who served refreshments, she had decided, for if she'd learned one thing about being a woman in a man's world, it was that she gained admission more readily if she brought along something to eat or drink. Her ticket to the upcoming talks was in the oven. She had refilled Tim Harmon's coffee cup twice without being asked and served her father's favorite pancake recipe just to keep the morning's preparation on a friendly and even keel.

"I think you would do better to go about your business. Visit with Sarah," Charles proposed affably. His tone suggested that he'd been neutralized by a good meal. "You have set a fine example for her. Good Christian women, the both of you. She and her children have been baptized, and now it's a matter of completing the transformation, showing the way to a better life. I believe your visits with her are helping to further our cause among the women."

Much of her father's rhetoric went in one ear and out the other these days, probably because it was never anything new. "Sometimes the happiest effects of our efforts are those we could not have predicted," Priscilla acknowledged absently. She lifted the lid on one of the big cast-iron kettles. Her last meeting with Whirlwind Rider sprang to mind immediately as she took up a knife and ran it around the edge of her raisin-nut bread. He had teased her about all the "white powders" in the agency rations. She'd pressed him to name one good thing that came from the agency allotment, and he'd allowed that he liked raisins pretty well.

"Smell the fruits of my morning's work," she told the two men at her table as she passed the heavy iron pan beneath their noses. They obliged and nodded and made the proper sounds of approval, little knowing whose ultimate satisfaction she actually had in mind. "The people expect a visit to begin with food, which the host—meaning you, Father—ought to provide."

"The people?" Captain Harmon leaned back in his chair and gave her his usual officious look. "This is not a social event, Priscilla."

"It may well be history in the making, and I intend to serve coffee and sweetbreads while I listen in."

"Suit yourself," her father said. "One never knows with the Sioux when an advance or a concession might be forthcoming out of all the drum pounding and smoke puffing."

"The people have their own way of doing things," Priscilla said.

"Which you know all about now, don't you?"

Priscilla turned, surprised by Harmon's mocking tone. Even more arrogant was the look in his eyes, as if he suspected her of undermining his authority somehow. As if he *had* some authority over her that she might undermine. She stood her ground wordlessly, for she owed him no justification.

Harmon settled back into himself and turned to her father across the table. "History will chide our sorry souls unless we make some progress toward persuading *the people*"—he spared Priscilla a pointed glance—"to name one man as their leader. A head chief of all the Sioux would be able to speak for them and to make agreements in their name."

"Red Cloud is the obvious choice," Twiss admitted.

"That would be history-making indeed," Priscilla quipped. Both heads turned at once. "Red Cloud is perhaps more popular in Washington than he is among the Lakota these days. His relations are called the Bad Face people, and it's becoming an insult to be counted among them." She shrugged, adding, "For some, that is."

"Who would say such a thing?" Twiss demanded.

"And where would *you* hear it, Priscilla?" Harmon put in. "Red Cloud's own people love him well. His efforts brought about the '68 treaty, and just look at all they got out of it." He gestured deferentially. "They got your father, for one thing. Here to see to their needs."

"It isn't as simple as all that," Priscilla argued. "You know that Red Cloud's people have relatives among the hostiles and that the so-called hostiles are unimpressed by the treaty."

Harmon slid his chair back. "So-called as they rightly be, Miss Twiss, the hostiles' days are numbered. These *people* you speak of should tell their relatives that."

"I believe they have."

He offered Twiss a man-to-man look. "Apparently your daughter has gained a new perspective during the course of this study of hers."

"Indeed," Twiss said with a nod of assent. "The very conclusion any enlightened individual must draw—that these people must be shown the way to a civilized existence." He put his thumb against the rim of his empty plate and flicked it away from the edge of the table. "I was shortchanged on the last ration shipment. Were you aware of that, Captain?"

"It doesn't shock me, considering how much bureaucracy there is along the way. Surely you don't expect to receive all that is shipped." Harmon lifted one eyebrow. "Or all that has been promised."

"I expect to be able to lure these people away from their hunting practices, which means that I must feed them. Generously." Twiss reached across the table, holding up a soft, pudgy palm. "Like luring a wild animal with a handful of cracked corn. Soon they will all come in from the Powder River country and take the hand we hold out to them."

Priscilla noted the gold ring, the blue veins underscoring smooth pink skin. It was her *father's* hand. When had it ever looked so powerless and barren? It was nothing but an empty hand, hovering over an empty plate.

Like luring a wild animal?

Not the Lakota she knew. Certainly not the man who had endured the rigors of the Sun Dance with eyes wide open and wounds gaping just as wide. Priscilla could not imagine Whirlwind Rider taking the hand or the handout.

A large canvas tent had been erected on tall poles to shelter those who would attend the negotiation session at the Red Cloud Agency. The army's purpose was to persuade the Lakota to name their leader, who would be considered their spokesman and decision-maker. The Indian Bureau's goal was to begin taking a census, which would require the hostiles to allow themselves to be registered and counted, and to relocate some of the agencies deeper in Indian territory. This was not a treaty talk, but a redefining of old terms. It required a few officers and adjutants, the Indian agents, and the tribal leaders. No one ever knew how many of the tribal leaders would show up, and Agent Twiss hoped he had provided a tent large enough to accommodate everyone.

Priscilla hoped she could keep up with the coffee.

The headmen did not arrive together, but grouped by their bands they came in small parties, successively claiming center stage. It was like a parade, with each unit trying to outdo the last. The horses were decorated with paint and quilled blankets. The old men were dressed in fringed shirts decorated with shells, hair locks, and strips of beads. Their magnificent headdresses were double-tailed and covered with fluttering eagle feathers. The younger men wore hairbone breastplates, fringed leggings, and fewer feathers, having had less time to accumulate their honors. They were a people who knew who they were, and they had come bearing that simple message.

Whirlwind Rider rode with the Oglala, for the Minneconjou had not sent a delegation of their elders, the Big Bellies and the White-Horse Owners. They were counting on him to be their eyes and ears. With his head held high, eagle feathers standing tall on his crown, the white fluff at their base fluttering in the morning breeze, he took pains not to notice the one woman who was present.

She had half a mind to call out his name and ruffle his feathers a bit harder. But she kept still. She knew she'd not escaped his eye and that his dignified bearing was for her benefit as much as for anyone else's. And benefit she did, for the show he made was heart-stirring.

Her father was right about the smoking. The pipe was passed solemnly, and once it had made the rounds, it was refilled by someone else and passed again. The officers insisted upon chairs, while the Indians sat on the ground. Whirlwind Rider sat with two of the older men. Henry LaPointe served as a middleman, accessible to both sides.

Priscilla played her role as inconspicuously as she had promised. This was not a picnic. She was not a waitress, her father had instructed. She was his daughter. She provided coffee and sweetbreads for their guests. Later there would be a disbursement of extra rations. She knew that if the Lakota had hosted the gathering, there would be a meal, and she wondered what they thought of her meager hospitality.

She wondered what Whirlwind Rider thought of it.

She stayed close to the wall, but she didn't feel much like a flower. It was hot, and no air stirred around her post at the back of the tent. Her tan dress blended with the colorless canvas, and when Whirlwind Rider accepted the coffee she offered him, he seemed not to recognize her.

Charles Twiss made the first speech. He spoke of friendship and cooperation. He praised Red Cloud as a wise leader, but he was careful to acknowledge each of the other leaders by name and to mention individual achievements. Priscilla was pleased to watch the heads bob in assent as Henry LaPointe translated her father's words, but what pleased her even more was the realization that she understood many of Henry's Lakota words. Even if she had not heard her father's speech first, she thought she still might have grasped the gist of what Henry was saying. It was hard to remember not to stare at anyone who was speaking, especially since Priscilla did not want to miss a single nuance, but neither did she want to seem unmannerly before Whirlwind Rider's elders. It surprised her to realize that she was hoping her efforts would not go unnoticed.

When Major John Bartell rose to speak for the army, tension in the big tent rose with him. He spoke of friendlies and hostiles, of protection for the people who camped close to the fort and of the bad feelings for those who did not. There was grumbling when LaPointe translated these words, and one of the men sitting near Whirlwind Rider demanded to know why the army had not turned the railroad crews away from Indian territory.

"You must name one chief," Bartell demanded. He took a swipe at a deer fly buzzing around his thick gray porkchop whiskers as he directed his comments to Red Cloud. "One man who can speak for all the tribes of Sioux. There are more decisions to be made, but there are too many decision-makers among you. We must know who speaks for you."

There was more discussion among the Indian men. The air was heavy with the gravity of the demand, the afternoon heat, and the residue of their smoking. Whirlwind Rider conferred with the men closest to him, then with LaPointe, whose collarless white shirt was beginning to chafe.

LaPointe pushed the thatch of short-cropped hair back from his forehead and turned to the white men, who sat in a straight row, shoulder to shoulder on their side of the tent. "We are all decision-makers, they say. No one man speaks for all Lakota."

"Red Cloud is a wise man." Twiss leaned forward in his chair and calmly cut off Bartell's inevitable military caveat. "He has led the way for the Oglala for many years.

Surely the leaders can see the merit of allowing one such wise man to speak for all the Lakota."

"The Crazy Horse people are Oglala, too, but they are not here," LaPointe explained, welcoming the opportunity to address the agent instead of the major. "Crazy Horse does not choose the white man's food. He will not wear the white man's clothing."

"Then Crazy Horse does not lead his people well, for the food is here for them, and the clothing is only a small gift among many greater gifts we bring."

LaPointe hesitated a moment before translating. It was Whirlwind Rider's contingent that responded most vehemently. Priscilla heard only a few words clearly, but she could tell that her father's criticism of Crazy Horse was not well taken.

LaPointe took his place again, cleared his throat, and made his report. "We want no more soldiers and no railroad. On this we have agreed, they say. The Father Agent may stay and bring his iron tools and his books. It is good when the wagons bring hardtack and sugar." He pointed to the tin cup in Red Cloud's hand. "The coffee is good. Sometimes the flour is not good. In those times we leave it to the creatures who live in it." He nodded toward a younger man who had been sitting through the entire proceedings with arms folded. "And my cousin says to tell you the beef does not make our hearts strong, like the buffalo."

"Beef is better," Twiss insisted. "You can keep the animals in a pen and have meat whenever you need it."

LaPointe's translation spawned some inside comments and a few chuckles among the Indians. Whirlwind Rider made a remark that had something to do with the white man's idea of a hunt, and Priscilla stifled a giggle behind her hand.

"This stalemate cannot continue," Major Bartell bristled. "There must be a chief of all the Sioux. We have been dealing with Red Cloud, and we shall continue to regard him as your highest chief." The major postured, arms akimbo, scanning the group like an overseer. Contrary to his claim, he passed over the old war chief with a dismissive glance. "Unless the Sioux cooperate with us, there will be more soldiers. More guns. *Bigger* guns. East of the Missouri River and beyond, we have more soldiers than could possibly appear in any of your dreams, and they all have guns."

"This is not what we want," Twiss said quickly, even before LaPointe had completed his translation. "Believe me, friends, we are men of peace. We don't want more soldiers to come."

"Then do not ask them to," LaPointe suggested without instruction.

Whirlwind Rider motioned to LaPointe, and together they conferred quietly with two of the older men. Shaking his head, LaPointe came forward once again. "My wife's brother, Whirlwind Rider, wishes to speak in his own behalf. He is one of the Tokala society, a warrior and a lance bearer, and he has brought honor to us"—he gestured in deference to his brother-friend, who was climbing over the robes and the knees of his bunched companions, making his way to the center space—"at a young age. He speaks—"

"Let them hear for themselves how I speak," Whirlwind Rider said. "This peace you have made is a small thing. You offer us what we already have. Food. Clothes to wear." He touched the sleeve of LaPointe's cotton shirt. "Land that is ours already. You speak of soldiers and guns, then again this peace. I am learning these words, and I ask the meaning of this peace." He turned slowly, sparing Priscilla a quick glance as he spoke. "I am told, it means not to fight. I am not . . ."

He lifted his hand in search of a word or a bit of enlightenment, but he did not find it in the stern faces of the white men. Closing his hand slowly into a fist, he shook his head. "You bring more soldiers not to fight. You have enough soldiers here, not to fight."

LaPointe stepped back, squatted among the seated elders, and quietly translated Whirlwind Rider's words.

"This Father Agent, he comes like the traders. Bringing gifts." Whirlwind Rider eyed Twiss. "But not like the traders, and not like the soldiers, he brings his family among us. He brings his daughter." There was a murmuring on both sides as his voice intoned respect. "And she walks among us, not afraid." Then, gently, "This means not to fight."

"My daughter has great regard for the Lakota," Twiss said cautiously.

"Regard," Whirlwind Rider repeated, testing the sound of a word he did not know. Then, with the bearing of a prince, he addressed the agent explicitly. "I would make her my first wife, so that our families will have the same grandchildren. This, too, will mean not to . . ."

Amazement struck much of the gathering with the pronouncement of the word *wife*. Whirlwind Rider felt it immediately. He saw the black- and gray-bearded heads turn, one to another, and he recognized the signs of indignation, the rumblings of disapproval. But the one sound that singed his ears like a flying spark was the feminine laugh he knew so well. As always, it sounded at once bold and bashful, but this time he was not amused by it. This time it was a rude and breathy squeal that blended mirth with stupefaction and speared him with humiliation in the presence of his elders. His face burned, and although the white men stared at him in horror, he knew the men of his tribe would have the decency to lower their eyes from his shame as he concluded, "That is all I have to say."

From what was no longer her inconspicuous corner of the tent, Priscilla clapped her hand over her mouth and watched in utter astonishment as Whirlwind Rider stood there in the awkward shock of silence, trapped by his own artlessness like a fish in a net. The thought of marriage had not occurred to her. Not with Whirlwind Rider. That was what had made their growing friendship such a pleasure. With Whirlwind Rider, she hadn't had to consider the bothersome notion of marriage. Not until this moment.

He'd made a public announcement, thrown down the gauntlet, and proposed what was tantamount to a political union without forewarning her, without giving her any hint that he'd had such thoughts. Slowly he pivoted in the center of the council, her people sitting in their blue uniforms, his bedecked in buckskin regalia, all watching. Their eyes met. Hers pelted a thousand doubts, and his betrayed their sting.

He turned away, heading for the sun-filled side of the tent. She scrambled to her feet and called his name, but he kept walking. Then she heard her father's voice in her ear, ordering her back to the house.

She tried to shake him off. "I must talk to him. I must explain . . ."

"Explain?" Twiss grabbed his daughter's arm and gave it a quick shake. "You'll explain to me, young lady, but not here. Not . . ."

The young men waiting outside the tent whooped in response to Whirlwind Rider's sudden exit. The tall, gangly youth who had been given the honor of horse tender was right on the spot with the roan. Whirlwind Rider took the reins from the boy and vaulted onto its back. Priscilla tried to call out to him again, but her heart was wedged in her throat, and she managed little more than a hoarse shout as she watched him ride away with the brother-friends who had claimed him.

Amid the confusion of exiting Indians and blustering officers, Priscilla became the object of more than a few scowls and stares. Captain Harmon shouldered his way past his fellow officers and helped Charles shepherd his daughter away from the mayhem. Together they marched her across the yard, Harmon huffing and puffing as he blasted Twiss. "It's a mistake to bring a white woman to an agency outpost. These people are not civilized. You never know what they might do, Twiss."

Priscilla kept looking back, straining to catch another glimpse of the departing Indians as she stumbled along between the two men. "It was such a surprise," she said, dazed. "So unexpected."

"The conference is a shambles now," Twiss lamented. "We'll have to start all over again."

"I think he misunderstood. I think—"

"Misunderstood?" Charles Twiss stopped in his tracks and turned to his daughter, silently asking the question he couldn't bring himself to phrase. In answer, Priscilla only lifted her chin defiantly. "I think it's time for you to go home," he said finally.

She demanded a choice, and her father gave her one. If she wanted a husband, Tim Harmon would make a respectable one. Otherwise he was putting her on the train back to Minnesota. From there, he said, she might make her arrangements for school. Any school at any cost. He was not a wealthy man, but he would find the means.

It was precisely what she had wanted ever since she could remember really wanting anything. It was a chance to study with the brightest young women, to be instructed by the best teachers available to female students. Now that she knew a little Lakota language, now that she had seen sights and heard sounds that few white eyes and ears had witnessed, her studies would take on a new importance. Now that she had come to know Sarah and Whirlwind Rider . . .

She'd hoped to see him once more before she boarded the train, but her father had forbidden her to leave the agency compound. She wanted to apologize, to explain, to thank him for the honor. To say good-bye.

Her trunk was loaded aboard the train, and the big locomotive was huffing and hissing and wasting steam. Her father seemed both anxious and distant, as though she'd already left him. She wasn't certain what she'd done, or what he thought she might have done. Several times during the course of their preparations for her departure he had stopped whatever he was doing and looked at her, hard, and his jaw would start working as though he might ask a question or offer some kind of truce. But each time he'd given up and turned away as words, for once in his life, had failed him. She discovered that it was a relief to wave to him through the window as the train lurched and bumped her about in her seat. It was good to be moving.

The train had built up a full head of steam and chugged a few miles down the track when she heard someone shouting. She sat up, glanced out the far window, then the one next to her. A soldier and a drummer sitting across the aisle from her did the same. The door at the back of the car flew open, and the brakeman stuck his head inside. "Looks like some fool's chasing the train!"

Priscilla couldn't see anything at first. The squat, gap-toothed soldier hopped across the aisle, stepped over the legs of the cowboy sitting in the seat in front of hers, leaned, and ducked, trying to get a look out the window.

"Bearing down out of them hills," the brakeman said, pointing southeast.

Priscilla looked again. She saw the rider's long black hair and the horse's burnished mane and tail flying freely as the pair streaked across the flat, headed straight for the train.

"Damn hostile!" the drummer exclaimed as he craned his neck, then dodged the droopy brim of the soldier's hat. "Damn red Indian. Shoot the bastard, somebody."

"Oh, my Lord," Priscilla whispered. "Rider." She noticed the trooper's movement from the corner of her eye, and she gasped. "Don't—" With a quick surge she braced one knee on the seat opposite hers as she lunged for the pistol. "No, you must put that away. He . . . I know him. My father is the agent at the Red Cloud Agency."

The soldier shoved her aside. "I don't care if your daddy's President Grant hisself, lady, that's a redskin devil lookin' to take scalps." He leaned just out of her reach and laid the barrel on the window ledge. "Easy as pickin' off buffalo."

"No!" PriscIlla dove halfway over the seat and knocked the weapon out of his hand and out the window. Whirl-wind Rider gained on the train. She caught her balance on the back of the seat, leaned out the window, and held out both hands as though she had the strength to push him back. But he kept coming. The stout roan kept pace easily with the locomotive. "Rider, go back! They'll kill you!"

He reached up and offered her something, touched it to her outstretched hand. Hard, smooth—she took it quickly, made a fist around it, and thumped it over her heart. There was a flash of triumph in his eyes as he dropped back and disappeared from her view.

The soldier grabbed her arm. "What's the matter with

you, girl? There's probably ten more o' them devils waitin' up ahead or somethin'."

"No, please, he just wanted to—"

"He's comin' around again," the drummer announced from across the aisle. "Hell, he's runnin' circles around the damn train."

"I'll get him," the cowboy proposed as though he intended to retrieve a dollar that had rolled under his chair. He drew his pistol as he climbed over the seat.

"Pick yer shot," the soldier said.

"No!"

"Shut up, girl." The soldier shoved her back down in the seat, then hopped up on the backrest in an effort to get a better view. "Take yer time but hurry it up, like they say down in—ooof!"

Priscilla used her elbow in a maneuver she'd learned from Sarah when they'd played Knocking the Ball. The soldier tumbled over backward as she flew across the aisle. "They're trying to kill you, Rider. Go! Go back!"

Gunfire exploded within the confines of the little car. The echo of the first shot magnified the report of the second. It was so loud it paralyzed her for an instant. "Stop it!" She clapped her hands over her ears, and her own shrill voice seemed distant. "Stop it!" Her heel slipped on the floorboards as she scrambled to reach the window.

"You get 'im?" the drummer asked nervously.

"Can't say fer sure." The tall cowboy peered out the window. "Must've hit 'im. Don't see where he fell, but he ain't ridin' that horse no more."

"No." Priscilla couldn't catch her breath, and her chest hurt with the dearth of air. She fell against the window and leaned into the wind.

The roan streaked across the flat. It might have been mistaken for a wild mustang, except that it was still blanketed, and there was a quiver or a scabbard strapped to its neck. Priscilla gripped the windowsill, muttering, straining to keep the horse in sight. She felt numb. "Rider, you can't be . . . Oh, no, Rider, no, what have you done . . ."

"Hell of a rider," the cowboy told the soldier, who was

picking himself up off the floor. "Made two full circles around us."

"Prob'ly countin' coups on the train, crazy bastard." The soldier turned to Priscilla, rubbing a sore elbow as he gave her a disgusted once-over. "I oughta thrash you, girl. Better tell yer daddy to keep them red devils in line. Likely they'll all end up like that 'un, sooner or later."

Nothing the men said made sense. It had happened too quickly. He was just *there*. He couldn't be dead. She hadn't seen him fall. His eyes, that fierce, proud look in his eyes ... He was not dead. She bolted for the door, stepped out on the platform, and watched the hills roll by. Nothing. Grass and buckbrush and sky and nothing. Yellow and blue and brown, all of it became a watery blur. She gripped the sharp-edged stone he'd given her until she made blood drip down the front of her dress.

"Riiii-derrrr!"

Chapter 7

*Standing Rock Sioux Indian Reservation
Summer 1971*

Cecily's helpers had deserted her. One minute they'd all been scraping away on the windowsills and the door frames of the old church, everybody straining, everybody sweating under the hot South Dakota sun. Suddenly the shout had gone up, "This side's done! Last one down to the river is a dead puppy!" and all hell had broken loose. Ladders had toppled, scrapers went flying, kids were diving through doors and windows, and Ellen Red Thunder was revving up her battered blue '59 Ford pickup.

Cecily's side wasn't done.

"You comin'?"

Ellen had no difficulty projecting her voice above the oversized engine's roar. From the first time they'd been introduced—Cecily, the summer intern, and Ellen, the on-site youth team leader—Cecily had envied Ellen her take-charge voice. Its low timbre complemented her dark beauty, her tall, raw-boned stature, her self-assurance. Cecily assumed they were close to the same age, but she'd never asked. Ellen could be as old as she wanted to be. She never had to raise her voice, and it never popped into the air like a shrieking rocket and shattered somewhere in the ionosphere. Ellen was powerful.

Cecily was steadfast.

"We'll never get this done if you guys keep quitting early!"

All she needed was another half hour to finish up. The little church on the prairie, too isolated to be of much use anymore, was still a piece of reservation history. It deserved a fresh coat of white paint.

"You keep at it, then. My side's ready for paint."

"You missed a spot, Ceci-lee." Tom Spotted Eagle aimed a finger at the sky. "Up there on the steeple. Better get that right away."

With Ellen at the wheel and a mixed bag of local kids and out-of-state summer volunteers whooping it up and waving cute bye-byes from the back, the rattletrap pickup had left her in a cloud of fine clay dust.

So Cecily Metcalf had missed the boat. She didn't like swimming in the silty Missouri River backwater, anyway. It smelled fishy. She preferred riding the mission school's horses during recreation time, but everyone else always wanted to go swimming. She also preferred to stick to the schedule, which made her the constant killjoy. The kids were always pulling something on her, teasing her about being "too uptight." But they weren't mean. They'd be back.

And if they didn't come back, she didn't care, because she was going to finish scraping around the windows of the old mission church so they could get on with the painting. Even though the afternoon sun was making her feel a little dizzy, she was going to finish. Even though her shoulders ached like crazy, she was *going* to *finish.* Even though getting left behind bothered her so little that she'd just cut her hand on the damn scraper—"Oh, shhhh-oot!"

The paint scraper slid to the ground, bouncing noisily along the metal ladder's rungs on its way down. Cecily lowered herself one notch, glanced down, and saw spots dancing around the tool she'd just dropped. A big red drop of blood splattered on the white handle. She looked at her hand. Another drop was gathering on the joint crease of her little finger. She gripped the ladder in her unscathed hand, flexed one knee, and cautiously dangled a bare foot in search of the next step.

She felt woozy. The space below her stretched and snapped back like a rubber band as her bare toes and the scraper in the grass vied for clear focus. Her blood splattered on both. She tipped her head back and looked up. Big mistake. The top of the ladder swayed against the edge of the roof, and the clouds swirled overhead like a square dancer's white crinoline.

"Oh, shhhh-oot. I'm going to fall."

Somebody behind her chuckled. Some male. Back just in time to get an earful from her, as soon as the spinning stopped. She closed her eyes and rested her forehead against a hot strip of metal.

"Why don't you just say it?"

She didn't recognize the deep, whiskey-warm voice. Either he was pretty tall, or she'd slipped a couple of rungs. The voice was close behind her.

"Say what?"

"Shit. Sometimes it helps." She felt something brush against the back of her calves. "I've got it."

"Got what?"

"The ladder. You gonna faint, or what?"

"No, I'm *not* going to faint. I dropped . . . I'm coming down."

"I'm waitin'."

She lowered her foot again and bumped her forehead down a rung, but she still couldn't find a foothold. "I think you're in my way."

"I think I'm in the way of you falling flat on your back and taking the ladder with you." A strong arm snaked around her bare midriff. She sank back against the promise of support, but she clung tenaciously to the ladder, which was familiar territory. "I've got you," the voice said. "Swing your leg over."

"Over what?"

"*Got what? Over what?*" Another deep chuckle. "This ladder can't be the only thing you're high on, honey. You got any left?"

"Don't be ridiculous." She closed her eyes, then opened

them again. Didn't seem to make a difference. Spinning spots. "I'm a little ... dizzy."

"Just relax."

He lifted her, guiding one bare leg in an arc, as though he were trying to get her to do some sort of tango. Short on choices, she went along. She dropped her head back against his shoulder and glimpsed patches of blue and white, mottled with black. It was the first time she'd ever been swept off her feet. It was sort of a disjointed, other-worldly sensation. All she knew for certain was that he was very strong, and she was feather-light. Both nice notions somehow, only she was afraid she might throw up and ruin the whole effect.

She landed in a saddle. She wondered how he'd managed to lift her into the saddle and slide himself behind it in one fell swoop. "I'm really sorry, I ..." She felt *so stupid*. "I have to ask you ... what exactly is going on?"

"You're passing out, little girl."

"I'm not ... either."

"Either what?"

"Either a little ... girl or ..."

"From where I was sittin', there were just two bare feet and a nice little butt." She turned, leveling what she hoped was a formidable glare. His insolent smile convinced her that her glare mechanism was malfunctioning. She probably just looked pie-eyed. Her smart-alecky good Samaritan, on the other hand, appeared to be about as tall, dark, and handsome as any dream she'd ever had.

Good Sam pointedly helped himself to a peep over her shoulder and down the front of her shirt. "Okay, where I'm sittin' now, I'll take the little-girl part back."

"I'm not passing out, either."

But she was leaning heavily against his chest. He gave a soft whistle, and the big horse moved into an easy lope. Cecily instinctively grabbed for the saddle horn, but there was no need. His arm was banded about her waist, his warm hand clasped to her side, left bare by the shirttails she'd tied up under her breasts.

Gingerly she rested her bleeding hand on her thigh.

"Where are we going?" Not far, she hoped. Cutoffs and bare feet were not the best horseback-riding attire.

"Find some shade."

"The church . . ."

"My horse doesn't like churches. Says the seats are too hard and the water tastes funny."

"This one doesn't have either." She glanced over her shoulder. Familiar territory. The ladder leaning against the steep-pitched roof, the little clapboard structure with its twin privies out back, the dilapidated picket fence—all of it fast sinking into the sun-drenched distance. "It's a landmark, you know. We're restoring it."

"Ain't no landmarks on the rez, girl. Just worn out shacks."

"That isn't true. There's a lot of history here. That little church is almost a hundred years old. A lot's happened . . ." She felt disoriented, and her usual cure for that—talk fast, the bearings would follow—wasn't working. She closed her eyes and let her head drop back, just for a moment, she thought. His shoulder was there.

"You okay?" His hand abandoned her side in favor of her wrist. "Make a fist."

"Is this a test?"

"Might stop the bleeding. You got an extra scrap of cloth or something we could tie around your finger?" She demurred with a glance. "Nothin' you wanna part with, huh?"

"Hot day," she muttered as she complied, squeezing hard around the stinging cut. "Down to the basics. Don't have a sock to spare."

"You know, you're right," he mused as he slowed the horse's gait. They were nearing a gnarled bur oak that looked as though it had been dropped in the middle of the prairie fifty years ago and never managed to coax any more of its kind to take root. "This place *is* history. Over and done with. Not a damn thing happens here anymore." He lowered his head closer to her ear, and his voice to a soft murmur. "Except every once in a while on a hot day some tender little white girl from somewhere east of the river decides to get down to the basics."

"Do I know you?" She hadn't thought to ask his name, and he hadn't thought to offer it. But she had a feeling it was something she already knew.

"In what sense?" His fingers stirred against her midriff, and his full lips curved in a sensuous smile. "If you make a habit of passing out in a guy's arms like this, you just might know me better than you realize."

"I did not pass out."

"Coulda fooled me." The horse picked its way through a tract of buck brush, snorting in disgust. "I've done it myself once or twice. I know the signs. Only your problem is too much sun."

Just shy of the shade tree, he handed her the reins and dismounted with an agile vault over the horse's rump. "Don't you have a hat?" he asked as he led their mount to a grassy spot.

"I left it in the pickup."

"And the pickup is down by the river with the rest of your crew." Sparing her bare feet from the treacheries hidden in the prairie grass, he lifted her out of the saddle, set her under the tree, and punctuated the whole cavalier act with a flourish by plopping his black cowboy hat on her head. "Now you've got a hat."

"Thanks." It was a little big. She adjusted it while she watched him tether the big stocking-footed sorrel.

He moved like a cat, loose-limbed and easy, smoother on his feet than most cowboys, who tended to be a little bowlegged. But he was broad-shouldered and narrow-hipped, and he wore his jeans like a cowboy, cut with just enough room to permit him to swing his leg over a saddle. His thick black hair was hat-creased, but neatly, almost rigidly trimmed.

"I'm Cecily Metcalf. I'm a volunteer with the student exchange—"

"I'm Kiah Red Thunder."

"Ellen's brother." Ah-ha, a corner piece of the puzzle. In the two months since she'd moved into the mission school dorm, she'd heard all about this one. "That's good. That's a relief. At least I *feel* like I know you."

"You don't look relieved. Fact is, you're lookin' a paler shade of white."

He sat down next to her and leaned back against the old tree's deeply furrowed gray bark. She pasted her knees together, tipped them to one side, and tucked her heels under her buttock, sitting as primly as she could manage in short cutoffs. He smiled deviously as he watched. She ignored the look.

"Did they send you for me?"

"Nah, I saw them head out. Saw them leave you behind. You're the do-gooder's do-gooder, aren't you?" He reached into his shirt pocket, pulled out a cigarette, and stuck it into the corner of his mouth, then went back for the matches.

"I'd like to see us finish more than one project before the summer's over." She felt silly about her hand. She was trying hard to ignore the throbbing, but it was like clutching a shard of glass. As awkward as it was to carry on a conversation, she was determined to rise to the occasion. "You're the one who's home on leave from the army?"

"I'm Ellen's only brother." He struck a match on his thumbnail, lit his cigarette, and drew a deep lungful of smoke. As he exhaled, his eyes narrowed behind the haze. "The one who wouldn't listen to her about going to college so he could save his people, or whatever the hell she's got in mind for me." He stretched one leg out and drew the other knee up close for an armrest.

"The one who's throwing his life away because he volunteered for the draft?" she asked. He gave her an affirming look as he took another long, lazy drag on his cigarette. She nodded. "Yes, I think she may have mentioned some of those things." If Ellen had mentioned *her* at all, he'd probably heard that she was gullible. He could spin any tall tale for her, and she'd swallow it. She'd even hand him the opening. "Why did you volunteer?"

"Something to do." He shrugged. "They were gonna take me anyway. I wanted it to be my choice. They made me some promises, but they only kept the one about getting a chance to travel. So I'm makin' the most of my opportunities." He glanced at her hand and bobbed his chin to indicate his interest. "You still bleeding?"

She opened her blood-smeared hand tentatively, extending it his way. Blood oozed afresh. "It's not as bad as it looks. It's on the crease."

He gave a sound acknowledging her plight as he plugged his cigarette back into the corner of his mouth. It bobbed between his lips as he spoke. "Why did you volunteer?"

"Same reason. Only you're going to Vietnam, and I'm just . . . What are you doing?" He'd just pulled the front of his red shirt open, popping all the snaps like a row of plastic bubbles.

"You're just slumming on the rez for a summer." He yanked the shirttails free of his belt. "Doin' good deeds, bein' real good-natured when the joke's on you, which it usually is."

"How would you know that?" His chest was smooth, tan, and so perfectly developed it almost took her breath away.

" 'Cause I've heard all about you. You're the serious one." He leaned back to allow for access to the front pocket of his jeans, and he noted her wide-eyed stare. "Jesus, not *that* serious. Compared to you, I was feeling overdressed." His little joke gave him a chuckle as he came up with a pocketknife, unfolded the blade, and tore into a shoulder seam. "It's an old shirt, but it's fairly clean."

"What are you *doing?*"

"Makin' myself a sleeveless shirt. Too damn hot for sleeves." He puffed on his cigarette as he examined the severed sleeve, picked a spot, and tore into it. "The sight of blood makes me nervous these days."

"For heaven's sake, you're tearing up a perfectly good shirt."

"Ain't the first time." He brandished a neatly torn strip of cotton for her inspection. "See? I do nice work. Give me your hand."

Mumbling something about the waste, she scooted her bottom across the grass while he took one last drag on his cigarette, then stubbed it out on the sole of his boot. He tore the paper off the unfiltered butt and salted the earth with bits of tobacco mumbling as indistinctly as she just had.

"What . . . what did you say?" It was her nature to ask. He looked at her as though she'd offended him.

"I'm sorry. I . . . I thought you were speaking to me." She glanced away. They both knew it wasn't true.

"Tunkaśila," he repeated as he took her hand into his care, laying it carefully on his thigh. "Old habit. Have you had your shots?" His scent was a provocative blend of leather, horse, and tobacco, and she wondered if anyone had ever tried to bottle it. He glanced up, smiling. "I'm all caught up on mine."

"I might need . . . What are you *doing?*"

He pulled a piece of sleeve from his mouth and laughed. "You left your glasses somewhere, right?" He shook his head as he cradled her hand and went about gently cleaning some of the blood away. "You ever watch one of those mimes?"

"Yes."

"I saw one on a street corner in San Francisco before I shipped out. Bet if you'da been there, you'da spoiled his whole act. 'What are you *doing?*' " he mimicked. " 'What *are* you doing? What are you doing *now?*' "

"You do such unexpected things," she mused, smiling absently as she watched him work. His hands were large and so deeply tanned that the contrast between hers and his was startling. But she doubted she could match his gentleness.

"Spit's healthy," he said. Then he looked up with a quick smile. "Saliva. It's clean. It fights germs. Mothers use it all the time."

"And fathers?" she asked. "And grandfathers? *Tunkaśila* means grandfather, doesn't it?"

"Yeah, but it also means—" He'd wrapped her finger in the strip of cloth and tied the ends. "Is that too tight?"

"It's fine. Did your grandfather teach you these things about"—she turned her hand, studying the neat bandage—"survival and spit and all?"

"Old Indian trick, learned from my grandfather." He

waited until she looked up at him, and then he laughed. "I'd like to be a fly on the wall when you go back home to Minnesota or wherever you're from and throw out all the Band-Aids in the house. You'll be tearing up your shirt and spitting all over it every time somebody gets a cut like this so you can show off what you learned when you spent the summer with the Indians."

He reached for the knife and his shirt and set about removing the other sleeve. She watched quietly, feeling stung. When he finished, he folded the knife, pocketed it, and finally looked up. "Feelin' any better?"

"I'd feel a lot better if you'd just stop"—stop what? acting, what?—"looking at me like that."

"I'm lookin' the best way I know how." He offered a slow, appreciative smile. "I'm not interested in the short shorts or the one extra button you've got undone there. What I'm lookin' at is long legs and damp cleavage." And he kept right on looking while he put his shirt back on. "You want me to look like some bashful country boy? No point in me blushin'. You wouldn't be able to tell, anyway."

"You can have your hat back." She snatched it off her head and thrust it out to him, as though the thing had chafed her. "You can either hide your face under it or hang it over that chip on your shoulder."

"Ah, the kitten has claws." He put his hat back on and adjusted the brim down low. "I like that."

"Do you?" Considerate one minute, cocky the next, he rattled her. She hoped it didn't show. "How in the world did you get to be Ellen's brother? I've seen her put guys like you away with a single word."

"And it sure as hell ain't *shoot.*" He settled back against the trunk of the tree. "You've already put me away, honey. I'm real worried about the chip on my shoulder."

"And I'm not slumming, either," she insisted, as though his invectives had all run together. "Slumming is in the eye of the beholder, right? That's not the way I see it."

"You came here for the great mystical Indian experience. I hear we're really in this year." He straightened suddenly and eyed her critically. "Don't try to tell me you came as a church volunteer to bring the Word of God. Not in that outfit."

"I don't think I'm going to try to tell you anything. I don't understand why someone as cynical as you would actually volunteer for the draft."

"Cynical? Me?" He laughed and settled back again. "Lady, that's a big word."

"You're big enough to handle it." His self-possessed smile was too aggravating to let stand. "But, you see, it doesn't fit. Nobody's volunteering these days except the most misguided idealists."

"Which I'm obviously not." He leaned closer, planting one elbow in the grass. "So maybe I'm just suicidal."

"I hope not."

"Maybe you could save me from myself."

"How long have we known each other?" She checked her watch. "Has it been an hour yet?"

"My time is short, honey."

"Like most soldiers'?"

"Like most Indians'." She did a double take, which he dismissed with a wave of his hand. "You're not interested in soldiers, so let's forget about them."

"I didn't say I wasn't interested in soldiers. It's just that I think the war is—"

"Don't." He raised a warning finger. "You don't know anything about the war. You might think you know something about politics, and maybe you do. But you don't know anything about the war." He rolled to his back, bracing himself on his elbows. "And I don't know anything about politics except that it sucks. The people always get screwed."

"What was your lottery number?"

"I missed the lottery. I got into the game before they changed all the rules."

"What would it have been?"

"What difference does it make? I'm going back to 'Nam for a second tour. The rules don't change over there." He slid his hat back as he looked up at her. "You know the Golden Rule?"

"Do unto others as—"

"Before," he corrected. He plucked a piece of dried nee-
dlegrass and wagged it instructively. "Do it unto them *before* they do it unto you. Makes good sense." Sinking
down between his shoulders as though he were settling
comfortably into his philosophy, he crossed his outstretched legs at the ankles and stared off somewhere.

"See, Indians never understood that, back in the old
days. You're interested in Indians, right?" He checked
back with her, and she gave him a nod. "You read a lot of
stuff about us before you came out here, about how noble
we were and about how war was kind of an honorable
thing and you didn't go around killing the other guy's
women and children and wiping out his whole family for
fun and profit. You know all about that, right?"

"Right."

"Bet you did a college term paper on it or something."

"I'm doing an honors project on the connection between
geography and native religions."

"Honors project," he repeated, considering the words.
He stuck the grass stem between his teeth and lay back,
setting his hat aside when the brim got in his way. *"Honor*
is another one of those big words. You can hide a lot of
gigis in the honor closet." He tucked his arm behind his
head as he glanced at her. "You know what a *gigi* is?"

"A ghost?"

"Are you afraid of ghosts?"

"No." She had no experience with them. "Are you?"

"Scared shitless." He chuckled. She decided it was another of his private jokes and that he probably had a million of them. "You wouldn't make a very good Indian if
you don't believe in ghosts."

"I didn't say I didn't believe in them. I'm just not afraid
of them. In fact, I like the idea of spirits from the past
being"—she waved her wounded hand in the air—
"around. With us, part of our lives. I don't think anything
is ever really dead. I think we have connections with"—
his chuckling grew merrier—"the past. You're laughing at
me."

Damn cocky male. She hated that male attitude thing.

"Maybe you would make a good Indian. Better than me.

Ask Ellen, maybe she'll get one of the old men to adopt you into the tribe. But you'll have to be careful for those *gigis*. Somebody dies, you gotta burn everything to keep those past connections from messin' with your mind."

"Burn everything!" She shook her head, and the skein of hair she'd clipped up off her neck flopped back and forth. "I love old things. Antiques. Things that have been around a long time, so you feel like they bring other people's lives into yours, like a continuation."

"Dangerous business," he warned. "Ghosts only hang around if they're unhappy."

"I don't think they *hang around*. I just think . . ."

"Is this all part of your honors project?"

"No, of course not." Gesturing eagerly, she shifted her hips and switched her legs to the other side as she spoke. "But doesn't that make sense? Life goes on, and nothing is really ever over because the effects are passed on, and people feel the effects. You know, something that happened to somebody a hundred years ago, and you're still feeling the effects—well, there's a connection."

"Sure, life goes on. And when I leave, things around here . . ." He plucked the stem from his mouth and rolled to his side and leaned back on one elbow, grinning up at her. "You know, the river just keeps on rollin'. The wide Missouri. You still wanna go for a swim?"

"I never *did* want to go for a swim. I don't like swimming in my clothes, getting them all wet . . ."

"We can fix that."

"Then you're soggy and wet for the rest of the day unless you . . ." But he was on his feet, dragging her up by the arm as he slapped his hat against his thigh and clapped it on his head. "Where are we going?"

"Downnn by the riv-er," he sang, decidedly off-key.

"I'm not taking my clothes off."

"Suit yourself." He tucked his thumb in his belt, and she followed the path of his gaze to the deep vee in her neckline, where sweat trickled into a little pool between her breasts. His shirt hung open in front, and he was grinning, cool as you please. "You're pretty soggy right now anyway."

"Well, it's hot!"

"Which is why we're going swimming. You can wear whatever you want." He retrieved the sorrel and extended a hand to her. "You go swimming with Kiah Red Thunder, the joke's not on you anymore."

"Oh, really." She hesitated, then gave a sigh of resignation as she ducked a low branch and accepted his hand.

"Really."

He had the decency to go behind a tree when he stripped off all his clothes. She told herself it was the seventies, after all, and she was the only prude left in the world. She went behind a tree, huddling with her indecision in the face of his rousing whoop and mighty splash. She was so busy zipping and unzipping her cutoffs, she missed the opportunity to score him on form.

After three false starts she finally tossed the shorts under a clump of butter-yellow sunflowers and hung her shirt on the jutting branch of a neighboring deadfall. Her flowered bra and panties looked just like a bikini, and if she'd had any chutzpah, she would have glided across the grass like a *Sports Illustrated* model. She had a flat belly. She had the right kind of legs. All she was missing was the Coppertone tan.

And the brass nerve.

"I can't quite bring myself to go all the way," she announced as she approached the riverbank. *Damn timid voice.*

He laughed, that damn cocky male chuckle. "That's far enough for now, honey."

She lifted her chin and took a deep breath, which had a certain positive effect. "Well, just so you know. This is as far as I go."

He was out there treading sun-dappled water, grinning like the porpoise waiting for his fish. His chin seemed to be resting on the water's surface, and he was squinting against the sun.

"You gonna stand there all day just to make sure I get an eyeful?"

"You did keep your underwear on, at least, didn't you?"

"Come find out for yourself."

"This is kind of a nice spot," she allowed as she waded in. First step, mud squishing between the toes. Second step, questionable hard thing on the bottom. Third step, no bottom. *Nice spot, my foot.*

"Every cowboy has his favorite swimming hole. Gotta be able to wash off the trail dust now and then."

"Oh, so now you're a cowboy, too."

"Can't you tell? I like being a cowboy better than I like being just about anything else you wanna call me." He circled her, sidestroking, keeping a distance. "Including a sonofabitch, which usually comes into the conversation somewhere down the road."

"What road?"

"The road to romance."

"Don't be ridiculous. You're home for, what? Another week or so?"

"I've got you down to your bra and panties already, and we've known each other, what? Two, three hours now?"

"Think of this as my bikini bathing suit, you sonofabitch," she said sweetly. He was closing in.

"Really? You're calling me by my middle name way ahead of schedule." Bobbing playfully, he aimed a tennis-swing splash and hit his mark.

"Oooh!" She lay back in the water and returned the favor with paddling feet. They circled each other like children squaring off, trading splashes instead of insults. Finally he jackknifed and dove deep, momentarily flashing his bare buttocks. He grabbed her ankles, and before she could kick free he'd grazed the length of her with his slithering body, front to front, bottom to top until his head broke the surface scant inches from her face. Floundering, she grabbed for his shoulders. He splattered her with a toss of his head and gave a sputtering but exuberant laugh.

"Um . . . you're buck-naked, cowboy."

"And my underwear is dry." Face to face, they bobbed together. "Are you smiling?"

Not quite. "Is that something I should be smiling about?"

But *he* was. The idea of keeping him at arm's length

might make her smile. She liked the idea of being chased and staying ahead of him. Yes, now that she thought about it. It was more risk than she was accustomed to taking, but for some reason, this far from home and with this particular man, she liked the idea. "Yeah, most women get that smile on their face when they call me cowboy."

Did they, now? "I'm not 'most women.'"

"Nobody is." He took her hands in his and ducked under her arms, turning his back to her in what could have passed for a dance step in an Esther Williams movie. "Current's pretty strong out here. Hang on"—with her arms draped over his shoulders, he tucked her hand beneath his chin and sang—"a little bit tighter, now, baby."

He went from dancer to tugboat, towing her in a path parallel with the riverbank, where the hoppers buzzed in the grass. The sun warmed their shoulders, but below the river's quiescent surface a swift layer of cold urged them to keep their feet moving. The air was so still and quiet that a trickling of water off the hand sounded like a waterfall. Hushed tones came naturally as they glided, propelled by an occasional stroke of his arm or flutter of her feet.

"Is this a good fishing spot, too?" she asked.

"Great fishing spot. You feel anything brush up against you"—his flirtatious backside grazed her stomach—"just ignore it. It's probably harmless."

"Probably?"

"Mostly. Unless you get it riled."

"How do you rile a fish?"

"You know, you act tough when you're in his territory. When you're a guest in his river, it's much better to just peacefully coexist. Don't knock him in the head if he happens to—" He drifted against her again, and she smiled, keeping her lips tight against the water's kiss. "Mmm, that's very nice," he said.

"What?"

"You know what. I don't usually let a woman get this close in the first three hours."

"You fight them off, I suppose."

"I coexist with women even better than I do fish, but *three hours*—" He did his pirouette again and came up facing her, holding her hands beneath the water's surface. He shook his head. His hair spewed droplets like a spinning umbrella, and he laughed. "Three hours is quick work, lady."

"On whose part?"

"Tell me what you plan to do for underwear when you get dressed." He grinned. "Feed my imagination a little."

"I plan to make do."

"What does that mean?"

"How much food does your imagination require, cowboy?"

"Good thing the water's pea-shrivelin' cold, or you'd be in deep trouble."

He figured it was up to him to get her back to the mission school dorm, which had been summer volunteer headquarters every year since he could remember. All he had was one horse, and with her wet underwear, he was looking forward to the ride back under that warm Dakota sun.

She figured she was already in deep trouble. Couldn't get much deeper.

Back at the girl's dorm, the news that she'd been swimming with Kiah Red Thunder did cause a stir. Kiah would have been pleased with the number of gasps and whistles his name generated. Then Ellen walked in on the parley, and the chatter shut down instantly.

Four teenagers—two white, two Indian—were all eyes and ears, but not a breath of sound until Ellen tossed Cecily's white sneakers on one of the six cots and flopped into the only chair. She relaxed, they relaxed. She looked up at Cecily and cocked her head to one side as if she were trying to read her face.

"We went back to pick you up, and you were gone. Looked like you'd dropped everything kinda sudden."

Cecily's face felt warm. "Actually, that's what happened. I cut my hand on the scraper." She displayed Kiah's improvised bandage and continued to regurgitate her defense like a sixteen-year-old. "And then I met your brother, who just happened to be riding by on a white horse, so to speak, because he really did come to the—"

"Kiah rides a big red stud."

"Kiah *is* a big red stud," one of the Indian girls quipped.

"How would you know, Deena?" Mary Feather prodded.

"Well, I don't." Deena shrugged her bony shoulders and shoved her hands into her pockets. "I've heard."

"Your *sister* knows," Mary said. Deena jerked a book of matches out of her pocket and threw them at Mary, who batted them back. Both girls scrambled across the floor after them as though matches had suddenly become a rare prize.

"I doubt that."

Ellen Red Thunder wasn't interested in a tussle over matches or reputations. She was tempted to sit back and ignore the whole thing, but looking at Cecily—wide-eyed and well-meaning, as usual—made it a little difficult. Maybe she shouldn't have left this little white chick out there all alone when she knew full well that her notorious brother—the damn chicken hawk—was on the loose.

"Kiah's pretty choosy," Ellen said. "He's used to taking his pick, Cecily, so be careful. He's here today and gone tomorrow."

Maybe it was none of her business. Ellen wasn't much interested in minding other people's business, even though, as youth supervisor, she was supposed to see that everyone followed the rules. She was supposed to try to head off the inevitable summer program romances at the first pass. But Cecily wasn't a kid. She was Ellen's age. She was a college intern, a student counselor, presumably a girl with some smarts. Her worst weakness was that she tried too hard. And she was tediously naive. Still, Ellen had signed on to shepherd the summer program's entire brood.

"He came along when I needed a hand, that's all. And then"—Cecily took the offensive with a look and a tight-lipped smile—"since my friends had all deserted me, he took me swimming. That's *all*." Having made her point, she relaxed, and her smile became genuine. "He's very nice."

"Kiah? Nice?" Ellen shook her head. "He'll charm the skin off a snake," she warned, and she used her mother's favorite stiff-fingered gesture to make it stick. "And an innocent lamb out of her fine white wool. You know it, too. You're not *that* innocent."

"Ellen, for heaven's sake. I'm not about to . . ." Cecily gestured impatiently, waving possible missteps away as she shifted gears. "You told me he was going to Vietnam. You didn't say he'd already been there."

"Special Forces. He asked for it, he got it." And she had yet to figure out why. "He wants to fight, he could do it right here, but he'd rather go off and get wasted in some rice paddy."

"He's not really"—Cecily hesitated to repeat the word—"suicidal, is he?"

"He tell you that?" Ellen cast her eyes ceiling-ward and laughed. She could just hear him, not saying it in a pitiful way, but in the style of an irresistible smart-ass. "What a line, Kiah boy. You are so full of it."

"I didn't really think he was . . . I mean, people who are suicidal don't *tell* you they're suicidal."

"He'll tell you whatever you wanna hear, like most men."

"He's your *brother.*"

"He's my brother," Ellen agreed. "You'll have to let me know if he's heavy."

"Ellen!" Equal parts shock and titillation shone in Cecily's eyes.

Cecily would pine for him, Ellen thought. She was as soft as fresh dough, and no warm-blooded woman was likely to refuse Kiah a bite of bread. Didn't matter who she was or where she came from. Kiah had that effect on women. This one undoubtedly assumed she would be the exception—*she* was different. Whatever Kiah had in mind for her, she probably had it coming.

Or maybe she would be the exception. Maybe she *was* different. And maybe Kiah had it coming. Two lovesick puppies pining away for each other with an ocean between them. Wouldn't that be cute?

"My mother's putting on a feed for him," Ellen said. "You wanna go?"

"A powwow?"

"Celebration time in Little Eagle. All kinds of food, dancing, local rodeo, and my brother in all his shining warrior's glory. You up for testing your defenses?"

"It was a hot day, so we went for a swim," Cecily insisted primly. "That's *all* we *did.*"

The drumbeat seemed to emerge from the center of the earth. It made the night feel eternal. They had driven across a long stretch of quiet prairie, feeling the drums before they'd actually heard them, leading the way to a place behind many hills. The sleepy village of Little Eagle seemed otherworldly, like a place out of joint with the time, but the drumbeat was all-time and the faces of friends and relations coming together for a festival belonged to all-people.

Set apart from the town itself—its small houses and unpaved streets—the thatched shelter of the bowery, which was the dance circle, was a broad purple silhouette against the red evening sky. A tall pole rose from the center, displaying Old Glory in the spotlight. Cecily wondered whether the flag was raised just to honor the local soldiers, but Ellen told her that every bowery had its flag. "Nobody honors the American flag the way Indians do," she said. "They like the colors. They believe the promises. They've been bleeding under it for a hundred years."

"They?"

"Whoever keeps raising it up there," Ellen remarked as she slammed the door on the battered blue pickup. "It's not me."

But Rebecca Red Thunder honored her boy in the traditional way. The Little Eagle VFW color guard marched him into the bowery. They wore a motley assortment of old uniforms—for some that amounted to the piece or two they could still fit into—but they all wore the cap of their local post. And they all took their roles seriously. A middle-aged veteran pushed an ancient one's wheelchair. The man and woman who carried the flags wore pristine white gloves. A drum group performed the traditional Lakota flag song, and Cecily could not, for the moment, remember a word of anti-military rhetoric.

Kiah did everyone proud, saluting smartly, maintaining an attitude of attention with eyes straight ahead. When it was time for the giveaway, he took his place with his family. His mother and his aunts had been stitching quilts for a year, and they'd made shawls and bought blankets and cigarettes, all to be given away in his honor. The announcer called the names of friends, elders, and supporters. Each came forward to accept a gift and shake hands with Kiah and his mother and sister.

Cecily admired the way he stood tall in his uniform with its battle ribbons and the stripes of his rank, his Special Forces beret dipping close to his eyebrow, his pants tucked neatly into the tops of his black boots, polished to a mirror shine. He was bright, beautiful hero material. He deserved homage. He deserved to have his pick of women. He deserved to be cast in bronze so that he could be just this young and strong and splendid for all eternity.

It took the recollection of his wicked laugh, his crude innuendos, and the water lapping at his natural, unpadded, ununiformed shoulders to bring Cecily's senses back. She caught herself smiling from the sidelines when she thought of his bare butt flashing in the river like freshwater trout, and she thought, *I know the real you, soldier boy.*

And then her name was called.

It was Ellen's doing. She'd whispered something to her mother just before she'd handed her a pink and blue star quilt. Cecily mumbled her thanks as she shook hands with the old woman with the long gray braids. Rebecca nodded. Ellen smiled playfully. Kiah was next. He stepped to the side as he accepted her handshake, moving her with him as though an extra foot gave them private space.

"This is a nice surprise," she said, absently smoothing out the stitched squares draped over her arm.

"So are you." He glanced at the quilt. "Looks like baby colors. You plannin' on any babies?"

"Not any time soon." She pulled her hand back and smiled apologetically at the old man standing behind her. "I'm holding up the line."

"Save me a dance," Kiah said quietly.

After the giveaway, Ellen grabbed her brother by the

arm before he could get away, even for a smoke. "You take care of my friend, will you? I need more signatures on this petition." She produced a clipboard from her big blanket-weave tote bag and flipped through the pages torn from a yellow legal pad. "Care to put your name down to support a cause that counts for something?"

"What's your cause this week?" He wasn't really interested, but with a look and a conspiratorial smile he made it clear that he was willing to take care of her friend.

"Decent doctors." She shoved the clipboard into his hands. "There's this one we need to get rid of right away."

"She thinks *I'm* militant," he complained to Cecily. Then he told his sister, "You barely get a couple of doctors for the clinic here, and you want to blow them away. Sure you don't want my M-16? It's quicker."

"I want your name, if you can remember how to spell it." She handed him a government-issue ballpoint pen. "He's really no good, this doctor. A little girl mouths off to him a little, so he ups and slaps her in the face. Of course the girl tells her grandma. Her grandma tries to tell the hospital administrator, 'We don't slap the children.' He doesn't listen. He says this doctor says he only tapped her a little."

"Maybe he did."

"The way we got tapped when we were in school?" The look they exchanged silently acknowledged any one of many mutual memories. Not that he wanted to remember, but she insisted. He sighed and put pen to paper.

Ellen went on with her story while she supervised his signing. "Same doctor, his dog gets hit by a car—some fancy pedigreed dog or something. He takes the dog into *our* clinic and X-rays him. This one old man comes into the clinic after he falls out of a car right on the highway like that 'cause his door wouldn't stay closed. But the old man, he has to sit and wait for this doctor to finish taking X-rays of his dog."

Kiah handed the petition back, then the pen. "So what happens if you get a thousand signatures, and they transfer the doctor?"

"We get another one." She tucked the clipboard under her arm. "Maybe he's better this time."

"It's the same old story, Ellen. They just shuffle the deck every so often."

"No, it has to change sometime." She was about half convinced. "This is the Age of Aquarius. Right, Cess?"

"So they say." She wondered why Ellen hadn't told her about the doctor and the little girl and the old man.

"You kids behave while I go look for more signatures."

She left them standing just outside the bowery, he with his hands in his pockets, she with her arms folded tightly around her new star quilt. With Ellen out of the picture, the moment suddenly became awkward. The announcer called out, *"Hopo!* Everybody dance!"

The drum rumbled steadily.

"What kind of dance am I saving you?"

He wasn't sure why he'd said that. He hadn't expected her to be there, but there she was, and he hadn't wanted to let her get too far out of his sight. "There's a white dance over at the gym. The band knows two songs, 'Hang On Sloopy' and 'I'm Your Puppet.' Take your pick."

She nodded toward the bowery. "I'd like to learn to do this."

He wished he'd brought along a change of clothes. A pair of jeans, maybe even a few feathers and beads. He wanted to be part of the Age of Aquarius, share her innocence and idealism, just for a week. She looked young and sweet in her miniskirt and the pale, gauzy blouse that was ironed just as crisply as the creases in his trousers. He felt like a tin soldier trying to make it with a ballerina.

He leaned closer to her ear. "I'd like to get naked and go swimming. What are you wearing under this pretty blue outfit?"

"None of your business!" She tried not to smile, but the light danced in her eyes.

"Them's fightin' words, honey." He slipped his arm around her waist. "Walk with me?"

Chapter 8

"So what did you think of all that fuss?"

Kiah's cap was already tucked in his belt. He was busy stripping off his tie the moment they'd ducked past a hot dog and frybread stand, part of the commercial loop surrounding the bowery where mostly non-Indian vendors offered everything from sauerkraut to salvation. "Did it embarrass you to watch as much as it embarrassed me, watching you watch?"

"You were hardly watching me watch you. I think you noticed me maybe twice." He'd given Cecily the admiring eye over the miniskirt. "Of course I was watching. The whole ceremony was wonderful—just brimming with tradition—and if you were embarrassed by the fuss they made over you, it didn't show. You played the part of the conquering hero very well."

"Conquering hero?" He chuckled as he made a neat sausage roll of his tie. "Not in this war, or even in this *life.*"

"I don't think they see it that way, so I don't see what could be embarrassing. Obviously your people are extremely proud of you."

He was leading her along a rutted path into the night's dark shadows, and she was following without question. She decided it was the uniform she was trusting.

"My people?" He shoved his tie into his pants pocket, jingling the change he'd meant to divide up among his cousin Tracy's kids. "You've been listening to my sister, and you're all hot on Indian customs and stuff. But you've got to be a little embarrassed about this particular spectacle, since you're against the war." She started to object, but he cut her off. "And I'm embarrassed because these old guys think the VFW is some kind of warrior society and I'm out there counting coups for them. They think they're gonna initiate me into their club."

"Well, you certainly qualify," she said.

He sighed and shook his head, and then he was quiet for a moment. He gave her right-of-way along the narrow path while he walked beside her, his boots swishing through the grass as he guided her way. He knew the path to the creek as well in the dark as he did in his troubled sleep, full of thoroughly mind-messing, subcutaneous homesick dreams. The crickets laid their song over the drums' steady track. Their lyrics were better than his—a lot less monotonous than the stuff that played in his mind continually unless he found some way to anesthetize it once in a while.

A woman could do that. Merely the sweet, fresh smell of a sympathetic woman could drive the *gigis* away.

"You know how they used to count coups?" He didn't wait for an answer. "They used to ride up to the enemy, touch him with a lance or a stick or something, and ride away. They were looking for honor, and that was a brave and honorable thing to do, a way to earn yourself all kinds of eagle feathers." He glanced back over his shoulder. The lights of the bowery were distant enough, but he spoke as though the ears of those who had honored him there might not be. "Sure way to earn yourself a bullet in the back, if you ask me," he confided.

"You're fighting a different enemy."

"Those guys in the color guard, they fought in Korea, World War II. Did you see that old guy who got up out of the wheelchair to shake my hand? He's a World War I vet. That guy's father's enemy was"—he shrugged—"probably your great-grandfather." There was more wonder in his voice than bitterness.

"Who probably didn't know, didn't understand anything about counting coups."

"Yeah, well, I don't understand about it, either. I understand about shooting to kill."

"Before they kill you."

"Before they kill me. Watch it now, the path sort of disappears as we head up this little ... Here—" He put his arm around her shoulders, and before she had a chance to guess what he was up to, he'd swept her up in his arms. "You're not dressed for sneakin' off in the grass."

"Are we sneaking?" If they were, for whatever reason, it was kind of exciting. She was wearing a pair of low-top moccasins, her legs were bare, and her skirt wasn't covering much butt right about now. But she felt like a princess in the strong arms of an improbable cavalier. "I thought we were just going for a walk."

"We're gonna sit," he told her as he mounted the little cutbank, heading for a cottonwood that stood on the high ground above the creek. His heels skittered a couple of times, and she clung to his neck. "Hang on to that blanket," he advised. "We're gonna break it in."

"We are?" She looked up at him.

The night breeze ruffled his hair as he smiled. "Like at a picnic, you know, give it the first mark of grass stain. If it doesn't wash out, it'll remind you of the night you took a walk with that cowboy, that, you know, what's-his-name."

"Kiah Red Thunder, who was only around for a week," she said. He let her feet slide to the ground, and for a moment their unnamed hopes and fears connected as they looked at each other in the moonlight.

What about this week?

Only around for a week, and then what happened?

"I've got another week," he said. "That much I can—" Her shoulders twitched with a quick shiver. He took the quilt from her arms. "Maybe we should put this around you instead of under you."

"No, I'm fine," she insisted, nervously tucking a piece of hair behind her ear as she reclaimed the blanket and shook out the folds. She spread it beneath the tree, and he fell to assisting, reordering her method in the process.

"You like rodeo?" he asked as he pulled the blanket up

closer to the tree trunk. "Bronc riding, bulls, that kind of stuff?"

"I've been to two rodeos this summer. My first."

"Wanna go to another one? Tomorrow?"

"I'm not sure what . . . whether I can . . ."

"I want you to come." He sat on the blanket, his back against the tree, while she knelt tentatively at the edge. He repeated his entreaty with an outstretched hand. "The best part of a celebration is the rodeo," he told her, then added softly, "Just come."

She glanced in the direction of the activity they'd left behind. From their vantage point they could see the spotlight over the bowery and a few small fires in the nearby campground. The drumbeat matched the resolute pounding in her chest—something that was always there, always taken for granted. Tonight the reverberation resonated inside her ominously, like an echo in a barrel.

"Don't you like the dancing?" On hands and knees she closed the distance between them. "I mean the traditional dancing, not 'Hang On Sloopy.'"

"I don't mind hangin' on to *somebody*." He slid his arm around her and drew her up next to him.

"Whoever's handy?" Her fragile tone fell short of the nonchalance she was aiming for.

"You." He nuzzled her hair and whispered her name, making it sound like something potentially juicy and delicious. Everything inside her tightened into a quaking little prune.

He wasn't in the mood for a prune. He kneaded her shoulder until it sank under his hand, then stroked her arm, soothing her as he spoke. "I used to dance Indian when I was a kid," he told her. "They made me this costume—big fluffy leggings with bells at the knees, big feather bustle with red plumes, big roach on top of my head."

In the dark his free hand painted pictures of a boy he remembered only distantly, a boy who loved being decorated. "Little Big Indian, that was me." He imagined the mirror they'd stuck in front of his face. How old? Six? Eight? He couldn't have been that young. Ever. "They'd dress me up, and I'd prance around like a prairie chicken.

Never was much for clothes, but, man, I've had all kinds of outfits."

"You're more comfortable in your ... swimming outfit?"

"Now you're talkin'," he said with a breezy chuckle. "I like boots and jeans pretty well." He stuck his foot out. Big, black, and spit-and-polish military. "Not these boots. These weigh a ton."

"Cowboy boots."

"Can't beat a good pair of broke-in Tony Lamas." That was the way he wanted her to see him. He shifted, turning her toward him. "I'm riding saddle bronc tomorrow."

"I hope I can come. I—"

"You can come." He brushed his lips against her temple and whispered, "You'll come for me."

"Kiah, sometimes you say things ..." She put her palms against him, feeling the hard breadth of his chest beneath his starched shirt, and she entertained a fleeting thought that she would push.

She should, she knew she should, but separation from him wasn't at all what she wanted. He felt warm and smelled earthy. A spicy, bottled tang mingled with the musky scent of natural man drew her arms around him even as she admitted, "The scary thing is, I know you mean them just the way they sound."

"I don't have time to make up a lot of pretty stuff." He looked down at her, but darkness confounded him until he touched her face with a blind man's fingertips, searching for every detail. "Wish I did. Pretty girls deserve pretty words."

"I don't want pretty words. I don't want—"

"Yes, you do." She'd taken him in her arms, after all, when he'd made his enticingly equivocal prediction that she would come for him. He lowered his head, his smooth cheek grazing hers. They both wanted the same thing. "You're not gonna make me stand on ceremony like they did at the bowery, are you?"

"They didn't make you." She was desperately reaching for assurances first, honest or otherwise. His warm breath on her neck made a quick shiver flash through her body.

"You did it out of respect for them. That means"—his distracting hands moved slowly up her back, banishing the tightness there—"a lot."

"It would mean a lot to me if you'd give me something," he whispered close to her ear. "Like a kiss."

"If you don't have time for pretty words, you haven't got time for—"

His lips touched hers softly, teasing until she tightened her arms around him. He nibbled, touched the tip of his tongue to the corner of her mouth and ran it delicately along the seam, parting her lips. "I've got all kinds of time for kisses," he whispered into her mouth, and the next one came harder, deeper, wetter, his tongue probing for a response from her. Her tongue darted instinctively to meet his, and she heard a quick catch in his breath. He shifted her in his arms and slid one hand over her hip, urging her body closer. He tasted of salt and smoke, as savory as wild game. He was an adventure.

The crickets crooned, with the drums rumbling steadily in the background.

He unfastened the big barrette that held the sides of her hair back, and the fine curtain cascaded into his hand. "I love long hair on a woman," he told her. A voice in her head tried to remind her that they all did, but she couldn't remember who *they* were. There was only Kiah, combing her hair with his fingers while he cradled her against his chest.

"I suppose you like long-haired men."

"It isn't . . . a deciding factor."

"What is?" He looked down at her again. "What have I got that I can please you with, Cecily?"

"Your mouth," she said. "Your kisses please me."

"I can do a lot with my mouth."

"Talking is good, too. Getting to know . . ." The white flash of his smile startled her as he lowered her back against the blanket. She clung to him like a baby possum, her voice trailing off in a whispered ". . . each other."

"I want to know this part of you." He slid his hand over her breast, caressing her, somehow managing to undo first one button, then another. Before she knew it, he'd made a button of her nipple with a sneaky thumb. "This part is so pretty, so responsive," he whispered, and she closed her eyes, delighting in the tingling truth of his supposedly un-pretty words.

"Oh, Kiah, that's not fair," she moaned. He pushed her bra straps over her shoulders and lowered his mouth to the valley between her breasts. "I can't . . ." But she didn't *want* to move her arms. He nuzzled the lacy cup aside, and all sensation spilled over it as he tongued her aching nipple.

"You taste good." He blew on the nipple he'd made wet, then took it in his mouth and suckled until she groaned from the deep pang of pleasure. "You should have babies," he entreated her in a voice that would gentle a man-shy filly. "Lots of babies, so they can go to sleep in your arms with the taste of you on their little tongues."

"Don't talk about babies. It's not a good time to think about having . . . wanting . . ."

"I don't know much about *having*." He loosed the hook between her shoulder blades. His hand wandered over her skin and over her clothes, rubbing cloth against skin, skin against skin. It was a game she'd played before, but she hoped he understood the rules. "I can't help wanting," he confessed. "Neither can you."

"No, I . . ." He was caressing her inner thigh, danger-ously close, delightfully close . . . *I want, but I can't, but this feels so good.* "Oh, Kiah, what are you doing?"

"I'm makin' it my business"—he kissed her mouth as he stroked his way closer, gradually pushing the scrap of a skirt out of the way—"to know what you're wearing, shhh—"

As soon as he touched slippery tricot, she clamped her thighs together. He persisted, his tongue skimming against hers, his hand coaxing her to relax. When she did, he cup-ped her mound in the palm of his hand triumphantly, as if he'd scaled a mountain, and he broke off the kiss.

Chest to chest they traded erratic breaths as he focused on her moonlit eyes, daring her to deny him. In the dark she was a timid wild thing, waiting for him to make the next move. And make it he would, goddammit. But not with her looking at him like that. He lowered his head and whispered hotly into the hollow of her neck, "Just let me touch you."

"Promise you won't . . . Kiah!" The word was couched in a breathless little gasp as he slipped his fingers carefully past the elastic leg band of her panties.

"I promise, okay?" His kiss had made her lips fuller, and they were sweetly parted. "Just say my name like that again."

"Kiah," she said, her voice still smaller because his stroking had taken most of it away.

"How does it feel?"

"It scares me, it feels so . . ."

"Don't be scared," he pleaded, pressing his cheek against her hair. He didn't want to scare her. He'd seen scared eyes looking down the barrel of his rifle, but never his . . . Good Christ, not his gun. He wasn't looking for conquest. He was looking for respite. "I want you to come just for me, that's all."

One false move and she'd jump away from him. Just the feel of her had to be enough this time. Just the soft, downy feel of her and the warm, weepy feel of her and the involuntary thrust of her hips and the desperate little feminine sounds. The broad pads of his fingertips had her panting.

"Put yourself . . ." He closed his eyes and relished the power to please, to keep the pressure slight and the rhythm steady, even as the pressure in his pants threatened to blow him apart. She was teetering on the verge. *Let it down, honey.* "I'll take care of it, Cecily. Just let me hold you in my hand."

He didn't think he could stand it if she impaled herself on his finger, but she was doing her damnedest. He wanted her so bad, Jesus, why wasn't he fucking her brains out?

"Kiah?"

In the charged silence she was asking him the same damn question.

"It's okay, baby. Let yourself go for me." She had no choice. His thumb was on the detonator, and he had a light but unrelenting touch when it came to explosives.

She was hanging on to him for dear life and calling his

name in such a breathy way that he thought he might jump out of his skin if she didn't stop. He was damn sure ready to jump out of his pants.

"Kiah . . . you can . . ."

"Shhh." He pulled her tight against him, caught her buttocks in both hands, and pressed his erection hard upon her. She buried her face in his shirt, and he absorbed her shudders with his aching flesh. The last frantic gasp gave way to quivery quiet. The night breeze and the crickets and the drums swirled around them.

"You'll be okay, honey," he whispered finally, then marveled at how foolish he sounded.

"Will you?"

No denying, she was sweet. "Yeah, in a couple of hours." He chuckled, wishing he could wrap her up in the blanket, just the way she was, and take her home. "Or sooner if I go behind a tree."

"Oh, Kiah." She gave a shaky sigh as she drew back, clutching one side of her blouse in the fist she held to her breastbone. "You shouldn't talk to me like that. I should have better sense, and we shouldn't be . . . because we just almost—"

"You're not on the pill, are you." As though she were remiss, she caught her lip between her teeth and shook her head. "I didn't think so. Some sophisticated college girl. And I didn't bring anything with me."

"Some worldly soldier. I'm not—" She was struggling so pathetically with her clothes that he felt as though he owed her an apology, just for messing them up. "I don't usually get quite so carried away."

"No?"

She turned from him as she sat up. "I keep forgetting that I just met you," she said, injecting a little false bravado as she plied unsteady hands behind her back as though she had no experience with the hooks she was trying to fasten.

"We're gettin' to know each other pretty well." He took over the two ends of her bra and deftly coupled them. Then he put his arms around her shoulders and drew her back against him. Back in his arms was where he wanted her now, where she ought to be. "All I've got's another week."

"Please don't do that routine on me, Kiah." She put her hands over his arms, not to deny him, but to embrace the part of him most accessible to her. He liked that. He shifted them both so that she was sitting between his legs, leaning back against him. With his arms around her, she didn't seem to be in such a hurry to button herself all up again. He liked that, too.

"Do you want to go back to Vietnam?" she asked quietly. He drew his breath in sharply, then controlled its gradual release, close to her ear, but he said nothing. He had no answer to such an artless question, but she wouldn't understand that.

So she persisted. "I mean, you said this was going to be a second hitch, and I wouldn't think that would be something you'd *have* to do."

"You wouldn't?" There was no point in getting angry with her. If she'd ever been ordered to do anything that made her want to puke, it was probably something like taking out the garbage. He could just hear her telling Daddy she didn't *have* to touch anything that smelled bad.

He knew she wanted him to talk to her about it, tell her what it was like. It was a demand no Southeast Asian woman ever made of a GI. Didn't have to. They knew things about war that he hoped this woman would never have to know. He had one more week to wallow in her innocence. One more week to tarnish it a little, but nothing it would take more than another week or so after he was gone for her to redeem. One week, and he'd return to the horrors and the whoring, and she would get on with her happy life.

He tried to think of some innocuous answer for it all, just to satisfy her, but there was nothing he could say that she could possibly comprehend. Nobody could, except maybe those guys in the color guard. Old Felix Catch The Bear in his wheelchair, lifting his gnarled hand to salute the flag—Felix would know what it was like to see a buddy get his balls blown off. He'd know how you felt like shit because you couldn't help thanking God it wasn't you.

"I wanted some time out," he said with a shrug. He knew it wouldn't make a damn bit of sense to her without the details. But the details, from where they sat under the starry summer sky, were not possible. "I couldn't wait another two months or a month. I had to come home. So I worked this deal, bought a little time here for more time over there."

"How much more time?"

"A year."

She turned in his arms and looked at him, aghast, as though he'd just grown another head. "Kiah, that's . . . that's crazy. A whole year?"

"What do you know about crazy?"

No. No, that wasn't what he meant to say because her answer, no matter what it was, wouldn't lead him where he wanted to go with her. Tonight, tomorrow night, the next. He had time. He smiled and touched her hair and lost himself in the moon-sheen in her eyes. "I had you a little crazy a minute ago, didn't I? Hmm? Didn't I?"

"Yes." She closed her eyes and sighed and settled back in his arms again. "It isn't the same."

"You got that right." He dipped his head down next to hers and rubbed her, cheek to cheek. "You know what I like about you? You've got this real fresh-scrubbed look. And innocent. Are you innocent, Cecily Metcalf?"

"I'm almost twenty years old. How can I be innocent? I'm a human being, selfish and greedy and opportunistic just like—"

"Whoa, whoa, I'm convinced." He hugged her and rocked with her, side to side. "So what's a nice guy like me doing out here with such a wicked, wicked woman? Hmm? Do I stand a chance of getting corrupted by you?" Chuckling, he nibbled her ear. "Just a little bit?"

"I'll go to the rodeo."

"That'll ruin me for sure."

Chapter 9

It might be her own ruin, but Cecily decided that if she were meant to have one fast and foolish fling in her life, it would be with a cowboy. *This* cowboy. The die was cast when she watched him climb over the top of the chute and lower himself into the saddle. It might have had something to do with the way his jeans fit that small, tight butt, or the way his long back tapered into his belt, or the breadth of his shoulders, or the fact that his striped Western shirt was new and crisp and still creased from the package. Whatever the attraction, she knew she was hooked.

She scaled the fence and said something cute like "Ride 'em, cowboy." Kiah gave her a wink to match her corny line, pulled his black hat down over his forehead, and told the gatekeeper, "Outside!"

Squealing and hollering like a high school cheerleader, she gripped the rail and watched him churn up arena dust, flinging his arm toward the sky. With each punishing jump he arched his long torso, as lithe as a dancer's. Lord, yes, this was the man.

When the whistle sounded, he popped out of the saddle and landed on his feet. The bronc hadn't bucked hard enough for his liking. He'd been looking for a ride that would rattle his back teeth and make his balls go numb. His teeth were fine, and there was a lot of life left in his balls. He knew that the minute he saw the glistening-eyed smile on the face that was peeking over the fence like sunrise. Fair, fresh-scrubbed Cecily. Her blond hair was caught up off the back of her neck in a pert rooster tail that bounced when she cocked her head to one side, looking for him to return the smile.

He did. He couldn't resist, and why try? He was paying a pretty steep price for a few days' chance to do some real smiling. It all felt like a dream anyway, like a few nice words stuck parenthetically in the middle of a string of vulgarities, but he'd be a damn fool not to enjoy it while it lasted. He'd just stuck his bronc and won the go-round, and he had a pretty girl waiting for him on the other side of the fence.

Either she had no idea what that look did to him, or she wanted it as bad as he did. Damn if she didn't look just as sexy in her hip-hugger jeans as she did in a miniskirt. He felt a pinch when he swung his leg over the fence and dropped to the ground. She *would* have to be standing there grinning up at him just when he needed to make some adjustments around the personal equipment his chaps didn't cover. He stuck his thumbs in his waistband and shoved the whole works down a little.

She was still smiling, and he was ready to take her to the far end of the field where most of the cars were parked and find one with a big back seat. He tugged at the brim of his hat and gave her a cocky-bastard grin. "You like that?"

The cockiness seemed to be lost on her. "That was a wonderful ride."

A shadow fell across his space as he worked over the buckles at the backs of his thighs. "Nice ride, Kiah," his sister said. "You haven't lost your touch."

"Ellen says your score will"—Cecily cast about for the exact expression as Kiah pulled the gaudy black and red leather away from his body—"put you in the money."

"It's all yours," he told Ellen. He wasn't competing for the money. He had enough to get him by, and he'd have given it to his mother, but it would end up with Ellen sooner or later. "You collect it from the rodeo secretary and put it toward a good cause."

"We're putting on a benefit dance for Sherman Elk Horn," she said. "His furnace blew up in his face when he tried to light it."

"You might try putting some decent tires on that pickup before they blow *out.*" It would probably happen on the way to the clinic with his mother in the throes of insulin shock, but he kept the worrisome thought to himself. If he said it out loud, Ellen would get in the last word, and it would be something about her taking care of everybody around here with no help from him.

"They've got a few more miles left on 'em." She elbowed Cecily, jerked her chin, and aimed a lip-thrust past Kiah's shoulder. "More'n I can say for this one. Here comes one of your fans, brother."

Kiah turned and greeted C.B. Whiteman with a handshake.

"You see this boy kick it out?" C.B. crowed. He clapped a beefy brown hand on Kiah's shoulder and wordlessly offered him a drag off the cigarette he'd apparently just lit. C.B. was already a little juiced, primed for an afternoon party. The red glaze in his eyes was a dead giveaway, as was the glib praise he sang for Kiah. "This marine knows all about kickin' ass."

"I'm not a marine, C.B." Kiah drew deeply on the cigarette and offered it back as the smoke trailed from his lips. C.B. demurred with a quick gesture, and Kiah plugged it back in the corner of his mouth, then set about working his chaps into a neat roll.

"I thought you was a marine." C.B. jostled Kiah's shoulder, as if to wake him up. Kiah shook his head. Then he sneaked a confederate lopsided grin Cecily's way as C.B. flapped his free hand against his side. "Hell, I joined the wrong outfit. Signed up yesterday." He waggled Kiah's shoulder again. "You wanna celebrate a little?"

"I've got another—" The hand on his shoulder tightened. It was the cowboy custom. The rodeo tradition—hell, what was the point of bustin' your ass if you didn't throw down a couple of belts with the boys? Kiah sucked another lungful of smoke, then blew it out in a long,

steady stream. Besides, this was a buddy who had signed
up for madness, damn his eyes.

"Sure." He glanced at Cecily, then back to his old
friend, whose expression reminded him that once he'd
made up his mind a man didn't look back, especially not
into the eyes of a woman.

But he wanted both. He didn't have much time, and today was his day. He didn't have to ask her for permission,
goddammit, nor did he have to ask her if she'd hold his
chaps for him. He handed them over, and she accepted
them. To her credit, she didn't say a word. But she was a
woman, and she couldn't resist questioning him with her
sweet blue eyes.

And he answered her with a question. "You're gonna
stick around for a while, aren't you?"

Cecily glanced at Ellen. Damn, he thought, women were
always in cahoots on these things.

"You're riding again, *aren't you?*" Ellen aped angrily.
"Break your stupid neck, you start your celebrating now."

He raised a warning finger in his sister's face. "I know
what I'm doin'. Cecily wants to learn to dance. Take her
over to the bowery for a while."

Cecily watched Kiah and his friend make their way past
the rumps of saddled horses standing around hip-shot and
twitching the deer flies away. Scowling, she craned her
neck and watched the two disappear in the congregation of
straw-colored cowboy hats and red bandanna headbands.
He'd *asked* her to come to this thing, and now he'd gone
off and left her standing there with a handful of leather
and a sister who'd told her so.

She turned to a pursed-lipped Ellen. "Have we been dismissed?"

"We—*you*—have been put on hold while the boys go
behind the horse trailer and pass the bottle." Ellen's arms-
akimbo, cocked-hip stance reminded Cecily of the horses
that were similarly on hold. Only most of them were
hitched somehow.

"They're little boys with big, throbbing dicks," Ellen
said bitterly. "If you think of it that way whenever they
come at you with that baby-I-need-your-lovin' routine,

you'll be able to laugh them right back into their little-boy huddle." She gestured impatiently at the battered trailers circled at the far side of the activity like covered wagons. "Where they'll just make their plans for another play."

"Ellen—"

"He'll be gone in a week." With a look, Cecily took exception to Ellen's choice of words. *"Gone,"* Ellen repeated with a cut-off gesture. "No good to anybody but our Uncle Sam. And Uncle aims to use him up."

That was exactly what the bull did to him on his second time out. Cecily knew Kiah was in trouble when he came back for his chaps and she noticed a funny gleam in his eye. He drew a spinning bull, and after a few seconds he lost his balance. One of the horns caught him in the shoulder when he couldn't get out of the way fast enough.

He had a three-cornered tear in his shirt, but the loss of blood didn't seem to faze him. If he'd lost anything important, it didn't show in his swagger. The rodeo secretary's first aid kit yielded peroxide and bandages, which Kiah turned over to Cecily as if he were in need of a service she performed for him every day. He picked a car at random, seated himself on the hood, popped the snaps on his shirt, and shrugged out of it.

Cecily eyed the bloody gash as he lifted the lid on the box of precut gauze squares. Nursing wasn't her thing, but—she glanced up and bought right into that brown-eyed smile—Kiah Red Thunder was. Ellen was right—she had to watch herself. Her perspective was easily warped by that smile.

He flexed his shoulder and looked down his nose at the injury. "Almost just missed me, but not quite."

"Almost took your arm off." He was even cute when he was tight, damn him. Somebody handed him an open can of beer while she was juggling the brown bottle of peroxide and the gauze squares. He tipped his chin and slugged back a long draft. "Obviously, you've had too much to drink," she clipped without looking up.

"Spoken like a true wife. Are you in training?" He chuckled as he reached over Cecily's head and passed the can back. She ignored both the remark and the unintelligible male rejoinder that came from behind. "Just kidding. Hey, thanks, Al."

Kiah braced his palms next to his hips. She could feel him watching her, waiting for her to melt before his wit, but it wasn't going to happen. She'd attend to the business at hand, and then he could pickle himself and ride elephants for all she cared. She didn't know why she'd stayed to watch him ride the bull, never mind listen to him throw it.

"I haven't had enough to drink," he claimed. "If I had, I'd be—ouch!" Cecily smiled. ". . . feelin' no pain." She waited for the initial sting to subside, then daubed around the wound gently, determining that it probably wasn't as bad as it looked. "Anyway, I'm okay. I'm still alive."

"Have you eaten anything?"

"Hey, I've already got a mother. I know when to eat."

"Hold this." She guided his fingers to the gauze she'd centered over the wound.

"I'm havin' a good time, okay?" He held the bandage in place and watched her tear into the adhesive tape with her teeth. "Did Ellen teach you how to Indian dance? Not much to it, the woman's step. You just kinda—"

She moved his fingers when she was ready to tape. She was totally attentive to her job, except for the part of her that could feel his eyes burning a hole in the top of her head.

"What's the matter?" he asked finally.

"Nothing."

"Nothing, hell. What did I do?" She glanced up at him as she bit a tear-starter into another piece of adhesive tape. He looked genuinely confounded. "Jesus, you wanna eat, we'll eat. Where's Ellen?"

"I think she's mad at you. Or maybe she's mad at me." With both thumbs she smoothed the end of the tape over his muscled shoulder. "Half the time I feel like I walked in on the middle of the movie with you guys."

"All of us guys?" He waited until her eyes met his. "Or just me and my coldhearted sister?"

"Your sister's not coldhearted."

"And you need to realize this is not a movie. You're not watching a Hollywood Western. We're the real Indians." Her retreating hand didn't escape his. "The real thing, see? Real blood." He glanced down at the stain that had soaked through the center of the bandage.

She gripped his hand. "Are you sure you're okay?"

"I'm fine." He pressed his advantage, sandwiching her hand between his. "Listen, we're not past Indians, you know like tipi-creepin', buffalo-chasin' *past* Indians. We're not gonna lift your scalp or your lily-white virtue, and we're more likely to pass the bottle than the pipe."

"Really." She glanced away, embarrassed.

"It's legal to sell liquor to us now. We're full-fledged citizens. We can even—" When she wouldn't look at him or laugh or whatever she was supposed to do, he squeezed her hand. "I'm not drunk, Cecily."

"You're not going to ride again, are you? Even if you're not . . ." He kept that steady pressure on her hand, that plea for a concession from her. She didn't know what to say. All she knew was that she didn't want him to go off with his friends again. Damn the political stuff right along with the war between the sexes; she wanted him to choose to be with her.

"I know you're not drunk." Saying the words aloud made them true for her. The relief she detected in his eyes made her smile. "I could go for a hamburger."

He bought her lunch, but for himself he opted for coffee and a cigarette. Coaxing him to take a couple of bites from her hamburger felt like an accomplishment. He seemed more interested in greeting old friends, introducing her around, and soaking up everything that was going on around him. "Smell that frybread," he would say, but he shook off the suggestion of tracking the scent down and trying a piece. "Listen to those jingle bells," he said when they stopped to watch a group of little boys competing for a fancy dance prize. "The look on that little guy's face— look at him, Cecily. He knows. He knows how fine he looks out there."

He borrowed a friend's horse—a rangy brown and white paint—and they rode double, just as they had the first day with Cecily mounted comfortably in the saddle and Kiah sitting behind the cantle on a wad of wool blanket fringe. With his arm around her waist, he was comfortable enough, too. They rode past the parking area, past the stock pens, past the campsite with its assortment of campers and tents, and past the small herd of horses cropping grass in the pasture surrounding the fairgrounds.

"When you see it all from the back of a horse, you kinda feel like nothing ever changes," Kiah said as he pushed back the brim of his black cowboy hat. "And you kinda hope some things never will." He rested his chin on her shoulder and tightened his arm around her waist as he guided the paint along the bluff above the river. "In the old days, Indian people used to court on horseback. They used to give out horses instead of engagement rings."

"Now you're talking about the past Indian people, right?" He gave a shoulder-rubbing nod. "Just so I have it straight."

"It's not that far back, most of it. The thing is, you guys have most of it wrong. So some of it still *is,* and some of it never really was." He chuckled. "That makes a lot of sense. Maybe I *am* drunk."

"No, I understand what you mean."

"Explain it to me, then." She laughed, and he nuzzled her cheek. Her hair smelled like the lemon drops one of his grandmas used to treat him to when he was a kid. He hoped he didn't smell too much like beer. "You make me feel a little drunk. I better hang on to you so I don't end up flying ass over teakettle again."

"This is a horse. You did fine on the horse." *But you can hang on to me anyway.*

"One of the things I really miss lately is being around horses, even just seeing them around. They don't have too many horses in 'Nam. 'Course if they did—" They'd get eaten, he thought. Or they'd get blown sky-high and come down to earth all ready for the dog-food can. He'd seen it happen to more than a few water buffalo. "Guess it's a good thing they don't. Just make us cowboys homesick if they did."

"But you get homesick anyway. That's why you bargained for another tour."

He'd just gotten sick. That was all. Plain crazy-in-the-head sick. He'd have killed somebody if they hadn't let him come home. Some pansy-assed clerk who never got anything under his fingernails but stamp-pad ink would have found out the hard way just how bad the need for a shot of wide open spaces could get.

They reached the spot he was looking for—a thick river-bottom stand of cottonwoods and wild plum bushes. "You wanna do a little fishing?"

"What'll we use for bait?"

"Anything you've got'll work just fine, honey." He'd done his share of courting on horseback, and he knew the time was right to let the horse take a good long rest. He helped Cecily down, because that was part of the ritual, then flipped the stirrup over the horn and unbuckled the cinch. The paint had barely broken a sweat, but it was getting a rest anyway. Kiah hitched it to a tree.

"Too bad they weren't giving away quilts today," he said as he pulled the saddle. "In the old days they used to wear blankets a lot. You always had a blanket when you needed one." He could feel her watching him. He felt pretty mellow, his head still pleasantly abuzz and the small talk flowing easily in the right direction. "So white people talk about blanket-bottom Indians, Indians goin' back to the blanket, stuff like that. White humor, I guess. But you always had a blanket." In this case it was a Navaho-style horse blanket with fancy fringe, neatly folded on top of a horsehair saddle pad. He tossed the pad over the saddle and shook out the blanket. "You mind a little horse sweat?"

"I'm white, Kiah."

He stared at her, unblinking. "I see that."

"I mean, I couldn't change that, even if . . ."

"You wanted to?"

"You wanted me to."

He dropped the blanket over a patch of sheltered grass and then went to her, the earnest beau taking her hands in his. She eyed the bower he'd fashioned with amazing expediency. "I don't want you to change anything," he told her. "I want you to be yourself and be with me, just for a little while."

"Be with you?" Being with him had already changed things. It would change her. He didn't seem to understand that, even though he was subtle in his coaxing, creating a tingling in the hollows of her palms where he rubbed with his thumbs. Maybe she was blowing it all out of proportion, being foolish and fanciful. That was, she'd been told often enough, her nature. "I guess that means you've had time to . . . prepare."

"Are you talkin' about—" His hands stilled, and when she looked up at him, he shook his head. "I had a couple belts with a couple buddies for the sake of old times. I wasn't gettin' whiskeyed up for—"

"I didn't mean that," she said quickly.

"I don't need anything to get me primed."

"I didn't say—" She lifted her chin, rolled her eyes heavenward, and sighed. "I do know what I'm getting myself into here," she said, mostly for her own benefit. "I *do* know."

"My arms." They enfolded her, and he rubbed his cheek over her hair, chuckling softly. "You think too much, college girl. I'll be good to you."

It was promise enough, she decided, because the tingling he'd created in one hollow place had transferred itself to another, then another. His body felt warm and sexy and hard against hers. The cove between her legs, first grazed, then hard-pressed by his arousal, needed more gratification. She put her arms around him and leaned against him.

He took her face in his hands and looked into her eyes. "I swear I'll be good to you."

It was his way of asking, she realized. Her lips parted for her answer, and he covered them with his, delving for the answer with his tongue and tasting it in the recess of her mouth. Sweet reception. He lifted his head and smiled. "That's good, isn't it?'

"Yes" was her answer, and "Oh, yes." And he took it as the answer he wanted, times two.

He kissed her again, lightly this time, his tongue playing over her lips while he unfastened her big barrette and dropped it on the ground. Her hair fell into his hands. He smiled and licked the heart-shaped curve of her lip. "I'll bet people like to play with your hair," he said as he slipped his fingers into the thick of it.

"What people?"

"Little girls. I'll bet they're always saying, 'Let me comb your hair, Cecily.'" She closed her eyes, intending to shake her head because she hadn't known any little girls since the time she'd been one herself, but she kept still. His fingers had reached the ends of her hair, and the waiting kept her still. Waiting for his next move.

"It's my turn to comb your hair, Cecily," came his warm whisper in her ear. He dispatched the zipper at the back of her neck. "My turn to undress you."

"What if someone—"

"Don't worry." He pulled her knit shell free of her jeans, gathered it at her waist, and peeled it over her head. She cooperated, but when the top came off she felt a sudden chill despite the heat of the afternoon. "No one will come here," he promised, smoothing her hair back with one hand while he reached around her back and located hooks and eyes with the other. He laced his fingers into her hair, massaged her scalp with his fingertips, and her bra went slack. "No one will see you but me."

No one but me.

He filled his hands with her breasts while he kissed her, his thumbs chasing her nipples while his tongue played tag with hers. Shallow breaths lifted her chest into his warm, damp palms, and her skin felt taut all over. She could have sworn she was growing in some places, shrinking in others. He caught her lip and gently sucked, trapped her nipples between his fingers and gently squeezed until a small whimpering sound escaped her throat.

The sound was nearly his undoing. He tossed his hat to the ground and went down on his knees before her, pressing a quick kiss to her belly. Banding one arm around her buttocks, he unbuttoned the jeans that rode her hipbones— feminine angles, hard points to be nipped and kissed until the jeans came loose and he could push them down, push her shoes off her heels, and push it all away.

He looked up. She was watching him. Her hair fell forward, covering her breasts. Light and shadow from the sun and the cottonwoods played over her skin and danced in her summer-blond hair. She knew her power over him. He could see it in her eyes, and he had a fleeting urge to beg her to be good to him, too. On his knees before her, he felt every bit as exposed as she, simply because he wanted her so badly. He slid his hands over the backs of her thighs, down, down to the inner curve of her knees, where he applied enough pressure to make them buckle.

He reached up in time to catch her and bring her to the blanket with him. Back to the blanket. Under different circumstances he might have laughed, just for the sheer joy of bringing her down right where he wanted her, straddling his lap. But it was hard to laugh when he was ready to burst out of his pants. He lifted his head to suckle her, took her buttocks in his hands to press her down on him, and drove them both to the brink of madness in a matter of moments.

She pushed her fingers into his thick hair and clutched his head to her breast. "Tell me how to please you this time, Kiah."

"Just touch me." She started to unsnap his shirt, but he flipped open his big Western belt buckle, found her hand, and drew it between them, pressing her palm to the hard ridge beneath the zipper of his jeans. "But make it real personal."

She undid his pants. It took both hands, and when she'd accomplished it, she glanced up, as if to ask further instructions. The look he gave her dared her to continue without instructions. She sucked her lower lip between her teeth as she slipped her hand into the breach. Like a pup craving her affection, his swollen flesh fairly sprang into her hand. He closed his eyes and lifted his hips to give her more access. Her touch might have been tentative but, Jesus, it felt good.

"Should I do . . . what you did?"

"If you want it to be all over before—"

She smiled. His admission put power in her hand, which she moved experimentally. She traced the length of him with her thumb. Her fingertips discovered his soft sac and prodded, gently abrading him with her nails. He groaned, pleasured by the knowledge that she was not afraid of him, that she was aware of him and wanted to do right by him, as he would by her.

He slid out from under her and laid her back on the blanket, his body following, yearning after her as he dug around for the condom he'd stashed in his pocket. Necessary nuisance, he thought as he secreted it in his fist. Bracing himself on his elbow, he slipped his free hand into the front of her panties. She looked a little glassy-eyed already. She unsnapped his shirt, muttering something about it being only fair. He smiled approvingly as she explored the contours of his chest, which swelled seemingly of its own prideful accord. She discovered his flat nipples. His smile went soft, his breath caught in his throat, and he could have sworn she'd attached jumper cables to his two little nubs.

"Who would have guessed?" she teased.

Ah, but he was stroking the cleft between her legs, and he had *her* little nub in the palm of his hand, at the mercy of his thumb. Her saucy smile was soon a thing of the past, too. He watched her face, watched the pleasure grow in her eyes as she arched into his hand and whispered his name. He felt her battling with his jeans, pushing them over his hips.

She was warm and wet and ready for him, and he wished he could just slide right in and make himself at home. But he was a big soldier boy, and he'd learned his lesson. Her eyes widened when she saw the condom.

"You didn't think I'd let you down, did you?" He kissed her temple as he dragged her hand from his groin to his buttock. "Hold me there, honey. I respond to the slightest pressure, like any good stud."

The muscle beneath her hand was like sculpted marble, but warm and alive. Oh, God, she was scared. She didn't want to stop him, but she wanted to tell him, ask him—something. She wasn't sure what. Be careful, I'm new at

this? Be kind, be ... be in love with me? He'd laugh.
Maybe not this minute, not with his obsidian eyes so full
of fire and his brow slick with sweat. She tried not to
think about what he was doing down there, but just to be
glad he had the good sense, more sense than she, more experience, more ... Oh, he was beautiful as he lifted himself higher, with his dark hair dipping over his forehead,
and the dark urgency in his eyes, and his touching, touching ...

"Open up for me, honey."

"Kiah ..."

"Please," he whispered. "I need you now, right now."

It wasn't the word she longed to hear, but it would do.
Need was a magic word, too. She closed her eyes and
opened herself to him. He made a swift, burning entry. She
curled her fingers, buried her nails in warm marble. It was
excruciating to know pain on the threshold of such pleasure. He muttered something about how good she felt. "I
do?" she gasped, and he dropped his face close to her ear,
his pleasured groan a sound of assent.

And so she squeezed her eyelids tight against the burning, both in her eyes and between her legs each time he
carved his niche deeper. *His* niche. Surely he knew.

"Relax," he exhorted her. "You're holding back on me,
honey, and I can't ..." He bore his weight on his arms,
and she felt a surprising tremor in them. And in herself,
too, deep where it hurt, surrounding the hurt, soothing the
hurt, came a small flutter of pleasure. She lifted, stretched,
gave the sensation greater access to her own core.

He accepted the invitation with a heated groan. Taking
full possession of her mouth, he matched tongue thrusts
with hip thrusts until the last and the deepest forced him
to arch away from her with a low cry that issued from the
deepest part of his chest.

She held him in her arms and stroked him. His back and
his buttocks were damp and slippery. She held him inside
her, too, as the pain subsided in the still interlude. She
knew it would hurt when he moved again, but he would
say something to make it okay. He would tell her how
wonderful she was and that he was changed now, too.

He braced himself on his forearm. With each heaving breath his chest touched her breast, retreated, then touched again. Her skin was soft and damp, like a baby's, but she smelled hot-sweet, and she looked like an angel, with her hair fanned all around her head. Getting inside her was a trip to heaven, all right. Getting out was the tough part. There was no such thing as a smooth move with a damn rubber.

He touched his nose to the top of her soft pink ear and whispered, "You okay?"

She gave a tight little nod. Clearly the angel wasn't quite ready to come down to earth. He touched his lips to the same curve of her ear. "Keep your eyes closed just like that for another minute."

He didn't look, either, but it was only a few steps to the river. Not until he got to the water did he notice the blood. The quick stab of panic was intrinsic to his upbringing. He cleaned himself off with the fury of someone who'd spilled caustic down the front of his pants. The man-to-man talk with his stepfather had been short and to the point. Watch yourself around women. *Because they can get pregnant?* Not just that. The bad ones can get other things, too, but good or bad, a woman's menstrual blood is dangerous to a man. Any decent woman will keep to herself during that time. End of lecture.

He felt a little sick. Either the beer or the damn superstitions were getting to him. Obviously, he'd caught her at a bad time. Obviously, she hadn't expected . . . Obviously, obviously . . . shit.

He stripped his shirt off, dunked it in the water, gave it a quick twist, and listened to the water trickle back to its source. He could hear the dance drums in the distance, speeding up, beating *damn, damn, damn, damn,* in perfect time with the beat of his anxious heart.

He went back to her and found her trying to poke both arms and her head into her pink top, all fighting for the same hole at the same time. The crazy terror fled, and his heart went out to her. He knelt beside her and tried to take over. "Let me help you."

"No, thanks, I can dress my—"

"It's inside out." Her struggle stopped. Her face was covered, and one arm stuck out at an odd angle. When he touched her, she shivered violently.

"My hands are cold from the water," he said, but he knew that wasn't the problem. Her arms came down slowly as he peeled the top back. Her hair fell across her face in bright yellow disarray. He pushed it back. Her eyes were closed, and her face was as pink as the top she clutched to her breast. An awful sense of helplessness nearly paralyzed him.

Her lips trembled in their valiant effort to smile. "Guess you've seen it all anyway, right?"

He hadn't realized he'd been holding his breath. He exhaled slowly. His whole face had suddenly turned to wood. "I'm not likely to get tired of lookin'," he offered gently.

She opened her glistening eyes and lifted them directly skyward. "It's a little embarrassing."

"This isn't . . ." It was his turn to glance away. Her panties were back in place, near as he could tell by the way she sat with her thighs glued together. He knew what she was trying to cover up. Unbidden, the image of a wounded GI trying to stem the loss of his own blood with his hands came to mind. He shook it off and sought a steady voice. "It isn't your time of the month, is it?"

"No."

"I didn't think so." He wasn't quite sure what to do now. What she would let him do. Touch her? Maybe she thought he'd touched her quite enough.

They stared at each other, mind-boggled, like two children who'd just gotten a peek at the physical difference between a boy and a girl.

"When?" she asked.

"When?"

"When did you not think so?"

"When it was long past too late."

He felt like a fool. He had this wet shirt in his hand because he wanted to . . . *do* something. But, damn, he was afraid of her now. She looked fragile, and he was afraid if he touched her, she'd shatter. Or worse, she'd cry. He didn't know what to say. Sorry? Somehow that didn't seem quite honest when just looking at her was making him hard again.

So he took the road he knew best, the best defense being the offense. "Why didn't you tell me?"

She drew a quick, shaky breath. "You didn't ask."

"I asked you if you were innocent." He'd thought at the time it was kind of a poetic way of putting it and wondered if she was impressed. "You gave me that whole line about being a human being and almost twenty years old. Christ, why didn't you just tell me you were a"—*careful with the word, now*—"virgin."

"Would it have stopped you?"

"You could have stopped me."

"I thought I would, but you said I think too much, and I said to myself, *permission to stop thinking.*" Her self-mocking tone turned disconsolate. "And that made me feel twice as much."

"Twice as much what?"

"Everything." She closed her eyes and tipped a little as though she were getting a bellyache. He took it as his cue to catch her and draw her face to his chest and hold her, just hold her close while she muttered dejectedly, "Everything, everything."

"Pain?" She shook her head, her nose tickling his nipple. "I hurt you, didn't I?" For one tense moment all breathing was suspended. Finally she nodded and pierced his heart with a soft sob. "I'm sorry."

A tear-filled gasp was the only reply she could manage. She clutched his arm as he lay down with her, stroking her tangled hair. "Shhh, baby, I'm sorry for hurting you. That much I can apologize for. I didn't mean to hurt you."

"I know," she said.

It was just something to say. At the moment she didn't know anything, except that his big body offered refuge, where she could hide her face from his. She wanted to crawl inside him and stay there. Damn it, she actually wanted to be *part* of him. He smelled of horse and smoke and beer and all things exotic and foreign to the starched world she'd lived in until this summer. She tried to imagine lying with him this way in the four-poster Chippendale bed in the guest room at home.

At least if it had happened there, she could have washed the sheets. It wasn't the pain. It wasn't his male ignorance. It wasn't even the fact that he hadn't said *one damn thing* that he was supposed to say—not *one line* that she'd been scripting for this event ever since she'd turned thirteen. It was the evidence on the blanket, of all things, that mortified her the most.

After a while he helped her with her bra and her top, but when he tried to take her panties down, she drew her legs up protectively.

"Let me do this for you," he pleaded, coaxing her legs apart. To the look in her eyes he responded, "No, I haven't done enough. I haven't cleaned up the mess I made."

"It's too—"

"Shhh. It isn't. It's my . . ." She relented reluctantly, opening her thighs under the pressure of his hand. He seemed equally reluctant to look, but he assured her, "It's mine to do."

Still not the right words, she thought, but endearing, nonetheless. They made her throat burn again. She lifted her head to see what was so cool and wet. "Your shirt," she said as she laid her head back on the blanket and gave a motherly *tsk*. "Your new shirt."

"Bought it this morning, ripped it this afternoon." He ministered to her gently, stroking upward. "I've always been hard on clothes. Hard on everything, from the looks of it." *Hard-on* was a poor choice of words, but he generally had a way of mangling words, too. "I didn't know if you'd, uh . . . if you'd come today. But I thought if you did, I wanted to be wearin' a flashy—" His hand stilled over the wet shirt. "You shouldn't have had to tell me. I should have known."

"I thought you'd be able to tell. Is that dumb?" She forgot herself for a moment, shook her head, and almost, *almost* laughed. "After all the times I said no, and then in an instant . . ."

"I held back as long as I could."

"Is that what you're supposed to do?"

"If you care about gettin' the woman . . . about givin' her what she needs, you, uh . . ." He tossed the shirt aside. "It'll be better the next time."

A heavy silence ensued. She adjusted her clothes. He stretched out next to her.

"Will it be you the next time?" Too late, she wanted to bite her tongue.

"That's up to you." He swallowed hard. "If you let it be me, I'll make it better. You've honored me with a gift, Cecily. Sort of like at the giveaway." He cupped her face in his hand and made her look at him. "I'm not sorry for taking it. Only for hurting you."

"The giveaway? Pretty cheap at half the—"

"No," he said.

"No," she echoed quietly. "I made a choice."

"How do you feel now? Still hurt?" She shook her head. "Do you feel different?" Again she shook her head, but she glanced up and smiled a little so he'd know it wasn't true. "You look a little different. You look like you belong to someone."

He was getting closer to what she wanted to hear. She smiled. "Some wild cowboy I hardly even know."

"You know more about me than I know about you." He traced the line of her jaw with his thumb. "You know my sister. You've met my mother now. This is where I grew up, pretty much. Two days and you've seen what there is to see."

"When you look at me like that I feel as though you know everything about me. You knew how to make me . . . respond."

He smiled wistfully. "Lucky guess."

"Couldn't you humor me and say something a little more sentimental and sublime?" She searched his eyes, hoping. "Something worth losing my virginity over?"

"Like what?"

"Never mind."

Women and their damn never-minds. How did they expect a guy to read a never-mind?

"I should've lit a candle or something," he said with a sigh. "There should've been music." He slid his fingers

into her hair and told himself it wouldn't hurt to say whatever the hell it was she wanted to hear. "Maybe you
should've had a ring on your finger."

"I know this wasn't a first for you, and I'm surely not
the last in a long line of—"

He gave a humorless chuckle. "Could very well be."

"But only over your dead body, and that isn't going to
happen." She looked up at him, such fierce certainty in her
eyes that he could almost believe she was some kind of
clairvoyant. "But if you'd let me believe that I was at least
memorable, because"—she glanced away—*"I'm* not likely
to forget."

"You belong to me today." It sounded like the worst
kind of bullshit, but it felt true. "I belong to you."

"Just for today?"

"What else can I promise you, Cecily? I have to go
soon. You knew that. And when I come home, you won't
be here." That look in her eyes had him tied up in knots,
which he guessed was fair turnabout.

He tucked his arm beneath her head and rolled to his
back, holding her close against his side. "Took you two
days to get under my skin. In two *years* I couldn't get invited through your front door. I don't know anything about
your family, but that much I can guess."

"My father's a real estate agent. My mother's an antiques dealer."

"What's that supposed to tell me? Hmm? Who are their
people? Whose people do they stay with? Do they still live
together? Does he drink? Does she make your clothes?"
She lifted her head and looked up at him, questioning his
seriousness. "You and me, we've got different basics,
honey."

"We have some similar basics." She touched the bandage she'd put on his shoulder. "What if I fall in love with
you, Kiah?"

"In a week?" *Or less,* was the response he saw in her
eyes. "I guess you'll have a problem when I'm gone," he
said quietly.

"Will *you?*"

"My major problem will be stayin' alive. Everything

else goes on hold." She nodded and laid her cheek against his chest, but he knew she didn't believe him. This was it. This was all the time they had. He tightened his arms around her. "You're not the kind of woman a guy keeps on hold very long."

"I'm not the kind of woman who has sex with just any cowboy, either. That's obvious, isn't it?"

"What's obvious to me is that you did it this time, with me." He rolled over with her, reversing their positions so that he could see her eyes. "I unlocked the door. I don't wanna go away thinkin' about who else you might let in."

"*I* unlocked the door. I don't have to let *anyone* else in." She lifted her hand to touch his face, and he wondered why it felt so cool. "Is there a chance you might fall in love with me, Kiah?" He closed his eyes. He ought to say no and set her straight, but instead he rubbed his cheek against her palm. "What if you do," she murmured, "in a week?"

"Then I've got two problems after I leave here. I'm still not sure why I bought the first one, and I sure as hell don't need the second." He slid his hand over her hip and drew her tight against him. "My body already loves yours, honey." Reflexively she arched just a little, just enough. "See there? Yours loves mine, too." He smiled. "That's enough. That's all we've got time for."

Chapter 10

Cecily gave Kiah her love on his terms. In the next week she ditched her work ethic and slipped away from the project to be with him whenever he came for her. He always came on horseback, plying his charm with all the young volunteers—the girls who thought he was gorgeous, the guys who wanted to be just like him, and even his sister, who returned his banter tit for tat. He was a battle-seasoned warrior, and no one questioned his right to claim Cecily's time and anything else she had to offer. The group got a charge out of her promises to be right back or to do her share later, but they were willing to cover for her. The seduction of Cecily Metcalf was the best entertainment of the summer.

She knew it, too, and much to her surprise, she didn't give a damn. She loved the way Kiah sought her out, as though being with her was the first thing he thought about when he got up in the morning. The journal she kept religiously hadn't been updated since the Friday they'd met. The passing of days was the last thing she wanted to note. Passing joy, passing excitement. Ellen called it a passing fling.

Whatever it was, it felt wonderful one moment and excruciating the next. There was a terrible sense of desperation in their need to be together, to be alone, to have sex wherever and whenever possible, as though they'd in-

vented something new and didn't have much time to perfect it.

"Not quite as overrated as you first thought?" he would
tease. And she would thank him for showing her what
she'd been missing and toss off a coy remark like "I'm re-
vamping my rating system." It was the kind of remark that
might make him laugh or set him brooding, depending on
his mood. There were times when he was full of wonder.
He seemed to drink in every nuance and soak her up sen-
sorially. At other times he would light a cigarette, sit back
against a tree, and ignore her for a while, and damned if
she could figure out what she'd said wrong.

The world was too much with him, she would say. He
was taking an R-and-R from the world, he would say. But
he could be persuaded not to waste another precious minute of it.

Early on the morning of his departure, Ellen came to
wake her. "He's outside," she said.

"Kiah? But it's not—" Sleep had been a long time coming, and the voice in the dark seemed like part of a dream.
"Is it morning?"

"It's almost four o'clock," Ellen whispered as she
tossed a pair of jeans on the bed. "I think these are yours.
Hurry up, now, I don't want anyone to catch him here at
this hour."

"They can't do anything to him now." Cecily stuck her
legs into her jeans as she rolled into a sitting position.

"Yeah, but they can send you home, my friend. I'm supposed to hand you a warning about your behavior.
Here—" Ellen dragged Cecily off the bed. "I'm handing
you your hippie shoes."

"Clogs. They're good for your feet." Cecily was trying
to stuff her nightshirt into her waistband with one hand
while she snatched her windbreaker off the back of a chair.
They crept past Deena's bed. "I can't go to the airport like
this. I can't imagine—"

Across the room Mary Feather's mattress coils creaked.

"Shhh." Ellen pushed Cecily through the doorway. "You
two are gonna lose me my cushy summer job. All he

wants is you and the pickup." She herded her down the dark hallway, but before they reached the back door, Ellen drew Cecily up short. "If he's thinking about—" She gave Cecily's arm a quick squeeze, and the narrow space was suddenly so charged with Ellen's will that Cecily was glad she couldn't see her face. "We've got relations in Canada. Kiah's never been there, but if he needs a place to stay, I know where they live."

"Did he say anything about—"

"No. All he said was he wanted you and the keys." She found Cecily's hand, and the keys chinked softly in her palm. "It's really his pickup. My dad left it to him, said it should go to the boy. Kiah never made any claim to it, but it's his whenever he wants it. Tell him to push it down the hill a ways before he starts it, or else it'll wake the dead."

Cecily nodded and tried to draw away, but Ellen still held her hand. "Would you go with him if he asked you?"

"He won't ask."

"You don't know what he's thinking."

"I don't know what either of you is thinking, Ellen. But I know Kiah's not going to Canada."

Ellen let her go. "You'd turn him down."

It was not an issue Cecily intended to discuss while Kiah waited outside. "If anyone asks, I went for a—"

"No one here is that stupid, my friend. They won't ask, either."

In the dark his cigarette was a bright orange beacon. He was leaning against the pickup, waiting for her to come to him. His kiss felt more like a prelude than a farewell, and he gave a lustful chuckle when he discovered her lack of a bra.

She didn't have to pass on Ellen's suggestion. He pushed the pickup away from the little row of white frame buildings that made up the mission school, past the steepled church, and over the hill with Cecily at the wheel. Once the vehicle started to coast on its own, she slid over and he jumped in, and they looked at each other and laughed like two mischievous pranksters, home free.

He turned off the gravel road, crossed a cattle guard, and stopped to pick up a bale of hay before proceeding through a couple of barbed-wire gates to a secluded draw. The headlights sent a jackrabbit scurrying for cover and gave one white-faced cow momentary pause in its grazing. Otherwise they were alone under the predawn sky. Kiah pulled the twine off the bale and kicked the hay loose in the back of the pickup.

"Come to bed with me." He gave her a hand over the tailgate as he deeply inhaled the scent of new-mown hay. "Alfalfa and sweetclover. Better than incense."

"I hate incense." But she liked the smell of Kiah. She went eagerly into his arms and savored the spicy scent he always wore for her. She'd never asked him what it was. "How much time do we have?" she whispered, unsnapping his shirt as she pressed her face closer and breathed him deep into every cell of her body. "When do we have to leave for the airport?"

"I don't want you to go to the airport. I asked one of my buddies to drive me up." She started to object, but he laid a finger over her lips, then kissed them, then drew her down into the hay. "I want us to say good-bye here. In private."

What he meant to say was that he didn't want them to say good-bye at all, she told herself. Maybe she couldn't quite read his mind, but that was the sentiment she read into the way he made love to her, for that was the way she knew him best. It was the one way he knew her as no one else did. He knew she wanted him to take her slowly. He knew how well she loved it when he took the time to tease her through her clothes, but he also knew when it was time for him to remove them. He understood how much she loved the feel of his lips and his tongue, and he realized that nursing him gave her great pleasure. He was sensitive to her modesty and her lack of self-confidence, but he coaxed her and whispered her praises and made her tingle exquisitely wherever his hand played over her.

But each time she reached for him, he stilled her hand, warning, "Not yet," and imploring, "Wait, honey, a little more . . . a little more . . ." Until she was so desperate for his penetration that she quivered. She cried out to him, and there were tears when he came inside her at last.

"Always remember that I was here first," he whispered against her neck, his breath hot with a demand that he would never make, except at this moment, when, yes, it meant everything because she was his, and she said, "Yes, I will."

"Look at me and say my name and remember it."

And she did, over and over again, with each searing thrust. He shifted her knees, steadied her hips in his hands, and made her take all of him as she spoke his name in loving and agonized tones, in complete satisfaction and abject misery. She would remember him as a powerful shadow silhouetted against the night sky, almost too much man for her, almost mystical, almost God-like and almost demonic. But the claim he made was earthbound and real. He needed her now, and she was his, and like it or not she took it to heart—*her* heart, a heart that was nothing if not fiercely loyal.

After their passion was spent they held each other and watched with dismay as the sky lightened and the stars grew dim. The horizon reddened. The sunrise came like a killing fire, melting the night away.

"I want to go with you," she said.

"How far?"

"As far as you'll let me."

He hugged her, amused by the notion of *him* letting *her.* "I've already had this discussion with my mother and my sister," he admitted. "Only they know better than to give me too much static. I'm going to make a quick, clean getaway, without a bunch of women hangin' on me."

"What makes you think we'd hang on you? You think we're all going to fall apart at the sight of your leave-taking?"

"I had this nightmare." Teasing came easily, naturally. He might have been dreaming, too; he wasn't quite sure. He was still drifting pleasantly on the high her sweet loving had given him. "Airport's full of people, the old lady's keening like I'm a dead man for sure, Ellen's cussin' me out, and you've got tears drippin' down your cheeks like some real sweet woman"—he pressed an open kiss where the tear might have been and tickled with the tip of his tongue until he could feel her smile—"whose no-good man's gone off and left her."

"I promise not to embarrass you."

"It wouldn't embarrass me." He lowered his forehead against her shoulder and rubbed it back and forth, drifting, just drifting. "It would break my heart. I'd go AWOL."

He'd meant to be kidding, but hearing himself say it, he was glad she couldn't see his face. In the morning light she might read a truth he couldn't admit. He wanted to stay with her. He wanted to take her somewhere, find a place like this that wasn't close to anything either of them knew and just be with her. Just *be*.

She combed her fingers through his hair. "I can be very controlled, you know, very reserved. I'm sure I could wave good-bye without shedding a tear."

"That would break my heart, too." He dropped a kiss on her shoulder and came up smiling. "Humor me. Let me have my fantasies."

"I have fantasies, too, Kiah. About where you're going." He couldn't smile anymore. Her fingers felt small and delicate as they moved over his face, touching the corner of his eye, his cheek, the top curve of his lip. He wanted to banish the sadness from her eyes, but he knew it was reflected in his. "I don't think I'll watch the news anymore," she said.

"Don't." He pressed his lips together and nodded once. "Keep it out of your head. A lot of it's just plain boring, anyway. Moving from one hole to another, waiting, watching the sky, watching your back. Trying not to think too much."

"Will you think about me?"

"Not if I can help it." Her eyes shifted away, and he caught her chin in his hand. "I'll try not to wonder if things are okay with you. I'll try not to imagine where you are and who's with you. You go crazy over there thinking about things you can't reach, can't have, can't do anything about."

"Take this with you." She reached behind her neck to unclasp a gold chain. "It's something you can hold on to. Something you can touch."

"I don't want any family heirlooms, honey. I can't promise . . ."

The chain went slack, and a bit of gold glimmered in the pale valley between her breasts. It had been the breasts that interested him—the plump curves, the rosy nipples—not the glint of any gold she might have worn from time to time. He knew he'd seen the necklace before, but in his mind it had no shape, and he permitted it no significance. He shook off the offer.

She kept pressing. "You don't have to promise anything. It has nothing to do with my family. It's just mine, something I treasure because—" She tucked it into his jeans, on the right side, where he always pocketed several condoms before he went to see her. There were two left, and he dove quickly to catch the little heart before it fell in with such mundane company.

Her hand stalled his. "No, it'll bring you luck. I bought this old trunk at an auction because I . . . I just had a special feeling for it. I found the locket inside, along with some old clothes, which I donated to a museum. But I kept the locket and bought a chain for it. It was an unexpected surprise." She smiled expectantly. "Like you and me."

"I don't want to take your treasure, Cecily. I might lose it. Somebody might steal it. You never—"

"It's too late, cowboy. You already took my treasure." Hay rustled beneath her as she squirmed and stretched, touching her lips to the corner of his mouth to show him she didn't mind. Holy Jesus, she was pretty with her hair catching the morning sun and her eyes searching his for something good and glorious, something he probably didn't even know existed.

"You won't lose it," she assured him. "You won't let anyone steal it, either. If you're ever afraid, maybe if you hold on to this, we'll make a connection somehow. Maybe not quite like we're doing now, but some kind of connection."

She settled back down, laying her arm over his chest, her ear over his thudding heart. "Are you ever afraid?" Her tender voice promised some kind of protection, perhaps from criticism.

"Sometimes," he admitted uneasily.

"But not very often. You're kind of reckless, like with that bull."

"A guy takes risks like that to prove he's invincible. Guess I'm not quite convinced." It was a dangerous thing to say aloud, but in the spirit of risk-taking, he took a chance. "I'm afraid of dying, just like everybody else. Making a bad end, disgracing myself, my . . ." He shook his head and sighed. It sounded like beer talk. "I don't know. A lot of things."

He felt like a haunted man. Too many abominations lived in the memory of his senses these days. The stink of burning flesh and bleeding flesh and rotting flesh. The piercing wail of a mutilated friend begging to die. The sight of children running scared, threatened by the weapon he used to create more shrieking and more stink. But he either had to use it or go down in terror.

Unspeakable horrors all, but the quiet, unbloody miseries could be just as bad sometimes. There were nightmares, and there was mind-bending loneliness.

He rubbed a handful of Cecily's silky hair over his face. "Now I'm afraid I'm gonna think about you, no matter how hard I try not to."

"Why is that so bad?"

He groaned. There was no way to explain how bad that would be.

"I'll write to you." She tightened her arm around him. "Will you answer my letters?"

He'd seen guys get letters for a while. He'd seen what happened to them when the letters stopped coming. "How much longer will you be in school?"

"Forever, maybe. I love school. I'm only a sophomore, and I'm already thinking about graduate school." She lifted her head and looked up at him. "When you get out of the army, you'll have the GI Bill. Do you think you'll use it to go to college? Ellen says—"

"Ellen knows damn well how much I hate—" He tucked his arm behind his head and drew a soothing, alfalfa-scented breath as he shook his head. "I'm not interested in her causes. I never gave a damn about school, and I'm not gonna be this, this . . . whatever the hell she wants me to be. She's the one who oughta go to school. She oughta get herself a degree or run for Tribal Council, or both. She could do both."

He'd said the same thing to his sister, but he knew that Ellen didn't take the idea seriously. That was the difference between Ellen and Cecily. Cecily was already thinking about graduate school. The women Ellen had grown up around weren't likely to dream of or suggest such a thing. He'd told Ellen to get off his back and do it herself. Probably hadn't sounded serious. Probably hadn't been.

"Her dad was a very traditional man," he said. "Kept a lot of the old ways. He could have been a leader, but he had no use for tribal politics. I got no use for it, either."

"How long ago did your father die?"

"*My* father?" He watched herringbone clouds drift high overhead. "If you mean my real father, I never knew him. Some Indian cowboy from Pine Ridge named Toby Rider. Lived fast, loved hard, and died young. That's all I know about him."

"Is that your plan?"

The idea made him chuckle. "Ol' Toby made a clean getaway, I'll give him that. My mom doesn't talk about him much, so I doubt if she shed too many tears. Moses Red Thunder was Ellen's dad. He took me as his son, gave me his name. He died of TB when I was sixteen. Ellen's been crusading ever since."

"Did Moses serve in the military?"

"World War II. They had Indian units. He was in communications. They'd send radio dispatches in Lakota." He'd seen it done in a movie once, only the guys had been Navaho, but the movie showed it just the way Moses had told it. It was like the Indians were America's ace in the hole. "I don't speak much Lakota. All I can do is load and fire."

"I don't want you to go back."

"Don't say that, Cecily." He turned her in his arms and made her look at him while he lifted her breast in his hand. "Don't let me think about it too much."

"Oh, Kiah, do you ever think about not—"

He touched her nipple lightly with his thumb. He felt the catch in her breath as she arched against him. "Let's make each other stop thinking."

"How much time—"

"Shhh." He kissed her and bred a spark of pleasured accord in her eyes. "That takes thinking."

He took her back before the morning heat had fully sucked the dew from the grass. She asked him to stop the pickup below the hill and let her walk from there. Then she wanted him to hold her once more and kiss her hard. He did, even though he wanted to cut this short. He needed to go somewhere and bathe his bruised heart in a shot of alcohol, toughen up his calluses again. He knew he could count on C.B. to get him on the plane.

But he held off on his leave-taking as long as he could because that, again, was the best he had to offer. And she held off on her tears until they burned her throat so badly that she had to let them go. He wiped them away with his thumbs, kissed them away, took them on the tip of his tongue, and told her they were treasures, too.

"Take care of yourself," he said, and she managed to gasp, "You, too." She willed him to ask her to wait for him the way soldiers were supposed to do. He didn't. He got out of the pickup and pulled her out after him and into his arms for another kiss.

"Go on, now," he said, his voice straining against all the pleas and promises he wanted to make. "Don't look back, okay?" She nodded. He shoved his hand in his pocket, then stepped back, brandishing the locket. Two loops of gold chain dangled from his fist, glinting in the sun. "I'll hang on to this," he promised, "to remember you by."

She walked a little way, then tried to run up the incline, but she slipped on the gravel and went down on one knee. Again he held himself back. He could feel the shape of the heart in the center of his palm and the chain cutting into his hand, but he kept still. She straightened her shoulders and walked over the hill without looking back, not even when she reached the top. She hesitated, and he found himself praying for her to turn around so he could see her face one more time. He thanked God when she didn't, then he cursed God when she disappeared from view.

And he cursed every goddamn fork in every goddamn rutted road he'd ever traveled as he threw the old pickup into reverse.

Part II

Rain, people, rain!
The rain is all around us
It is going to come pouring down,
And the summer will be fair to see.
The mocking bird has said so.
                    —TIGUA SONG

Chapter 11

Nebraska Territory, Summer 1873

Whirlwind Rider's heart had long been cold with anger. It was not a good way for a man to live, even though the railroad surveyors with their parties of soldiers had surely earned every act of retaliation he had initiated. While Red Cloud insisted that he could not foresee victory for the Sioux, others disagreed. Crazy Horse of the Oglala, Big Foot of the Minneconjou, Sitting Bull and Gall of the Hunkpapa—these were the leaders Whirlwind Rider chose to follow, for they refused to become loaf-around-the-fort people. Becoming an agency Indian was no way for a Lakota to live.

None of his people ever mentioned the offer Whirlwind Rider had made for the white woman. It had been a rash move. Since that day, he had gained a reputation for taking bold risks, but only in battle. He had not taken a wife, even though it was time. No one questioned his reasons or his intentions. No one knew how heavily the matter weighed upon his mind.

He had spoken of this with Crazy Horse, who understood the plight of a man who longed for a woman he could not have. For many years Crazy Horse had carried love in his heart for Black Buffalo Woman, who had chosen another man. It was well-known but rarely discussed among the people, for the entire affair had caused much anguish.

Crazy Horse did not ask about Whirlwind Rider's relationship with Agent Twiss's daughter. Such a question would have been ill-mannered, and it was well-known that the young warrior had kept his own counsel since the time he had ridden alone against the iron horse and come away with a painful bullet wound. From that day on, the surveying parties had been his personal enemies.

This was not good, Crazy Horse told him. The intruders were enemies of the people. The miners' insults to the land and to the people were worse than those of the surveyors, and the white promises made on white paper were lies. To fight on behalf of the people was the mission of the Tokala and the other warrior societies.

But personal hatred would poison a man's life, Crazy Horse said. "I carried this thing in my own heart until it caused our people to take sides, her husband's family against mine. It was no good."

Whirlwind Rider knew of the feud. Black Buffalo Woman had chosen No Water, but later she had left him and gone to Crazy Horse. Everyone remembered the night No Water shot and wounded Crazy Horse as a time of terrible turmoil, for the rivalry might have torn the band apart had it not been for Crazy Horse's insistence that there be no trouble. Black Buffalo Woman had returned to her husband, and No Water had sent two fine horses to Crazy Horse's camp in the proper way of putting things aright.

"You chose another woman," Whirlwind Rider said quietly as he passed the pipe between them. Crazy Horse's wife had left the two men to speak privately. "Have you forgotten the first?"

"Not forgotten. I have settled my heart by untying it from her. I spoke with her once, telling her that there were no more bad feelings. The anger is replaced with a sad-sweet memory of how determined I once was to turn her head my way. I wanted to boast more, to make a show for her, but it was not in me. I thought, Be patient. She will see who is the man for her."

"I made a show for her." They spoke of two different

women, recalled the two very different *hers,* but the only real difference for the two men was that one heartache was fresher than the other. Whirlwind Rider shook his head slowly as he watched the flames lapping at the hearth rocks. "I made a fool of myself."

"We all do." Crazy Horse, almost ten years older and wiser than Whirlwind Rider, offered a mentor's smile. "We greet each morning the same way, happy as pups, until that fateful day when we glimpse a certain look in a certain pair of eyes. Nothing is ever the same after that."

"Now you're sounding like an old man," Whirlwind Rider warned.

"Sometimes I feel like one." Crazy Horse rubbed an itching shoulder against the willow backrest, then relaxed with a sigh. "Remembering those days is like filling my head with the scent of sweetgrass smoke and the song of the crickets. For all the heaviness in my young heart, life was simpler then."

Crazy Horse was speaking of the times, Whirlwind Rider realized. Not of his woman troubles. "I have been waiting, but for what?" he mused. "It's time I took a wife, just as you did."

"When you do, you must tell her what is in your heart." Crazy Horse tapped the pipe bowl gently against a rock. "Let her decide whether it is enough for her," he suggested as he emptied the ashes of the smoke they'd shared. It was the customary signal that it was time to conclude their visit.

This he would do, Whirlwind Rider decided, in good time. He would seek advice from Two Bear Claw, his uncle and stepfather, and he would smoke with his friend LaPointe and talk over the prospect of marriage. LaPointe knew how he felt about Priscilla. Sarah knew. And Whirlwind Rider understood that this feeling was a weakness in him. He could neither kill it nor reason it away. But as trouble continued to brew on the Dakota plains, it became clear that Lakota blood and white would never be a happy blend.

Neither was the blend of Lakota blood and trade whiskey a happy one. When Whirlwind Rider reached Two

Bear Claw's camp on the White River, he found that a whiskey seller had already been there, plying his trade against the white agent's so-called regulations. If anger were poison, then whiskey was surely anger in liquid form, Whirlwind Rider thought disgustedly as he surveyed the damage his cousins had done to their own camp after a night of drinking the stuff. There were women and children hiding in their lodges while their men behaved like crazed beasts, raving and fighting one another, knocking down drying racks, turning over cooking pots, frightening the young, and profaning the sacred.

It was as though the camp had been attacked by an enemy. Whirlwind Rider was sickened by the discovery of the bleeding body of one brother and the corpse of another. Their mother knelt beside them, her arms furrowed with the self-inflicted gashes of one in mourning, wailing in unspeakable sorrow. In their whiskey-induced madness, her sons had done this thing to each other.

Whirlwind Rider found his cousin Little Wolf crouching on hands and knees like a helpless child, retching himself inside out. There was no talking to him. There was no talking to anyone. The *akicita,* who should have been keeping order, had been among the first to succumb. Some of the people had fled the camp. He followed their trail and found his mother, Shell Track Woman, and Two Bear Claw, who had led a small party to safety. For this much Whirlwind Rider was grateful.

"Why did you let them do this?" he demanded of his uncle.

"I could not stop them," Two Bear Claw said. The old gray head wagged sadly. His befuddlement was unsettling, for this was a man Whirlwind Rider regarded with deep respect. "No one could. They passed the whiskey from one to another, like a challenge. 'Try it,' they said. Once they started drinking it, they could not stop."

"But they know this." Whirlwind Rider gazed at the grass rippling serenely on a nearby sidehill. The calamitous scene that lay only a short ride beyond this peaceful valley haunted him. "We have all seen this before. Of all the things the agents wants us to forbid the people to do, this is the one ban that makes sense."

"*Hau*, I agree with you, *cinks*." Two Bear Claw laid his hand on the young man's shoulder and called him "my son," thinking how good it would be if Whirlwind Rider would bring his strong will and able body back among the Oglala. They desperately needed such men now. "Agent Twiss says the whiskey is not to be brought here, but these traders come anyway."

"What they say means nothing, and they ignore everything we say." The reins jerked in his hand as his horse claimed more slack in pursuit of a bite of grass. But it wasn't time to fill either of their bellies. He could not abide one night in Two Bear Claw's camp, not under these conditions.

He vaulted onto the roan's back. "If they intend to destroy us," he told his uncle, "we cannot let them do it by our own hand."

The whiskey seller knew he was trespassing in Indian territory. It was the best place to find Indians. His wagon's wheels creaked under the load of goods he'd procured in return for the one trade item that couldn't miss. Corn or rye whiskey might be hard to come by, but any form of grain alcohol was salable, and there were plenty of customers in Indian territory besides Indians. Soldiers and miners had a taste for it, too.

A wise trader kept moving, looking for new customers. Every once in a while a bad batch of firewater could stir up a hornet's nest. Soldiers occasionally dropped dead of alcohol poisoning. Mining partners might take after each other with their picks. And, of course, the Indians nearly always went wild over the stuff. Once he'd done business in an Indian camp, a wise trader moved on quickly, and he generally watched his back for the first few miles out.

But it wasn't his back they fired on first. It was the whiskey barrels. The whiskey trader trespassing in Indian territory managed to get off a few shots before they plugged a hole in him, too.

* * *

From the porch Priscilla saw the riders' dust cloud. She was about to stick her head back in the door and call her father, but when she realized that it was a party of Indians, she held off for a moment and watched them ride. Gliding in on the wind, she thought, with the leader's hair outstretched like a raven's wing. The sight of a Lakota brave on horseback was bittersweet, but she welcomed the stinging joy it brought her. In the two years since she'd gone away to school, her heart had been purely functional. Nothing had bruised it. Nothing had lifted it, either, until now.

As the riders drew closer, even before she could see them clearly, she sensed something impossibly familiar about them, about the leader in particular, as though she were about to revisit a dream. It was her favorite dream except for the last part, the part with the riderless horse. If she went inside, she would spare herself. Mistaken identity was surely just another version of the riderless horse. But she couldn't turn away. Her feet were stuck to the porch planking.

By the time the horse slowed to a walk, she knew there was no mistake, but she was afraid to believe. The handsome, bare-chested rider showed no emotion, no sign of recognition. He looked a little older than he did in the dream. Maybe she did, too. Or maybe he couldn't see her. Maybe *she* wasn't really there. She lifted her skirt and stepped off the porch without taking her eyes off him.

"Whirlwind Rider?"

"Your memory is good." His words were clipped and sharp. He gestured to his party of three buckskin-clad warriors. "We have come to see your father."

His announcement made no immediate impression. The words *He's alive* echoed like church bells in Priscilla's head. Her lips moved of their own accord, and she heard a voice that sounded remotely like her own. "It's good to see . . . that you are well."

He nodded once. "You have been here long?"

"No." She took a deep breath and turned her head only far enough to allow the breeze to sweep the hair off her cheek. She dared not take her eyes off him for fear he might vanish. "Only two days. I haven't seen Sarah yet, or . . . or anyone."

Priscilla fought to hold herself in check as she squinted into the late afternoon sun. She was fairly bubbling inside, from her stomach to her throat, for his face was so beautiful it nearly took her breath away.

And he was alive.

His eyes seemed to soften a little at the mention of his sister's name. With her heart wedged in her throat, Priscilla managed to smile casually and offer the correct invitation. "Please come inside. My father is—"

"I do not pay visits to the agency. Only to my family. Tell your father I have—" He glanced away as the door opened again.

"What is it, Priscilla?"

She forced herself to turn in the direction of her father's voice.

Dressed in his shirtsleeves, his braces looped over his ample hips, Charles Twiss raised his hand to shade his eyes as he surveyed the mounted party. "Are you from Two Bear Claw's band?"

"You have said the army will stop the whiskey traders," Whirlwind Rider stated without preamble. "You have said there will be punishment for selling whiskey, but still they come."

"If they come, they must be reported," Twiss warned. "Not murdered. Would you know anything about the white trader who was murdered?"

"Was he the man who brought whiskey to the Oglala camp on the White River?"

"I don't know. Had he been taken into custody, there would have been an inquiry. A hearing. It is our way to listen to both sides of a story. If the man did, indeed, trespass and trade in contraband—"

Whirlwind Rider gestured impatiently as the roan shifted beneath him. He was not painted for war, nor did he carry the trappings of his *akicita*. He wore fringed leggings and a breechclout, and a single eagle feather fluttered from a thong tied in his hair. "Your fast talk means nothing, agent. I know that murder means to take a man's life. I know that whiskey poisons our people."

"I know that, too. I have forbidden them to drink it."

"You forbid many things. Your friendlies live like camp dogs. All they do is sit outside your door."

"There will soon be schools for the children, and with the tools and seed for—"

Whirlwind Rider made the cut-off sign with a stiff hand. "Keep the whiskey away from our land."

"I try, but there are the soldiers, and the buffalo men and"—Twiss regarded the faces of each of Whirlwind Rider's companions, as though memorizing them—"and some others. You are clearly a man of some influence. You must tell your friends not to trade for whiskey. Tell them it is poison."

"They have eyes. They see this." Whirlwind Rider leaned forward, his quiet threat intensified by the dark look in his eyes. "You will stop the whiskey traders, or we will stop them ourselves."

"We must keep the peace. Two Bear Claw is a friend of mine. You are his relation. You could help. You could—"

"I came to tell you this in your language. I am not one of your friendlies, agent. But I have learned your language better than you think."

"I remember," Twiss shot back as he stepped to the edge of the porch, arms akimbo.

The old man's bluster brought a slow smile to Whirlwind Rider's face. The man thought to protect his child, who'd been struck nearly dumb by the appearance of one she thought to be a ghost. "Watch out for your daughter."

Laughing, he sought her eyes. Just as he remembered, they were as big and as transparent as the windows in a white man's house, and what he saw in them startled him. A child no more, she looked appreciatively upon a man. His chuckle was caustic. "She speaks *my* language better than you think."

At Whirlwind Rider's signal the party wheeled their horses and rode away as they had come. Priscilla watched, stunned by the way her own heart tagged after him. So much to say, and she'd barely been able to utter a sensible word.

Charles Twiss laid a heavy hand on his daughter's shoulder. "What did he mean by that, I wonder?"

Priscilla stiffened. "Is that something you wish to discuss now, Father?" She turned, feeling a coolness rise inside her when she saw the same look she'd seen in his eyes the day Whirlwind Rider had offered to make her his wife. It was a look that had said "How shocking, Priscilla. How disgusting, Priscilla." And the eyes belonged once again to a man she realized she really didn't know as well as she'd once thought.

"Two years ago when you sent me packing, you made it clear that you did not wish to discuss anything but my speedy departure." She shook off her father's hand, stepping away as she watched the riders top the distant rise and drop out of sight, one by one. "He is Sarah's brother. I helped him with his English, and he taught me some Lakota."

"And proposed to make you his squaw. I would not have agreed to this visit of yours, Priscilla, if I had known he was anywhere in the vicinity."

"He was my friend," she said distantly. There had been the promise of more than friendship, but that was all. Just the promise. "And I thought ..." *I thought I'd witnessed his death. I've thought of him every day since.* "I learned a great deal from him." Under her father's scrutiny she added quickly, "And from Sarah. I came back to see Sarah, Father. And you, of course."

"And this man, this ... What is his name, Priscilla? Does he have a decent Christian name?"

"Decent?" His name was perfectly suited to him. Just seeing him made everything spin around her, as though she were standing in the vortex of a maelstrom. "No," she admitted softly. "I didn't expect to see him."

"His name?"

"You said you remembered him."

"I certainly remember his speech at the meeting we had here. I've not seen or heard anything from him since." He turned to go back inside, grumbling, "Not that I expected to."

"He did not mean to insult you," Priscilla insisted as she

followed a few steps behind him. "Or me. I was not insulted by his suggestion."

"Indeed." Twiss paused at the door, then faced her abruptly with the paternal bearing she was quickly learning to resent. "When did we begin keeping secrets from each other, Priscilla? Why do you not trust me with this man's name?"

"It's not a secret, Father. You can find out easily enough."

"He'll be back with the hostiles by the time I do. They've been skirmishing with the surveyors' escort details, raiding the Crows, playing Hide and Seek. Someone murdered a damn whiskey drummer." He sniffed as he reached for the door handle. "I can't protect the Indians unless they cooperate with me."

"Protect them from what?" She stayed his hand. He gave her a look that said the answer should be self-evident. "Isn't that the army's job, Father? Why should there be whiskey sellers and railroad surveyors in Indian territory? Isn't there an agreement—"

"The hostiles jeopardize the agreement whenever they attack men who are simply trying to do a job."

"Like whiskey sellers?"

"Like whiskey sellers. The scum of the earth, but a dead one becomes an issue. Another excuse to reinforce the garrisons." With a sigh he seemed to tire of his own pompousness. "I have made very little headway. They must abandon their savage practices, or all may be lost."

"They need time, Father."

"There is no time." His shoulders sagged. Even the weight of the front door seemed to tax him as he tugged at it, muttering, "There is no time."

Whirlwind Rider was not dead.

Priscilla hummed the words over and over in her mind like a doxology. Praise God, he was not dead. When Two Bear Claw and his family returned to the agency after their hunt, Sarah would be with them. Priscilla could then ask her friend the myriad questions that had been cartwheeling through her mind all evening.

Or she could ask Whirlwind Rider now. For when she went to her small room and closed the door, she could feel him waiting there in the shadows. Her heart pounded. She was both frightened and exhilarated by the notion that he had summarily dismissed her by day and stolen back into her life by night. He stood in silence, a dark shadow waiting in the corner like a mountain cat, full of potential power that she could feel and smell. The air fairly sizzled with his presence. She closed the door softly and leaned her back against it.

"You should not be here, Rider," she whispered as she closed her eyes and thrilled her senses with a deep, unsteady breath. "It's too dangerous for you."

His voice was like a rumbling in the dark sky. "When there is danger, I can feel it in my blood and on my skin. I do not feel any danger now." She heard the swish of leather fringe stirring against his leggings. "Do you?"

"I'm not afraid of you. I know you wouldn't hurt me."

"Your father drinks the red whiskey and sleeps like the dead. How is it he is not mad from it?"

"He has always enjoyed his port, but he drinks only a glass or two at a time." She gripped the doorknob as though she were hiding some secret treasure behind her back. "I believe you when you say it poisons your people. I have seen this happen in Minnesota."

"They are agency Indians, where you come from, the Santee of the Dakota people. They are my cousins."

"Your alliances stretch across great distances." As did her hand, reaching tentatively in the dark.

"The Santee and the Lakota are allied by blood," he told her, ignoring her gesture. "I have no alliance with you."

"Except friendship," she said softly.

"You seek my friendship?"

"Yes."

"You reach for me now?"

"To touch you, yes." Her fingertips grazed the hard contours of his chest. "To make sure you're real. Rider—" She held her breath when he grabbed her arms. The promise of his embrace made her light-headed. She flattened her palm against his warm, smooth skin, and she would have melted against him if he had not stiffly held her apart from him.

"We are of different blood," he said as he turned her to the small window. She heard the sharp intake of his breath as he clamped his arm around her shoulders, grabbing the puffed fabric of her short sleeve and pulling her back against him. Slowly he slid his other hand down her arm, testing the feel of her. He lifted her wrist and held their arms side by side up to the light. "Look, Priscilla. Your skin catches the light from the moon."

"Yours takes its color from the sun."

He turned her in his arms, but still he held himself apart from her. The moon's white light sharpened the angles of his dusky face. "The sun and the moon were once secret lovers, it is said. But their love could not be." He searched her eyes for some acknowledgment, some understanding. "They were banished from their homeland, and now they chase each other in an endless circle across the sky."

"The way you chased the train?" She wanted to put her arms around him, but he held her fast. She could only reach his chest. His skin was like a rock, still warm from basking all day in the summer sun. "All this time I had thought you were dead. I tried to stop those men from shooting. I knocked the gun from the soldier's hand."

"I saw you do this thing."

"But the other man had a gun. I tried to stop him, too, but then I saw that your horse was galloping away, and you were not on his back."

"Sometimes I ride on his back, sometimes his side. He is my war pony. My shield."

"The man said he had . . . shot you."

"I was struck by a bullet that day." He guided her hand under his arm to a place on his side, toward his back. "Here."

"Oh, Rider." The puckered ridge of proud flesh singed her fingertips. "Was it bad?"

"It is a scar to remind me that I was once a foolish boy." The visible scar had helped him regain his honor, but he carried another scar. A private one. "It was bad the day you shamed me with your laughter."

"I didn't mean to laugh, Rider. It was only because I was surprised. We had not spoken of a marriage . . . such as you proposed."

"We spoke of many things."

"Yes, we did. I've missed our . . ." He pressed her hand firmly against the scar and held it there. She could feel the tension in every tendon of his body. ". . . our time together, Rider. Your English has gotten even better. How do you manage this?"

"I speak with LaPointe and with a black robe who comes among our people. It is a small thing. A gift, they say. I have a mind for this, and I do not forget what I learn."

"If you went to school, you could learn so much more. I have been in school, learning ways to teach. I want to teach Indian children to read and write." He started to back away, but she followed, and he gained no distance. "Rider, the time will come when they will need to know these things."

"No, Priscilla, the time will come when you are not safe here." She tried to touch his face, but he stayed her hands, securing both of her slender wrists in the grip of a single hand as he spoke gently. "You must go back, *wigopa*. Follow the Iron Road back to your school."

"There must not be any fighting. If you fight them, more soldiers will come."

"More soldiers *have* come. They say they will make another Iron Road."

"My father can help your people, but you must not hinder his efforts by"—eyes closed, she whispered in fear—"by killing whiskey traders. Did you do that, Rider?"

"A man does not speak with a woman about such things. A Lakota woman would know this."

"I am not a Lakota woman, although sometimes I wish I could be." But she knew she was too cowardly, too spoiled, too . . . "Have you taken a wife?"

"Have you taken a man?"

"No. I have too many other things to think about," she insisted as she twisted her hands from his grasp. He relented, and their eyes held each other fast in the moon-light. Slowly she lifted trembling fingers to his cheeks. "I have not forgotten your face. Sometimes I can feel it, the way it felt when you touched my face with yours."

"I will take a wife soon."

He didn't scare her. His hoarse voice lacked conviction. She smiled. "You have chosen one?"

"She will be a Lakota woman," he said, lifting his chin as he suffered her to slide her soft touchings down his neck, testing his forbearance. "She will not speak of schools. She will know how she must speak to her hus-band, and when he speaks of important matters, she will not laugh."

"I will finish school and become a teacher, and I will laugh when I please." She slipped her arms around his neck, beneath his heavy hair. "Do you kiss?"

"Kiss?"

"Touch lips, yours to mine, before you go. It is a way to say good-bye."

"Show me," he whispered, and his mouth softened as he lowered his head to hers. "Like this? Is this what you want?" His lips were a whisper away.

She'd scarcely moved her head in assent when his full lips parted and covered hers and caressed them hungrily. In truth, she knew little about what she wanted, but the tangy flavor of his lips was surely part of it. "Just this and no more," she whispered when he broke the kiss and his lips grazed her cheek.

"You will go away from here, *wigopa.*" He pulled her tight against him, and his breathing quickened close to her ear. "Away from me."

She rubbed her cheek against his and scarcely breathed at all. Her arms were filled with a near-naked man. He was all muscle and sinew and heated flesh, and he made her feel utterly unfamiliar with herself, as though much of her body were just awakening.

"And you will take a Lakota wife," she muttered as she brushed her lips against the side of his neck. Nothing ei-ther of them said made any sense, or any difference. Now

that he permitted himself to hold her, now that her dream
had become flesh, their senses were greedy for each other.

He moved her toward the small bed. She would have
fallen back on it had he not aligned her hips with his and
drawn himself up, arching against her, hard, so hard that it
created a tremor deep inside her. She made a small, soft
sound of astonishment.

"You have not known a man this way."

"I have no husband." She tightened her arms around his
neck and offered herself to the stimulating pressure of his
body. "I don't want a husband. I want you."

"If I take you, I will keep you." He took her face in his
hands and made her look into his eyes, even as she clung
to his neck. "You will bear my children and stay with me
among my people."

"Yes," she said, for it was the only answer in her head.
It would feel good to know him; that much she knew.
"Take me with you tonight."

He studied her for an interminable time, taking his turn
to touch her face, outlining her features with a forefinger,
a gentle thumb. He drew a long, deep breath and said at
last, "It is a dream, my sweet one. A dream."

She tried to shake her head, but he held her chin still.
Tears of frustration burned in her throat. "You could stay,
Rider."

"I would have to leave you before dawn, just as you
have always left me before dusk. We would chase each
other to the ends of the earth and never quite meet."

"Yes, we will," she insisted; her lower lip trembling.
"Here. Tonight."

Her stubborn hold on his neck made him smile sadly. "I
cannot do this. You have touched my heart, and I cannot
count coups on you this way."

"Stay with Red Cloud's people. Stay with your father's
people, please, Rider." She pressed herself against him and
groaned as she gave in to hot, mortified tears. "Please."

"Your father is my enemy."

"No, not my father."

"You are a strong woman." He enfolded her in his arms,
tucking her head beneath his chin. "You must take your fa-

ther away from here. He cannot keep the soldiers from this land. Only our warriors will keep them away. I came to tell you that I do not wish to kill your father."

"You must not fight, Rider. You cannot beat them all."

"You do not know me."

"I know that you pierced yourself and prayed that your people would live. I know . . ." Blindly her bold fingers discovered the scars on his chest. His eyes seemed to challenge her to make something of them, so she did. She lowered her head and kissed each scar reverently, then looked up at him. "I respect you for this. I also know that you can build a house here and grow food. If you do this, others will follow your example, and the soldiers will leave you alone."

"You believe this?"

"Yes." She touched his shoulder, then trapped a lock of his hair between her fingers. "Yes, I believe it. My father has devoted his life to this cause."

"Take your father away, *wiǧopa*. He is not a warrior."

"Will I see you again?" She had no experience with seduction, she realized. She'd never thought to attempt it, and now she was making a bad job of it. "Will you meet me by the river, the way we used to?"

"We were like children then. We had our own world for a time." He brushed her hair back from her shoulder, mirroring her gesture as he captured a lock of it in his fist. "Those days are gone. If I see you again, you will know a man. A Lakota man, who would fill your belly with a Lakota child."

Was that what she wanted? She closed her eyes, clasped his hand in hers, and moved it to her waist, then down, over her skirt, pressing his palm to her abdomen. "Here?"

He rested his forehead against hers. His strong hand submitted to her small one. His fingers flexed, but only slightly. It was enough to send a waterfall of excitement sluicing toward her feminine core.

"This is not what you want," he whispered. She pressed harder, but he pulled away. He grabbed her shoulders before she could turn from him, and he shook her and spoke to her as though she were a child who didn't know her own mind. "If I did not care for you, I would take you

now, because we want each other *now*." His voice became
gentle again. "I would take what I want before you go
away again."

"But if you stay—"

"No, *wigopa*. You want your white ways. You cannot
have them with a Lakota man." She looked at him plain-
tively, and he shook his head. "I am still a Lakota man."

"I painted your shirt. I have kept it." She drew away
from him, taking one hesitant, backward step, then another, hoping he would pull her back when he found he
couldn't let her go this time. He did not. Her face burned
furiously as she turned and knelt beside her trunk. She felt
around inside and found the buckskin shirt. It triggered a
flow of her tears, the way it always had. She'd painted the
figure of the fox through tears.

"I mourned you, Rider," she told him as she rose
slowly, bearing the shirt like an offering. "I thought you
were dead."

"Shhh." He took the shirt in one hand and pulled her
face against his shoulder with the other. "I am dead, and
you are gone from this land. Do you hear this, *wigopa?*"

She groaned, rubbing her tears into his skin as she
shook her head. He lifted her chin and brushed his lips
softly against hers. "I see that your people can have tears
for mine. I see that there is a heart and soul among them.
I will remember this."

"I will be here a little longer," she said quickly as he
moved decisively toward the window. "I won't see you
from the train window this time?"

"No. You will not see me."

She did not take him at his word. She expected him to
return. She looked for him in every shadow, thinking he
would ask her to change her plans, trying to decide what
she would say. If he were willing to stay at the agency,
what then? If not, what *then?*

She saw Sarah several times, but Whirlwind Rider did
not come again. Within a month her friend bore her the
news that he had found a wife among the Hunkpapa.

Chapter 12

Dakota Territory, Summer 1875

It felt like a homecoming, even though the Red Cloud Agency had been moved to the plains of the upper White River. Priscilla had finished her studies and had taught among the eastern Sioux at a Minnesota mission for one school term. The impoverished families of her students were the same Santee Sioux whose uprising in 1862 had inspired the whispered fears she remembered from her childhood. The land they were permitted to occupy had been whittled down by a series of treaties and agreements, and the promise of annuities was as poorly kept in Minnesota as it was in the territories.

Still, the Great Sioux Reserve in Dakota Territory remained largely intact, and in Priscilla's memory it was a place where the Lakota people still had a chance to determine their own destiny. In her singularly well-educated if minority view, it was right that they should. And in her young and idealistic heart, she had never really left the vast rolling prairie or forgotten the ties she had there.

But the news from the West had been disturbing. Lieutenant Colonel George Custer, hoping to regain national attention and his wartime rank of general, had led an expedition into the Black Hills and reported the presence of gold to the Eastern press. The inevitable fever was ignited.

Against the terms of the treaty, more miners poured into the area, spilling through the huge cracks in the ring of forts that encircled the Sioux Reserve. The men in Washington had stopped making treaties in favor of offering "agreements," which always resulted in shrinking Indian territory. Now there was talk that a new agreement would soon open up the goldfields. All this meant that Charles Twiss's work was more pressing than ever. Priscilla had come to help him.

To her surprise, he did not welcome the kind of help she offered. Their relationship had changed since her first visit to the agency. They were no longer "two intelligent heads ultimately of one mind," as her father had once boasted. She attributed much of the change to her growing up and his growing older. Her attraction to Whirlwind Rider was not an issue for discussion—not with her father or anyone else. It was what it was. Her own secret star, perhaps, safely out of her reach. Meanwhile, her letters to her father had been cordial, and his replies had unwittingly convinced her that her mission was not in Minnesota at all, but rather on the Great Sioux Reserve.

"You've promised schools, Father," she insisted as he picked through the crates of books she'd brought with her. "We must provide schools."

"*I* haven't promised schools. The treaty promises schools. Let us see what the next agreement promises before we hurry to build anything more." The lid clattered on the box he'd just pried open. "Is there nothing in any of these for your father, dear girl?"

"A number of books that should interest you. I thought it best not to transport any spirits."

"No spirits, eh?" With a dry chuckle he dumped himself in his favorite chair and rocked back, peering up at her. "What delightful irony, my dear. Do you speak of ghosts or liquor? Either way, this place is burgeoning with spirits."

"I brought you some chocolates," she announced absently as she searched for places to put things. The house was similar to the one her father had occupied on the Platte. The furnishings were, of course, the same, but her father's personal habits had changed. His books were strewn about, some stacked in piles against the walls. His desk was laden with scraps of paper, a tin mess plate, cups, and trinkets. But there was no inkwell. No lamp. No signs that this was a workplace for a man of letters, a man who had records to keep and correspondences to maintain. "I see I shall have to help you get organized here."

"Well, who knows how long we'll be here, hmm? They can't seem to grow a crop. I've tried—some of *them* have actually given it a go. This is a hostile place for farming, I'm afraid, and they are not farmers, these western Sioux."

"Neither are you, Father." She watched him rocking, rocking back and forth as he stared into the cold stone hearth and stroked the white beard that desperately needed a trimming. The pouches under his eyes sagged halfway down his cheeks. He was less and less the man she'd known when she was a child. "What kind of an agreement is in the offing?"

He glanced at her, then looked away again. "A congressional commission is on its way to negotiate the purchase of the Black Hills."

"Purchase the Black Hills from the Sioux?"

"I know. Not even Red Cloud will discuss it. I believe the hostiles' numbers are increasing, along with their resolve."

"And the army?"

"Military minds insist that we are headed for another Indian war, and I must say that some of the officers are fairly licking their chops over the prospect. It's too bad Tim Harmon was transferred. He could have watched his predictions become reality." Charles tapped a chunky fist on the arm of the rocker. "The coming negotiations will be crucial."

Priscilla knelt beside the rocking chair, grasping the arm to stop the motion and make her father look at her. "You can't give up. War would be disastrous."

"That depends on how we look at it, my dear." He smiled, a peculiarly humorless, fish-eyed smile. "When it comes, I have no doubt that it will be over quickly. The hostiles will be subdued, if not eliminated. The rest of the people will finally be receptive to adopting more civilized ways."

"First it's the whiskey traders who are permitted to do their business here, and now it's the gold miners." With half a mind to test for the presence of a pulse, she touched the back of her father's hand. "You speak of yourself as their Father Agent, and yet you talk of eliminating some of them, as though they were chess pieces simply to be removed from the board." She paused, but he stared at the brass buttons on his vest and offered no rebuttal. "It would not be that neat," she said finally. "There would be blood spilled."

His round belly rose and fell on a sigh. "Well, these people are used to spilling blood. They do it all the time. We've seen them do it, haven't we?"

"If you're speaking of the Sun Dance, that was a ceremony," Priscilla said.

"And maybe war is a ceremony. Out with the old blood, in with the new." His grating chuckle prompted her to withdraw her hand, her chin dropping a notch in horror. He shook his head. "I can't stop it from happening, Priscilla. Even if the commission gets what it wants, that may not stop it."

"But the *people* . . ."

"They are a stubborn breed. Some of them will survive." It was a toneless, unfeeling observation, followed by a sad mockery of his old enthusiasm. "The survivors will make good citizens, don't you think?"

Endless thinking and postulating now seemed like futile activities. Priscilla made two decisions. She had come to Dakota Territory to stay this time, and she had her own work to do among the Lakota people. She wasn't sure what it was, but she knew that four years of preparation had opened her mind, and her two summer visits to the plains had opened her eyes and ears.

She knew that language could be a barrier or an inroad, and her father, for his five years of service as an Indian agent, knew far less Lakota than she did. The teachers at the mission school in Minnesota had criticized her for her willingness to speak with the students in their language, even to allow them to improve her Lakota vocabulary as she returned the favor in English. While the others followed the policy of punishing the students for speaking their native tongue, Priscilla used the language to the children's advantage. They were learning to read faster under her instruction than anyone else's. Only the students appreciated her success. She had no friends on the school staff, and no one seemed sorry to see her go.

She didn't need a school building, she decided. She didn't need an employer to tell her how to do her job. And a teacher's pay wasn't much more than room and board anyway; that much she trusted she could wrangle from the agency. Her father wasn't going to let her starve. All she needed was students. Once again she sought out her friend, Sarah LaPointe.

Like many of the agency Indians, Sarah and her husband had built a cabin, but they were among the few who actually lived in it. Most of the people used the tipi as their dwelling and the cabin for storage. But Henry LaPointe had built a stone fireplace and a bed, and Sarah served meals on a rough-hewn pine table. Still, Sarah said, if the people should strike camp and move deeper into Indian territory, the LaPointe family would move with them.

"It would be difficult to run a school under those circumstances," Priscilla mused as she accepted the coffee Sarah offered her. "I would either have to follow the children around or wait until they returned."

"My husband learned from the missionary teachers. Some of them did as you say. They followed our camps." Sarah stood at the open door and watched little Joseph tumble in the tall grass with a flop-eared puppy. There was another baby on the way now. Another child to feed, another child whose future would be uncertain.

"Times are hard," Sarah said. "There is more sickness, it seems, and less game. I have thought, when they make the schools they have promised us, this learning for my children would not be a bad thing. But they don't bring the other things they promise. And I think back on the summer hunts and the winter camps." She turned to Priscilla again. "Our people to the north and west can still hunt buffalo. There are not as many as there once were, but where there is a good hunter"—she smiled wistfully—"the family can still eat every day. That's better than we have it here sometimes."

The image of a good hunter sprang to Priscilla's mind. A man who was called hostile because he chose to feed his family. "Is Whirlwind Rider still living among the Minneconjou?" She avoided Sarah's eyes in the hope that it sounded like a casual question.

"Yes."

"I remember"—Priscilla cleared her throat—"that he took a wife two years ago, or he was *about* to, you told me then. I wonder . . ." She looked up and spoke cautiously. "Do they have children?"

"My brother's wife died. That first winter she got the coughing sickness."

Died. Lord forgive her for the way her mouth went dry so that she could hardly utter, "I'm sorry." *Oh, Rider, I am sorry.*

"My brother's spirit is not broken by this. He is a leader in the old way. He gives away what he does not need. He sings the kit-fox songs and carries out his duties. He will not accept rations. He will not accept the agency. He will not surrender." Sarah stood over Priscilla and studied her face for a moment, as if some story were written in her eyes. "I see that you are as strong-minded as he is. It is a strange thing, but I think you belong with him, Priscilla. Is that why you came back?"

"Does he ever speak of me?"

"He has hidden his heart away. I believe he carries you there."

"He was right, though. It's impossible." She had dreamed of him so often, his fire-and-buckskin scent, the sound of his voice in the dark, the touch of his lips on hers. But whenever she *thought* of him, she tried to be sensible. "A life together would not be possible."

"The life my brother lives is not possible. So says our Father Agent." Sarah smiled triumphantly. "Still, my brother lives."

"Will you tell him I'm here?" Priscilla rose from the table, surprised by her own hasty request. "And tell him I'm not leaving. I'm here to stay."

Welcome late summer rain tapped on the rawhide walls of Sarah's tipi. Seated on the hair side of a buffalo hide, Priscilla reshuffled her letter cards and worked *rain* into her reading lesson. Eleven-year-old Pierre LaPointe had brought a new friend today, along with four others who had participated in previous lessons. Sarah usually took part, too, but today she was busy in the cabin. It surprised Priscilla when Sarah interrupted the class to call the boys outside. She offered no explanation. She simply told the boys to hurry along.

The boys filed out, and Sarah backed away, her eyes flashing with a conspirator's smile. She held the door cover aloft, and Whirlwind Rider ducked inside.

For weeks Priscilla had been anticipating this moment, but now that it was here she almost panicked. She could read nothing in his eyes. There was no greeting, no curiosity, none of the joy she felt simply in the chance to lay eyes on him after two long years. It was almost like the first time, except that she was the one caught by surprise. She lowered her gaze and recognized the fox she'd painted on his rain-damp shirt. It was a greeting of sorts.

Nervously she gathered her alphabet cards into a pile and tapped the edges against her knee.

"You look well," he said at last.

She glanced up quickly and offered a grateful smile. "You look fine, too." A bit more lean in the face, perhaps, but as disturbingly handsome as he had been the very first time she'd seen him.

"My sister tells me that you will stay now."

"Yes. I've come to stay."

He sat down next to her on the buffalo hide, crossing his legs and bracing his elbows on his knees, and together they listened to the gentle tapping of the rain. After a long silence, he asked, "What will you do here?"

"Teach the children." She watched him out of the corner of her eye. From what she could see in the strong lines of his profile, he was unimpressed with her plans. "I think it's important that the children have access to . . . to books, and that they understand what is being said by the white people who come here. The way you do. Not that you couldn't teach them yourself, but . . ." He glanced her way. "I have decided to make this my life's work."

"Work." He gave a caustic laugh and shook his head. "Your father has work. The soldiers have work. Their work is to destroy the Lakota."

"I promise that what I teach will not harm the children." He leaned back, planting one elbow on the shaggy rug. A teasing smile danced in his eyes. "Speaking another language has not damaged you, Rider. Neither will reading and writing bring any harm to the people here."

"Why?" he repeated indulgently. "Why are you here?"

Softly, candidly came her answer. "Because I cannot be anywhere else."

"It is a hard life here now."

"I know."

"But not for a soldier's wife, they say. Some of them bring their women now." He glanced at the alphabet cards. "Will you be a soldier's wife?"

"No."

"I said I would take a Lakota wife."

"And you did. Sarah told me." The news had stunned her at first. She'd told herself she had no reason to be hurt by it, but she was. She couldn't even bring herself to mention the marriage in her journal. But now seeing him and hearing the sadness in his voice, she wanted only to share his grief. She touched the back of his hand, which rested on the rug, close to her knee. "I'm sorry you lost her, Rider."

"The white man's sickness takes the old ones first, then the young ones. Like your whiskey, we have little power against it."

She glanced up apologetically, her fingertips lingering on his hand.

"I think you do," he said. "I think you have power over these things, and you will not die."

"But we do die, just like—"

"I speak of *you*, Priscilla." He turned his hand and caught hers. "I speak of you."

She remembered the meteoric happiness she'd known in the past when he had held her in his arms and spoken of her. She had not felt that way since. "I am just as mortal as the next person." *Mortal and human, and I want to feel that way again.* "But I came here to live and to work. Not to die anytime soon."

"Good." He sat up, moving closer. The sound of his breathing made her shiver inside, as did his question. "You have no man at all?"

"No, I have . . . not." There was only one she wanted. Nothing had changed since she had confessed this to him the night he had come to her room. She had wanted him then, and she wanted him now. She would have no other. She offered a prim smile. "As I'm sure your sister had dutifully reported to you."

"I have told you to leave me, but you have come back. I have tried to wipe you from my mind, Priscilla, but you are always there." He touched her cheek with the backs of his fingers and softly traced her cheekbone with his thumb. She sat very still, as though she feared that any movement would scare him away. "You are much trouble for me," he told her, smiling.

She pouted. "Then stay up there with your mother's people and don't interrupt my classes."

"I think you would follow after me." His fingers strayed to her hair, probing to see how the fat knot of fine, silky stuff was secured to the back of her head. He withdrew a wire hairpin, examined it briefly, then dropped it carelessly on the rug and went searching for another. "I think you would ride into Crazy Horse's camp or Sitting Bull's camp, with your two legs on one side of the horse and your little hat, and you would look our wise ones straight in the eyes." Her eyes widened, and again he smiled. " 'I have come to be Whirlwind Rider's woman,' you will say."

She squared her shoulders. "I would do no such thing." But she smiled, too, as she bent her head to give him access to more pins.

"And they will shake their heads at me, and they will say, 'Cousin, you will need all your strength.'" The knot uncoiled in his hand. "Is there no husband for you among the whites, *wigopa?*"

"I didn't come here to find a husband," she insisted, tossing her head to shake her hair into a tawny, rippling fall. "I don't need a husband."

"You need a man."

"I could have *had* a man. Any number of men. But I was busy with school, you see, and I—" She closed her eyes as he combed his fingers through her long hair, grooming her. "I wanted to be here. I wanted to study at a fine school, and I did that. I did very well. I presented my paper on . . ."

She was nervous. She was eager. She was babbling, and yet she felt compelled to explain the direction she'd taken, for it seemed that he might understand, better than anyone. "I tried to describe the indescribable. To explain the inexplicable. They were interested in my work, in a rather detached, academic way." She turned to him and discovered, to her surprise, that he was listening. She touched his square chin. "I'm afraid my words and my drawings did not do you justice, my magnificent friend."

"What is *magnificent?*"

He knew. She could tell by the light of abiding confidence in his eyes. "Special," she told him. "Uncommon. To my knowledge, the one and only Whirlwind Rider. You and your people have changed me, and no matter how much time had passed, I always came back to this place in my dreams. I wanted to be here."

"You are still the daughter of my enemy, *wigopa.*"

"Does it matter?"

"No. Not now."

She understood what that meant. She was ready. As irrational as her inclination was, it had been there, intrinsic in every move, every plan, every decision she had made for such a long time. Her destiny had been bound up with this man since the moment their eyes had met at the forge, and she would not be a whole woman until he made her so.

He removed his wet shirt and tossed it aside.

"Rider, the children." She glanced toward the door. "If they come back outside, they might . . ."

"My sister has taken the children away, and the door to this lodge is closed." He took hold of her shoulders and lowered her to the buffalo-hide pallet. His hair slipped over his shoulder and mingled with hers, dark with light. "We will not be disturbed. The afternoon is heavy with rain."

"I love the sound." She laced her fingers in the curtain of his hair and turned her cheek to it, tickling her nose with it. "I love the smell of rain in your hair, and on your skin."

"I know your scent as well, *wiǧopa*," he whispered as he nuzzled her neck. With one deft hand he began freeing the small buttons that ran along her breastbone. "The sweet smell of flowers, the soft scent of woman. If I found you asleep in the dark of night, I would know you before I touched your face."

"Rider . . ."

"I would know you before you called my name."

"Whirlwind Rider." Wonderful name, she dimly recalled telling someone. Suited him perfectly. Baring his chest came naturally for him, but must he bare hers? Instinctively she clasped her hand to her bosom. "Don't—"

"Don't?"

"Don't uncover me . . . all the way."

"How will I learn you, then?" He looked down at her, smiling as though her modesty amused him. With a kiss he moved her hand aside and continued his quest. "You seem so small. I must see for myself if it is a woman I hold in my arms, or just a girl."

"You've known me long enough to realize . . ."

He came to the button just above the waist of her dress, dispatched it, and the bodice fell away. "What is this?"

It was her turn to be amused, to be comfortable with being the teacher again. "The dress comes in two pieces. I have several bodices"—she cleared her throat, calming herself with the call to instruct—"several tops for this dress because"—he touched the gray silk and cotton stripe, rubbing it between his fingers as she explained—"because fabric, of course, is dear. One would be foolish not to make use ..."

His smile cut deep grooves in his sun-bronzed cheeks. She wasn't sure whether he was amused by something she'd said or something he'd discovered as he undid the buttons at her waist. "Oh, Rider, I did not imagine ... How much must be removed?"

"How much do you wear?" He stretched out beside her, bracing his elbow on the rug, propping his head against the heel of one hand while the other, spanning her midriff, drifted up and down her corset. "What is this? It feels like my breastplate, but the bones go up and down. Does it protect you?"

"Obviously not." She could not help smiling. She wasn't sure why she found the laugh lines at the corners of his eyes so endearing.

"Does it come off?"

She showed him where the hooks were, and he went after them diligently.

"*Ŏhan.*" Triumphantly, he peeled the underpinnings of fashion away. "I have found a woman."

They gazed into each other's laughing eyes. She was a woman now, yes, a woman with her own mind, her own body to share as she pleased. And she pleased. The light in his eyes told her so. She may have seemed odd to him in some superficial ways, but by virtue of some strange quirk in them both, they pleased each other. She laughed until he bent his head to kiss her breast through her thin chemise. There was an audible catch in her breathing, a mingling of hesitation and expectancy. He slid the ribbon in the neck casing from its bow as he kissed away the last vestige of her smile.

He touched her breast, cupping it, molding it as though he were creating it. He brought it to life with his thumb, rubbing the tip with a light touch until it tightened into a tender bead. His kisses were hot and moist, his tongue delving into her mouth like a shock of flame. His hand slipped down, down over the fluff of her light crinoline.

She guided his hand to a tape at her waist, and he

quickly untied it and pushed it away. His caress stirred something distinctly pleasurable deep in her belly. He moved his mouth over her breast and tongued her aching nipple. The belly-pleasure intensified. He was not as adept with hooks as he was with buttons, but he kept peeling back clothing in search of fine, smooth skin. Finally together they shoved the pile of fabric aside, like a wad of excess, trimmed away.

He accosted her in earnest with his kisses now, nipping at the curve of her lower lip, diving deep with his tongue as though he would use it to count her teeth and measure the roof of her mouth. She gripped his shoulders as he slid down to become gentle and winsome again, suckling her like a hungry babe. The delicious tugging at her breast increased the pleasure in her belly, making it spin, marking it as his namesake, a small but unrelenting whirlwind.

With a quick pull he freed the thong that held his buckskin breechclout. She watched it fall away from his waist, her curiosity giving way to wide-eyed awe. He gave a quick, guttural laugh as he moved over her. She slid her hands over his smooth chest. Hard muscle was his breastplate. His belly was long and lean. No hair, although she'd noticed a nest of it around the part of him that sprang forth like a mystic, secret spear when he'd undressed. He hovered over her, submitting himself patiently as her inquisitive fingertips idled, pressing him low in the belly.

His dark eyes smoldered. "There's more."

"I know," she whispered. "I saw."

"Now touch. I will trust you."

"Trust m-me?" But he was the man. He was the one whose long, hard shaft would soon pierce her. That much she knew.

"Touch me first," he invited in a strained voice. "Before I touch you."

She closed her hand around him carefully. His eyes drifted closed as though he were on the verge of either savoring something wonderful or losing something vital. What could she take? What could she do to him? She moved her hand experimentally and found that his stiff weapon was encased in a sheath. The sharp catch in his breath surprised, then empowered her. Emboldened, she traced the warm shaft to its coarse-haired nest and the velvety pouch protected therein. He moved his thighs apart, straddling her, giving her free access to him.

"You're very soft here," she said in a small voice.

"Tender," he said. "Even a hand as small as yours might leave me helpless."

"With pain?"

"Or pleasure." He nuzzled her temple and whispered, "The choice is yours."

"Pleasure." Instinctively she caressed him, making him moist at the tip. "Is this good?"

"Lila waśte." He slid his hand between them and possessed her feminine mound beneath his palm. "Very good. Trust me now." She gasped as he slipped one finger into the cleft between her legs. His touch felt at once pleasant and perilous, and squirming only intensified the sensation.

"Oh, my," she breathed.

"Ŏhan." He chuckled, nuzzled her neck, and touched her some more. He touched her until she was on fire and embarrassingly wet and completely a-tremble. She hid her face against his arm and whispered his name.

"Nimitawa ktelo," he answered. "You will be mine, Priscilla," he translated as he penetrated her with the first swift thrust. He took her startled breath into his own open-mouthed kiss and groaned appreciatively as he rocked his hips, his sensuous rhythm slowly mounting. *"Ohinniyan,"* he crooned close to her ear over and over, plunging deeper inside her. *"Ohinniyan, ohinniyan.* Always, forever mine, *wiǧopa. Ohin . . . ni . . . yannnnn."*

They listened to the rain pelting all around them as they lay in each other's arms, hands sliding smoothly over skin still dewy from their frantic attempts to absorb each other, to become completely and wholly one flesh. They were two again, enraptured with the wonder of discovering each other. This rainy afternoon and this cozy, conical shelter were all theirs, and in this place each knew the other's serenity, contentment, wonder, and more. He sensed the discomfort he'd created for her. When he left her side, it was only to pull the door flap aside and catch cupped hands full of cool rain with which to bathe the maiden's blood from her thighs.

She lifted her head and smiled gratefully, feeling newly baptized. He had not given her a name, but she knew his heart was hers.

"You have touched me with your woman's blood," he said reverently as he caressed her delicate skin. His long black hair lightly swept her pale, damp thigh. "It is a powerful medicine. A man must seek his medicine, but a woman is born with it." His eyes sought hers. "Your power is like lightning. Beautiful and frightful. A man cannot resist it, but he must be cautious in its presence."

He buried his fingertips in the hair between her legs, sheltering her private place with his hand. "I have entered a sacred circle," he said solemnly. "Life begins here. From today I will defend you with my life."

"Is this a vow, Rider?"

"It is, yes." He lay down beside her again and pulled her into his arms. It gave him great pleasure simply to smooth her long, silken hair down the length of her back.

"Why have you waited, *wiǧopa?*" He knew. Deep down he had always known. But he wanted to hear her say it. "Tell me why you have saved this gift for me."

"It was not something I thought about in my head, exactly." She wouldn't have dared think it, *exactly.* "I thought about you, of course. Even when I thought you were dead, I thought about . . ." She brushed his hair back from his temple and smiled, lost in his eyes. "You. Both sweet and sad thoughts of you. I thought about the night you came to my room, the way you tried not to hold me in your arms and let me touch you, but finally you did, and, oh, what magic there was when we were pressed close together for just a few fleeting moments. I remembered the way it made me ache inside."

He weighed her small breast in his palm and teased her nipple until her breathing fluttered a bit. "Here?"

"Mmm, yes."

Smiling, watching her face, he slid his hand to her belly. "And here?"

"Yes." She shifted closer. "I could not think of another man touching me. Not this way. Even though I knew you had a wife—"

"Shhh." He touched a finger to her lips. "If we speak of the dead, we disturb their souls."

"And our own, perhaps?" She tipped her head back and looked up. "Did you think of me, Rider?"

"Yes."

"Even when you were married to someone else?"

"A man may take more than one wife." He mirrored her quick scowl. "It is not so for the white man?"

"Only if his first wife dies."

"Ah, well, this is easy to understand. A man who takes a second wife must be a strong breeder and a good provider. These soldiers and these miners of yours provide nothing but trouble."

"They are not *my* soldiers." Disclaiming all other males, she snuggled contentedly into the harbor of his warm embrace. "I have nothing to do with miners, either."

"You have to do with me." He reversed their positions, smiling as he tucked her beneath him. "You have chosen a hunter and a warrior. Come with me. I will provide for you." He nibbled at her ear and promised, "I will breed you often and well."

Oh, yes, she wanted that. "You speak English as well as Henry does. If you live among the Oglala, the army will make you a scout."

"My cousin Crazy Horse is Oglala. He does not stay among these agency people."

"Crazy Horse is a renegade," she reminded him.

"Whirlwind Rider is a renegade, too," he answered readily.

"I don't think so." The sensual lips grazing her cheek made it hard for her to remember what *renegade* even meant.

"Ah, then my aim was true. My spear was won us an ally." His chuckle turned to a grunt when she playfully shoved her fist into his gut. "A touchy one," he allowed.

"You're the touchy one. But you're not like Crazy Horse."

"You know him?"

"Of course not. He doesn't come to the agency."

"Then you will try to understand that I *am* like him. He is Lakota." He looked into her eyes and explained what she already knew. "I belong to the Tokala. I carry the lance. I protect the helpless ones. When something difficult must be done, I am there first to seek the task. These are some of the words of the song I sing." He caught her chin in his hand. "Why do you look away? Is this a small thing to you?"

"No. It's an honorable thing." She closed her eyes. "It frightens me."

"You belong with me now, *wigopa*. You must know who I am. You must know that I am Lakota. I am no agency loafer."

"If you stay near the agency, just ... even close by, where I can ..." Her eyes pleaded with his. "We can be together somehow. I know we can. But if I go with you, my father will send the soldiers after me."

"Tell him you have chosen me."

"It won't matter. It's the one choice he would not permit me to make." She saw the doubt in his eyes, and it frightened her. "Rider, there is another meeting planned. Another council meeting, only this time there will be men from Washington. Important men, like your White-Horse Owners and Big Bellies, the ones who decide."

"We have heard of these plans. They want the headmen of all the bands to attend. Again they want Red Cloud to speak for us." He lay back on the rug and stared at the top of the tipi, where the smoke hole was shielded outside by a storm flap. This was the only shelter he knew, the only kind of home he ever wanted. But he wanted this woman, too. He sighed. "What do they want?"

"They will propose to buy Paha Sapa."

"*Buy?*" It was an absurd idea. "With pay-money?"

"Money and more annuities."

"More promises?" He rolled his head back and forth on the buffalo hide and gave a mordant chuckle. "Red Cloud's people have not eaten well on these promises."

"It may be different this time." The simple act of saying

the words made her realize she didn't believe them any-more. She turned her head and pressed her cheek against his arm. "If you refuse, they will . . . I'm afraid they will find some other way."

Her fear was more important to him than the threat, which did not come from her. In response, his song rose in his throat. He sang it for her softly.

The Fox, I am.
Whatever must be done for the people, I will do,
but a hard time I am having.

Chapter 13

Journal Entry, September 20, 1875

The Army has done almost nothing this summer to keep the hundreds of fortune hunters out of the Black Hills. Lieutenant Colonel Custer, who is posted at Fort Abraham Lincoln on the northern boundary of the reserve, made an expedition into the Hills last year and announced to the world that gold fairly lay in the grass, ripe for the taking. Earlier this summer a geologist named William Jenney confirmed the news, which from all reports is spreading across the country like wildfire. Rumor has it that some of the soldiers have turned their own hands to prospecting.

Father says that the 1868 treaty was a promise made to be broken. It disheartens me to hear him say this. He has changed so much in the last four years. He scoffs at my attempts to provide some schooling for the children at his agency. He is now of the opinion that the children must be taken from their families and placed in boarding schools, far away from "savage influences." Knowing Sarah LaPointe and some of the others as I do, I cannot abide this idea. Taking away their children would be worse than taking away their land.

Senator Allison and his commission have come for

their treaty council. New federal laws prohibit the making of more treaties, but the commissioners hope to make some changes in the 1868 treaty, which fixes the limits of the Great Sioux Reservation. They are accompanied by soldiers, journalists, photographers, and even a few women. Not surprisingly, I also met a beef contractor whose interest in the proceedings is, as he put it, "purely business." He added, "All them savages need do is make their mark, and I'm in business." His smile seemed somehow chilling, and it occurred to me that I would not wish to have this man standing between me and my next meal.

The commission and its military escort have set up their square canvas tents on the White River. They chose a place between the Spotted Tail Agency and the Red Cloud Agency to avoid showing favoritism to either the Brule or the Oglala chief, since they are both leaders of "friendly" Indians. The government has decided that these two men are leaders of the Sioux.

The old and oft-repeated demand that the hostiles gather at the agency for a census to be taken among the Lakota was renewed in the months before the council. The Oglala friendlies sent emissaries to their cousins in the north, took them gifts, and asked them to come to the big council. So far the northern bands—including the Minneconjou, the Hunkpapa, the Sans Arc, the Two Kettle, and the Blackfoot Sioux—along with Crazy Horse's renegade Oglala, have refused to put their names to any government papers.

But they have an interest in this council. They have come in closer, like a flock of wary birds, and although some of their headmen were present at the first day's session, men like Crazy Horse and Sitting Bull will not come to the meeting tent in person. They do not trust these proceedings, but they have seen to it that everything that transpires will be reported to them and that their wishes will be made known. I suspect that they are camped somewhere nearby. The plains and valleys for miles around are filled with colorfully decorated tipis. The autumn-gold hills are thickly dotted with Indian pony herds.

Since the treaty requires that three-fourths of the Lakota must agree to any changes made in the accord, the commission is generally pleased to see a large turnout. Their charge is to secure a lease or purchase agreement for the Black Hills. In today's meeting Senator Allison proposed a lease agreement in which the Sioux would effectively turn over all mineral rights to the United States government for "a fair sum." Once the concept of leasing was explained, Spotted Tail declared the offer to be laughable. He asked whether the senator would consider offering him a team of mules on similar terms.

The commissioners believe that they are dealing with an ignorant and defenseless people. How wrong they are!

After the talks ended on the first day, Whirlwind Rider rode north to Crazy Horse's camp. There he met with the young Oglala leader and with the *akicita,* the warrior societies, including his Tokala brotherhood. He explained the proposal for leasing the land so that the gold the whites love so much might be chiseled from the bosom of Paha Sapa. He related Spotted Tail's words, and those who shared the circle with him laughed and allowed that perhaps Lakota blood did still run in the veins of the agency chief. But they listened silently as Whirlwind Rider reported the rest. The commissioners wanted more Sioux lands. They wanted the hunting grounds that extended south to the Platte River. They wanted the Powder River country and the hunting grounds east of the Big Horn Mountains. In return they offered pay-money and annuities of food and clothing.

"They have promised these things before," the brave warrior called Little Big Man said. "But look what happened last winter. It was up to us to keep our agency cousins alive. No supply wagons came. The snow was deep, and it was a bad time for all of us, but our cousins had nothing. Many of them died. If we had not taken them food and robes, there would not be one left to speak of selling the land."

"That is what the *wašicun* want." Crazy Horse shook his head and spoke quietly, as was his custom. "They are killing all the buffalo. They tell the people to stay close to the agency and they will be fed. They wait for wagons that do not come."

"Except to bring whiskey," Whirlwind Rider said. "The whiskey traders' wagons roll across the land no matter what the season."

"And the soldiers, and the ones who grub for gold. They are not stopped by the snow."

"They will be stopped by this." Little Big Man brandished his rifle. "We must ride into their camp now and kill these commissioners before the agency chiefs sign any of their papers."

But Crazy Horse reminded them that the Lakota had agreed to the council, and that there were Lakota families camped close by. "When they meet again, we will give them our answer. We will show them that one does not sell the land upon which the people walk. Our cousins who loaf about the agency will hear us, and maybe they will remember what it is to be Lakota."

The council did not reconvene for three days. There was much arguing among the agency Indians. Each day the commissioners waited, but first Spotted Tail refused to come to the meeting tent, and then Red Cloud refused. Whirlwind Rider was growing impatient with it all, but he was beginning to understand the narrow path the leaders of the people were given to walk these days. The white world could not be ignored. Like a torn sack of their flour, its contents steadily sifted out and drifted into Sioux country on the slightest breeze.

He himself could not ignore it now that he had taken one of their women to his blankets. He was no better than the agency chiefs, for now he had his own selfish reasons for wanting peace with the whites. His reason was not as bland as their flour. She was sweet. More like their sugar.

They met at night and in secret. Whirlwind Rider found a secluded spot sheltered by an overhanging clay bluff. LaPointe led Priscilla to meet him even though he doubted the prudence of such a rendezvous. He warned his brother-friend that Agent Twiss seemed to pay particular attention to every move Whirlwind Rider made as he was translating for the representatives of the northern bands.

"You shocked him once," LaPointe said. "He looks for you to make another surprise move."

"Let him watch me. Do you think he will see who I am?" Whirlwind Rider held the bay mare's reins while Priscilla dismounted. He turned, chuckling as he hooked his arm around her shoulders and pulled her close to his side. "I am the man who will be the father of his grandchildren. Twiss is a man who cannot see what he *will* not see."

"Be careful, my friend," LaPointe warned genially. "One day he may see the way his daughter looks at you. She, too, watches your every move, but her eyes shine for you like two blue stars."

Priscilla gave a shy laugh. "Aren't they supposed to?"

"Yes, *wigopa,* your eyes are meant to shine for me." A lovers' look passed between them. He held her gaze, nodding toward his friend. "LaPointe's mother took a white man for her husband. I wonder why he thinks we are so different."

"You know why," LaPointe said. "Their women are their property. My mother was my father's possession. In their eyes, she did not take him; *he* took *her.* Of course, my father came to realize that a Lakota woman will not stay unless she chooses to, and so he learned to treat her with respect. And she loved him."

"Your father was an honest trader," Whirlwind Rider recalled as the three stood together under the starlit Dakota sky. "He put a fair price on his goods, and he did not trade whiskey."

"Times have changed."

"This council will bring more changes. I feel it, just as I feel the coming of winter in the air."

Priscilla felt the chill, too, but she rejected all sense of foreboding. "After today, I think there's every reason to hope that the people will stand together." She looked up at Whirlwind Rider, hoping to reassure him. "Red Cloud and Spotted Tail don't want to sell the Hills, and they realize that a lease would amount to the same thing. After all, possession is nine-tenths of the law, they say."

"What does this mean, nine-tenths of the law?"

"It just means that the law recognizes the claims of those in possession. Those who occupy the land are the ones who own it, for all practical purposes. And the Lakota people occupy the land."

"Until we are removed," LaPointe said flatly.

"But you *won't* be if you don't *agree* to be," Priscilla blithely contended. "You have the treaty on your side. Tell them to stick to it. I don't care what my father says, a promise is a promise."

"If we choose not to sign their papers, will they go and leave us in peace?"

His mocking tone made it clear that Whirlwind Rider knew better. In his world such a choice would be respected among those who had agreed to live side by side, but it was probably too much to expect from a people who permitted their own women and children so few chances to choose for themselves.

"I don't know." Priscilla sighed. His question tempered her optimism. "You might have to give them something. I don't know what."

"Will they take promises? I can make as many promises for them as they make for me."

"Whatever they take will be taken tomorrow," LaPointe said. "They have a plan to see that Spotted Trail and Red Cloud both start out from their camps at the same time tomorrow."

"Then the Tokala will be there." Whirlwind Rider cast a glance at the rim of the bluff. "The agency chiefs will not ride alone."

LaPointe left them to enjoy the few stolen hours they would have together. Priscilla was becoming a fixture among the people, finding ways to teach effectively right in their midst. She often stayed with Sarah. They had become like sisters. LaPointe had tried ribbing Whirlwind Rider a bit lately about her presence in his household, suggesting that his brother ought to claim his woman soon or LaPointe himself might start thinking he had a second wife.

Whirlwind Rider's only response had been a look stern enough to freeze the broth in his sister's cooking pot.

The whole situation was a bit tenuous for LaPointe's taste. His road between worlds was precarious enough. But he knew that, try as he might, this indomitable warrior was now powerless to shake this woman loose from his heart. LaPointe did not question his obligation to help his wife's brother, his lifelong friend.

Whirlwind Rider picketed Priscilla's horse near his roan and took her to the grassy place where he had spread his robes beneath the stars. They undressed each other and made a cocoon of his buffalo-hide pallet, wrapping arms and legs around each other in their desperate need to saturate their senses with each other in the little time they had.

He loved to kiss her breasts and tighten her nipples with the deft featherings of his tongue. He reveled in his capacity to make her sigh with pleasure. It was small reward for her unstinting willingness to turn his most excruciating need into blissful satisfaction.

"You risk everything whenever you come to me, *wiǧopa*," he whispered into her soft, night-bright hair.

She pressed her lips to his shoulder, and he was enchanted by the soft tickle of her tongue. "No more than any woman who shares her love with a man."

The feel of her fingers laboring to make their small dents in his buttocks made him groan. "More than most, I think."

"Oh, but you're worth the risk," she said, feeling deliciously full of female sauciness. "A bit more than most men are, I think, although I wouldn't know for certain."

"You don't know about me, for certain."

"I would accept your promises, Rider." She pressed her palms tightly into the small of his back and pushed them slowly upward. She loved the firm feel of his long, lean contours and his firm muscle. "Make me some wonderful promises."

"I promise to make you a happy woman tonight." He stroked her from breast to hip, enjoying the simple freedom to do so. "I promise to make thunder rumble low in your woman's belly and lightning flash in the heaven you carry inside your head."

"Oh, my." She'd once called him a poet. She'd been so right. "Can you promise to love me, Rider? That's what I want most. I want you to love me."

"As long as I draw breath I will love you, *wigopa.*"

And he made slow, nerve-blistering love to her beneath the luminous arc of a white bow moon. He made her reach for him and call for him. He made her weep for him and come for him. He made her a happy woman, and when she told him how very desperately she loved him, she made him a happy man.

"Are you cold?" he asked later as he settled her in his arms. "I can build a fire that will make no smoke, but the light is difficult to hide."

Had they been lying in a snowdrift, she would not have let him move away now. She was pleasantly languid, utterly content. "I'm warm here with you. It feels as though summer lingers just for me tonight."

Night sounds were as soothing as warm flesh. A pack of coyotes sang in the distance. Nearby, the rattle of leaves spoke of their single season's passing.

"Do you hear the voice of the cottonwoods?" Whirlwind Rider asked. She nodded against his shoulder. "Stirred by the slightest breath of wind, they speak softly in the ear of the One Above. It is a prayer. For this reason we use our brother the cottonwood for our Sun Dance pole."

"I would say that's a good reason."

"One of the white commissioners prayed when he started the meeting." Absently he stroked his woman's slight arm as he recalled the curious way this prayer had been made. "He asked his god to open the hearts of the Indians to what his people had to say. He did not pray for wisdom in his own heart. Why is this?"

"He was not sent here by God." Priscilla bit her lip. The truth came as an unexpected revelation to her as she said it aloud. "He was sent here by the government in Washington. He was really asking God to see that the commission gets what it came for. If they do, they will say that it is destiny, that God wants it this way."

And it wasn't so. The truth struck her suddenly and undeniably. The God of her faith had not, nor would He ever ordain the destruction of Whirlwind Rider's people. If her government should seize the land, it would be an act that God played no part in. She knew this as surely as she knew that her union with this man was her destiny, and that it was blessed.

"We do not pray the same," Whirlwind Rider said, mystified. "We pray in search of the wisdom that begins with Tunkaśila, not with the Lakota." He turned to her, possessively clutching her arm. "I also know what I want. I want you for my wife, and I will not hesitate to fight for you. I am not afraid for myself. But I have prayed for wisdom in this."

"Have you found it?"

"I have found that my heart is full of love for you."

"Then that must be the answer to your prayer." She lifted her hand to his hair. "I believe that love comes from God. I find of late that I cannot contend with anything more complicated than that. All I can think of is that I love you."

"Listen!" He laid his thumb against her lips, and they attended to the night's soft whisper. "The tree speaks a prayer for us. Whatever comes tomorrow, we know that the cottonwood has wished us well."

The council reconvened the following day. The commissioners, preoccupied with the words they would say, took their places in the tent on their chairs, the symbolic high ground, and the soldiers lined up behind them. They remarked about the Indians' concern over equal status and chuckled over the "ruffling of the big chiefs' feathers."

They seemed oblivious to the growing commotion outside, but Priscilla noticed it. Even from the back of the tent she could see the cloud of dust rising on the ridge above the river valley.

She made her way toward the open side of the big tent and hurried outside, out of her father's sight, away from the posturing soldiers and the government officials with their mutton-chop whiskers and their black hats. Such men no longer interested her, if they ever had. Her heart yearned in the direction of the ridge, where, bathed in late morning sunlight, a long wall of armed warriors galloped in tightly controlled, close order, followed by a second wave, then a third. The Lakota were coming to the council tent, and they meant to show those inside exactly who they were.

This was not an attack, for the men were not stripped and painted for war. This was a demonstration of strength and self-determination. It was a declaration: We are the Sioux. It was a demand for respect. Black and white honor feathers fluttered along the lengths of the lances, staffs, and trailing headdresses. The horses were painted with the symbols of ancient warrior societies.

It was an impressive collective showing, but like many of the Lakota women whose trilling celebrated pride in their men, Priscilla had eyes for one special man. She recognized him first by his magnificent prancing roan. He wore a kit-fox skin around his neck, and the fur brushed the hard lines of his resolute jaw. She knew better than to hope that he would take notice of her now. Last night he had been her lover. Today he was a leader among his people. It was hard to believe that the hand bearing the lance of the Tokala was the same one that hours ago had gently soothed her trembling body, but the sweet paradox made her thrill all the more to the very sight of him and the secret understanding that he was her man. She loved the proud way he sat his horse. She admired the sentiment of the war song he sang with his Lakota brothers as they approached the tent.

"Paha Sapa is my land. This land I love, I will fight for it, hoka hey, heya hey."

Onlookers jumped aside as the warriors approached. For a moment it seemed as though they would overrun the tent, but they turned aside and circled it once before some of the men dismounted and turned their horses over to the young attendants to lead them away. Spotted Tail and Red Cloud made their appearance, leading the procession of those who would meet with the commissioners. Whirlwind Rider took his place among the representatives of the northern bands. The rest of the horsemen surrounded the tent. The Indians smoked and talked among themselves. No one seemed eager to initiate any serious talking. The white contingent strove to keep up their dignified appearance in the midst of what they clearly considered a crass spectacle.

Whirlwind Rider listened and watched, waiting for the appropriate time to deliver the only true Lakota answer to the demand for the sale of Paha Sapa. Thus far the agency chiefs had shown some solidarity with the northern bands, even though many of the loafers had been saying that the land was already lost and they ought to take whatever they could get for it. But such cowardly talk was only muttered in hushed tones.

Suddenly there was a break in the circle of mounted warriors, and one man came charging through. It was Little Big Man, stripped to his breechclout, armed with a Winchester, and painted for battle. The white commissioners blanched at the fierce sight, and the Lakota talk-makers heard his warning: "I will kill those who would steal the land! I will kill the first man who speaks for selling Paha Sapa!"

This was not what Crazy Horse and the others had intended. There were too many innocents close by. Little Big Man was known to be hotheaded, to take matters into his own hands, to spoil the hunt by rushing the signal.

Like a man venturing into a bear's cave without so much as a blade for a weapon, Whirlwind Rider rose to his feet and stared Little Big Man down. "This is not the time, cousin. This is not the place."

But for the restless horses outside, all was silent. The air was thick with tension. From his place among the counseling chiefs, Young Man Afraid rose, holding his blanket around him. "This is foolishness. Go to your lodges, my young friends, and let your heads cool."

Those outside heeded the advice of their leaders. One after another, individually and in small groups, they wheeled their horses and rode across the valley and up the ridge. Finally, with a collective sigh of relief as Little Big Man retreated, the white commissioners gathered their papers and their black hats and hurried away, calling the soldiers after them.

The big council was over. The commissioners demanded that the Indians meet with them behind stockade walls, but only the agency chiefs complied. The northern bands refused, saying the snows of winter were drawing close. They headed for the creeks and valleys in the north while there was still time to do a little hunting, believing that the council had broken down without reaching a consensus.

Before he left, Whirlwind Rider met Priscilla at his sister's cabin. "You must choose now, *wiǧopa*. Soon it will not be safe to travel the in-between road, and I cannot go your way." He touched her cheek, almost in apology. "If you want me, you must go mine."

He was all she wanted. "I choose you."

"Then come with me now."

"The army would use me as an excuse to mount a campaign against you." She wanted him desperately, but she wanted him alive, and she wanted his people to live. "Give me time to find a better way."

"If anything happens to you, *I* will mount a campaign. A one-man war against anyone who tries to keep you from me."

"The way you stood up to Little Big Man, I don't doubt it." She took his strong hands in her small ones. "Your people will be my people, Rider. I don't want my presence among them to be the instrument of their destruction. Priscilla Twiss must cease to exist."

"You will help us, LaPointe?"

Whirlwind Rider's brother-friend nodded in assent.

* * *

Journal Entry, September 29, 1875

The talks proceeded for a time without full representation from the northern bands. Red Cloud said that the loss of the land, especially the Black Hills, would make his people poor. His price, he said, was enough to feed the next seven generations of Lakota. Senator Allison submitted a written offer of six million dollars, which the agency chiefs rejected, ending the talks. Clearly, however, the issue is not settled.

Journal Entry, November 15, 1875

In his cups this evening, Father confided to me that the news from Washington is not good. Interior Secretary Chandler has proposed to Congress that Sioux rations be cut off entirely until they agree to relinquish the Black Hills. General Sherman has stated that Congress has the right to abrogate the treaty since the Sioux "have not lived at peace." Father predicts that the army will make no more attempt to restrict miners and settlers from invading the Hills.

For my own part, I am hoping for enough snow to keep the miners and whiskey drummers in their dens all winter. An early blizzard would suit me fine.

Journal Entry, December 10, 1875

We have just received word that Interior Secretary Chandler has issued an ultimatum to the northern bands. They must abandon their hunting grounds in the Powder River country and return to the agencies on the Missouri River by January 31 or they will officially be declared hostile to the United States, and troops will be sent out against them.

It is an unconscionable demand. The snow threatens to be deep this winter. Travel on the plains would be hazardous now.

Priscilla closed her journal, but rather than stow it in its customary place in her steamer trunk, she tucked it into her saddlebag with her reading primers. She would be ready whenever the time came. The gathering of wintry clouds in the high plains sky was no threat to her. It was a promise.

Chapter 14

Dakota Territory, Winter 1876

Charles Twiss sat staring into the fire, rocking his squat, heavy body in his favorite chair and sipping a glass of the whiskey he had recently procured from a drummer who was trespassing in Indian territory. The whiskey traders were becoming bolder all the time, but occasionally their desire to do business could be useful. A gift for the agent in return for a blind eye. Twiss insisted upon "the good stuff," which he knew most of them carried for their more discerning clientele. He would have preferred port, but he couldn't be too choosy when his sources were limited. No more sweet wine until spring, when he would tuck his tail between his thick thighs and go home to Minnesota.

He permitted Priscilla to serve him his supper on the small side table. It was the third time she had offered. She had already eaten her own meal, long before he was hungry. It was hard to be hungry for bean soup with salt pork night after night, and it was hard to sit across the table from a once-adoring daughter who now offered little conversation. Owing to the influence of her Indian friends, she seldom even managed to look him in the eye these days. But then *they* wouldn't look him in the eye, either.

Priscilla insisted that avoiding direct eye contact was a matter of respect. It was another of the "cultural vari-

ances" she found so interesting. The truth of the matter
was that the government had failed to deliver rations even
remotely adequate for their needs, and they all blamed him
for it.

Priscilla, on the other hand, seemed to be enjoying some
measure of success as a teacher, although he suspected that
she had learned far more of their language than they had
mastered of hers. They had given her gifts, among them a
pair of moccasins and a set of leggings, which she had actually taken to wearing because, she said, they were practical. At times it almost seemed as though she were
gradually becoming one of them.

"Utterly ridiculous," he muttered aloud as he stirred his
soup to cool it.

"What is?"

"Did I say . . . ?" He looked up at the golden-haired
woman sitting across from him. She allowed him her company but paid him less than half a mind. Leaning close to
the lamplight, she pretended to be quite busy writing in the
journal. He'd once thought she favored her mother, but
somehow the likeness seemed to be vanishing. She was serenely beautiful in her own right, but it was a curiously
distant beauty, at once familiar and alien.

"Indeed yes, ridiculous," he muttered.

But she glanced up from her writing. He'd gotten her attention, and he almost felt favored.

And compelled to lie.

"I was thinking of Red Cloud's demand for a new agent.
Whom does he expect? Saint Paul himself to come and civ-
ilize him? If he's not careful, he's liable to be dealing with
Sherman or Custer."

"Eat your supper, Father." Her nose was back in the
book again.

"I won't be treated like a child who must be fed, Priscilla. I draw the line there." His spoon clattered against the
rim of the bowl. "If I were to resign, you would have to
give up your teaching mission."

"I have my own work here," she said calmly.

"Only by my leave. Your efforts are simply an extension of my efforts."

She spared him a harsh glance.

He felt bereft when she took even *that* away. "If we do go back, I believe we might start a school. The Twiss Academy for Indian Children. What do you think, dear girl? How would that suit you?"

"What I think is that you ought to set the whiskey aside and eat your supper."

"Bean soup and hardtack." He eyed the stuff in the bowl disdainfully. "I long for a nice fresh leg of spring lamb with mint jelly."

"Don't even mention fresh meat, Father. It's too depressing. There have been no supplies since the council meeting." Priscilla closed the journal and pushed it to the edge of the lamp table. "How are these people supposed to survive? The government tells them to come to the agency in the dead of winter, but for what? They have not sent any food in months."

"The freight wagons can't get through in the winter."

"The *miners* get through."

The miners were of no concern to him. Let them have the damn Black Hills; there was no farmland there. He had promised to turn the Sioux into farmers.

"If they had only tried a little harder, we could have grown a crop, I'm sure of it. But they wouldn't work at it, damn their lazy hides." A wild notion struck him as he sipped at his whiskey. He chuckled giddily. "Maybe the Sioux should take up prospecting. Wouldn't that be a sight? The commission told them that gold was of no use to them; yet they offered them money for it. Wouldn't it be something if the Sioux decided to dig up their own money?"

"They love the land," Priscilla said, her voice sounding strangely tinny and hollow in Twiss's ears. "Red Cloud told the commissioners that the land was worth more to him than anything we have to give him for it. It's unthinkable for them to dig it up."

"Except to pull up their wild turnips and whatnot." He took up his spoon and sullenly stirred the thick contents of the bowl. "Well, I suspect they'll go hungry this winter.

The army will undoubtedly be rounding up the hostiles before spring thaw."

"The northern bands have taken it upon themselves to procure their own food, and for that they will be hunted down," Priscilla said disgustedly. There being no response, they lapsed into a cool silence. Cooler still was Twiss's soup, but he ate it because it was all there was.

Priscilla was almost ready to follow her new custom of taking to her room as soon as she had seen to it that her father had eaten something when Henry LaPointe came to the door. Twiss's brain buzzed as he listened in on the polite greetings. He found the friendly tone in his daughter's voice more than a little irksome, so he took his time about finishing his whiskey and heaving himself out of his chair. Priscilla's latest braided rug tripped him on his way to the door, but he caught his balance and kicked the menacing thing out of his way. He straightened his vest and met LaPointe at the door with a curt nod.

LaPointe's report was equally curt. "A distribution of food will be required at once, Red Cloud says."

"What game is he playing with me now? The old man knows the wagons haven't come yet."

"There is no *game* in this country anymore. The people are hungry. The agent must open the storehouse doors now, he says. Unless this is done, he cannot prevent more of his people from joining their cousins in the Powder River country, Red Cloud says."

"The unceded territory is no longer available to the Lakota for hunting." Twiss made the cut-off sign with a fluttering hand. "Off-limits now, by order of, uh . . ." He couldn't remember whose signature had appeared on the directive. "Surely Red Cloud must realize that the hostiles have brought this down on all our heads. It appears that those renegades will not give up until every Lakota man, woman, and child lies bleeding in the snow."

LaPointe stared at the floor impassively. "Better than to lie starving in the snow."

"All right." Charles tucked his thumbs in the armholes of his vest and assumed an imperious, if slightly teetering posture. "Tell them I will distribute one pound of flour per family member tomorrow."

"The people also need blankets," LaPointe informed him.

"There are no more blankets. What are they doing with their blankets? Trading them off for whiskey?" With an impatient gesture he waved the whole matter away. "Flour and perhaps a little hardtack. That's all there is." He swayed slightly as he turned to toddle back to his chair. "That's all we have. That's all."

"Tomorrow, then," LaPointe clipped, his eyes ablaze. But he calmed himself quickly in deference to the shame he saw in Priscilla's eyes. "My wife says that the children are well enough to have school again."

"That's good news. We shall have class tomorrow."

Along with the look in his eyes, his subtle nod toward the door indicated that there was more.

"Oh, and I want you to take something to Sarah for me, if you wouldn't mind," she said brightly. "I'll have a few other things to load up in my saddlebags tomorrow, and . . . well, it's just a bit of yard goods. I'll fetch it."

"I'll wait outside."

"The weather is quite unpredictable lately," Twiss called out to her from his seat by the fire when he heard the door close. "You cannot be riding around from pillar to post with your portable classroom. Not until it warms up a bit."

Priscilla emerged from her room, donning her cloak as she tucked a package under her arm. "I refuse to sit here and do nothing, Father."

"You think I could be doing something more, don't you? My efforts have been thwarted, but my ideas are sound. I can save these people from ruin if they will only cooperate," Twiss ranted as he struggled to focus his own uncooperative eyes. "Once the army brings the hostiles to heel, Red Cloud will turn to me again. I will send the children away to school. Their minds will be purged of the ways of the past. Here at home we shall give each man a plot of land, and he will learn to get his living from it." He lifted his glass in one hand and stabbed a point-making finger toward the floor with the other. "They will become decent Christian citizens by the grace of God and Father Agent, who is and shall ever be foremost among the friends of the Indian. If I leave them to their own devices, they will be sorry. Very sorry indeed."

"Yes, Father." Priscilla clenched her teeth as she drew a pair of mitts over her fingerless gloves. "Excuse me. I want to catch up with Henry. I have these sewing materials for Sarah."

"Good." He thumped his glass on the side table and poured himself another whiskey. "Sewing materials. Teach her to make shirts and pants. Decent clothing for decent citizens. The women are our best hope for . . ."

As if she could teach Sarah LaPointe anything about sewing, Priscilla thought. Sarah, who had shown her how to cut two shirts from a piece of calico that should have yielded only one. She stepped off the porch and skittered across the icy yard to the little picket fence, where LaPointe stood with his horse.

"He has come for you," LaPointe said simply.

A quick, deep breath of cold air shocked her lungs. "Where is he?"

"He waits for you at my lodge. He brought meat, thank God." He lowered his voice. "You are ready to do this thing?"

"Yes." She did not hesitate, but he did, and the winter silence seemed ominous. "You don't think it'll work?"

"I think you are both foolish." The stocky mixed-blood shook his head and glanced at the dreary evening sky. "But it is useless to try to interfere with the foolishness born of love. I'll wait for you behind the barn."

"I shouldn't be too long. Father retires early and sleeps late these days. When he wakes up, he'll assume that I left for your house at first light." She tipped her head back to survey the nondescript sky and measure the gathering darkness. It seemed to crowd in close and whisper some nebulous prophecy. "Will the skies give us what we need tomorrow? It's not terribly cloudy. It's not even terribly cold."

"It will be. It's in the air now. Do you feel it?" In the still of the winter dusk he whispered softly, taking care not to disturb the thing in the air prematurely. " 'Priscilla Twiss should have known better,' they will say. 'The signs were clear.' "

"It's my first winter here, and there are those who think I'm quite headstrong. Others think I'm foolish." Despite the lip-stiffening chill, she offered a smile. "But I believe God has a special place in his heart for those who are fools for love."

"For all our sakes, I hope so."

The west wind pushed clouds across the inky sky as Priscilla followed LaPointe over the trail he was supposed to have taken home hours earlier. It was the same trail she would be presumed to have taken much later, *if* all went according to plan.

She knew the way to his cabin as well as he did, but for safety's sake he had waited for her, as his brother-in-law had asked him to. She had given up her sidesaddle in favor of a regulation army campaign saddle, which Tim Harmon had given her father as a parting gift when he was transferred. She would give this up, too, along with her mare, all according to plan. She was taking precious little of her old life with her, perhaps because so little of it was actually precious to her anymore. She would miss her father. She would pray for his health. But it was long past time she left her father's house and made her home with the man she loved.

Whirlwind Rider was waiting for her. There wasn't much time for emotional reunion or farewell scenes. They were racing to beat the storm that would cover their trail. He'd brought a fine spotted mare for Priscilla to ride, and a packhorse, which he loaded with provisions while she stood close by under the roof of the lean-to that served as LaPointe's barn. They exchanged glances as he secured a rawhide bundle with a deftly tied half-hitch.

"You're looking at me as though you're not sure," she said warily.

He nearly smiled. "I was thinking the same."

"I'm quite sure," she told him. "I've never been more sure of anything in my life than I am of you. And, as you know, I've always been a woman who knows her own mind."

"A woman who thinks she knows just where she's going." He peeked over the saddle, the promise of a smile dancing in his eyes. "But always she comes back to me."

"Well," she said lightly, "the mind and the heart must reach an accord sooner or later."

"This is a woman's job," he muttered as he ducked down again. "This packing."

"It doesn't look hard." She'd been watching him. LaPointe had been right about the way her eyes followed him, especially his hands. Nothing delighted her more than Whirlwind Rider's marvelously masculine hands. "I'm sure I can handle the packing next time."

He circled the packhorse once more, checking the fastenings and weighing the balance of the load. Then he came up behind Priscilla, laid his hands on her shoulders, and drew her back against him. "I cannot tell what may happen to us, *wigopa*. When they come against us, I will fight. I will be fighting your people to protect mine. How will you stand?"

"With my husband." She closed her eyes and dropped her head back to his shoulder. "Always."

"Against your father?"

"My father is not a soldier."

"He may send them after you."

"No, he won't. He won't know. He'll never know."

"He will mourn you, then."

"He would anyway." She turned to him, taking him in her arms. "I would follow you, Rider. I would search for you until I found you. If you hadn't come for me, I would have . . ." She looked up, trapping his gaze with the fervor of her own. "I love you so fiercely."

"Ah, my woman is a she-fox." He smiled and touched her cheek with a warm, horse-and-leather scented hand. "I will fight them if they come for you. You are like the contrary, the one in every camp who does the opposite of what is expected and thereby completes the circle."

"My people have no place for the contrary. They would

either shun me or lock me away. Either way, I would be a lonely woman."

"And so you choose a dangerous path," he said as he undid the buttons beneath her chin.

They barely noticed Sarah and Henry LaPointe, who had come bearing a few more items to add to the provisions. They waited quietly for their chance to say goodbye.

"Yes, I choose." Priscilla turned to their friends. "I should be able simply to tell my people that, shouldn't I? This is the man I choose."

"They would call you a captive, and they would try to take you from me. My uncles tell me that the soldiers have done this before." He slipped the heavy black cloak from her shoulders and handed it to LaPointe. "Is this not so?"

"It has happened." LaPointe traded a buffalo robe for Priscilla's cloak.

"Priscilla Twiss must die today so that Whirlwind Rider's woman may be born." He wrapped the robe around her slight shoulders, smiling when she made a face to show how heavy the hide was. "She will be born with a strong back."

"Be forewarned," Priscilla began, returning his smile, "that she has a strong will, no matter what name she goes by."

She turned to Sarah, hugging her with one arm and clutching the robe about her shoulders with the other. "You'll mourn for me, my friend?"

"I will mourn the passing of a friend and rejoice in a new sister."

LaPointe's task was to stage Priscilla's demise. He performed as admirably as any stage player. He had found Priscilla's mare after the blizzard, he said. He'd searched to no avail. There was no telling how far the horse had wandered. He wondered aloud why Agent Twiss had permitted his daughter to leave the agency that morning. Poor Twiss, who had slept most of the morning away, insisted that he had *permitted* nothing. He'd heard nothing, seen nothing, suspected . . . nothing.

But he had lost everything.

The search was hampered by the weather. One of the soldiers found Priscilla's black cloak. LaPointe lamented that the snowdrifts were so deep that they would probably find no trace of her body until spring, if the wolves left anything at all to be found. Twiss was heartsick. His daughter was a martyr, he said. She had given her young life to the cause of civilizing the Indian. He would write about her, immortalize her on the dedication page of a new tract. In the name of Priscilla Twiss he would plead for the cause of saving the poor little Indian child from the uncivilized ways of his parents and grandparents.

But deep in the Dakota Badlands there was a small winter camp, tucked safely away from wolves and search parties and prying eyes of any description. There, in a snow-bound tipi the color of parchment, Whirlwind Rider made slow, methodical, careful love to his wife. And afterward, as they drifted intimately in mutual satisfaction and campfire dreams, she kissed his hand and held it tight to her belly. There was a husband's question in his eyes, a wife's answer in hers. And she whispered to him of the child she carried.

Chapter 15

❧✿❧ ✿❧✿

A brown snake slithered past Cecily's foot just as she shoved a box labeled "Kitchen" onto the wrought-iron landing at the door of the trailer house. A belated hop put her on the second step, a safe place from which to watch the creature thread its way through a curling gap in the corrugated metal skirting and disappear underneath her weather-beaten new home. At least the thing wasn't rattling its tail at her. If she had any luck, it was a bull snake looking for mice. It had come to the right place.

Cecily had been warned that housing in Fort Yates was in short supply and that VISTA workers were at the bottom of the priority list. She had never lived in a trailer house before, but then she'd never had a place of her own before, either, so the little trailer represented a double milestone. It even had a spare bedroom, which was fortunate since there wasn't much storage space, and she had a U-Haul full of indispensable treasures.

The place had been a shambles when she'd first walked in. In the process of scraping up everything from cake frosting to used condoms, she had concluded that somebody had had quite a going-away party. She had scrubbed

212

walls, floors, cupboards, and commode until the creases in her knuckles burned from the disinfectant. Then she'd thought of rubber gloves.

It felt good to be back in the Dakotas. She noted the feeling with a sense of relief, because she'd surely had her share of last-minute doubts. The thought of returning had always seemed to linger in the back of her brain, even when she was busy making other plans, sending out applications, looking for that golden opportunity to further her education. But a longing for the Dakotas harried her like an itch that wouldn't go away. The day she'd gotten the news that she was only an alternate for the graduate school program she'd set her sights on, she had signed up for VISTA, stipulating that she would serve on any reservation in the Dakotas. In the back of her mind she had given fate a little test, and her assignment did not surprise her. She had drawn Standing Rock again.

And the first familiar face to appear on her doorstep was that of Ellen Red Thunder. Cecily actually saw her shadow first when she looked out the window, but she knew who it was. Beautiful and bold as ever, Ellen's statuesque body unconsciously assumed an assertive posture, and Cecily could feel her dominating presence even before she reached the door.

"Heard you were back," Ellen said with a grin. She shaded her eyes and peered up at Cecily. "Thought you might remember me."

"Ellen! Of course I remember you." Cecily stepped back and made a sweeping come-on-in gesture. "I wrote to you, but . . ." She shrugged, unwilling to accuse Ellen of shirking any duty at all. "I thought maybe you'd left."

"Left the rez? Imagine." Ellen laughed as she took a seat at the little table that, together with a TV stand and a built-in sofa spanning the end of the trailer, was the extent of the kitchen-dining-living room furniture. "No, I got your letter. Answered it, too. Just never got around to mailing it."

She changed the subject with a nod in a down-the-road direction. "I was just over to the Housing Authority. They said you might want someone to share the rent on this place."

"You?"

"I told them I knew you. I've got a new job, too. Aide, over to the hospital. I hate to have to drive back and forth from Little Eagle."

"That's too far," Cecily affirmed, recalling the vast distances from pillar to post in this part of the world.

"Yeah, well, housing is real hard to come by in this town. They try to get singles to room together."

"But this is"—Cecily waved one hand, since there wasn't room to wave two—"so *small.*"

"Far as they're concerned, there's an unmarried woman taking up a two-bedroom unit. That's like a vacancy." Ellen flipped her single long braid back behind her stout shoulder. "Besides, when you college girls join up with VISTA, you're expecting to rough it a little, aren't you?"

Cecily glanced toward the bedrooms. "Yes, well, this is really—"

"So you graduated and everything, huh?"

"Yes. Three weeks ago."

"Hear you're taking over the rez rag."

"The *Standing Rock News.* My title is editorial adviser."

"Be careful. They ran the last guy off when he published an account of the Tribal Council's travel expenses. Seems the councilmen like to go to a lot of out-of-state conferences, but they don't always like to attend the meetings or whatever. The guy they kicked out was a graduate student. Real gung-ho." She crossed her ankle over her knee and tugged on the flared leg of her bell-bottom jeans. She wore low-top moccasins. Cecily noticed a ring of dirt around her ankle. Ellen rubbed at it, absently peeling it off like dead skin as she spoke. "Thought you were going to be in college for six years straight through. That's what you always said. Did you miss us?"

"I *did* miss you. I especially missed getting teased unmercifully." She opened the dwarf-sized refrigerator door and quirked an eyebrow Ellen's way as she pointed to the shelf full of canned pop.

Ellen held out her hand, and Cecily filled it with a can of cola, then grabbed a can of diet for herself.

"I applied for a graduate program in journalism and made alternate," she explained. "I decided to get some practical experience, and this way I had a chance to come back to the Dakotas."

"So who did you miss most? As if I couldn't guess."

"I missed everybody."

Ellen's guffaw was punctuated by the burping of pop-tops.

"I really missed the wide-open spaces," Cecily insisted. Ellen's eyes glittered above the rim of the can as she slurped noisily. Cecily laughed. "Okay, I'll ask. Is your brother still in the army?"

"Nope. He just got out. You mean you've been in town more than ten minutes, and you didn't know he was back? Funny you two should both happen to wander back to the rez almost at the same time."

"Purely coincidental, you can be sure." Cecily bumped the refrigerator door shut with her hip. "He didn't answer my letters, either. I finally gave up on him."

"Yeah, well, so did I. Men are just little boys with big"—the teasing lights danced in the eyes that said, *Dare me*—"socks. *Big* socks to cover up their biiig, loooong, get-cold-at-the-last-minute feet." She laughed, throwing up the hands she'd used to delineate. "Wonder if my brother with big cold feet knows you're here."

"I wonder if he even remembers my name." Just wondering didn't mean she actually cared. "I'm not really eager to run into him. It might be a little awkward. What's so funny?"

"You're funny, Cecily Metcalf. You don't mean to be, but you are. That's why I like you." Ellen nodded for emphasis, rapping the bottom of her pop can on the table as she surveyed the close quarters, ceiling to floor. "So do I get to stay, or not?"

"If you think there's room."

Ellen hopped up from the chair and peeked into the bedroom off the kitchen and beyond that to the room at the far end, where the built-in bed was already made up. "Plenty of room. I don't have much stuff. God, have *you* got stuff."

She moved through the doorway, noting the stacks of boxes. The old steamer trunk caught her eye. "What're you dragging this around for? It looks like an old grandma's trunk. My grandma had one just like it, full of old junk."

Cecily followed Ellen into what was no longer the "spare" room. They stood side by side, looking down at the trunk as though they were trying to figure out whether it would fly.

"I got this one at an auction. It was like buying a grab bag. The auctioneer said it had been locked for a hundred years. The story was that the family was afraid to open it after they'd had its owner declared dead, so they stuck it away in the attic." Cecily folded her arms across her chest as she looked up at Ellen. "I don't believe that, do you? I'm sure they would have opened it. There might have been something really valuable in it."

"Was there?"

"Just some clothes and a few books and pamphlets, but they were *old*. There were some interesting things. A woman's things. There was only one piece of jewelry." The locket. She wondered whether he still had it. "I gave that away."

"That's good. When a person dies, you give the stuff away or burn it to keep the *wanaği* away," Ellen said, and Cecily flashed her a puzzled look. "Ghosts. That's the traditional way."

"I think someone *did* mention that practice to me once." Someone named Kiah Red Thunder, whose every word uttered to her was probably, for better or for worse, etched in her memory.

"That's what we did with most of my mother's stuff."

"I didn't know your mother had died." Cecily touched Ellen's arm. With a brief nod Ellen shrugged away, leaving Cecily feeling awkwardly exposed. "I'm really sorry to hear that," she offered quietly.

"She'd been sick for a while." Ellen sighed and shook off the loss as she nudged the trunk with the toe of her moccasin. "There might be ghosts in this thing. You ever feel kinda spooky about it?"

"Not spooky, really, but there's always been something about it, some kind of"—she cast about for a word that didn't sound too silly—"magnetism or something. It's been like a friend to me. My mother deals in antiques, but I just like old things. It's like they have a story to tell, you know? About the past. About how we got to be who we are."

"You're a romantic." Ellen grinned broadly. "Wait'll you meet my boyfriend, Bobby. He's a romantic, too. Guess I've got a real soft spot in my otherwise unsentimental heart for guys like you."

A week later Cecily heard something going bump in the night. Initially it scared her. She was neither awake nor asleep. At first she took the squeaking for an animal noise, and the brown snake slithered into her hazy consciousness. She sat up. After a few quiet seconds, the squeaking started again.

"Ellen?" Silence. "Ellen, are you okay?"

There was a low male chuckle; then, "Shhh."

"Whoever you are, I've . . . got a gun."

"I've got one, too-oo."

The man's sing-songy tone was no comfort.

"Well, why don't you just . . . put yours away and leave quietly. My gun is pointed at the door, and I have a phone right beside my bed." Her whole body was suddenly sweatier than a long-distance runner's. She would have felt much better if any part of her claim had been true. "I'm calling the police."

Now there were two voices laughing, and Cecily recognized the one that said, "See, I told you she was a laugh a minute. There's no phone in there."

"Ellen? I thought you were gone for the weekend."

"I'd invite you to come in and say hello to Bobby, but I don't think you want your innocent baby blues to see where *his* gun is pointed."

"Oh." It was only when she slid back down between the sheets that she realized how hard she was trembling, inside and out. "It sounded like we had mice or something." She permitted herself one long, deep sigh. "Pleased to meet you, Bobby."

The man chuckled. "Pleasure's all mine."

"Go back to sleep, and we'll be as quiet as mice," Ellen promised.

But they weren't. Cecily lay awake half the night listening to squeaky springs and gratified groans. The trailer was too small for two people. The walls were too thin to provide any privacy. Not that she was any prude. Not that she didn't understand lovers willing to do whatever they had to do to be together. She just didn't want to have to listen to it. She didn't want to remember what it was like, and she especially didn't want to imagine what it might be like again. The fact that Kiah wasn't far away was a constant irritant, an itch she hadn't found a way to ignore. She'd been telling herself that scratching it would only make it worse, but she figured it was only a matter of time before she ran into him.

The sooner, the better.

Utterly exhausted, she emerged from her bedroom the next morning determined to let the two lovers know that she was just a bit put out. Ellen's radiant grin was no consolation, but the coffee she set on the table in front of Cecily did help.

"Bobby's gone," Ellen said.

"Oh. Sorry I missed him."

"No, you're not. You would've been red-faced as hell." Ellen chuckled as she cracked an egg on the rim of the skillet she'd prepared for cooking. The egg hit the hot grease with a tantalizing sizzle. "But you *are* going to meet him. He's got a job for us this weekend."

Cecily groaned. "I don't need a job this weekend. It was like pulling teeth to get that paper out, and I need a weekend off."

"How about an adventure? Isn't that what you came to the rez for? Exotic adventure among the natives?"

"I came for the experience." She sipped her coffee, then reconsidered. "All right, what kind of an adventure?"

"You've heard about the Broken Trust protest movement?"

"They've taken over a town, haven't they?"

"Where've you been lately? Sitting in council meetings listening to those guys drone on about whose brother-in-law gets the next do-nothing job?" Ellen spared her roommate a knowing smile. "They've taken over the community of Red Creek. They're using that little church we worked on that summer as their headquarters."

"Oh, no," Cecily moaned. "All our hard work."

"Yeah, right." Ellen sipped her coffee as she flipped the eggs. "They're finally putting the place to good use. We're taking a stand, Cecily. Making the kind of statement the Tribal Council doesn't even want to hear, never mind the state or the federal government. If we want to put an end to this game of Screw the Sioux, it's time to start kickin' ass and takin' names." She waved her spatula for emphasis. "Bobby's one of the leaders. Surprised the hell out of me to see him last night. The FBI would love to get their hands on him right about now."

"You mean he sneaked out under cover of darkness just to see you? That *is* romantic."

"It was stupid." Ellen chuckled mischievously. "And I told him so right before I unzipped his jeans. Damn, that man's *really* hot when he's hot." She sucked a breath between her teeth, then gave a saucy grin. "When he's on the run like that, it's like he thinks it might be the last time he'll see me, so he's gonna make the most of it."

"I don't think I need to know all this."

"What you need to know is that the people behind the barricades are running low on food, and the federal marshals have agreed to let the churches bring in food and medical supplies once in a while. That's where we come in." She set two plates of fried eggs and toast on the table, then took the chair across from Cecily. "I work for the hospital now, see? And you're white, so they'll trust you. You'll be driving."

"*Just* food and medical supplies?"

"We'll be picking the stuff up from a *church*, Cecily. What else are they gonna send in there?"

"Do you think I can get a story? Some interviews, maybe?"

"Media attention is what this whole thing is all about," Ellen said eagerly. "That's why they had to take over a town, take a couple of hostages, and claim some white-owned business property on the rez. It's the only way we can get anybody to listen. You can get a terrific story, but I wouldn't try to publish it in the rez rag if I were you. You'll probably be out of a job if you do."

"Why?"

"Because the protest is about Indian rights, and *this* particular Tribal Council is about playing politics with those rights."

"Hostages," Cecily said, awed by the word and hard-pressed to imagine the reality of her friend's boyfriend being involved in such a thing. "They haven't hurt anyone, have they?"

"Not so far. The people they're holding are all locals down there, and they're using them mostly to keep the cops and the feds from rushing the place. It's not so different from the takeover of the student union at that college back East that time, remember? It's power to the people. We have to take a stand somehow."

"I'm surprised you're not in there with them."

"I want to be." Ellen sipped her coffee, then added, "But then I'd probably lose my job, and I've been trying to get on at the hospital for a long time. I want to make my life count for something. I want to do something useful."

Cecily broke her toast in half. "It's about the Black Hills, isn't it?"

"It's been about the Black Hills since the Laramie Treaty of 1868 acknowledged that they were ours." Between bits of egg shoveled onto her toast, Ellen expounded. "The Black Hills are Lakota land. They always have been, and they always will be. Back a hundred years ago, the U.S. government wanted the people to sell them, and everybody refused, except for a few old guys who were tricked into signing a paper. That was back in 1877, after they'd haggled over it for years, tried to starve everybody out, and . . . well, you know about Custer."

"I guess everybody knows something about Custer. Whether anyone knows the truth—"

"The truth is, he was a butcher, and he got his. But then we lost the Black Hills. Red Cloud had said the loss of the Hills would make his people poor, and sure enough, we've been poor.

"But back in the 1920s some slick white lawyer decided to talk the tribal governments into letting him take their case to court and get them a bunch of money for the Hills. Get *himself* a bunch of money for the Hills—that's what he really meant to do. So this whole legal crap has been going on ever since, with different white lawyers and judges arguing it out."

She dropped her fork on her plate and leaned closer. "But, see, Paha Sapa is Lakota land. We can't take money for it. These lawyers are asking the Indian Claims Commission to compensate us because the land was taken illegally." She paused, assessing Cecily's attention, which was undivided. "How much do you think the Black Hills are worth?"

"They're priceless." Cecily felt vaguely embarrassed by the admission. She looked down at her plate and poked at her egg yolk with the corner of her toast. "I mean, really, there isn't enough money—"

"At last! A white person who thinks like an Indian."

"Well, I mean, they *are* a national treasure."

"Belonging to the Lakota Nation." Ellen leaned back in her chair. "But these lawyers work for the Tribal Council, and so do you because the council controls the newspaper. Around here, anything that isn't wrapped up in Bureau of Indian Affairs red tape is probably being screwed up by the damn Tribal Council."

"The councilmen are elected by the people, aren't they?"

"These days most people vote for their cousins or their in-laws, thinking that'll get 'em a bigger piece of some tribal program. The people on the council, they've got *iona* cousins. Many, many. And they'd sure like to get their hands on a nice fat Black Hills settlement. The Broken Trust movement is about showing the world that our claim to the Black Hills is legitimate, and we're not selling out. We want to force a recall of the whole Tribal Council. We want the BIA to listen to the people. Those lawyers don't represent the Lakota people. We won't settle for anything less than the land that rightfully belongs to us." Ellen gave her friend a hard look. "So, are you in?"

Cecily swallowed equally hard. "Why me?"

"I don't know. Being Indian is in these days, but I don't think you're here to play Indian. I think you're an honest friend." Ellen tipped her head to one side, considering. "And you're a journalist, right? I think someday somebody out there might listen to you, so I wanna make sure you've got something to say that's worth saying."

"You'll probably want to make sure I stay alive, then, huh?"

"I'll keep your skinny little ass covered," Ellen promised with an indulgent smile.

The church donating the supplies loaned them a Volkswagen bus with its name emblazoned on the side. Cecily assumed that it was the stylized winged dove that got them through the roadblock with only a cursory search. Beyond the right-of-way fence, derelict cars formed a barricade in the lush, early summer prairie grass. Across the flat, less than a mile beyond the barricade, stood the little white church.

Young Indian sentries wearing bandanna headbands and boot-cut blue jeans waved their rifles, signaling down the line that the van would be allowed to enter what looked like a war zone. The blacktop became gravel road, and the van's tires skittered over the washboards. A tall, lanky man ambled over to meet them as Cecily pulled up close to the church's front doors.

"This is Bobby Blue Bow," Ellen announced with a flourish.

"Hey." Bobby cocked two fingers in a diffident greeting. "Sorry about last night. Thanks for helping out here."

"I don't suppose you'd let me take a few pictures?"

"You kidding?" Ellen jerked the van's side door open. You might as well take a few fingerprints while you're at ."

Bobby laughed. "The feds have all our fingerprints. If we let 'em catch us, we'll disappear into the jaws of the ustice system. Might be a good idea to let her take some pictures, just so's down the road somebody can prove we xisted." He braced one arm on the roof of the van, gave he contents a half-interested glance, then turned to Ellen. 'Did you ask Kiah about joining up with us?"

She snorted in disgust. "He's hopeless, that one. He ays he's had enough fighting. I told him he'd been fight-ng the wrong damn war, but he says one losing battle is ust like any other."

"So what's he doing?"

"Kickin' back, he says." She slid Cecily a quick glance and couldn't help but notice that she was all ears. "He's noled up out in the country. Hidin' out, I say."

"Out to your mother's place?" Ellen nodded. "We sure could use him. He used to be hell-on-wheels in a fight, and that was before he went to 'Nam. Bet he *really* kicks ass now."

"I can kick ass just as good as he can," Ellen insisted. "Let me stay."

"You're more useful to us on the outside." Squinting against the sun, he turned to Cecily. "You, too, girl re-porter. Somebody has to tell the world what's goin' on."

"Yeah, but the world doesn't read the rez rag." Ellen sounded indignant, as though she didn't like the idea that Bobby had favored Cecily with a special assignment.

"I'm thinking of doing some free-lancing," Cecily said.

"Good," Bobby replied. "We'll let you take your pic-tures, but when you leave here, you stash that film where the sun don't shine, or you won't get it past their little Checkpoint Charlie out there."

Cecily noticed the variety of weapons the protestors carried—mostly hunting rifles, but a few assault weapons. She appreciated their jovial attitude toward posing for pic-tures. Most of them were young men with long hair and easy smiles, and the uniform of the day seemed to be red bandannas, tie-dyed T-shirts, and well-worn blue jeans. There were also a few women on hand, along with some old men who looked the part of the traditional Indian.

The group had taken a few white hostages, including a storekeeper, a mail carrier, and a priest who insisted that he was there by choice. Bobby pointed out that they had let the storekeeper's wife go and that no one was tied, bound, gagged, or bruised in any way. Without the hostages, no one on the outside would care about the fact that they had taken up a post on the reservation to make their statement.

Now they were carrying out the business of living day-to-day under siege. It wasn't the first such incident the group had staged. They didn't know whether it would be the last.

After a leisurely unloading of the van and a lingering farewell, Cecily and Ellen presented themselves at the roadblock again. In her rearview mirror Cecily noticed that Bobby had followed them on foot at a safe distance. Just as they had been earlier, both women were asked to step out of the van while a sheriff's deputy searched the interior.

He opened the side door and flashed a light under the front seats while Cecily and Ellen looked on. Cecily's denim tote bag was one of the few things left in the van to search. He opened it up and peered inside. "What's this?"

"It's my camera." *Obviously.* Cecily resented the intrusion into her personal effects. She squeezed her hands into fists until the ignition keys cut into her palm. "There's no film in it."

"Really." He popped it open and found that she was telling the truth. "How can you take any pictures if there's no film, and what would you be taking pictures of in that rat hole, anyway?"

She reminded herself to stay calm. "I work for the Standing Rock newspaper. I always remember the camera and forget the film."

"Oh, yeah?" The pig-nosed blond deputy dropped the camera back into the bag and adjusted his aviator glasses as he worked over a piece of gum with his back teeth. "Thought you worked for some church."

"I'm a VISTA worker. I'm always volunteering for something, you know. Whenever, wherever."

"Oh, yeah? Where you from?"

"Minnesota."

"You a hippie or something?"

"No. I'm a VISTA worker."

"She's just driving the van, that's all," Ellen told him quietly.

"And you work for the hospital," he said, repeating what he'd been told as though he wasn't sure he believed it anymore.

"That's right."

He reached under the passenger's seat, felt around a little, and came up with a bullet. Cecily managed to stifle a horrified gasp as he brandished his find high in the air and snapped his gum like a testy truckstop waitress. "What kind of medical instrument do you call this? Maybe it's some kind of a suppository, huh?"

"Where did you get that?" Ellen asked. "Out of your pocket?"

"It was on the floor in there." He signaled to his dark-haired partner, who had stood by disinterestedly, fully expecting to let the van pass. "Now both of you put your hands on the vehicle and spread your legs way apart."

"You've got no call to—" Ellen jerked away from the burly blond deputy. "You're not touching me."

"Ellen, just do as he says," Cecily put in, trying to maintain a calm voice. Her only previous run-in with the police had been for a traffic violation. Being called to task by a man with a badge was a bit demoralizing, but all you had to do was cooperate, and everything would be just fine. "We've got nothing to hide."

"This sweaty-handed redneck is not touching me." Ellen backed away. "No man touches me unless I *say* he touches me."

The deputy drew his sidearm. "You ready to back me, Collins?"

"Why don't we call for more backup?" The dark-haired

officer closed in behind Cecily. He noticed a second police car approaching from the west. "Here comes Harroldson. Let's just calm down and—"

"Take your hands off her, hey!" Bobby shouted from the other side of the road. All heads turned in his direction, the policemen automatically dropping into a crouch. The second car screeched to a halt, and the door on the driver's side flew open.

"I only see one redskin back there," Harroldson shouted as he emerged with a rifle. "Jesus, he's—"

Bobby leaped over the barricade. Harroldson took aim and fired. The deafening blast made Cecily jump just as Collins caught her arm behind her. She jerked her head around in time to see Bobby crumple to the ground. It all happened too quickly, too unexpectedly for Cecily's brain to keep up with what her eyes were seeing. She couldn't duck, couldn't help, couldn't even move. All she could do was watch in mind-numbing horror.

"Bobby!" Ellen shrieked. She lost one of her moccasins in the road as the big blond deputy dragged her toward his police car, which was parked at a right angle with the van. He threw her against the car, bent her over the hood, and handcuffed her. She wasn't fighting. She was straining for a glimpse of the man who had fallen. Her dark eyes were all Cecily could see above the roof of the police car. "Bobbyyyy!"

Somebody down on the protestors' side of the road shouted, "Bobby's down! Don't shoot! They've got the women."

Cecily couldn't see anyone behind the barricade.

"Let's get these two out of here," the deputy barked.

"Put your hands behind your back," Collins told Cecily as he brandished a set of handcuffs. She complied without question.

"They shot Bobby," Ellen wailed.

"Where are you taking us?" Cecily demanded. And then it occurred to her that they were actually under arrest. "We haven't done anything! Why are you doing this? What about—" She was actually being shoved across the road like a wheelbarrow. "What about our rights!"

The blond cop pointed toward the shooter, who stood ready for another target to pop up from behind the barricade. "Put the white girl in Harroldson's car, and let's get out of here."

"No! You've gotta help him. Call for an ambulance." Arms pinned behind her, Ellen managed to jerk free of her arrester's hold. "Let *me* help him."

He grabbed her and shoved her against the car again. "You're getting in here, Pocahontas."

"I don't wanna go to your jail. Take me to Fort Yates. Turn me over to—"

"Yeah, right." He opened the back door of the patrol car. "This is a county road; you're on state land. You've got a right—"

"Tell Kiah," Ellen shouted as she was being pushed into the car. "If they let you go, find Kiah."

Through the back seat window Cecily glimpsed the terror in Ellen's eyes. Absolute raw terror. The siren was already wailing as the car rolled past with Ellen's face pressed to the window. Cecily read her lips. "Find Kiah."

Cecily was hustled off in the second police car and taken to the county courthouse. She knew Ellen was there somewhere, too. Twice she heard her shouting, and she thought, Settle down, now. Settle down, my friend. This is a bad dream. It'll all be over soon, and we'll leave this place together. Together we'll find out about Bobby.

But Cecily spent less than an hour in a small holding cell before she was taken back upstairs to the sheriff's office.

"I would like to call a lawyer," she told the man wearing the sheriff's badge. The little courthouse was crawling with law enforcement officers of all descriptions. This was probably the most excitement the desolate reservation border town had seen in years.

"Go ahead," the sheriff said as he tossed her keys across the desk. "They brought your van in and gave it a thorough going-over. Everything but the complimentary car wash. You're free to go."

Cecily snatched up the keys. "What about Ellen?"

"We're charging her with resisting. She bit one of the officers."

He was shuffling through papers, avoiding her eyes.

Her nerve was on the rise. "I find that hard to believe."

"You didn't hear all the screaming?" the portly man asked as he shoved a file into a drawer.

"This whole thing was completely unnecessary. Has Ellen been allowed a phone call? She has a right to call her—"

He closed the drawer carefully and drilled her with a decidedly patronizing look. "I suggest you move along. This woman is in trouble. Those hoodlums stood by while we scraped her boyfriend up off the road.

"Is he alive?"

"Far as I know."

"Have you at least *told* Ellen that he's alive?"

"I don't owe these people anything." He waved his hand in a vaguely all-inclusive direction, as though *these people* were all around him. "They keep making trouble like this, all they get is just exactly what they deserve. Now take that hippie bus and get on outta here before I charge you with something."

Her first inclination was to call a lawyer, but she didn't know any around here. She hoped Kiah would. It occurred to her that the politics behind the whole sorry mess was more complicated than she had imagined. She didn't know who was on whose side. Kiah was the only person she could trust to be on Ellen's side.

It was getting dark, but she knew her way to the town of Little Eagle, where it seemed like such a long time ago that Ellen had taken her to a powwow, and Kiah had coaxed her to return for the rodeo . . . and more. She would head for Little Eagle again. Once she got there, she would have to ask directions to the Red Thunder place.

Chapter 16

Kiah Red Thunder was a certified, decorated, locally celebrated, and nationally ignored Vietnam war hero. The first thing his sister had suggested when he came home was that he ought to use his medals to his advantage and run for tribal councilman. Throw the do-nothing incumbents out and make some changes, she'd said. But he had dropped all the honors in the bottom of the one chest-of-drawers in his mother's three-room house and told Ellen to forget that noise. He was going to raise cattle, just as soon as he got his head straight. That was his only reason for coming back to Standing Rock. He'd been a cowboy before he'd become a soldier.

If he'd had any imagination, he might have devised a different plan, one that would have taken him anywhere else but back to the reservation. As bombed-out as his brain was, he couldn't come up with any alternatives. He was back home. But he wasn't ready to see anybody or go anywhere or explain anything.

He'd only been home once in two years—a year ago for his mother's funeral. He felt a little guilty about staying away until the word came that she was gone. He'd known how sick she was, and he could have asked for leave sooner or even tried for a hardship discharge. But he didn't figure he could have done the old woman any real good. The best tribute he had to give her was to make his ap-

229

pearance at her funeral all decked out in his dress uniform, wearing every damn ribbon he'd received. Even Ellen had to admit that their mother must have been smiling down on him that day.

That made one day in how many? He'd never been good for much but kicking ass and raising hell, which was what he'd thought the war was all about until they'd abruptly started pulling U.S. troops out. It was then that it had finally occurred to him that he'd been fighting too damn long for too damn little.

On the other hand, it felt weird to be home. He didn't fit, not even on the rez. He felt like a guy who'd just had the shit kicked out of him on national television, and everybody thought he'd taken a dive. People were too embarrassed to look him in the eye. Even when they were saying, "Welcome home," you could tell they were thinking, "Now go hide your face in shame. Don't you know America never loses?"

Most of America hadn't been there, so most of America didn't have a clue. On his way back to 'Nam after his mother's funeral, the year before Nixon decided to pull the troops out of Southeast Asia and bring Kiah home for good, one jerk in an airport had actually asked him if he'd ever killed a baby. As he was picking himself up off the floor, the guy had promised to sue the army, prompting Kiah to recite his name, rank, and serial number and invite him to go ahead.

"Then you can take my place, okay? Since my ancestors learned about skewering babies from your ancestors, I'll bet you'd do real good. See, those Asian babies, they look a lot like Sioux babies."

He'd released a handful of T-shirt and given a curt nod as the asshole straightened the wrinkles out of his peace logo. "You're messing with the wrong cowboy, Mr. Peace Man," Kiah had said. He remembered heading for his plane feeling pretty cocky. He was going back to work.

But it had turned out that all the President's cowboys and all the President's Indians had not been able to rout the Red menace. Kiah felt like an insect, scooped up out of the jungle and shipped back to the States in a glass jar.

People either stared or shrank back in disgust. Nobody was impressed. Nobody was interested in the nightmares he'd brought back with him.

So he'd decided to put them to rest at his mother's place—the little house he and Ellen had grown up in, which probably had tons of ghosts in residence already. He figured he'd drink himself to sleep every night until the nightmares were either dead or pickled, and then he'd raise cattle. He kept telling himself that all he'd ever really wanted to be was a cowboy.

He hadn't done a good enough job of anesthetizing himself the night the pounding in his blood-drenched dreams turned into knocking at the door. It was the middle of the night in the middle of nowhere. At first he was sure he was hearing things, so he turned on a light, which usually banished the *gigis*. But not this one. He pulled his jeans on and splashed some water on his face before he opened the door.

It took his eyes a few seconds to adjust.

Jesus, another dream.

"Hello, Kiah."

"Cecily?" He'd had this dream before. It always started out nice, but it was deceptive. Usually left him feeling pretty shame-faced when he woke up.

"You remembered. May I come in?"

"Sure." He stepped back, opening the door just wide enough to admit a slender wisp of nighttime fantasy. In the dim light from the bedroom she looked even prettier than she had the last time he'd conjured her up. "What time is it, anyway?"

"It's late, but this isn't a social call. Ellen asked me to find you. She's been arrested."

"Shit." He raked his fingers through his hair as he headed for the kitchen. This dream was on its way to becoming a nightmare faster than usual. Such was the way with reality.

"What, is she mixed up in that mess down at Red Creek? I told her to stay out of that. She's got herself a good job now, and she doesn't need—"

"We delivered some food and medical supplies donated

by a church," she explained as she trailed him from one small room to the next. "We were promised safe passage. We got in okay, but on the way out they searched the VW bus the church loaned us and came up with a bullet. One bullet. I have no idea where that came from."

He offered an incredulous double take over his shoulder, but she seemed to miss the point. Damn. Her eyes were bigger and bluer than he remembered, and her summer-blond hair, curling softly over one shoulder, was even longer now.

"Anyway, they started to take us into custody, and before I knew what was happening, all hell had broken loose." She seemed confused, as though she were still trying to put all the pieces together into a complete and sensible picture.

"What's 'all hell'? My scrappy sister?"

"They kept her, and they let me go."

"Figures." He snatched the white enamel pot off the stove and took a blue can down from the shelf above it. "I need some coffee. You want some?"

"I'd really like to get back to the county courthouse. That's where they're holding her. She needs a lawyer, Kiah. She needs—"

"I don't know any lawyers." And he sure as hell didn't need any part of Ellen's politics, or all the factional bickering that went with it. But he wasn't about to let his sister sit around long in a white man's jail. Coffeepot in hand, he spread his arms and smiled a little when her gaze skipped from his eyes down to his bare chest. "What you see is what she gets, but I've gotta have some coffee before I go anywhere."

"Bobby Blue Bow got shot."

"Is he dead?" She shook her head and started to elaborate, but he cut her off as he turned away. "Those guys are askin' to get shot. Ellen thinks it's a game."

"I don't think she does. I think she believes in what they're doing."

He could tell she wanted to hurry him along. While he was trying to find cups and a spoon, she'd picked up the pot and started looking around for a sink. He had news for her. It wasn't going to materialize.

But she was more interested in getting her point across. "I also think she's terrified of being in that jail. She fought like crazy."

"That's the way she always fights. Like crazy. And there's no running water. I haul it from town." He nodded toward a ten-gallon cooler with a spigot on the bottom. When she was headed in the right direction, he went on. "Indians don't usually do very well with white cops, white lawyers, or white juries. That's why she's scared. *Damn* that Bobby Blue Bow."

"It wasn't Bobby's fault. He was trying to look out for her, I think. He was . . ." Her voice drifted as the water drained slowly into the pot. Mesmerized, she added quietly, "It was awful. I don't know why they let me go and held her."

"Get off it," he scoffed. She jerked her head around, surprised. "You know exactly why. They think they can do whatever they damn well please to her. It's always been that way." He gestured impatiently for her to hand him the pot. "Wake up and smell the coffee, Cecily. It's *always* been that way."

"It felt awful."

"Yeah, well, if you don't wanna see how it feels, you don't go walkin' on the side of the fence where the cactus grows, honey." He spooned the coffee grounds into the pot, jammed the lid on, and slammed the pot on the stove.

He looked up to find her staring in disbelief.

"You put the coffee right into the water."

"You're in for a treat, sweetheart. Old-fashioned cowboy coffee." He lit the burner with a wooden match and adjusted the blue flame. "You just stand here and watch this while I get dressed. When it starts to simmer, turn it off."

"Could you hurry, please?"

"Once you turn it off, it has to sit for about five minutes." He reached for the washbasin. "I'll wash with cold water, but that's as much hurrying as I'm gonna do. Five extra minutes ain't gonna change a damn thing."

Cecily folded her arms, hugging herself around the middle, belatedly trying to steady her insides. She'd told herself she was going to see him sooner or later, that she was ready any time. But she'd forgotten how stunning his presence was. When the door had finally opened, his eyes, his scant smile, his brawny bare torso had assailed her all at once. It was hard not to remember the way they had last been together, harder still not to reach out and invite him to take her in his arms the same way again. But she had contained herself. She was *still* containing herself, holding herself in.

She wanted to look around, to get a feel for the place where he lived, but she didn't dare leave her post. She'd noticed a wood stove in the front room, along with an old brown sofa that was sagging in the middle, a couple of chairs, and a few framed photographs hanging on the garish green walls. She glanced up at the bare light bulb and followed its cord to the single outlet in the kitchen. Clearly the house predated the advent of rural electricity.

"Five years."

"What?" Cecily turned with a start. Kiah stood in the kitchen doorway, tucking the tails of his white Western shirt into his jeans.

He smiled and glanced at the light bulb. "We've only had electricity out here for about five years. Before that we used kerosene. Then the government got us hooked up, and the REC brought the wonder of rural electricity into the kitchen and said, 'Here. Plug something in.' I'll have to figure out how to wire up the rest of the house one of these days. 'Course, this shack'll probably go up like a pile of tinder." He nodded toward the stove. "Coffee's ready."

As though she'd shirked her duty, Cecily fairly leaped to turn the burner off. "Why don't you just hire an electrician?"

"Yeah, right, college girl. What's an electrician?" He chuckled, wagging his head. "You find me one who'll come out here, and tell him to bring the plumber with him while he's at it. You're drivin' a VW bus, you said?"

"Yes."

"We'll take my pickup." He buckled his belt, then rolled his cuffs to the middle of his forearms. "Listen, you'd better keep your head down when we get to the courthouse. I don't have much money, and I sure don't have any connections. I may have to bust through a wall and drag my sister out."

"You'd do that?"

"Never know what I'll do till the time comes. Wearing moccasins and beating on the drum is one thing, but Ellen's wasting her time over this damn protest." He took two cups down from a small cupboard. "On the other hand, I'll be damned if I'll let my sister sit in jail over a lost cause."

Kiah wore a new straw cowboy hat that he'd shaped to his liking. The crown barely cleared the roof of the cab. It was the same old blue Ford that Ellen had been driving two years ago. He started it with the same keys he'd claimed from his sister when he'd come to say goodbye to Cecily in the wee hours of the morning. As he backed it away from the house now, she glanced over her shoulder into the truck bed that contained a roll of barbed wire, a few tools, and some scrap lumber. For one night that big blue box had been a lovers' bed filled with fresh-cut hay that had left a few scratches on her backside. She hadn't noticed them until after he'd gone, and then they'd only been a minor irritation compared with the emptiness she'd felt.

He shifted gears, and she turned and caught him watching her, reading her mind. She wished she could do the same, but his dark eyes were as unreadable as they were beautiful and unnerving. The roar of the old pickup's engine mercifully filled the silence, and Cecily remembered Ellen saying that Kiah had been "chosen" to inherit the vehicle. It fit him. He drove an old pickup with a past, a tough-skinned transport with a stubborn heart. Like the cowboy hat and boots, it fit him perfectly. He looked so good in his tapered shirt and jeans that it was hard to imagine him ever wearing or driving any GI green.

He fished a cigarette out of his breast pocket, stuck it in

the corner of his mouth, then thought to ask, "Will this bother you?"

"Not if you roll the window down," she said.

He struck a match and lit the cigarette, squinting through the smoke as he watched the patch of road illuminated by the headlights. The brief flame cast a flickering glow over his angular features.

He caught her noticing every handsome detail just before he blew out the flame. Damn him, he knew exactly how the taunting smile in his eyes charmed her. She could tell by the way it tugged at the corner of his mouth as the smoke from his first deep drag trailed out the window.

"Why did you come back here?" he asked without taking his eyes off the road. "Christ, you've got your education, you've got everything goin' for you now. What are you doing here?"

"I'm not finished with school. I'm going back after I get a little experience under my belt." He slanted her a dubious look. "Graduate school, you know. I do enjoy school."

"Sittin' at a desk all day? You enjoy that?"

"It's different when you're studying the things you're interested in." She decided not to let him intimidate her. "I truly *enjoy* school," she told him flatly. "I could be a professional student if anyone would pay me for it."

"Sounds to me like you need a life." He slid her another cool glance. "I've got news for you, honey, you're not gonna find one out here."

"Maybe your definition of *a life* isn't the same as mine. I have a mind of my own. I like to do my own thing. I don't follow the crowd." She fixed her eyes on the road ahead and added distantly, "I don't even know the crowd, and they don't know me."

"Well, there's no crowd out here, so maybe you *have* come to the right place."

Long moments of silence passed between them. Kiah finished his cigarette, and Cecily watch the broken yellow line flash by like a picture rolling monotonously on a faulty TV set.

After a while the silence got to him. He searched for some music on the radio, but all he found was static. "Either they've all signed off, or the damn thing's shot," he grumbled.

"That didn't work very well . . . before." He glanced her way, and she added, as if she thought he'd forgotten, "When I was here before, and Ellen . . ."

She turned to the front window again, staring past the headlight beams, into the darkness. "Did you get my letters, Kiah?" Her voice was so soft and shy, it made him hurt a little.

"Yeah." He drew a deep breath, seeking an air of indifference. "It was nice there for a while, gettin' some mail."

"Why didn't you ever answer?"

"I'm not much of a letter writer."

She didn't say anything for a moment. He hoped that meant his answer had satisfied her.

Wishful thinking.

"Did you think about me at all after you left?"

"Sure." He'd thought about her a lot. He'd thought about the kinds of things that drove a guy crazy.

"Did you miss me at all?"

"What do you mean *miss* you?" *Good Christ, what a question.* "What good does that do? You had your life, and I had mine."

"I thought you said I needed a life. Now you're saying I had mine, and you had yours." She shot him a surprisingly fierce look. "Make up your damn mind."

"I made up my mind. When I left here, I walked off the edge of the world. You know what that's like?"

"No."

"No, you don't," he argued, ignoring her answer. "And I don't know what your world is like, either, but I found myself wondering about it. Imagining you, imagining the college boys with their clean hands and their draft deferments." He gripped the steering wheel. It was his turn to slip her an accusatory look. "I didn't even have a picture of you. Why didn't you send me a picture?"

"I would have if you'd asked me. I didn't know . . . I didn't want to just *foist* my picture on you."

He laughed derisively. "You didn't wanna be over there with me. No way, shape, or form."

"That's ridiculous," she snapped.

They exchanged hot stares.

She was the first to glance away, but not in defeat. "Do you still have the locket?"

"Yeah. You want it back?" He'd meant to be flippant, but it came out more cautiously than he'd intended.

"No. I gave it to you."

"For luck." He carried it with him everywhere. He could have returned it to her on the spot if she'd said yes. He forced himself to relax, to give her at least a hint of a smile. "Must've worked. I'm here. No parts missing."

"That's good." He gave her another doubtful look, and she reassured him with a tentative smile. "Well, it is. All your parts are very nice."

"You should know." He could almost hear walls cracking as he returned a smile that was almost as shy as hers. They shared a look of sweet remembrance. "I liked your parts, too. I had to try not to think about them getting into the wrong hands."

"The wrong hands?"

"Or the *right* hands, probably, you wanna be realistic, but ... to be honest, it took a while for me to get real about the whole thing. About you." He was about to trip over his own tongue and fall into another bottomless pit. If he wasn't careful, he'd end up telling her how difficult *getting real* had been.

Staring at the road ahead, he rubbed the back of his hand across his chin and told himself to lighten up. Then he gripped the wheel with both hands again. "What it took was bangin' every whore in Thailand."

"Well." Her tone turned to ice. "That must've been quite a job."

"Hell of a job, hell of a job."

"But somebody had to do it?"

"Never got VD once," he boasted. "Proud of me?"

Maybe he'd forgotten *how* to lighten up. Even in near darkness, one quick, awkward glance into her eyes told him he'd veered way off the high road.

"Hey, what's wrong? You can't take everything I say seriously. I was just kidding."

"About what? Which part was a joke?" She folded her arms around her middle as though she were pulling back, protecting herself. "You weren't joking. You were trying to humiliate me."

"Nah, I was trying to be ..." Damn, she looked small and sweet, sitting on the far side of the cab and cradling her breasts in her arms. He swallowed hard and looked back at the road. "I don't remember how to joke around women like you."

"Really? I don't remember that you ever knew how."

"Yeah, well the ten days you knew me wasn't exactly the funniest time in my life." He shook his head, chuckling humorlessly. "That's all we had together, you know. I figured ten days, hell. Nobody belongs to anybody after ten days."

"No, of course not." She stared at the road, too.

Again he hoped her momentary silence meant that she would drop it there.

Again it was wishful thinking.

"Just how many whores are there in Thailand, if you don't mind my asking?"

"I didn't count." He was trying hard not to give a damn about the wounded edge in her voice, but it wasn't working very well. Besides, no matter how mean he felt, he hated to bad-mouth Thai women. There had been one or two who'd gotten him through some rough times. He shrugged. "Not too many."

The sun was rising when they reached the courthouse and the county jail. The doors were locked. Since there were cars parked outside, Kiah knew there must be people inside. But the doors wouldn't open until eight o'clock.

"Now what?" Cecily asked nervously.

"We wait in the pickup." He slid down in the seat and pulled his hat down over his face. "Story of my life. Hurry up and wait."

"We all have to wait sometimes." She stared at the courthouse steps. "Anyway, I'd rather wait in a pickup than a jail cell."

"I doubt that your wisdom is based on experience on either count."

"Listen, mister, you are the last person I wanted to go looking for in the wee hours of the morning, but I did it because Ellen asked me to."

"You also went to Red Creek because Ellen asked you to."

"I went to Red Creek to see for myself what was going on. So I could gain some wisdom. Through *experience.*"

"You sure get your share of that when you come out here, don't you?"

"I've wised up about men, thanks to my experiences with you."

"I pride myself on teaching the ladies well. Did you put your experience to good use?" He pushed his hat back and looked up at her before she had a chance to say something he didn't want to hear. "Sorry. That was a cheap shot. I'm sorry."

"This is a difficult situation."

"Yeah." He offered a conciliatory smile. "Was I really the last person you wanted to see?"

"I didn't say that." She stared out the front window, pouting. "I said I didn't want to go looking for you. I thought maybe you'd pay me a visit."

"I probably would have." He, too, stared past the hood of the pickup. "Sooner or later."

"That's comforting, considering I beat you to it."

He chuckled. She smiled, eyes still straight ahead.

They might have been watching a drive-in movie together the way the little prairie town just beginning to stir held their attention. Somebody was cranking up a lawn mower. The flag was climbing the pole in front of the post office across the street. A hearse was approaching, turning, pulling into the alley behind the courthouse.

"What the hell . . ." Kiah sat up slowly, scowling at the black, wheeled vulture. He turned, and his eyes met Cecily's in mutual fear. They both flung the pickup doors open at once. Side by side they marched up to the courthouse door just as the janitor unlocked it.

Sheriff Tom Hodges was just hanging up the phone when they approached his desk.

"You're holding my sister. I want to see her."

Visibly distraught, Hodges rose from his chair. "Who are—"

"Kiah Red Thunder." He pulled his billfold from his pocket and produced his driver's license. "What'll it cost me to bail her out?" With a pointed look, he added, "In *cash*, so you don't have to be looking for references."

"Um ... Mr., uh, Red Thunder ..." The desk chair drifted back on its casters as Hodges hiked up his pants. "I don't know the best way to tell you this ..."

"Try straight out."

"All right." The sheriff's round face reddened as he drew a deep breath, then abruptly released it. "Your sister hanged herself in her cell last night."

A deafening silence fell over the three like a fisherman's net, momentarily tangling them all together in the horror of the news.

"You're shittin' me." Woodenly Kiah took a step back from the desk. "Where's Ellen?"

"I'm sorry, Mr. Red Thunder. She's dead."

"She couldn't ..." An appalling image dangled like a shadowy phantom in Cecily's mind. "How could she ... have ... hanged ..."

"She used her own clothes. Her shirt, her"—Hodges dropped his hand immediately when he realized it was on its way to his own chest—"her brassiere."

"Did you tell her that Bobby wasn't dead?" Cecily demanded. Then she turned abruptly as a familiar voice posed a threat from behind.

"She didn't ask," the pig-nosed deputy claimed. His partner, Collins, stood just behind him in the doorway. "All she did was cuss us out and raise a ruckus back there. Then she got quiet, and we thought she'd worn herself out."

Now that reinforcements were close at hand, Hodges ventured out from behind his desk with a sympathetic overture. "I know what a shock this is. Would you like to have me call a minister or—"

"I want to see my sister," Kiah said flatly, his eyes shuttered.

"I don't think you want to see her *right now*. Maybe give yourself a little time to just—"

"Maybe you didn't hear me, Sheriff." Kiah dismissed the two in the doorway with a cursive glance. *"I said* I want to see my sister."

Hodges stepped back. "We were getting ready to move the body. It looks . . . You don't want to see her the way she is now, son."

"I just did two tours in 'Nam. I'm not anybody's son, but I'm Ellen Red Thunder's next of kin, and I want to see her *exactly* the way she is. Right now."

A dawn of new awareness claimed Hodges's whole demeanor. "You're *that* Red Thunder." He glanced at Cecily, as if he were checking for confirmation. "Read about you in the papers. I always say, you people make the best damn soldiers." He nodded toward the door, and the two deputies took the signal to clear the way. "I guess you have a right to see her, if that's what you want."

Kiah spared Cecily a skeptical glance, but he didn't question her decision to accompany him down the steps to the basement, where the jail cells were located. Toward the end of the corridor, one barred door stood open.

Cecily's eyes were glued to Kiah's back. Strangely, she felt Ellen's presence. She didn't need to see what was inside the cell. The dank air reeked of the remnants of her friend's anger and fear. The ringing in her ears shut out the ominous sound of shuffling footsteps. She tasted bile. For a moment she couldn't move, couldn't breathe the cloying underground air.

Kiah stepped away from her, grabbed one of the bars, and stood rigid, his face unreadable. Cecily wanted to run, but she didn't. She moved to Kiah's side and shared with him in viewing the hopelessly still body that lay on the cot.

The sheriff pulled the white sheet away from Ellen's bruised face. No one had had the decency to close her eyes. Kiah snatched the sheet from the startled sheriff's hand and snapped it off his sister's half-naked body. The bruises all ran together—breasts, neck, face, everywhere.

"Leave us alone for a minute." There was a killing edge in Kiah's quietly controlled tone.

"We still have to take some pictures."

"Get out," he growled without taking his eyes from his sister's face.

"I'll be right outside. I can't let you, uh . . ."

It was Cecily's angry look that sent the sheriff into the hallway.

Mechanically, Kiah removed his hat and knelt stiffly beside the cot. With a steady, careful hand he removed the bra that was knotted around Ellen's neck. He closed her eyes with the same hand, a brotherly hand that lingered over her face as though he wanted to shield his young sister from seeing what she had done to herself—or what had been done to her. Cecily lowered her gaze to the thick braid that spilled over the side of the cot and trailed several inches across the floor. As long as she lived, she would remember that shiny black braid lying on the white tile.

"It's not possible," Cecily whispered. "She was alive when I left her. Now she's so . . . quiet and still."

"And dead." His hollow voice echoed within the confines of the barren cell. "She didn't die quiet and still. She died fighting."

That much was clear. The question was whether she died fighting real demons or imaginary ones. Cecily shuddered, but she could not tear her eyes away from her dead friend. The agonizing strain was fixed on her face as though the expression had been frozen in time, fixed like the hands of a broken clock at the moment when time had stopped for Ellen Red Thunder. This was Ellen's testimony.

Kiah's hand moved gently over the length of her body, from a bruise on her shoulder, to the India ink dots long ago tattooed on her knuckles, to the lifeless fingers, to the frayed pocket of her jeans, to the skinned toes of her bare foot.

"She lost one moccasin in the road," Cecily said in a thin, bleak voice.

"Shit." His hand closed slowly around Ellen's foot. He

tightened his grip until his hand shook. "Goddamn them, *tankśi*," he whispered, calling her little sister the way his stepfather had taught him when she was a baby. "Goddamn them all for this."

Cecily's heart ached too painfully for tears. Kiah held his inside. She stood behind him, her hands on his shoulders, and waited until he was ready to move on.

His face betrayed no emotion when he confronted Hodges and his deputies once more. "When can I take her home?"

"After the autopsy is done, you can claim the body."

"Who beat her up?"

"No one beat her up. She resisted arrest. She had to be restrained." Hodges was hiding behind his desk again. "Death by strangulation doesn't make for a pretty corpse, I'm afraid. That's why I said—"

"It took three of us to get her in the cell," the pig-nosed one reported from his post near a tall file cabinet. "She threw herself around like . . ." He wagged his head with ostensible regret, but there was a contemptuous gleam in his eye. "She was a hellcat, plain and—"

Kiah let his right fist fly, knocking the rest of the statement down the man's throat. The ugly piggish snout suffered the second hit as he stumbled back against the file cabinet. Kiah was no less a hellcat than his sister. Collins tried to help the sheriff restrain him, but without Cecily's help they wouldn't have had a chance.

"Don't, Kiah, please," she begged as she came between his cocked fist and the deputy's suddenly not-so-smug face. "They'll lock you up, too."

"Who murdered my sister?" Kiah jerked his arm away from Collins and turned his accusations on the sheriff. "Huh? Which of your goons had their hands on her? She would never take her clothes off like that. Not in a place like this. Not with . . ." He glared at each man in turn. "Who did this thing?"

Hodges was rattled. "The matter will be thoroughly investigated. I'm sure the FBI will have their agents—"

"The FBI," Kiah spat. "Is that supposed to impress me? When was the last time they ever arrested anyone for killing an Indian? Never happens. It's either suicide or it's just Indians killing Indians, so what the fuck." A muscle twitched in his jaw. The black rage in his eyes was as intimidating as a loaded gun. "I'll do my own investigating."

"Kiah, please."

Cecily's hand on his arm made him flinch. He looked at her through unseeing eyes, a look so full of fury that it frightened her.

"Please try to . . . calm down. I know it's—"

He made a tormented sound, deep in his throat. She dared to touch him again, and this time he allowed her hand to rest on his arm, even as his hot stare betrayed his doubts.

"I know," she repeated quietly. "But you can't let them lock you up, too."

"We will if we have to," Hodges warned hastily. "Anderson shouldn't have said what he said. We'll call it even."

"My sister's dead." For the first time Kiah's voice cracked. His chest heaved with one long, deep, cleansing breath, which enabled him to demand as steadily as ever, "You call that *even?*"

"I'm sorry. We're *all* very sorry about your loss." Hodges nodded at Cecily. "Take him home."

She slipped her arm around his waist. He looked at her. His eyes glazed over, but she felt some of the tension in his body dissipate, as though her proximity might have absorbed some measure of it.

"Please, Kiah. Let them do what has to be done. We'll make arrangements to bring her home."

His nod was almost imperceptible. No one spoke to them as they left the courthouse with their arms around one another, each spontaneously supporting the other. He opened the passenger door for her, and she blinked back the tears that this gesture, of all things, brought to her eyes.

They said little as they drove back to Little Eagle. Cecily watched each square-topped butte sprout up from the horizon, expand as they drew closer, then slide past. Yellow-green fields and tan-green pastures rippled under the summer sun. Kiah's silence was heartrending, but Cecily dared not intrude. He drove the pickup as though he were part of it, an extension of its machinery. It was a relief when he finally rolled the window down and lit up a cigarette.

He parked the pickup next to the VW bus, shut the engine off, and stared at the humble clapboard house. Daylight exposed the peeling, broken details of its shabbiness. He was too tired to care. Very much.

"I'd invite you in, but ... well, you saw already, the place is a mess."

"You don't think I'd notice, do you?" Cecily laid a consoling hand on his shoulder. "Or care. Let me make you some breakfast."

He gave her a sad smile. "You don't think I could eat, do you?"

"I want to do *something*."

"So do I, but you stopped me from doing what I wanted to do."

"Kill the one with the pig nose?" She shook her head. "I really didn't want to stop you. I wanted to watch him bleed, but you can't always get what you want."

"Sounds real sensible." He sighed and glanced out the side window at the clump of chokecherry bushes growing by the creek that ran behind the house. The cherries would shrivel in the sun this year. "I don't need any food right now. What I need is"—*no less than a quart of Everclear*—"to be left alone for a while."

"I don't think that's such a good idea."

"You don't, huh?" He covered her hand with his, squeezed gently, and nodded toward the bus. "Go on home, college girl. I'm not gonna do myself in."

She stared absently at the bus. "You do know, don't you, that you were *far* from the last person I wanted to see when I came back here?"

He touched her cheek and nodded. "Get some rest. You've had a long night."

Reluctantly she left him. It was a long road back to Fort Yates. Long and desolate. She wondered what Ellen would have done, whether she would have stayed to look after him, no matter what he said. Probably. Ellen was a strong woman. Cecily had simply done what she was told. She'd left him. She'd left them both. Both times she came away feeling as though she were the one who had been left out.

God, they were so much alike. She wondered if Kiah realized how very much like him his sister was. They both had a way of reaching inside her with just a look, never hinting at what they found there. She wanted to know, but she seemed to lack the nerve to ask.

Memories of Ellen seemed to crowd the long stretch of highway reflected in the rearview mirror. Memories kept replaying in Cecily's mind, particularly the image of the last time she'd seen her alive. She'd never seen fear in Ellen's eyes before. Antipathy, yes. Anger, certainly. But never raw fear. *Ellen was a strong woman.* Strong-willed, unflappable, unsinkable. The corpse on the cot in the jail cell bore only a remote resemblance to the Ellen Red Thunder Cecily knew. It was hard to realize, hard to believe she was dead.

And impossible to return to the little trailer house they'd shared for such a short time. Ellen had never once made her bed. The first thing Cecily would see when she walked through the door was that bed, those sheets still rumpled just the way Ellen had left them.

She had driven fifty miles when she slowed the VW bus for a railroad crossing. She wasn't paying much attention to the tracks, and the train that burst forth from behind a hill and came barreling across the road nearly scared the life out of her. She slammed on the brakes just in time. The engine stalled, and she sat there shaking for a few minutes, watching the cars roll by before she started the bus again and executed a U-turn worthy of a stock car driver. A thick cloud of dust followed her back down the narrow gravel road.

She drove the fifty miles back to Kiah's place. If he wouldn't let her in, she would sit outside in the van. At least she wouldn't be alone in the trailer.

When he opened the door, he said nothing. But he stepped back and let her in. She looked up at him, her vision blurred by her tears. All her explanations and demands were stuck in her stinging throat. He took her in his arms, and they stood for a long, long time, just holding each other.

Chapter 17

❧❧❧ ❧❧❧

"I don't want to be alone now," Cecily sobbed. "Please let me stay with you."

"Okay."

His answer was tentative, but he could feel the way she latched on to it and held it tight, almost the same way she clutched his bare back. It was a hot, dry afternoon, and her hands felt cool against his skin. But she wasn't supposed to be there, not now. As soon as she'd left he had stripped down to his jeans and had himself a drink. Not a glass— more like a fast chug. He didn't think she could smell it on him, the way she was pressing her face against his shoulder and flooding him with her tears.

"I shouldn't have left her," she muttered desolately.

"You came to get me." And now you've come back, he marveled as he stroked her hair. "That's what she asked you to do."

"I should have made sure she knew that Bobby wasn't dead. I should have called a lawyer right away. I should have—"

"You did what she asked you to do. Ellen didn't kill herself over Bobby Blue Bow." He drew back and lifted her chin so that he could see her face. Could she really believe her recriminations could even touch his? He shook his head. "She didn't kill herself at all. She got mixed up with that bunch of rabble-rousers and got herself killed sure as hell."

What was that question he saw in her eyes? *What did he intend to do about it?* Hands on her shoulders, he set her away from him, then turned on his heel and headed for the kitchen, tossing the answer over his shoulder. "Short of gutting the fat rednecks who'll never go to jail for killing her, there's not a goddamn thing I can do about it."

The admission disgusted him.

"Surely the investigation will turn up some explanation." Cecily took a swipe at her tears with the back of her hand and followed him. "I mean, it's obvious she was beaten. It's obvious—"

"She was raped?" He eyed the bottle he'd left standing on the kitchen table. It had been a while since he'd resorted to the gut-purging power of straight Everclear, and he was having trouble getting the stuff down. He lifted his gaze to hers. Was that shock or fear in her red-rimmed eyes? Both, maybe. She was entitled to both.

"She was raped, Cecily. I know that, just as sure as I'm standing here in my mother's kitchen." He sighed as he reached for the bottle. "And I'm pretty sure I'm standing here, at least for the moment."

"If she was raped, the autopsy will—"

"The autopsy will show what the sheriff said it will show. Death by strangulation, self-inflicted. You actually think they'll go lookin' for any semen or find any bruises they can't explain away?" He tipped the bottle to his lips, swallowed a mouthful of the high-proof drink, and grimaced. "Semen? Wonder where that came from?" he questioned mockingly. "Who could it possibly belong to? Had to be some Indian guy, right? After all, she'd just left Red Creek, hadn't she? There's a bunch of horny Indians holed up at Red Creek."

"I was with her at Red Creek."

"Well, brace yourself for a brand-new reputation, baby. You left Sugarplum Fairyland behind you." He waved the bottle in a generally easterly direction. "Maybe you oughta think about hightailin' it back there, huh?"

"Maybe you oughta think about slowing down a little."

"It's not working, anyway. The one time a guy really needs to get himself royally bombed, and it doesn't seem to work." He checked the label, just to make sure the stuff was what it was supposed to be.

Sure as hell. Same old firewater.

"Where are my manners? Can I offer you a drink? I think I've got a clean glass around here somewhere." With a nod toward the open shelves, he offered her the bottle. "You wanna get drunk with me? You're old enough, aren't you, college girl?"

"I'm old enough, but it doesn't, um . . ." She wrinkled her nose and gave her head a prim shake. "I'd just get sick, and then we'd both be sick, and we don't need that."

"Sensible Cecily." Except when it came to being in the wrong place at the wrong time, and sure as hell with the wrong lonesome cowboy. "I don't get sick. If you do, I'll take care of you." He made the offer again, pressing the bottle on her. Getting drunk together was the only way he could arrange to head off the bad stuff. His head was always full of bad stuff. "You wanna stop seeing her face, don't you? You want those big, black, staring eyes to go away, don't you?"

She took the bottle and set it back on the table. "I just don't want to be alone with those eyes."

"Maybe they're not lookin' at you the way they're lookin' at me." Maybe she didn't need him to take care of her. Maybe she was too good to be touched by any of the bad stuff.

Not that his sister's eyes were bad. They were just too damn grievous sometimes, especially when they looked at him. Even when they couldn't fucking *see* anymore, some terrible timeless wailing echoed from their hollow depths.

He could still see, and that was the whole goddamn problem.

He sighed. "She used to say that a true Lakota would scorn alcohol because it killed the spirit. So I told her— just last week or so, I told her—you oughta go spend a couple of years losing a war, and then come tell me what kills the spirit."

He turned away from the bottle on the table, away from

Cecily's eyes. They were not the same eyes—they were blue and full of life—but they were the eyes of a woman.

It didn't matter which way he turned; he couldn't escape the memory of Ellen's vacant stare. "Maybe she was losing her war, and maybe she *was* telling me. Maybe that's what happened last night."

"I was too scared to fight," Cecily told him. "Ellen was scared, too, but she fought anyway."

"You didn't have as much to fear as she did."

"Maybe not, but I'm a woman, too. They were all men. I hadn't done anything wrong, and I didn't want them putting their hands on me, but they—"

"Oh, Jesus, Jesus, Jesus." He grabbed her shoulders and nearly lifted her off the floor. "Honey, you've taken up with the losing side."

"Don't say that."

"You didn't even know there *were* any sides, did you?"

"I know about prejudice."

She knew *of* it, maybe. He let her go and turned away. "Stick around, and you'll get to know a lot more."

"Well, the autopsy will *have* to show something. I mean, the report will have to explain how . . ."

"You want answers, right? You and me, we're gonna go in there and *demand* some answers, right?" She nodded. He took a pack of cigarettes off the counter and shook one out. "Do you know how to do an autopsy?" She shook her head. "Neither do I. And I don't know anybody who does, which means we probably have all the answers we're ever going to get.

"Hey, look, Indians are always hanging themselves in the white man's jails," he told her offhandedly as he went searching for a match. "It's supposed to be one of our favorite pastimes, like drinking and raising hell. We do these things to accommodate you guys, so you can shake your heads and say 'Jeez, it's too bad these once noble people are doing this to themselves.' "

"Don't look at me and say, 'You guys.' I'm not like that."

"Okay. Some other guys. Not you."

"Maybe we should hire someone." They both spotted a

ook of matches on the windowsill, but since his reflexes
were somewhat diminished, she got to them first.

"*Hire* someone?" He put the cigarette between his lips
and stuck out his hand.

Flashing a demure smile, she struck a match. "A lawyer
or a private detective, maybe." She struck three times be-
ore she achieved fire and was able to offer him a light.

"How about a hit man?" Amusement flickered in his
eyes as he lowered his head to meet her flame. He drew
deeply on the cigarette until the tip glowed, then watched
her puff out the flame as if it were a birthday candle.

"No, wait a minute," he said, smoke trailing from his
lips. "*I'm* a hit man. That's what the army hired me for.
Best damn executioner—" Cigarette in hand, he tapped his
chest with his thumb. "You can't buy an aim like mine on
the mercenary market. Most of those guys are hacks."

"Kiah, don't." She tossed the matches on the counter.
"Don't call yourself that. You weren't a hit man; you were
a soldier."

"I could go back to the courthouse and take those guys
out"—he snapped his fingers—"right now, no problem."
He shrugged, his expression turning serious. "That's all I
can do. That's all I *know how* to do. And I'm her brother.
Nobody else'll get 'em for what they did."

"Oh, Kiah." Cecily leaned back against the counter,
bracing her hands on either side of her hips—a woman
standing her ground on a woman's turf with a woman's
philosophy. "The worst thing you could do to Ellen right
now is to throw your own life away."

"I can't disappoint Ellen anymore. She's all done worrying about whether I'm ever gonna make something of myself."

"She loved you."

So there it was. The be-all and end-all of a woman's
legacy. He hooked a thumb in his front pocket and shook
his head. "She had no faith in me. None." He turned toward the window. "She wanted too much from me. She
wanted my goddamn soul, that's what she wanted. Hell,
she wasn't even my mother or my wife. She was just my
sister."

He dragged deeply on his cigarette, dammed the smoke up in his chest for a moment, and then sent it out the window, into the bright sunlight. "Women are too damn much bother, you know that?"

"Let me make you something to eat. What would you like?"

"The question is, what do I have in the kitchen?" he said absently. "You notice there's no refrigerator."

"There's a stove."

"You know what you could do?" He turned and cocked a finger in her direction. "Write a story. That's what you do best, isn't it? Write a story about what happened to Ellen. Don't let them bury the truth with her."

"Okay." She repeated the threat he'd made at the courthouse. "I'll do my own investigation. If I don't come up with all the answers, I'm sure I can plant some damn good questions in people's minds."

"There you go. Now you've got your mission." Just like that, she'd taken his empty threat, legitimized it, and made it her mission. And he was without one. Without any power but his brawn, without any plan, without any vision. He shook his head, sinking further into his private morass. "Why don't you go on home now, Cecily? Give me some down time, okay?"

"Go into the bedroom and close the door. Lie down, close your eyes; you won't even know I'm here." He let her take the last of his cigarette and squash it into the plastic ashtray that was already brimming with the ashes of his earlier attempts to calm his insides. "I left Ellen," she said quietly. "I'm not leaving you."

"I don't *need* you here now." He wanted to laugh at her when she brushed her hands together and pushed the ashtray back from the edge of the table. Hell, nobody had *asked* her to touch the damn thing. But he didn't feel like laughing. He felt like having another cigarette, getting totally bombed, and then, hell, getting royally laid.

And here was his prospective princess, reading the labels on his meager stock of canned goods.

"What are you doing back here, anyway?" he dehanded. "Why did you come back to the Dakotas in the first place, huh?"

She glanced at him, reading his mind, sure as hell, like was just another damn label.

One corner of his mouth curled into a sneer. "Was it to other me? You do bother me, you know."

"How so?"

"You remind me of a time when I was ..." She'd turned back to the food, studying the top shelf. Her head was tipped back, and her hair ... damn, her hair. He remembered how silky it felt when he pillowed his face in it. "When I was very, very stupid."

"How so?" she repeated.

"I was just stupid, that's all." They were such bitter-sweet memories, and tagged to them were the tender feelings that he'd tried so hard to bruise and discard so he wouldn't have to deal with them anymore.

She turned to him, clutching a can of ravioli to her breast. "Let's be honest, Kiah. *I* was the fool. I wrote to you; you never answered. But I actually thought the time we had together meant something to you." Her lips hinted at a wistful smile. "It did to me."

"I was your first lover." He jammed his thumbs in his belt and affected a casual shrug. "From what I hear, women don't forget the guy who took their cherry."

The wounded look in her eyes made him feel like the worst kind of bastard.

She lifted her chin. "And from what *I've* heard, men give each other more locker room points for—"

Neither one of them was talking any sense. He closed the distance between them in a single stride, took the can away, and set it aside. Then he grabbed her by the shoulders and kissed her, his tongue fully claiming her mouth and tempting hers to claim his the same way. It was too late for sense. He was too damn hungry, too damn horny, and *damn* his hide, too damn anxious to score on her, just the way she'd been about to suggest. On the strength of a groan, he tore his mouth away.

"So, see," she whispered brokenly. "You weren't so stupid."

"I just made a stupid remark." Without releasing her, he relaxed his hold. "I'm feelin' mean as hell, Cecily. You should get as far away from me as you can."

"Are you going to hurt me if I don't?"

"I don't know." He closed his eyes and cupped her cheek in his palm. He didn't want her to go. "Not with my hands. I'll be good to you with my hands."

"I'll be good to you, too." She rubbed the tip of her nose against his smooth cheek and whispered, "You need someone to be good to you, don't you?"

"Yeah, I think I do." He tucked his chin and touched his forehead to hers, rolling it back and forth, relishing the cool feel of her skin. "I need you, Cecily." Her arms went around his neck as she insinuated herself between his thighs. "Oh, sweet Jesus, I need you."

He caught her hips, pulled her tight against him, and moved her back and forth across his erection, showing her how bad it was, letting her imagine how good it would be.

"Me, too," she whispered, prompting him to lift her straight up off the floor and carry her to his rumpled bed.

There was none of the timidity or the innocent joy of that first summer. There was mature need and anger and the fresh gash of grief, and together they kindled a fire that raged against the pain of loss and the dread of more loss. There were no ardent claims or chancy concessions. But there was goodness shared. There were long, wet kisses and reverent caresses. There were embraces too familiar to be anything less than loving. There were voluptuous sensations traded and enjoyed as they tasted each other intimately and pushed each other to the limits of pleasure and beyond.

And finally, after the last of the shock waves had drifted into the heat of the afternoon, there were tears to soothe raw places. Kiah could not remember the last tears he'd shed. They embarrassed him now, but he couldn't hold them back, even as he kissed hers away.

"It's a losing battle, I'm afraid," Cecily whispered as she swept her thumb across his damp cheek. "It's best to just let them come."

"Sounds good to me." He lowered his head next to hers,

drying his face on the silken hair that fanned across his pillow. "I let you come, you let me come, and it was the best, all right," he murmured, his lips close to her ear. "The best. The very best."

"I know what you mean, but I was talking about the tears."

"Yours?"

"And yours."

He rolled to his back, sprawling off to her side. "I ain't cryin', honey. Cowboys don't cry."

"Whatever you say." She rubbed her cheek against his shoulder. Replete with physical fulfillment, they lay side by side, cooling off gradually as the sweat evaporated from their skin.

"I'm going to miss her, too," she said, disturbing his lethargy. "I didn't want to face that trailer. I'll pack her things for you."

"For me?" He tucked his arm behind his head and stared at the curly outline of a water stain on the ceiling. "Hell, I don't want 'em. Anything you want, you can keep. The rest you can give away or burn."

"That's *your* job, isn't it? I mean—"

"I'll do it if you don't think you can"—he knew better, but he said it anyway—"find the time."

"I know that's the traditional way, and it's what she'd want done. I just don't know exactly what the . . . procedure is."

"The procedure is to say, 'Anybody want this stuff?'" He sighed, genuinely disgusted with himself.

But disgust didn't change his perspective. "I'm no expert on the *traditional way*," he confessed. "Put an ad in the paper. You work for the newspaper now, don't you?"

"I want to help out, Kiah. If that's what you want, I can certainly take care of that for you."

He wasn't sure what he wanted. When his mother had died, it had been easy to let Ellen decide. "She didn't have much, did she?"

"She didn't own a lot of *things*, but she had so much . . ." Cecily pressed her face against his shoulder.

"Oh, Kiah, she had so much heart and courage and . . . and you could just tell how hard she fought."

"The women always pay the highest price. It was that way in 'Nam. The women and kids got hit the hardest." He felt the catch in her breath, and he knew he'd made her cry again. He took her in his arms. "Shhh, it's okay. You'll be okay."

"I *am* okay," she insisted. She scooted close to him, as close as she could get. "Perfectly safe, perfectly okay. All because I . . . took off and . . . left her in that place with those . . ."

"Stop it, now," he said gently. He brushed her hair back and kissed her forehead. "There was nothing you could have done to change anything, Cecily." He dried her tears on the corner of the bedsheet. "Come on, now, I'll fix you something to eat. I'll show you what I can do with a can opener and a stove."

They dragged their jeans and T-shirts back on and picked over the pantry shelves, rejecting the ravioli. He made coffee, and she heated up some soup and made sandwiches from canned chicken. They were both ravenous by the time they sat down to eat.

"I'll help you get in touch with relatives if you want me to," Cecily offered as she sliced her sandwich in half with a table knife. "Are there many we should notify before her name hits the news?"

"A couple of calls to a couple of cousins will get the word out." He devoured half his sandwich before elaborating. "There were just the two of us. My mom had two miscarriages and one baby born dead. She named him Moses, after my stepfather. She couldn't have any more children after that. She probably had no business getting pregnant as many times as she did, with her diabetes, but who'd have the nerve to tell her that? She did things her way. Ellen was a lot like her." He watched her nibble at her food while she listened intently. "How about you? Do you have a big family?"

"Aunts and uncles, cousins I seldom see. I'm sort of a maverick. My family thinks I'm too much of an idealist, and they're not particularly impressed by what they call my crusader politics." She picked up a piece of chicken that had strayed from her sandwich and munched on it. "Ellen was the real crusader. I'm just a recorder. A witness, I guess."

"Like I said before, college girl, you've got your mission in life." He spared her a glance as he sized up the balance of his sandwich for another bite. "And it all sounds real noble."

"It's not noble. I'm too much of a coward to stick my neck out, the way Ellen did."

"You don't think you were stickin' your neck out when you drove those supplies down to Red Creek?"

"Like a turtle, maybe. I pulled it back in pretty fast when the authorities started hassling us."

"Ah, the turtle. The Lakota symbol of long life. When a baby's umbilical cord fell off, they used to sew it up in a beaded turtle and give it to him for luck."

The idea enchanted her. "Do you have one?"

"Used to. Don't know what happened to it." He shrugged. "I don't believe in that stuff." Nor did he dismiss it entirely. He picked up his soup spoon and turned it in his fingers, catching a ray of sunshine streaming over his shoulder through the window at his back. "I was kinda glad I had that locket, though, when I was in 'Nam. I had this crazy notion that I had to have it on me all the time or I'd get my head blown off. That's how superstitious you get when you're gettin' shot at on a regular basis."

"I say, whatever works."

"Very practical. I like that."

"Ellen said I was a romantic."

"I like that, too." He smiled wistfully. "And I like the way your eyes sparkle, and the way your hair turns gold when it catches the sun. You should've sent me your picture."

"You should have answered my letters."

There was a kind of assent, maybe even an apology in the way he lowered his gaze.

"What about family on your father's side?" she asked.

"I always liked to think of Moses Red Thunder as my father. When we were kids, when Ellen would get real mad at me she used to say, 'He's my dad, not yours.' She knew that would get a rise out of me." He took a bite of beef broth and noodles, then reached for a cracker. "My real dad was dead before I was old enough to know him. I guess you could say he self-destructed. Other than that, I don't know much about him. That's all past history, far as I'm concerned."

"Maybe, but I'm interested in 'past history,' " she said eagerly. "I think that's why I came out here in the first place. I loved working on that old church, hearing the stories people tell."

"People around here are great storytellers. Half of it's bullshit, you realize." She scowled at him, and he laughed. "You can't tell the difference, can you? You'd better figure it out before you start printing news articles full of bullshit."

"I'm learning fast, thank you very much." She helped herself to a saltine. "I've read a lot about the history of your people, but most of it was written from the non-Indian standpoint."

"The history of"—he paused for a sip of coffee, then tipped his head in deference—*"my people,* as you say, is pretty embarrassing."

"To *my* people, yes."

"To me." He set his cup down carefully and studied it for a moment. "Once when I was on R-and-R, I was mistaken for a Hawaiian, and I let it pass without setting the record straight. I don't like this 'Indian plight' thing. I don't like people feeling sorry for me."

He pushed his plate back abruptly, as though he were rejecting the crumbs that were left. "I don't like the way they just gave up. They had a treaty. They had the Black Hills; they had . . ."

He waved the rest of it away with a sharp flick of the hand. "I don't have much interest in fighting for Indian causes, the way Ellen did. Just another losing battle."

"I don't think it's the same," Cecily said.

"Same as what?"

"The same as the war we just lost."

"A loser's a loser, you ask me." He leaned back in his

chair. "I'm all done losing. I'm not asking for anything I
know I can't have, and I'm not putting my ass on the line
for any bunch of people who can't agree among themselves what side they're on. For every Indian who wants
the land back, there's another one who just wants his share
of the money."

"There are bound to be differences of opinion."

"Yeah, well, they've been bickering over it for fifty
years, and they'll bicker for another fifty." He lifted a single finger, then a second one. "A *hundred*. Hundred and
fifty. Do I hear two?" With a derisive chuckle, he shook
his head. "Hell, this is one cowboy who's not about to pin
his hopes on any pie in the sky."

Nor did he pin any hopes on the inquest into the cause
of his sister's death. The autopsy revealed that, although
the body was widely battered, the cause of death was
strangulation. There was no mention of any trace of semen
on the body. Several witness, Cecily reluctantly included,
testified that Ellen had resisted arrest. The arresting officers displayed their own bumps and scratches like battle
scars, allegedly inflicted by the deceased. Her death was
ruled a suicide.

Kiah didn't believe it, but he accepted the ruling with a
stoical sense of resignation since he could not prove otherwise. He wasn't sure what Ellen would have chosen to
have done with her body, short of raising her to the sun on
a scaffold. Since that was not a legal option, he decided to
have the body cremated, then to scatter the remains somewhere in the Black Hills. He chose Bear Butte, which was
a natural monolith that stood apart at the northern boundary of the Hills, and Cecily was the only person he invited
to share the journey there with him. They climbed the
steep path together. Along the way they noted the many
small scraps of red cloth that had been prayerfully tied to
tree branches by other Lakota visitors.

At the crest of this ancient holy place, a strong summer
breeze assisted Kiah in scattering Ellen's remains. It occurred to him that he should have brought some red cloth,

some tobacco, some sweetgrass—*something* to make this feel right.

Then from the primal part of his brain came a song. It started deep in his throat and rose to tickle his soft palate and force its way out through his nose. There was no holding it back. He'd never sung Indian before, but he'd heard enough of it over the years. There were words—he had no idea what they meant—and there was anguish and passion in the unleashing of a lament that had been dammed up within his chest too long. Endless sorrow echoed in the valley below. Not just his, but all humanity's.

Neither of them spoke as they made their way back down the hill. They stopped at a café in Sturgis and shared a quiet lunch. He was ready to eat his words about having nothing to do with traditional ways, but she made no mention of his bald-faced but totally involuntary display of traditionalism. He was grateful for her discretion. She had shed silent tears, and he didn't mention those either.

After lunch they took a drive through the Hills because she said she'd never seen them.

"This is it," he said as he negotiated the winding curves amid the craggy, pine-covered slopes. "This is the land all the fuss is about. They're kidding themselves, the ones who think we've got a prayer of ever getting it back. But it sure is beautiful."

"The parts that haven't been desecrated by pickaxes and billboards," she said. They'd just passed a mining area and a slope that had been clear-cut and terraced by bulldozers.

"Most of it's still pretty. It's where Ellen belongs. Maybe it's where I belong, too." He glanced at a roadside sign promoting a Deadwood casino. "I'll bet if you hauled all that commercial crap out of here, nature would take over, and it would look the way it once did in no time."

"Except for the presidents."

"Except for the presidents. Well, we'll let them stay. What do you think they'd say if they could see themselves carved in stone like that?"

"Pretty scary," she guessed. "I wouldn't want to see my face that big."

"I don't think Crazy Horse would want to be carved in stone, either. 'Course nobody knows what he looked like, so I imagine if he ever saw the statue they're chipping out of Crazy Horse Mountain, he'd get a good laugh when they told him that was supposed to be him."

"*If* they ever finish it."

"If they ever finish it," he conceded with a chuckle. "What a godawful thing to do to a perfectly good mountain. But you can't stop 'em, you know?" He gave a quick, harsh laugh. "We gave it a damn good shot at the Little Big Horn, which was all the excuse they needed to run right over us." He gave a clucking sound as he shook his head. "Gotta live with 'em; can't shoot 'em. When they do something really stupid, you just have to laugh."

"I'm assuming *they* includes me."

He slid her a dubious glance. "Are you workin' on a statue up here?" She shook her head. "Panning for gold? Painting signs that say, 'Only ten more miles to Sitting Bull Cave'?"

"None of the above."

"Then *they* doesn't include you," he said with a warm smile. "Congratulations."

It was late when Kiah parked his pickup next to her trailer. She invited him to come in, and he did. They took turns showering in the tiny trailer-house bathroom, shared a three-in-the-morning breakfast, and made maple syrup—flavored love in Cecily's bed. There was ample comfort for him there. There was soft-spoken solace from the woman who had trusted him in her innocence but still seemed to care for him. He regretted that he had cultivated so little goodness in himself to offer her in return. He could give her good and tender sex, but that was about all. And so, when he had suckled her breasts and touched her intimately until she cried out, "Love me, Kiah," he did so, but he could not *say* so. And when he had built the tempo of his thrusting nearly to the point of madness for her, she cried out again, "Oh, Kiah, love me."

He did. But he would not say so.

* * *

After he had tortured himself for a while with watching her sleep and thinking how easy she made it look, he went outside to have a cigarette. Leaning back against the trailer, he watched the false dawn lighten the jagged butte-edged horizon while he tested his immunity to a growing awareness of his own loneliness. In Cecily's bed he could surely find a hundred ways to delude himself, but there was no way this interlude was going to last any longer than it had the first time. He hadn't written to her for the same reason he wasn't manning a barricade down at Red Creek.

He was a realist.

Cecily loved waking up to the smell of coffee already in the making. Apparently Kiah liked his strong and early. The only problem was, he'd had to move to the kitchen to make it, which meant Cecily couldn't have her coffee and Kiah, too. She dragged herself out of bed, brushed her normally tame hair gone wild overnight, jumped into a pair of cutoffs and a T-shirt, and followed the aroma.

She discovered Kiah before she got to the coffee. He was kneeling beside the old steamer trunk that stood in the corner in Ellen's room. Sipping his coffee as he ran one hand over the brass fittings, he seemed intent on examining them for damage. His interest in the trunk was unsettling somehow. Unexpected and completely uncharacteristic. He didn't even look up when she stood beside him.

"I've boxed up Ellen's things," she said quietly, in lieu of *good morning*. It felt like the answer to an unspoken question, even though the cardboard box containing Ellen's property was a pale shadow of her own marvelous trunk. "If you want the box burned, I don't know if I can do that myself."

"Give it away, then. Like I've told you before, it's not that I'm superstitious about it. I'm just not very sentimental. Can't see keeping useless stuff around."

But he traced the carving in the trunk's leather covering as though he were reading a story in Braille. Then he realized that she was staring at him, and he pushed himself to his feet.

"I take it Ellen didn't have anything you wanted."

"I put a few special things aside. Some beadwork, a few pictures, things like that. I'll keep them for you if you like."

"Keep them for yourself. It's nothing I can use." He eyed the trunk. "I don't need any keepsakes to remember her by."

"No, I'm sure you don't." She slid her hand beneath her hair and lifted it off the back of her neck in a restless gesture. She wasn't sure why she felt as though she had some ground to defend. "That trunk is at least a hundred years old. It belonged to the lady of the locket."

"The lady of the locket, huh?" He gave her a slow-to-warm smile. "That just might make a good song title."

"Or maybe a poem." Cecily spared the trunk a melancholy glance. "I often wonder about her. The lady of the locket."

"What do you wonder?"

"Who she was. How her life turned out."

"She ended up dead," he pointed out matter-of-factly. "That's all there is to know."

" 'That is all ye know on earth, and all ye need to know,' " she recited, gratefully slipping into her scholarly comfort zone. "That *is* a poem. Keats. But he was talking about beauty and truth, not death."

"Death is the ultimate truth. I don't know about beauty."

"I disagree," she said as, like a pied piper, she led him away from her trunk and into the kitchen.

"That's because you're a romantic."

"So was Keats." She opened the utensil drawer. In her quest for a spoon, she shoved aside the jumble of letters she'd lately been dropping into the drawer. "I guess I'd better look at some of this mail that's been piling up since . . ." A particular envelope caught her eye. "I didn't see this."

"What is it?"

"It's from . . ." She took a table knife from the drawer, ripped into the envelope, and unfolded the letter.

"Oh." She reread the first sentence, just to make sure. "Oh, wow."

"Did you win the grand prize?"

"Al-*most!*" She beamed at him. "I was selected as an alternate for a terrific graduate program, and now they have a space for me. Immediately, it says."

"Congratulations are in order again."

"Well, I don't know." She glanced down at the letter, then looked up at him for a more definitive reaction. "I don't know what to do. Do you think I'd be leaving the newspaper in the lurch?"

"You've been here, what, a few weeks?" He shrugged. "I think they'll be able to muddle along."

"What about ..." He met her gaze, but his eyes betrayed nothing. No feelings. No wishes. Lord, how she wanted him to have wishes. She wanted him to ask her to stay. "Do you think I should accept?"

"I think it's up to you. Make hay while the sun shines. Can't tell you who said that—probably somebody on 'Hee Haw.' " He turned away. "Do what you want."

"It's only two years. It's like *the* best program for journalism."

"Sounds good to me."

"Kiah, tell me what you want." She grabbed his arm. He permitted her to turn him toward her. "Tell me how *you* feel."

"I don't want anything. I don't feel much of anything, either." The vacant look in his eyes was certain testimony. "So, you see, college girl? Truth isn't necessarily beautiful. And I think you should do what's best for you."

Cecily's throat burned as she stared at the letter in her hand. The words blurred a little. She turned her back on him so he wouldn't see the hurt she felt. Was it asking too much for him to utter one small word of regret at the prospect of seeing her go? Just *one*. She drew a deep breath, listening hard, willing him to imitate her gesture, to touch her and bid her turn around again.

But, damn him, he didn't.

He *didn't*.

She held a terrific opportunity right there in her hand, and, by God, she was going to take it.

Chapter 18

Dakota Territory, Spring 1876

Priscilla watched her footing carefully as she made her way down the steep hillside. Her head was still swimming from the climb. She had been gathering wild onions to flavor the soup she would make with the fresh meat her husband would bring home soon. It would not be buffalo, for none had been sighted in weeks, but when Whirlwind Rider went hunting, he always returned with food. And Priscilla always prepared their share, even though the aroma that bubbled up from the boiling pot sometimes forced her to excuse herself from the lodge.

Her weak stomach was such a bother these days. She had work to do, and she fully expected her body to function as any healthy woman's should. She was determined to push it, gently but firmly, until she had the situation completely under control. Her friend Red Sky Woman needed no help putting up *her* tipi, and she was further along than Priscilla was.

Whirlwind Rider was forever admonishing her to rest, but now that the long winter was over, she wanted to get out more. It was hard to keep up with the other women when they went gathering wild turnips and the tender spring bulbs of the sego lily and the wild onion, but her friends had shown her what to look for. They had taught her to leave every third plant in the ground so that the food would multiply again.

The breeze off the spring-fed lake below cooled her damp face. Her gathering apron tapped against one hip as she walked, and two empty buffalo-bladder water pouches swung freely from her shoulder. As she knelt by the water's edge, her little friend Brings Mouse popped out from behind a stand of red willow.

"I am watching for you," the young girl announced cheerfully. She claimed Priscilla's water bags and set about filling them. "I am to carry these for you, my uncle says. They are too heavy for you now."

"I won't put up a fight, Brings Mouse, thank you. I'm just a little"—she couldn't remember the exact word for *embarrassed*—"red in the face. My husband worries about me too much."

"That is as it should be. He is a Tokala. He watches out for the helpless ones."

"I'm not always this weak." She stood up carefully, fighting the black spots that clouded her vision.

"He has a special duty to you. While you carry his child, he pays close attention to your safety." With a girlish giggle, Brings Mouse adjusted the thong straps of the water bags over her shoulder. "Shall I tell you what he said about you?"

Priscilla smiled. Ten-year-old Brings Mouse was her teacher as well as her student and friend. "Do I want to know?"

"It's something funny. He says that your needs are special because you carry a good, strong Lakota child in the narrow little purse of a white woman's hips."

"There are many white women with hips wider than mine, and I'm sure mine are not the smallest, by far. I'm certain this has nothing to do with the problems I'm experiencing. I'm feeling very well today, actually."

Brings Mouse led the way along the path to the Minneconjou camp. "My uncle says this thing with a smile in his eyes," she reported. "I think he means your hips no disrespect. My grandmother does say that he babies you too much, but she thinks this is because of the one who died."

"His first wife. I have never heard her name." She knew that speaking it would be taboo. "Did she have small hips, too? Or did she seem better suited to this business of . . ."

"She was not as small as you are, but she was pretty. She came from the Hunkpapa people, and for a time my uncle stayed in their camp." Brings Mouse shrugged and glanced away. "Anyway, that one had the cough."

"Poor Rider. Now he has a wife who cannot keep her food down. I keep telling him it's just because this is my first baby. Sarah says it gets much easier after the first one."

Their lodge stood in a grove of cottonwoods, off by itself as though it were still occupied by newlyweds. Priscilla suspected that Whirlwind Rider kept them outside the perimeter of the camp circle so that people wouldn't notice how much of the woman's work he took upon himself. She insisted that she needed to practice erecting and dismantling the tipi so that she would eventually be able to do it as efficiently as the other women did, but since the day she'd explained that her frequent illness was due to her pregnancy, her husband had not permitted her to touch a lodgepole.

"Someone has gathered the wood already," Priscilla noted as they approached her tipi. "Did you do this for me, too, Brings Mouse?"

The girl shook her head quickly and pointed to the stout roan that was picketed on the far side of the lodge. As if on cue, Whirlwind Rider emerged from the door.

"You must have had good luck," Priscilla said to her husband. She noticed the white curl of smoke rising amid the tips of the lodgepoles. She wished she had been there to greet him when he came home. He had only been gone a short while, but her heart still pounded like a new bride's, and she knew she was blushing. "I'm glad you're back."

He took the water pouches from Brings Mouse, who giggled and scampered on her way.

"Your cheeks wear the kiss of the sun today," he said as

he led the way inside. "Or is this the flush of carrying things you are not supposed to carry?"

"All I'm carrying right now is a good, strong Lakota child. Am I not supposed to do that?"

"I'm not certain." He hung the water bags on their forked pole. "I don't know what usually happens when a Lakota plants his seed in the belly of a small white woman, so I'm not sure what you are supposed to do."

"Something wonderful happens." She took his hand and placed it on the barely discernible swell of her stomach. "I felt our baby moving inside me today."

"Good." His fingers stirred against her soft white elkskin dress. "That's good. Perhaps the bloom will linger in your cheeks now. When I saw you last, your face was the color of this dress, and your hands were trembling." She had tried not to wake him, but he'd known she had been sick again when she'd gone outside during the night. "It made me uneasy that you sent me away."

"It made *me* uneasy when you suggested changing your plans. I will not keep you from doing what *you* are supposed to do. But thank you for sending Clear Water Woman. She gave me some wonderful tea, and I do feel much better." She nodded toward the bulging water bags. "I really *can* carry my own water. You don't have to baby me, Rider. You have everyone thinking I'm made of glass."

"Like my signal mirror?" He pulled his shirt over his head and tossed it aside. "I dropped it once, and it broke. I have only a small bit of it left." He smiled as he untied his leggings. "I take very good care of that small piece. I wrap it in a scrap of rabbit fur. I 'baby' it."

"Clear Water Woman says that you baby me. She said this to Brings Mouse, much to my embarrassment."

"Who said it to you because no woman can keep such a thought to herself," he surmised as he tossed the leggings the way of his shirt and turned his attention to her belt fastenings. "I baby you, do I? What else do these female relations of mine say, hmm?" Her belt, along with the gathering apron stuffed with onions, joined the pile of castoffs.

"What if they saw us now?" He brushed her hair aside
and touched his lips to the curve of her sun-damp neck as
he pulled her shoulder tie loose. "Would they say that
Whirlwind Rider humbles himself before this new woman
of his? Would they guess that she fills his head so completely that he actually let a buck get away from him this
morning?"

She tipped her head back and loosed a throaty giggle.
"Oh, no, did you?"

"If I were a boy, they would have given me a foolish
one's name today." He smiled, and the mischief-light
danced in his dark eyes. "But I am not a boy. Luckily, few
dare to mock me." Still smiling, he shook his head. "Except LaPointe."

"Was he with you today?"

"He was." With three appreciative fingers he touched
the shoulder he'd just bared as he recalled the morning's
expedition. "The grin on his face was not quite so big after I chased an antelope down. He tried it himself with the
next one we saw, but his agency loafing has made him too
slow."

"You ran an antelope down *on foot?*"

"It cannot be done on an open flat. I can run like an antelope only for a short distance. I ran him into a trap." He
showed her with his hand, using her shoulder as the trail,
her neck as the natural wall. "Steep cliffs. He could not
get away."

He loosened the other shoulder tie and slid his hands
down her slender arms, pushing her dress to the floor. She
stepped out of it as he lowered her to their sleeping pallet.

"I had no idea you could run as fast as an antelope. I'm
surprised I was able to catch you."

"I think you used my own hunting tricks against me. I
rushed headlong into your canyon." He lifted his brow appreciatively as he ran one hand between her thighs. "And
I found a beautiful place. I think it must be like the place
where you say your god lives."

"Heaven?" His long hair fell over her face like a bright
black curtain. She smiled at him as she reached up to tuck
it back behind his shoulder. "The way you put it makes for

a very awkward"—she caught her breath as his thumb reached its destination in the cove of her legs—"oh, but a very poetic comparison."

"One does not wish to leave such a place. Not even for a little while." He drove his fingertips into the crisp hair that covered her woman's mound. His eyes devoured the sweetness he saw in hers. "You are the hunter of my heart, *wigopa.*"

"Where is your heart?" she teased, boldly exploring his hip and thigh. She knew her way around him, too. His breechclout allowed her small hand easy access, especially when he moved his legs apart to invite intimate pursuit of the part of him that she would make her plaything.

She smiled as she claimed it. "Is this it? I know this is the part that keeps running headlong into my canyon."

"It is the part that fits the best. It gives the rest of me transport to the place where my heart now lives." He lowered his face to the shallow vale between her breasts and drew a line with the tip of his nose. "This is why I must taste you and touch you and breathe you. I am part of you now."

"And I am part of you as well. I want always to be part of you. That way I can be all the things I'm not." She stroked him, making him longer and harder, making his eyes burn holes in hers. Her smile was triumphant. "Strong as a bull. Cunning as a fox. Quick as an antelope."

"Mmm, rest in me, then, and I will be all those things for you, and more. My power is small next to this power of yours to nurture my heart." He slipped his hand over her belly. "And *this* power . . . to quicken my seed."

"God does that."

"Yes, but He does it in you, not me. Through you I will live in my children's children."

"It doesn't matter anymore that I'm not . . . a Lakota woman?"

"All that matters is that you are *my* woman, and this is our child." He nuzzled her breast, took her nipple between his lips, and tongued the tip into a hard bead. "Sweet and tender," he murmured.

"More tender than sweet." She closed her eyes, willing the urgent tension to squeeze out the pain, and he groaned softly as he drew away. It wasn't what she wanted, and she told him so by stroking him the way she wanted to be stroked. "Don't stop," she whispered. "I love being kissed by a man who can run as fast as an antelope."

"A hungry man"—he slid lower—"does what he has to do"—and rubbed his cheek over her belly before he nipped the hard point of her hipbone—"for the taste of something sweet."

"Even chase a train?"

"If it carries what he wants." He held what he wanted between his two hands. Her pale thighs, her slight hips, her wonderful female secrets. "No train will take you from me again."

"No. Never again."

The small fire at the center of their circular home burned down to soft-glowing coals while Whirlwind Rider made love to his wife. He went slowly with her, employing his patience and cunning to the fullest to make her pleasure last. He knew how bad she was feeling most of the time these days, and he wanted to make her feel good. He wanted to hear her whisper his name as though he were a deity who made miracles. To that end he touched her with deft fingers and enticing tongue until his name became her litany. She came to climax delicately for him, time after time, quivering beneath him like a small, frightened animal.

When he could no longer hold himself apart from her, he moved beneath her and sat her astride him, positioning her carefully, inviting her to impale herself on him carefully and ride cautiously and take him only as deeply as her need required.

She required all of him. She required his well-oiled rhythm, his shuddering pleasure, and his warm, wet release. She came harder this time, crying out in exquisite misery. She swore he'd not hurt her, but he wasn't sure he believed her. He held her in his arms for a long time, stroking her the way he would a colt who had smelled the blood of the hunt for the first time.

Ah, how unbearable it was for a man to love a woman this much and to feel completely powerless in the face of the mysteries that troubled her.

"If there were to be no children in our life, I would not love you less, *wiǧopa.*"

"But there will be." She lifted her head from his chest and looked into his eyes. "Don't scare me that way, Rider. We have a child on the way."

"I know." He slipped his hand between them to feel her belly again. "I am trying to watch out for both of you. A man knows little about these matters until the woman who carries his child lies with him in his blankets. It's good to know that the child moves." He paused, then added gently, "Because I also know that there has been blood."

Instantly her face turned pink. She buried it against his neck. "Just a little," she confessed, "and none for a long time now."

"And you have pain."

"Not often," she said too quickly. He touched his lips to her shoulder and forgave her lie with a kiss. "Not too often," she amended softly.

He closed his eyes, and his lips lingered close to her skin. "I have never known such great joy or such terrible fear. For this I have taken a vow to dance gazing at the sun."

"I shall be there to sing for you."

"I will rely on you to sing for me." He lifted her chin and made her look at him. "I want you to give me a song to take with me to the Powder River country, and while I am there, I want you to make prayers for me." He put his finger to her lips before she could object. "No, now, you must obey your husband in this matter, *wiǧopa.* You must stay with my sister. You cannot make this journey."

"But someone from the agency might discover me."

"LaPointe will keep you safe. After the Sun Dance celebration, I will come for you. When you are able to travel, we will join the buffalo hunt."

She tightened her arm around his middle, and he saw the fear in her eyes. "Rider, the soldiers have been tramping over Lakota land ever since they declared the northern bands hostile last winter. They are determined to make war on those who do not stay near the agencies."

"We knew this from the beginning, you and I."

"Yes," she said fiercely. "And knowing this, I want to be with you."

"You will always be with me, *mitawin.*" His love for her brightened his dark eyes. He brushed her hair back from her face. "My wife. It is no longer any secret that your voice carries a great distance. The love words you whispered in my ear last night still filled my head this morning."

"Let me go with you and whisper to you every night."

"After the child is born and you are strong again, you will learn to make meat. You will see that your husband is too much hunter for one woman, and you will plead with me to bring a second wife to our lodge to help you with the work."

She rewarded his teasing with a frown. "This is a dream you've had lately?"

"Even after the poor tail-tiers claim their share from my kill, there will be hides and meat"—he lifted her hair in an expansive gesture—"more than *two* wives can handle, and I might have to take a *third* . . . ooof!" Her small fist against his hard middle put an end to his boasting. He laughed. "I see that one woman is trouble enough."

"I don't mean to be trouble for you, Rider." She lowered her eyes and her voice. "If I'm not strong enough, or"—he was spared a brief glance—"pretty enough . . ."

"Ah, now you pout. This is a sure way to coax a man to kiss you any way you wish to be kissed," he said, touching his lips to her fingers before planting a soft kiss in the center of her palm. "And to make him tell you that you grow prettier in his eyes with each day that passes."

"If I'm not with you, I won't. The pretty women will be those close at hand."

"Is this the kind of man you have taken for a husband?"

"No." She touched his cheek, then outlined his angular jaw with one finger. "Truly, I have married the most honorable man I have ever known." To his knowing smile, she replied, "Admittedly, my experience is limited, but I have *observed* a variety of men, and ... Oh, Rider, I want to be with you, no matter what happens."

He turned his face slightly, closing his eyes.

"Rider?"

"No matter what happens," he echoed.

"I'm afraid that if you leave me ... if we're not together ..." It was her turn to bring his face around with a persistent hand. "I know it must sound foolish to you, that I'm afraid to be separated from you, even for a short time."

"A man has his fears, too. Does that sound foolish to you?" She stared into his eyes. "A man must provide for his family. He must protect the ones he loves. His deepest fear is that he will fail when the test comes." He glanced away. "Loving me may yet bring you harm, *wigopa*. That is my fear."

"Lay your fears to rest," she said as she laid her head on his shoulder and snuggled into his arms again. "I was born to the task of loving you. I intend to do it very well for many, many years to come."

His hand strayed to the soft swell of her belly. "My love for you has brought you this."

"Yes. Thank you."

"How do you thank me for pain?"

"Shhh." She reassured him with a hug. "We'll be fine. I just want you to be here when the baby comes. That's all."

"I want to help you with this. If I stay, all I can do is walk the soles off my moccasins while the women make the medicine only women can make." His hand stirred over her affectionately. "I have done all a man can do. I have made my vow to dance standing tied, with two thongs attached to my back and two in my chest—"

"Oh, Rider—"

"No, this is nothing." He pressed his lips to her forehead, hoping to kiss away her concerns. "Nothing like bearing a child. It is only a small piece of my body, but I will offer it with my whole heart."

And he would offer it in a faraway place. When the Minneconjou struck camp and headed west, Whirlwind

Rider went with them. He did not tell his wife that he knew the Lakota would have to fight their way to the summer gathering place in the Powder River country to the north and west of Paha Sapa. General Crook, whom the Lakota called Three Stars, had been hounding the people all winter, and now he was camped with his soldiers in the midst of Lakota territory.

Crazy Horse advised against attacking the soldiers in their camp, but it was well-known that sooner or later the soldiers would come in force against the people, and then there would be fighting. The Minneconjou, the Hunkpapa, and Crazy Horse's Oglala followers expected this. Some of the restless young men from the agency camps—from Spotted Tail's Brule and from Red Cloud's Oglala—had even joined the so-called hostiles.

When they converged on the Rosebud River, they formed an impressive camp. They were met by a few of their Cheyenne allies, the followers of Two Moons and Old Bear. The camp moved upriver, seeking fresh grass for the huge pony herds. They made a Sun Dance, and Sitting Bull of the Hunkpapa had a vision of many soldiers falling into camp. The soldiers he saw were dead, and they were without ears, for it was well-known that white men never used them anyway.

So be it, Whirlwind Rider decided. When they came, he would fight. He danced standing tied, in keeping with his vow, but his prayers were not for victory over the soldiers. He sang, as he always did, asking that his people might live. But he prayed fervently that Wakan Tanka might watch over his wife as she bore his child. He danced until he had to fight to stay on his feet. The more acute the pain, the closer he felt to Priscilla. He imagined easing her pain by prolonging his, by tugging constantly at his bonds to intensify the pain and by bearing it with all the honor she had attributed to him.

Not long after the Sun Dance, Whirlwind Rider followed Crazy Horse into battle against Three Stars. After a long fight, the Lakota left the battlefield to Crook's bleeding troops and headed west, toward the Valley of the Greasy Grass along the Little Big Horn River.

When word of the fighting reached the little camp on the White River, Priscilla, who was a closely guarded secret in Henry LaPointe's household, was not told. There were rumors of a victory over the soldiers, first on the Rosebud, then on the hills overlooking the Little Big Horn, but no one knew which Lakota warriors might have fallen. There was much buzzing among the friendlies who camped closer to the agency, stories that the yellow-haired Custer, notorious for his attack on a peaceful Lakota village on the Washita River, had found the women and children guarded by warriors this time. Ah, then he must have been disappointed when his plans to put more babies to the sword were hindered by fighting men. Crazy Horse was more than a match for any cowardly woman-killer.

Hopo! the old men said, recalling their own past victories. There were still Lakota warriors to be reckoned with.

Henry LaPointe regretted that he had not been there to fight beside his brother-friend. Three Stars Crook had put out the word that the army was looking for Indian scouts. Traders' sons, like himself, were always the first to be recruited. They were only half Indian. They spoke English, and they "knew the score." Anyone who volunteered would be given a uniform with stripes, pay-money, and extra annuities for his family.

It was hard to turn down the annuities. LaPointe knew the score, all right. These were hungry times. He had the look of an Indian, but inside he was also the son of a white trader. He knew the value of the goods being offered, and he knew that they would become even scarcer now that the negotiations over the land had ceased. He knew what was coming. He knew who would get the land. But he could not turn himself inside out and ride against his mother's people, so he stayed away from the fort and avoided the call for volunteers.

Entrusted with the duty of watching out for his best friend's wife, all he could do now was huddle in his cabin and wait. Wait, watch, and listen to the terrible sound of a woman in agony. LaPointe longed to follow the same path the children had taken hours ago to his cousin Brown Wolf's lodge, but instead he added more wood to the stove

and boiled more water for medicinal tea. He knew that
Priscilla's labor had already lasted much too long and that
the women were worried. But he was only a man, and
there was little he could do. It was his duty to stand in for
Whirlwind Rider, to keep watch over the women who
were making women's medicine.

Three trade blankets had been hung from the sod-roofed
cabin's rafters. Behind their curtain, Sarah LaPointe and
Clear Water Woman tended Priscilla through her labor. It
was a rainy July afternoon, and the occasional drops that
blew in through the open window felt good on Priscilla's
face. The breeze lightened the cloying scent of Clear Water Woman's sweetgrass smoke, and the nausea drifted
away. Priscilla was certain now that her child did not
want to be born. She could tell by the restraint written in
the eyes of her two attendants that this was turning into
the kind of childbirth every woman feared. She knew that
she was fighting for her life.

Between contractions she tried to focus her thoughts on
her husband. She recalled his stamina during the first Sun
Dance she had witnessed in what now seemed a very distant past, a time when she had known so much and understood so little. She imagined him pushing himself now
through another step, another step, another step. She understood. One step at a time. This was how it was done.
This was how one endured. The pain was nothing. It
would be gone tomorrow. The blood would replenish itself. The flesh would heal. Whirlwind Rider would come
back, and she would be waiting for him.

Another step. Another step. Another step.

Journal Entry, July 1876

*My little boy never drew breath, and there has been
no word from my husband. I cannot think that I have
lost him, though. He is Tokala, the Fox. He is swift
and clever, difficult to catch. We have heard that after
the battle, the camp broke up into smaller bands, and
now the people are on the move, hounded by army*

troops. I must regain my strength, so that when I join him, I will not be a burden.

Journal Entry, August 1876

Henry LaPointe has spoken to some of the agency Indians who were with Crazy Horse and Sitting Bull at the Little Big Horn. Some of these "friendlies" have been trickling back from the Powder River country, tired of the circuitous chase with the soldiers. I am assured now that my husband is safe. He follows Crazy Horse, who has given refuge to many families who have suffered in their skirmishes with the troops.

I keep hoping that Whirlwind Rider will appear at the cabin door, but Henry reminds me that Crazy Horse needs the akicita now more than ever, especially the Tokala, whose job is to protect the helpless ones. He promises that he will take me to my husband as soon as he can, for I refuse to spend the winter apart from him.

Henry also tells me that my father has been replaced by a new agent. Henry and two of his friends quietly appropriated my trunk from the household goods that were waiting to be shipped back to Minnesota. It was a kind gesture—he thought that the return of some of my possessions might cheer me—but most of the goods seem alien and frivolous to me now. As I convalesce, I am learning to apply a beaded design to the yoke of the buckskin dress that my extraordinary husband so patiently helped me to make last winter. (How I do miss him now!)

There were a few books in the trunk, along with some of my father's old tracts. I only wish I had more schoolbooks. There is more talk of new agreements over the Black Hills. The agency Indians are as hardpressed by soldiers and negotiators as the northern bands are by columns of troops. I am neither fighter nor missionary, and I may never achieve motherhood. But I am a teacher. There is something I can do. I intend to remain inconspicuous for now and hope that the unrest will somehow be resolved without more bloodshed. Then, wherever my husband and his people are, there I shall be, and there will my portable school be, also.

Journal Entry, September 1876

The northern bands' refusal to come into the agencies gave the army the excuse it needed to mount its campaign over the last several months. Custer's defeat has apparently turned the campaign into a quest for revenge. Henry says that some of the young men at the agency have been urging the others to seize what weapons they can and join the northern bands, but the few headmen whom the army recognizes as chiefs have said the effort would be futile.

It was these few, including Red Cloud and Spotted Tail, who met with another commission from Washington. I cannot help but think that if my father were still here, he might have stood with Bishop Whipple, who is a member of the commission. The bishop denounced the army's war against the Sioux, but still he advised the chiefs to sign the agreement, promising that the "friends of the Indian" would see that protection and care would be provided for the people.

The agency chiefs pointed out that most of the Lakota were not present at the council. They said that no agreement could be made in behalf of those who were not there. But the commissioners said that the northern bands no longer have any say in the negotiations. They have been officially declared hostile. When the chiefs would not sign any papers, they were offered a little whiskey under the table. The commission threatened to remove all the Sioux bands to the Indian Territory in the south unless they agreed to sign the papers. The chiefs, LaPointe said, responded with wonderful, defiant speeches.

Then the doors of the stockade were locked. The chiefs were told that if they did not sign the papers *relinquishing the Black Hills, the Lakota children would not eat. In the end this was the threat that broke them. The helpless ones could not be left to starve.*

In November, the Moon of Falling Leaves, LaPointe took Priscilla to Bear Butte country, just to the north of Paha Sapa. As they rode into Crazy Horse's camp, she felt that she was coming home. She saw many familiar faces. When at last she saw the face of the man she had come home to, she wept for joy. Wordlessly he reached for her. She slid from her horse and into his arms, and he made a deep, gratified groan as he enfolded her within his wearing robe. In full view of the entire camp he closed his eyes, rubbed his face against hers, and eagerly filled his lungs with deep breaths saturated with the scent of her.

"You feel thinner," she said, clasping her arms around his waist.

"I have been fasting." He leaned back so that he could see her face. "I have stopped thinking of food. I need very little these days."

"I see that you still have your shirt." She smiled as she slipped her hands beneath it, spreading them over his tapered back. "Are there new scars?"

"Only from the piercing. I think this shirt you made must protect me in battle. The bullets have been missing their mark."

"I thank Tunkaśila for that."

He searched her eyes. "Are you all right, *wiĝopa?*"

She nodded. Her lower lip trembled as she studied the fox she had painted so long ago. "I lost our baby."

"*We* lost a child. I know." He waited until she looked into his eyes again, and he allowed her to see the depths of his sadness in them. "My heart aches with yours, *mitawin.* I know what a difficult time you had. You are well now?"

"Yes."

"Then I thank Tunkaśila. It is for this that I have danced and fasted and prayed. With every breath I take, I ask that once you are well, Tunkaśila will keep you safe." He ugged her close again. "But now here you are, and this s not a safe place."

"You're here." And that was enough for her.

But it was not enough for him. This was a poor camp full of hungry people, who would grow hungrier before the winter was over. If his wife were the only one he had to feed, he could do that, but he was a Tokala. He had many mouths to feed.

"We have heard that the agency chiefs have signed more papers," he said. "When the soldiers catch up with us, they will claim that we are walking on *their* land now."

"Yes, I believe they will say that."

It was not true. He wanted his wife to know this. "We fought well on the Greasy Grass. We kept the soldiers from harming the helpless ones."

"I know," she whispered. "We heard about the victory."

"But since that day, there has been nothing but trouble. No time to hunt and make meat. There is little food set aside for winter." It had been too long since he'd held her, but even as he cherished her in his embrace, he felt obliged to make the terrible appeal that might keep her safe. "I want you to go back to the agency, *wigopa*. Go back to your father."

"My father has already gone back to Minnesota."

"Follow him," he insisted, but his arms would not open, and the words brought him a sick feeling.

"I am not a little girl anymore. I am a woman, and a woman belongs with her husband. I shall follow you."

His heart soared, but in his gut he felt as though he had swallowed a stone. "My people have lost their home. I have no place to take you."

"Then we shall stay here. Whatever happens, Rider, we are one flesh."

"How can this be?" He leaned back, letting his robe fall about his shoulders as he laced his dark fingers with her pale ones and studied them together. "How can two so different be part of each other this way?"

"We had a child." She squeezed his hand and fought to keep her voice steady. "If only I had been a little stronger. If I had just had—"

"You are my strength, *mitawin*." He brought her hand to his lips. When she lifted her eyes to his, he whispered, "You have a woman's courage for living. A man seeks his vision of life, but a woman carries it with her from birth." He caught the tear that fell from the corner of her eyes with his thumb. "Do you envision a life with me, Priscilla?"

"Yes, I do."

"The only life I have ever known . . ." Again he pulled her close against his chest. "What is it like, this life you envision?"

"It's unlike any life either of us has known." She drew a deep, unsteady breath and sighed. "Your world will never be the same again, Rider. And I'm never going back to mine. I guess we'll have to make a new one somehow."

"If it were just the two of us, I would know how."

"You'll know how." She looked up at him, smiling through her tears. "From the first moment I saw you, I knew you would change my life. I have much to learn, maybe a few things to teach, and someday I want to have another child. Your child."

"I want to give you another child, *wiǧopa*. I would not leave you with a fatherless Lakota child, but if the soldiers don't kill me, I want to—"

He shook his head before she could refute the truth he wanted her to face. "They will come for us. There is the chance that they will keep shooting until we are all . . ." He touched her cheek. "And there is the chance that they will not see that you are one of them."

"I am not one of them," she said. "I am your wife. That's who I am."

"But there is the *chance* that—"

"There are all kinds of chances. I love you, Rider. That's all I know for certain." She adjusted his wearing robe on his shoulders. "Do you have a place for us to sleep? I want you to plant another seed."

It was a great relief to laugh after such a long time of having nothing to laugh about. But now she would lighten his heart, this wife of his. "You will try to make a farmer of me, woman?"

"I will try to make a *father* of you. That is my woman's vision. Are you up to the challenge?"

"I think you know the answer to that, *wiǧopa*." He tucked her under his arm and nodded toward a lodge that stood by itself against the reddening autumn sky. "I am up to the challenge of loving you, and that much will never change."

Part III

Amid the rising smoke, my grandfather's footprints
I see, as from place to place I wander,
The rising smoke I see as I wander.
Amid all forms visible, the rising smoke
I see as I move from place to place.

—OSAGE SONG

Chapter 19

North Dakota, July 1980

The six-thirty flight from Minneapolis was late. Kiah Red Thunder had neither the time nor the patience to be cooling his heels at the Bismarck airport. He hadn't thought about Cecily Metcalf much lately, not until she'd called him about doing a story on the Supreme Court's startling decision regarding the everlasting legal battle over the Black Hills. Hearing her voice over the phone had stirred up a whole legion of ghosts he thought he'd laid to rest, and he'd already begun to regret his initial willingness to cooperate with her plan.

She hadn't asked him to pick her up at the airport. He'd *offered*. But the minute he'd hung up the phone, he'd wanted to kick himself. He could just imagine her telling some newspaper editor that she'd once known this guy who might be a good contact for a story about the Indians' Black Hills claim.

She had known him well, and more than once in the proverbial "biblical sense," but she wouldn't have gone into detail with her boss. Not Cecily. She had done her homework before she called, too. She knew that he was on the Tribal Council now. To her credit, she hadn't mentioned his former aversion to Indian politics. Neither had she bombarded him with questions of any kind over the phone. She had asked him for an interview, and that was all.

The smartest thing for a tribal councilman to do these days was to avoid the press. The Supreme Court had just handed down its judgment on the Sioux Nation's long-standing suit, affirming the Court of Claims ruling that the U.S. government had taken the Black Hills illegally back in 1877 and awarding the Sioux $106 million in damages. Now everybody and his brother suddenly had an opinion on the matter. The attorneys, of course, were claiming that they had performed a minor miracle for the greater good of the Sioux Nation. It was a victory for the lawyers, no doubt about that. They had triumphed against the U.S. government before the highest court in the land, and they themselves were now multimillionaires.

But the Lakota were still a poor people. And they were, as they had been for a hundred years, mystified by the strange workings of the government. Indians had become U.S. citizens in the 1920s, and the federal government had overseen the organizing of tribal governments in the 1930s. Over the years there had been many suits and a few settlements. There was "pony money," paid out not to the people who had gone hungry because their horses had been confiscated way back when, but to their grandchildren and great-grandchildren. There was the "six-fifty" payment per tribal member for land flooded when the Corps of Engineers had dammed up the river. There had been an attempt to terminate the reservations back in the fifties. Then there was the Indian Civil Rights Act back in the sixties. One policy flip-flop after another had been declared "for the good of the Indian."

It seemed that every time the government changed a policy, there were lawyers on the spot telling the Lakota leaders that they'd have some money coming if they took *this thing* to court. Often *this thing* amounted to a windfall for the lawyers, the used-car salesmen, and the liquor stores. Sometimes the tribe's share was divided among its members. Other times they'd used it to set up programs that were supposed to benefit the people. But no matter how the money was used, it never changed anything.

This time the *thing* at issue was the Black Hills. It was the ultimate claim, the most basic of disputes. It was a question of the intrinsic values of two nations. The federal government was offering the Lakota a final once-and-for-all cash settlement.

"*Tóksa,* Black Hills," was the old Sioux joke, the answer you gave somebody when you owed him money. "Pretty soon, Black Hills." But now the money had actually been offered. A lot of it. Some people were saying, "Take the money. They've already taken the Hills." Others, especially the more traditional people, recalled Crazy Horse's answer the first time money had been offered. "One does not sell the land on which the people walk." Accepting the money, it seemed, would be tantamount to accepting a hundred-year-old theft as a sale. Or sellout, depending upon your point of view.

Not a day went by that Kiah didn't think about resigning from the council. It was a no-win situation. Dealing with dissatisfied Indians was bad enough. Talking to the mainstream press—most of whom didn't know a Lakota Sioux from Tonto—was even worse. But here he was, slouched down in one of a long row of hooked-together chairs—the single brown face in a sea of white ones—watching for something to fall out of the big summer sky. And he was actually waiting for a *reporter.*

Are you going to take the money? That was always the first of their "penetrating" questions. They didn't really want answers; they wanted an angle. If you said yes, they wanted to know how you could call yourself an Indian leader. Wasn't that like selling Mother Earth? If you said no, they wanted to know how you could call yourself an Indian leader. Wasn't that like taking food out of the mouths of Indian children?

As Kiah understood it, the land wasn't being offered. It was more like, Here's the money we think we've owed you since the last century, plus interest. So now we're even. A hundred million can buy you guys a lot of used cars.

That was the kicker. The next question was always, If you take the money, what are you going to do with it? *May I make a suggestion?*

Fire away, he'd say. Better yet, write it up, and I'll add it to the file. It was amazing how many ways people could think of to save the Indians. For a small fee.

Tȯkśa, Black Hills.

From the air, the towns in North Dakota looked like small irregularities in the pattern of a giant yellow-green-tan quilt. Cecily hated heights. The only time she ever looked down was from the safe vantage of an airplane window. She imagined that this was how God saw the earth, zeroing in like a plane making its descent. From this perspective, Bismarck's most striking feature wasn't the network of streets or the mall or the state's single skyscraper. It was the lazy curve of the Missouri River. From a distance it was clear that the town was just a dot on the plains, but the mighty river had no visible end. It dominated the landscape like a vital cord, pulling the quilt together.

From a distance it was easy to put things into proper perspective. But when the plane was on the ground and Cecily's feet touched North Dakota real estate, the big picture narrowed. She stepped out of the jetway, and for an instant the forest only had one tall, slim tree, wearing a straw cowboy hat and a cocky smile. She would have greeted Kiah with a hug, but he offered her a more discreet handshake.

"Good to see you," he said, and she responded in kind. "So, did you finish school yet?" He made it sound as though she'd been tying up the bathroom while he'd been waiting to take a shower.

"For the time being." She'd forgotten how unsettling it was to look straight into his dark eyes, but she wasn't going to let him rattle her. She smiled pleasantly. "I can always find an excuse to go back to school and take another course or two. A person can always use more education."

"Sounds about right." The crowd was headed for the baggage-claim area, and they were moving with the flow. "If you need an excuse, you go off to school. Whenever you want more *education,* you know where to come for that." He nodded toward the observation window, which overlooked blacktop runway, a few green trees, and a lot of prairie. "Welcome back to the school of reality, Cecily Metcalf. You did say it was still Metcalf, right? You're not one of those feminists who sticks with her maiden name?"

"I'm not married."

"Neither am I." He offered her a nettling glance. "In case you were wondering."

"You notice, I didn't *ask*."

"You didn't have to, newspaper lady. I can read your face just like a book." He let her go ahead of him, her pumps clicking, his cowboy boots clopping on the stairs. "Always could," he muttered above her head.

"Okay, time out." She adjusted her purse strap with one hand and tugged on his arm with the other, retreating from the baggage-claim procession. "I'll make a deal with you. I'm here to get the facts. I won't jump to any conclusions if you won't."

He laughed. "Indians don't jump to conclusions. That's fact number one."

"But you just did."

"I made an observation," he said. "A conclusion isn't that easy to come by. We're not even sure that such a thing exists. You hungry?"

"I turned down the mystery meat they were serving on the plane."

"Good." They were on their way again, trailing the crowd down the sunny corridor. "You're about to get a little fat to chew on for your story. You're not gonna take any notes or ask any questions," he cautioned. "You just listen in, okay?" He jammed his hands in the front pockets of his jeans as he slowed to a halt on the periphery of the luggage-toting crowd. "I'm taking a gamble on you, Cecily Metcalf."

"Oh, really?" Now that he'd established her marital status and the state of her appetite, it was nice of him not to consider her a sure thing.

"Yeah, really. I'm hoping you're the hotshot newspaper lady you claim to be, syndicated and all that."

"I am." At least, she'd made a good start. She was still trying to make her mark.

"And I'm betting the honesty's still there. You were idealistic, but you were always honest."

"I was also naive." She looked him straight in the eye. *Honest and then some.* "I'm older and wiser now."

"That doesn't scare me." He gave her that lopsided smile she'd always found alluring. "In fact, I'm countin' on that, too."

"Good. Older and wiser inevitably command respect." She countered with a foxy smile of her own. "So where does the fat come in?"

"We're gonna meet a couple of crafty businessmen for supper. Chew the fat, you know? A lawyer and some friend of his. I don't know what kind of song-and-dance they've got planned, but the kinds of shows I've been treated to lately have been pretty entertaining. You'd think I'd just won the sweepstakes or something." He glanced at the crowd around the luggage carousel, which was thinning out. "Trick is to take it all in with a few grains of salt."

Kiah seldom made any apologies for being late. If he was supposed to be somewhere, he'd get there eventually. People either waited or they didn't. He knew that the two businessmen he'd promised to meet at the Townhouse Restaurant would wait. For the privilege of buying him supper and bending his ear, they would have waited in the bar until closing. Of late the smell of money around tribal councilmen had upped Kiah's social rating considerably.

Paul Weeks was one of the attorneys who had devoted much time and effort to representing the Sioux in federal courts. He was a small man with a bald head, a shiny red face, and a quick smile. He signaled the hostess that his party had arrived as he introduced his lean, hungry-looking friend, Tom Meecham, who hailed from the Twin Cities. Weeks was a take-charge kind of guy.

Kiah introduced Cecily simply as his friend. He could tell that Weeks expected something more, but he wasn't getting it with Kiah's introduction. It often amused him to watch people ferret out information for themselves, and he was curious to see how Cecily was going to respond to the predictable conversation they had in store with these two.

But it was Tom Meecham who turned the charm on Cecily, establishing that she, too, had flown in from the cities, that they both lived in the suburbs, and that she hadn't been following the Twins this year because she wasn't much of a baseball fan. Kiah admired Cecily's cool reserve. She was more confident than he remembered, more poised, certainly more mature. Maybe even more beautiful, if that were possible. He hoped she hadn't changed too much. He'd always thought she was classy, even when she was just a kid, but it was a natural kind of class. He hoped she hadn't lost that, even though, right now, that polite, polished reserve looked great on her. He liked the way ol' Meecham wasn't getting anywhere.

"Just what is it you do, Tom?" Kiah interjected as the menus were handed out. "You wrote a book, didn't you?"

"I wrote a little thing called *How to Get Your Fair Share*. Sort of a handbook for the man who wants to be on the cutting edge. Man or *woman,*" he amended with a quick glance at Cecily. "I added a special chapter for women in the second revised edition. The book is doing very well. New decade, new cutting edge."

"Tom's an entrepreneur," Weeks explained.

"Entrepreneur," Kiah echoed, dragging out each syllable as if he were pulling the word apart to air it out. "Does that mean you like to go around starting things?"

Meecham gave an arrogant chuckle. "I'll start anything but trouble, Kiah."

"It's always good to set some kind of limit."

"Well, the sky's the limit for the enterprising man." With ravenous eyes Meecham spared Cecily another glance over the corner of the menu. "Or woman."

"That's kinda what Paul's been saying about the Black Hills claim. The sky's the limit." Smiling, Kiah set his menu aside. "So now we know. You hit a hundred and six million dollars, you've reached the sky, right? That's the limit."

"You know as well as I do what we're about to have on our plates here, Kiah." Weeks folded his hands as though he were about to pray over the salt and pepper. "This is an award for damages, and it's a handsome sum. It opens up all kinds of possibilities for economic development on the reservations." He nodded absently to the waitress offering water. "This is what we've been fighting for, man. This court battle has been going on for sixty years, and we've finally won. This is a great victory for your people."

"A lot of them don't see it that way," Kiah said. "Of course, some of them do. Some of them say, 'Fine, give me my share,' like Tom's book. But some of the people don't want the money, and they never did."

"You're a reasonable man, Kiah. You know you're never going to get the Hills back. That's just not feasible. Besides, a lot of it's parkland. Everybody has access to it, you know, and that's the American way. You can go up there and camp or, you know, do what"—his quick gesture over the middle of the table made the candle flame bob briefly—"whatever your people like to do there. Commune with Mother Earth, you know, in your own very special way." He nodded thoughtfully. "I admire the Sioux. From my heart, I respect and admire them, and I'm just glad I was able to help, in some very, very small to bring this whole thing about, this great victory."

Weeks paused in his diatribe long enough to permit the waitress to take their orders. Then he started in on Kiah again. "Have you given any thought to how you might put all this money to use?" Kiah lifted his brow. "I mean, I'm sure you *have*. I was just wondering . . ."

"The councils of all the tribes involved will have to vote on whether to take the money."

"The money's *there,* Kiah. It's an award, for pity's sake. If you don't take it, it'll just sit there and earn interest." The lawyer glanced at the entrepreneur. "But, you know, you could put it to better use. I mean, interest rates . . ."

"As I understand it, over the past sixty years, it's been one lawyer after another saying, 'Here's what we do.'" Kiah paused, looking at Weeks as though he could see through his bald head. "So tell me about land values and interest rates, counselor. For pity's sake."

"My firm has an agreement with the tribal leaders. We were hired to represent the—"

"I know, I know." Kiah helped himself to a celery stick

before he passed Cecily the relish tray. "Don't give yourself indigestion over this, Paul. You'll get your fee off the
top whether we take the money or not, am I right?"

"You're damn right, but the point is—"

"The point is, Paul, that I listen to the people at Standing Rock every day, and they all know exactly what they
want." The celery stick became a pointer. "Trouble is, they
don't all want the same thing."

"You're elected to represent their best interests."

"What does that mean, Paul? *For pity's sake,* do you
know what it means?"

"*I* think it means you take that money and put it to good
use. Take the damn bull by the horns and relieve the plight
of the Indian, for crissake."

"Oh, for *Christ's* sake. Now, that's different. Relieve the
plight of the Indian for *Christ's* sake sounds a lot better
than, you know . . ." A smile danced in Kiah's eyes as he
chewed a bite of celery. "It's better than *pity. Pity's* kind
of a cussword for me, so you wanna stay away from that
one. Better to say it in Indian. *Unśica.* It goes down better,
you know? Indians respond to a person who's *unśica* in a
way that doesn't leave him even more *unśica.*"

"I didn't mean—"

"I know." Kiah's smile was infectious, especially when
he had the upper hand. "I like your style, Paul. You run
the bull into the chute, and I'm the one who's supposed to
take him by the horns." He turned to the other man. "So
what's your angle, Tom? You've got the solution to all
this, right? Just give me the book, and tell me what page."

Meecham took a sip of water. "Actually, I do have an
idea that I think you're going to like, Kiah."

"I'm willing to listen."

"And that's just one of the things we Anglos could learn
something about from you Native Americans. Listening."

"Can't argue with that," Kiah agreed. "But around here,
you're *waśicun,* not Anglo."

"Sorry," Meecham said. The quick response delighted
Kiah. Here was a white man apologizing for calling *himself* the wrong thing, but still hardly missing a beat in his
pitch. "There's something about Native Americans that the

rest of the world has always been fascinated with, Kiah. Something everybody, no matter where they're from, *everybody* admires. You people have something we all want."

"E'en it?" Kiah drawled, deliberately injecting a little "rez talk." "Jeez, I thought you *wašicun* had just about cleaned us out, Tom."

"Now, don't misunderstand me, Kiah, I appreciate the fact that Indians—Native Americans, pardon me—have not been treated fairly over the years. But times have changed, and most of us grew up playing cowboys and Indians, watching the Westerns, going to summer camp, and learning all about the way your people lived in perfect harmony with nature. I'm sure you still *do,"* he added hastily. "Anyway, those were good times for us—when we were Boy Scouts or Girl Scouts, Y-Indian Guides, whatever. We get really nostalgic when we think about our old Camp Gitchigumi days. So now here we are, we're stressed-out CEOs, or dentists, air-traffic controllers . . ." Meecham gestured Cecily's way, inviting her to put in a word.

"Writers," she supplied.

"Writers, whatever. And we're out of touch with the whole primal-spiritual-childhood thing."

"That's where we come in," Kiah supposed.

"You're damned right, that's where you come in. You have this ancient *insight,* this powerful mystique, this, this . . ."

"Medicine?"

"Medicine. Great word. People think medicine, they think balm. Restorative. Cure. Great word."

"So how can we"—Kiah gestured inclusively—"my tribe and you, the, uh, entrepreneur—how do we all go about dispensing this medicine?"

"We build a resort on the reservation," Meecham announced, thoroughly intoxicated with his own acumen. "Not an ordinary resort, you understand, but one where we can facilitate traditional Indian weekends and vacation packages. A place where people can really sink their teeth into the whole Native American experience. *You* know what I mean, Kiah. You've been there."

"Most of my life," Kiah said.

"Right, wonderful. You put people up in tipis. You've got your buffalo wandering around, you've got your Indian guides, your craft classes, your souvenir shop. You offer horseback riding, canoeing—"

"Buffalo boats," Kiah corrected patiently. "Not too many canoes around here in the old days, but the Mandan had these round boats made of buffalo hides."

"Oh, yeah, great. People appreciate authenticity."

"Not too many Mandan left, though. You're talking a real Sioux experience, right?"

"Right. I'm talking Sioux. The Prince of the Plains."

"I like the sound of that." He glanced at Cecily just in time to catch the sparkle in her eyes.

"You serve the traditional food around the campfire," Meecham continued with solemn enthusiasm. "You bring in the medicine man, the dancing, the drums, the whole nine yards."

"How about the *inipi?*" Kiah wondered. Meecham returned a blank stare. "The sweat."

"Like a sauna with the little sweat lodge?" The light dawned in Meecham's entranced eyes. He hardly noticed dinner being served. "Great touch. People would love it."

"We could offer a Sun Dance for those who are willing to bleed a little." Kiah picked up his steak knife without cracking a smile. "Skewer their chests, tie 'em to a pole, teach 'em the songs . . ."

"Well, now, you'd get into some problems with liability insurance. I think you'd want to keep it all basically pretty tame while providing sort of a soupçon of the culture. You know, a harmless sampling." Meecham leaned over his plate. His blue tie drooped within half an inch of his sour cream and chives. "Kiah, you'd have people coming here from all over the world. I kid you not, you would have a veritable gold mine."

"A *gold mine?*" Kiah's knife went still halfway through a slice of steak. "Not like the gold mines in the Black Hills."

"Well, not . . . not *literally.*"

"You gotta watch that, Tom." Kiah went back to cutting

his medium-rare beef. "There are certain words and expressions that sorta set Sioux blood to simmering, if you know what I mean."

"Well, I can understand that," Meecham indulged.

"I'm sure you can." Kiah savored several bites of his steak before he finally popped the all-important question. "So where do you fit into all this, Tom?"

"I'm like a facilitator."

"I thought *we* were the facilitators."

"Of the actual experience, yes. I facilitate the business. There's the construction; there's information gathering and dissemination; there's management."

"That's all your department."

"That's where you utilize my expertise, that's right."

"Sounds like a gold mine to me." He shared a conspiratorial look with the woman he'd introduced as his friend. "What do you think, Cecily?"

"I think that's a fair comparison."

"He's pulling your leg, Tom," Weeks said. "That's a little Indian humor."

"Paul knows all about Indian humor," Kiah allowed. "You wanna deal with Indians, you gotta learn to appreciate Indian humor."

"Of course, Tom's plan presupposes that you accept the Black Hills award and get on with your lives."

Kiah laughed. "Our lives haven't exactly been on hold for the last sixty years, just waiting for you lawyers to save the day."

"I know that." Weeks shifted in his chair and offered his bottom-line, man-to-man look. "We did what we could, Kiah. This is not the best of all possible worlds. It's hardly ever fair. The high courts have ruled that the taking of the Black Hills from the Sioux was 'the most ripe and rank case of dishonorable dealings' in our country's history. But this is 1980, and we have to live in the real world." He made an openhanded gesture. "Tom's plan is just an idea. There are lots of ideas. The money can make a difference. It can help you change things on the reservation."

* * *

Cecily had only nibbled at her plate of red snapper and
ce pilaf, but she left the restaurant feeling as though
he'd had a bellyful. Kiah had allowed her to see what he
was dealing with, but she didn't know whether he wanted
to hear her opinion of what she'd observed. Don't take
notes, he'd said. Just listen. Maybe it was too early for an
opinion. She kicked off her shoes and made herself comfortable for the long ride home.

"New pickup," she noted as he backed it out of the
parking space.

"Not new, just new*er*. Had to put ol' blue out to pasture," he said with a chuckle. She imagined the trusty old
pickup sitting under a tree in his backyard.

The radio softly played a melancholy country tune. Kiah
steered the pickup through the curves of the two-lane river-
bluff road that took them past the site of old Fort Lincoln.
It was from this post that Lieutenant Colonel George Custer
had led the Seventh Cavalry to its defeat at the Little Big
Horn. The restored blockhouses stood on the hills overlooking the river in dark silhouette against dusk's rosy sky.
They were silent sentinels, watching over the present road
like eyes from the past. They reminded Cecily of the antique
steamer trunk she'd recently had restored.

During the restoration its tray had been found to have a
secret drawer, which contained the journal of a woman
named Priscilla Twiss. At some point Cecily intended to
share her find with a historical society, but not yet. She
had always felt an uncanny attachment for the steamer
trunk, and she was determined to find out more about the
woman who had once owned it.

Priscilla Twiss had been a woman who had, in effect,
disappeared from one world into another. She had also
been an eyewitness to the taking of the Black Hills, and
she offered a unique perspective on the background of the
story Cecily intended to write. But it was a personal perspective. It was a woman's life. Priscilla Twiss, whose
trunk had been sitting in Cecily's various rooms for nine
years, had come back to life after a hundred years when
Cecily read her journal. She felt as though a friend had
just begun to confide in her, and she wasn't ready to share

that confidence with any historian or archivist. Not yet.
Not until she discovered what had become of the first
owner of her antique trunk.

But she did long to share her discovery with someone.

"Do you still have that locket I gave you?" she asked
casually.

"Sure. Somewhere. You said you didn't want it back."
He glanced at her askance. "Changed your mind?"

"No, I just wondered." She figured he'd lost it, or
maybe given it away. "Just one of the things that popped
into my mind since I first called you about this visit."

"I wonder if you've been remembering any of the same
things I've been remembering." He reached over to turn
off the radio. "Would you care to compare notes?"

She gave a tight smile and shook her head.

"All right, then, let me hear what your impressions are
of our Mr. Weeks and Mr. Meecham."

"Tweedledee and Tweedledum." She shrugged them off
with a chuckle. "They strike me as real opportunists."

Without taking his eyes off the road he nodded, mulling
over her choice of words. "Now tell me how you're different from them." He slid her another quick glance. "I almost forgot. You're different because you're Alice, right?
Welcome back to Wonderland."

"I've grown up, thank you. You were quick to observe
that I'm no longer *college girl.* I'm now *newspaper lady.*
I'm here to write an honest story." She laced her fingers
together and hooked her hands over one knee. "By the
way, I appreciate the fact that I've advanced from *girl* to
lady, but my gender really has little to do with my pursuits
as student or journalist."

"Don't you want an Indian name?"

"Like yours?" she asked lightly. "What does Kiah
mean, anyway?"

"Kiah?" With a dry chuckle he shook his head. "It's
from the Bible. Haven't you ever heard of Saint Kiah, the
patron saint of dubious honors?"

She offered a dubious look.

"Seriously, Red Thunder's my only Indian name, and it
came from my stepfather. No ceremonies or quests." He

odded in her direction. "But you keep coming out here,
ou should have an Indian name. Women used to have
ames like Blue Eyes Woman or Talks Big Woman. You
now, real descriptive handles."

"You were usually being sarcastic whenever you called
e college girl."

"*Me?* Sarcastic?"

"Maybe it's what Weeks called Indian humor."

"Or maybe it's something else." He studied the road for
moment, then added quietly, "Maybe a little jealousy,
aybe a few regrets."

"Jealousy? You didn't seem to be interested in college
or yourself, at least according to . . ."

The look they exchanged acknowledged the presence of
is sister's ghost. *According to Ellen Red Thunder.*

"Did I seem to be interested in you"—he glanced at the
oad, then assessed her perception with a look—"for my-
elf?"

"You didn't ask me to stay."

"You didn't offer to."

On that note they rode in silence for a while. *It's just as
vell you didn't,* they both thought. They had both been
oung and infatuated, passionate without restraint. Realis-
ically, things had worked out for the best. She had only
ome back because she had a job to do.

And *he* had a job to do. Surprisingly, he represented the
eople in exactly the kind of association he'd once
hunned.

"How did you ever get involved in tribal politics?"
Cecily asked at last.

"I needed a job." Simple as that. No burning ambitions,
no illusions. "I picked up a petition to run for office the
same day I got turned down for a loan to buy cattle." He
remembered how surprised he'd been at first whenever
anyone was willing to sign the damn petition. But he'd
been a warrior, and Ellen's advice kept ringing in his ears.
"I got elected on the basis of my easy handshake and my
medals for bravery."

"Both good leadership indicators."

He chuckled as he downshifted for a hill. "I wanted to *buy* a bull, and I end up throwing it."

"No, no, taking it by the horns," Cecily insisted with a smile, recalling that it was exactly what he'd done at dinner. "Maybe our leaders should always be cowboys."

"I thought that was *heroes*. My heroes have always been cowboys."

"Mine, too." She turned toward him, braced her elbow on the back of the seat, and propped her head against her hand. She liked the way he wore his hair, trimmed collar-length, the way he chewed on a toothpick instead of a cigarette, the way he managed the pickup's big steering wheel. "I liked the way you handled those two rustlers tonight."

"Thank you, ma'am," he said with a grin and a tip of the hat. "Weeks is very good at his job, but he doesn't speak the same language as his clients."

"You mean Lakota?"

"I mean good ol' Native American English. Don't lawyers think in Latin or something?"

"Who knows? For sure they think in dollars, and it sounds like they got you a pile of those."

"Which I've done my share of chasing in my time," he admitted readily. "Most people hear that hundred million figure, and they say, 'Hey, don't look a gift horse in the mouth.' What they don't realize is that Indians have a lot of experience with government gift horses. The catch is that they started out by taking our *own* horses away first."

"That was a long time ago."

"Yeah, I know. I used to say that, too, remember? I used to tell Ellen, 'Forget it, it's all water under the bridge.' " He adjusted the floor shift again, and the engine purred an octave lower. "This lawsuit wasn't my idea. Nobody seems to know whose idea it was, and nobody can agree on what we expected to get out of it. Since the beginning, the lawyers have been insisting that we had some money coming, but that's all. They say we have to understand that. Just money. That's all we get."

"They're saying that it doesn't matter whether the government had the *right* to take the land," she added. "It was taken, and that isn't going to change."

"They're saying that I have to accept that." He glanced at her meaningfully. "Nobody tells me what I *should* want or what I *have to* accept. That's up to me."

"But the money's there, and you know you're not going to get the land back."

"Right." Eyes back on the road, he gave a long sigh. "Follow the money. Money is power. The lawyers get their ten percent, and Cecily Metcalf gets her story."

"I promise to write an honest story, Kiah."

"You'll have a field day with Indian politics. The press always does."

She would be fair, and she knew that was all he expected. That was why he had agreed to this. She had seen the view from the other side. "Whatever happened to Bobby Blue Bow?" she asked.

"He did some hospital time, then some jail time after the Red Creek occupation caved in. He's married. Works as a janitor at the Indian community college. He and his wife take classes."

"Was anything else ever said or . . . or done about Ellen?"

He gave her a dark look. "Was I supposed to do some crusading?"

"No." She glanced away. *Investigating,* she wanted to say, but the tone of his voice invited no alternative suggestions. "I just wondered."

"We let her go." She could feel his eyes, even as she avoided them, but he wouldn't let her avoid the image. "Remember? You and me together. We scattered her ashes up on Bear Butte."

"I remember." She could still hear his song echoing across the gulf of space and time and unwelcome change. She could still feel the emptiness. "I'll write an honest story," she said softly. "I promise."

Chapter 20

Kiah dropped Cecily off at the Warrior Motel in Fort Yates, where she rented a room that was clean and cool, if not fancy. As long as it provided the basics—telephone, electrical outlet for the typewriter, a shower, and a bed—she was set.

During the next several days Kiah included her in most of his plans. She attended a full council meeting and several committee meetings. She interviewed a host of people, some who held office, others who were simply members of the Standing Rock Sioux Tribe. There were all kinds of opinions on the matter of the Black Hills. It was an emotional issue for some people and a subject that others were just plain sick of hearing about. But no one seemed to be without an opinion. Cecily observed Kiah's meetings, he listened in on most of her interviews, and they compared notes.

After she'd filed her first story, Cecily got a call from her editor, who reminded her that her series would appear in over fifty Midwestern newspapers and that she needed to "dig deep."

"Dig deep?" she repeated, rankled by this unprecedented lack of trust. "What's that supposed to mean, Harold? I've just gotten *started,* for Pete's sake."

"It means *dig deep.* We're talking about a lot of money here. The Sioux can't really think they're ever going to get he Black Hills back, so find out what it is they really want. What do these tribal leaders have to gain by refusing he money?"

"They haven't decided to refuse the money," she re-minded him. Hadn't he read the piece beyond the first paragraph?

"Yeah, but the fact that they're even thinking about turning it down, for crissake, this is real *money*. There must be some interesting motives lurking in some dark corners out there. You need to show the plight of the victims and really expose the loggerheads—you know what I mean, the ones who use their office for personal gain." Harold chuckled. "A politician's a politician, whether he's wearing a golf hat or feathers, you know what I mean? When you talk about 'diverse opinion,' you mean they're bickering among themselves, right?"

"They're listening to all sides."

"But there's no real leadership, right? The tribal government is like a dog chasing its own tail. Meanwhile those people continue to live in poverty. I didn't really get the true picture of the plight of the Indian from your first article." Harold paused for an audible drag on a cigarette. "You know, Cecily, this could be an award-winning series. Those people are not making any progress, and you're going to show us why that is."

"The first article dealt with the facts of the court case," she explained, schooling herself to be inquiring rather than indignant. Since Harold usually trusted her instincts, she was as curious about *his* motives as she was about anyone else's. "I'm going to write more about the historical background and how that relates to the present situation. I'm not ready to say anything about progress or the lack of it, Harold. This really is a different culture."

"Well, maybe that's the problem. They're Americans, aren't they? Native Americans. They ought to have a shot at the American dream, just like everybody else. But they're still living in the nineteenth century. They're getting poor health care, poor education, poor *everything,* and they're talking about turning down over a hundred million bucks!"

"They're talking about a lot of things. That's the way they do things around here." Cecily leaned back against the headboard and stretched her legs out on the bed. "I told you before, Harold, nothing is a given in this story. Not even the question of progress or the value of money. My intention was to start the story with a blank page."

"Don't overlook any of the unpleasant details. Those are the kind that sell papers."

"I realize that. I don't intend to overlook anything."

"I'm not going to run this until I see more of it."

Cecily studied the *End of the Trail* print that hung above the small television set across the room. "Am I supposed to be lending credence to some particular editorial position on Indian affairs that I don't know about?"

"We are a Midwestern news service." Another pause, another puff at the other end of the line. "Treaty rights and Indian sovereignty are touchy issues at the local and state level these days. We want to be fair. We want to be accurate. If tribal governments don't function effectively, if Sioux leaders don't lead—if they're corrupt or inept— we're not afraid to show that."

"What if they aren't? Or what if it's not that simple?"

"I told you, we want to be fair and accurate." Another instructional pause. "And I know you will be, Cecily. You're an excellent journalist."

That much was true, but the compliment rang pretty hollow as she dropped the receiver back into place. It had been tacked onto the end of a lecture Cecily didn't need. Harold knew her work to be thorough, and he knew that she was a stickler for accuracy. She always double-checked her facts and sought backup sources. It was her job to present the readers with news and information. She was expected to present it objectively. In the end it would be up to the readers to be fair.

Cecily had spent most of the morning interviewing the agency superintendent at the BIA office. Where the bureau officials were concerned, Kiah had told her she was on her own and wished her luck. "The BIA speaks a language all its own," he'd explained. " 'Bossin' Indians Around' we call it, and they use more double-talk than a split-tongued

orse trader. I usually come away thinking, What the hell
id he say?"

She assumed she was on her own for the weekend, too,
ut the knock on her door proved otherwise.

"How'd it go?" Kiah wondered, forgoing a more per-
unctory greeting. Cecily stepped aside to let him in.

"About the way you said it would."

He smiled and nodded absently. She closed the door.
They looked at each other, and suddenly the motel room
with its functional furnishings seemed very small.

Kiah nudged his hat back with his thumb. "How long
are you planning on staying? You know, you don't have to
stay in a motel."

With a look Cecily invited alternative suggestions.

He shrugged and glanced away. "You're welcome to the
spare room at my place. I've added on. I've even got a
bathroom now. Running water, all the conveniences."

She took a deep breath. "That might not be such a good
idea."

"Why not? We're sensible adults."

"I was a sensible kid, too. But then I met you, and
I ..." Put it mildly, she told herself, and she contrived a
breezy tone. "As I remember, I lost my head."

"You got it back, though." He smiled and touched the
smooth curve of hair that touched her shoulders. More
stylish these days, he thought. But still natural. He lifted
his brow approvingly. "I just thought if you were planning
to stay awhile, you might be more comfortable in a house
instead of ..." In an abrupt move he jammed his hand in
the back pocket of his jeans and shrugged one shoulder in-
differently. "Not that it's anything fancy, but it's not a motel room."

"I have to be objective with this story. I'm not writing
Harold Severson's story—he's my editor," she explained.
"And I'm not writing your story. I'm writing—"

"I don't give a damn what you write. You said you'd be
honest, whatever that means. I guess I'll see what it means
when I read the paper. If it gets into print, it must be true.
Isn't that right?"

"Not necessarily." She turned toward the desk, and a

leather-bound book caught her eye. "But if it's written in somebody's private journal, that's different. I'd say that's probably honest writing."

The journal lured her slowly toward the desk. "Do you remember my old steamer trunk?"

"The one that belonged to the lady of the locket?"

"Yes. The lady of the locket." The one he had around *somewhere*. With her forefinger she traced the initials stamped in the leather, parched by the passage of time. "I didn't know anything abut her until I had the trunk restored. The fellow who did the work discovered a nifty little secret compartment. The mystery lady's name was Priscilla Twiss."

Cecily lifted the book off the table and carried it to him as though she were handling a sacred object. "This is her journal. The first entry is dated 1871."

"Quite a find."

"It's more than that, Kiah." She was determined that his lack of excitement would only be a temporary letdown. "This woman's father was an Indian agent at the Red Cloud Agency. She became the wife of a man who actually fought at the Little Big Horn."

"If he was with Custer, she had a sad tale to tell," he surmised with a complacent nod.

"His name was Whirlwind Rider. He rode with Crazy Horse." Her enthusiasm swelled as Kiah's eyes widened considerably. "Have you ever heard of anyone by that name?"

"Whirlwind Rider? The Red Cloud Agency was at Pine Ridge, where my real father was from." He considered the book in her hand with new interest. "My grandfather must have been some relation. His name was Marcus Whirlwind Rider. Because of the way the regulations worked when I was born, they enrolled me as a full-blood with the Standing Rock Sioux, from my mother's Hunkpapa side. It's kinda confusing because I'm half Oglala, probably with some other bands mixed in from way back. But, anyway, I'm one hundred percent Lakota Sioux, and I've got the good looks to prove it." He looked up with a grin, but then he puzzled for a moment. "Was this woman a captive or something?"

"Far from it. She faked her own death and went to live with her husband's people."

"Jeez." Again, his eyes widened. "I've never heard of any white women with Crazy Horse's band. They were considered hostile until they surrendered about a year after Little Big Horn. Crazy Horse was murdered just a few months later. There were a few white *men* marrying Indian *women* back then, but the other way around was less"—he shook his head and added softly—"acceptable, I guess. Hard to believe this woman married one of the hostiles."

"I think she was a well-guarded secret." The unfolding mystery made Cecily's fingers tingle as she gripped the book. "I haven't shown this to anyone, Kiah."

He looked at it again, warily, as though it might be an animal threatening to bare its teeth.

"I know this sounds crazy, but I've had that trunk for nine years, and I feel as though this woman is like a friend to me now. We've made some kind of connection. And I don't believe in ghosts, so I don't think she's haunting me. I just think that in a way she crossed a bridge back then. Between cultures. And now she's crossed a bridge between her time and ours."

Before he had a chance to refute any of her fancy, she handed him the journal. "I have a feeling she'd want you to read this."

He turned the book over in his hands, examining the binding. "Is this like the part of the movie where everyone in the audience screams, 'Don't open that'?"

"If ghosts do exist, this one means you no harm. Do you still have the locket?"

"It's my, uh . . ." He shoved his hand in his pocket and came up with a small leather pouch, along with some change, keys, and a pocket knife.

Not only did he still have it, but he'd gone to some trouble to protect it. She touched the suede, then folded his fingers over his cache and offered him a gratified smile.

"It's kind of embarrassing, the way I hang on to this thing for luck." There was a soft chink as he dropped the stuff back into his pocket. "It doesn't have anything to do with ghosts. It reminds me of an old friend." He weighed the journal in his other hand. "You want me to read it now?"

"Let's go to your place," she suggested on impulse. "I'll cook supper for us while you read. Once you start, you won't put it down."

She was right. He gave her the run of the kitchen while he planted himself in his favorite easy chair. With one long leg draped over the arm, he read. When Cecily offered him a cup of coffee, he paused long enough to find out about the Twiss-Varner estate auction. Then he went back to his reading.

"This woman sounds like you," he called out to her at one point. "Running back East to go to school, but always coming back."

"Yes." Cecily popped her head around the kitchen doorway and gave him a prim smile. "I noticed that similarity, too."

" 'Course, she held out longer than you did."

"Whirlwind Rider was a gentleman," she said curtly.

"Yeah, well—" He took great care in turning another antique page. "Wonder what she looked like."

"I know what *he* looked like," she said with complete assurance. Kiah glanced up quizzically. She tossed a dish towel over her shoulder and smiled, dreamy-eyed. "He was incredibly handsome. You can just tell by the way she talks about seeing him that first time in the blacksmith shop. He had muscles that wouldn't quit."

"And a gentleman to boot." Kiah clucked his tongue, acknowledging the rarity with amusement. "What a guy."

He kept reading. She peeked in periodically just to satisfy herself that he was still absorbed. Her interest in nineteenth-century Americana had prompted Cecily to read many a dry journal, but Priscilla Twiss was a wonderful writer, and her ink sketches added detail, color, even humor to many of the entries. Even the ever-unsusceptible Kiah Red Thunder seemed fascinated with her story.

"This part about the baby . . ." He ran his tan, masculine

fingers over the fine script on one cream-colored page. "I guess women had it rough in those days. Did she ever—"

"Keep reading," Cecily coaxed gently.

Unwilling to distract him until he was finished, she stood quietly at the kitchen window for a long time watching a black cow graze in the shade of the shelter belt near the creek. A white-faced calf was curled up in the grass nearby. Cecily wondered whether they were Kiah's. Since her last visit he'd made some improvements in the house, and it looked as though he'd put up a new corral. She didn't remember seeing a pole barn out back when she'd been there before, but there was one there now. She wondered if he had qualified for a loan after all.

She leaned against the door frame and watched him finish reading the final page, then asked, "Shall I warm up the spaghetti sauce again?"

He closed the leather-bound book slowly. "It just stops." He looked up. "What happened to them?"

"I don't know. At some point the trunk was returned to Minneapolis. There's a letter—" She crossed the room and knelt beside his chair, taking the book in hand. The folded letter was still inside the front cover where she'd found it. "There's no date on it, but it must have been written shortly after her husband's band surrendered." She sat back on her heels as she unfolded the paper. "Listen to this:

" 'Dear Father,' " Cecily read. " 'I am alive. I had to let you think that I was dead so that you would not send any soldiers against my husband. I hope that you will forgive my deception and try to understand that I have made the only choice a woman who loves a good and upright man can possibly make. Wherever my husband goes, there will I be. I trust that you will honor my wishes and refrain from interfering in any way.

" 'I have decided to send you my trunk as soon as I can find the means. It contains some keepsakes—some treasures I want you to have—along with some of the less practical remnants of my old life. I hope that when you read my journal, you will understand the choice I have made. Now that most of the Lakota have complied with the government's demands, I hope that the weapons of war will be put away and that my husband and his people will be permitted to live in peace in the land that is their home.

" 'You will know by this that your first grandchild died before he had the chance to live. By the time you receive this letter, perhaps I shall be carrying another child. I surely hope so. I cannot help but think that my father, whom I know to be an enlightened man—and, what is more important, a kind man—will, in his heart, give his daughter his blessing. I pray that our union may be blessed with more children, but in Lakota families the children are a joy that is shared in a special way. Already I am called sister, aunt, and cousin, and I share the family's children the Indian way. I shall continue with my teaching. Please understand that I can conceive of no future for myself other than that which my husband and I will share.

" 'My husband's relations among the "friendlies," as you were wont to call them, have assured those who have surrendered that there is to be a new agency here in Dakota. After a bleak and hungry time last winter, even Crazy Horse is looking ahead, having taken a trader's mixed-blood daughter as his second wife. Black Shawl, his first wife, is terribly ill with consumption. (My own husband assures me that one wife is enough for him.)

" 'I realize that in light of my situation you may well decide to continue to count me among the dead. However, I do hope that the news that I am, indeed, alive and well will overshadow the misgivings you are bound to have. In the spirit of that hope, I ask you to use whatever influence you may have to persuade the United States government to keep its remaining promises to the Sioux. The Black Hills have been taken now. It would be a travesty of American justice if the people were to be removed south to Indian territory. But if this happens, I shall follow my husband.

" 'I do love you, Father. I pray daily for your health and prosperity.'

"And it's signed with a *P*," Cecily concluded. She handed Kiah the letter and folded her hands over the crisp creases in her slacks. "I'm wondering whether her father ever found the journal."

"If he did, he obviously chose to keep it hidden away. Didn't you say the trunk had been locked for a hundred years?"

"That was what the auctioneer claimed. I never really believed it." She sighed. "I'd love to find out what happened to her."

"She must have died somehow, and he took another wife." There was a new note of sympathy in his voice. "It's over a hundred years ago, Cecily."

"I know. But when this was written, she wasn't very old. This is six years of her life, but there's more. There's a lot more between the lines and . . . just a lot more." She wouldn't let him banish Priscilla so easily. "It's a wonderful story, but it still leaves a lot of mystery left to be solved. Isn't that exciting? And somehow these people might be related to you."

"It's a small world out here. I'm related to a lot of people." He swung his leg from the chair's padded arm to the floor as though he were dismounting. He handed her the journal. "But not her. She was white."

"What happened here after 1877?"

"Sitting Bull went to Canada, but he came back in the early eighties, surrendered, and was held prisoner for a couple of years before they let him come back to Standing Rock. He was assassinated in 1890. Some of his followers fled and joined up with Big Foot's Minneconjou. They all surrendered at Wounded Knee, and then, of course, they were massacred. The reservations got smaller and smaller, and the people"—he braced his hands on his knees—"just made do. Crazy Horse was assassinated not long after that letter was written. Any of the leaders who were fighters became targets.

"If they were alive today, Crazy Horse and Sitting Bull would line up with the traditionals. And the traditionals are kind of the keepers of the faith," he explained. "Up until lately they've kept to themselves, pretty much ignored by the people who consider themselves to be more progressive.

"I wonder if Grandma Emma's still alive," he said, finally rising from his chair.

Cecily followed suit, levering herself off the bare wood floor.

Kiah's eyes narrowed, his attention fixed on a memory. "Grandma Emma would have been Marcus Whirlwind Rider's—" He pondered a moment. "I don't know if they were really brother and sister or what. I grew up around my mother's family, mostly, so I never bothered to get all that straight on the other side, and the older women in the family are all just 'grandma.' *Unci.* It's been a long time since I've seen Grandma Emma. She used to have a little place out in the country down there at Pine Ridge."

"What about your grandfather?"

"I never knew him. Never knew my father. I guess I told you that."

She nodded, pleased by his growing interest and the promise of more discovery.

Noting her pleasure, he gave a self-satisfied smile, as though he were handing out rewards. "What do you say we go down to the Hills for the weekend, take in all the sights?"

"I'd say that I'm here on business, and it's not up to you to entertain me." Being entertained by him could be risky, in fact. She wanted to stick with investigating family history.

"Then I'd say take the weekend off." He stepped closer, the easy, seductive smile still lurking in his eyes. "I wasn't planning on entertaining you. I was planning on getting to know you a little better."

"Good grief, here it comes." She challenged him with a look. "Getting to know me *how,* Kiah?"

"Maybe some ways we haven't tried yet," he said suggestively as he put his warm hands on her shoulders. "Seems like after we jump all over each other's bones, one of us always has a plane to catch."

"Jump"—she sputtered—"each *other's*—"

"Okay, after *I've* jumped *yours.* Does that sound better?"

"No!" She looked him straight in the eye and tried to sound indignant. "It sounds awful, and that's not the way it was."

"Let's compare memories. You show me yours, and I'll
show you mine. Does that sound awful, too?"

"It sounds as though you haven't changed."

"I have, and I haven't," he said, smiling mysteriously.
His fingers stirred over her shoulder blades. "Typical Indian paradox. You're here to find out what that means."

She couldn't argue that point, but he figured that the
reason she was hesitating—he wished she could see the
half-scared look she was giving him—was that she wasn't
sure how much *she'd* changed. He shrugged and stepped
back in a strategic retreat. "I just thought we'd spend some
time together in the Black Hills, that's all."

"Would we visit Grandma Emma?"

"If you promise not to play reporter." He raised an admonishing finger. "If you promise to listen and not ask too
many questions."

Cecily did not stay with him that night, but she went
with him when he came for her the next morning. They
headed south, through western South Dakota, bypassing
the best part of the Black Hills in favor of sticking to the
most direct route to Pine Ridge Reservation. They would
come back to the Hills, Kiah promised. Cecily nodded absently. She was more interested in visiting the present
home of the Oglala and in meeting someone who might remember something about Priscilla's husband.

Since the small house sitting out on a windswept flat
south of the South Dakota Badlands had no phone, there
had been no way to call ahead. There was power in the
vast austerity of the place. The low-lying hills were dotted
with scrub pines, and weathered clay cutbanks were rem-
iniscent of the moonscape they had just driven through.

"She lives here alone?" Cecily asked.

"Last I heard there was a nephew moved his family in
with her, but I don't see a car or anything around. I hope
she still lives here." Kiah parked the pickup on the shady
side of the house. "Assuming she does, just remember, it's
respectful to nod and listen. Try not to look her in the eye
while she's talking to you. Even if her eyesight's worse
than I remember, if you stare at her, she'll know it."

The door opened, and a gray-haired Indian woman leaned out and hissed at a barking dog. Then she adjusted the thick glasses over the bridge of her nose and waited as Kiah approached with Cecily in tow.

"Unci," he greeted her, instinctively using the Lakota word for grandmother. "It's good to see you. You're looking fine today."

She peered up at him as he shook her hand. "Which one are you?"

"I'm Kiah Red Thunder, from up on Standing Rock."

"Toby's boy? Eeee, long time since I seen you. Come on in." She offered a nearly toothless smile as she backed over the threshold. Kiah felt like a wishbone, with the old woman tugging on one arm while he reached back to hold the door open for Cecily with the other.

"Last time I seen you, you were just small." The old woman bent slightly and held a stiff hand two feet above the floor. "Then pretty soon they said you got to be a soldier. Didn't they have a big doings for you up at Little Eagle a while back when you were going to fight that war? But I see you came back all right."

"Yes, Grandma. They shot at me and missed."

"Ayyy, that's good they missed. I had to miss the doings. I was sick that time." She adjusted her slipping glasses again and looked him over closely. *"Tuki!* So this is Toby's boy. You look like him. He was a real looker, that one."

"This is my friend, Cecily Metcalf, Grandma. She's from Minnesota."

"That's a long way to come. Sit and rest yourself." She indicated the motley collection of chairs around the small table that took up half the front room.

Cecily was eager to comply with all directives, so she sat, but she wondered whether the old woman realized they'd been sitting for hours in the car.

Emma kept chattering as she disappeared into the kitchen. "Virgil and his bunch went over to the powwow, but one of Mary's girls just brought me some frybread and *wōjapi.* I have coffee." She came back with a plate of donutlike frybread and a plastic bowl of soupy Juneberry

udding. "Do you remember Mary?" she asked Kiah, who
was still stretching his legs after the long drive. "She's one
of my granddaughters."

"I've kind of lost track." He took the food from her and
set it on the table. "So you're a *great*-grandma."

"Oh, yes, I've lived a long time. How many kids you
got?"

"I don't have any children, Unci. One of these days,
though."

"You'd better get busy, *takoja,*" she said, claiming him
as her grandson, as was her right in the Indian way. "Toby
only had one; his father only had one, and *his* father only
had one. You don't want to be the last one, do you?"

"The last one, *what,* Grandma Emma? Moses Red
Thunder raised me. I don't know much about Toby Rider
except his name, and even that's questionable."

The old woman toddled back into the kitchen. Kiah
risked a glance at Cecily, sitting quietly at the end of the
table and letting him set the tone. He'd told her not to ask
too many questions, but in the time since he'd read the
journal, he'd thought up about a hundred of them.

Grandma Emma came back with coffee.

"Why did he change it?" Kiah asked as she handed him
a cup. "Wasn't his father's last name *Whirlwind* Rider?"

"Marcus." The old woman lowered herself painstak-
ingly into a chair opposite Cecily. "Marcus was a soldier,
too, you know. He went to France when they had that First
World War over there. I went to the doings they had for
him when *he* came back. That was a long time ago."

She looked up at Kiah, who took the cue, finally, to seat
himself at the table.

"Yes, Marcus went by the name of Whirlwind Rider. He
kept his whole name. Toby, well . . ." She smiled, remembering. "Toby was a good kidder. He liked to get into a little trouble sometimes, but he was a good boy."

Turning in her chair, she touched the corner of a picture
frame, tipping it askew on the green wall just above her
head. "He bought me this one time from out in Colorado."
It was a yellowed print of a Rocky Mountain landscape.
"He went to a big rodeo there. Won first place in the bull

riding. He said Toby Rider was a good name for a rodeo cowboy."

Kiah's eyes widened as he scanned the print. "He took first in Denver, huh? Wonder what year that was."

"It was 1947." She poked his arm with her finger. "See, you think I'm just an old woman, but I remember these things."

Kiah laughed. "I think you're a foxy old woman, Unci." He glanced at Cecily for her approval. She was nibbling at a piece of frybread. With a look she deferred to his lead, and he continued. "Tell me about Marcus. Was he your brother the Indian way, or . . ."

"He was older than me. My mother, my grandmother, they both spoiled him. He was an only son and a warrior in the new way. We were not yet American citizens, but many of the men volunteered to fight that time. They brought home many honors. Marcus wore the boots and hat," she said, raising her hands above her head to describe the shape of the World War I campaign hat. "Oh, he looked fine. But inside his shirt, he carried his medicine bundle. His father was an old man. He waited for his son to come home from that fight, and when he did . . .

"I remember the way the red, white, and blue flag at the top of the pole kept popping in the breeze. All the old ones came. They came from Standing Rock and Rosebud, Cheyenne River and Crow Creek. It was an important day, that day when Whirlwind Rider made a celebration for his only son.

"It was a grand sight to see. The drums sounded good and strong again, like the heart of a young man. Whirlwind Rider sang an honor song for a returning warrior. Father and son led the people slowly around the bowery." She held up two fingers and bobbed her hand in a circle to demonstrate. "Two warriors," she recalled. "The young one wearing the uniform. The old one"—she touched the back of her head and made as if to comb her hair—"a long trail of eagle feathers down his back. A fox cape around his neck. A hairbone breast collar. He danced as straight and tall as his son, that one."

"Were there many by that name then?" Cecily asked,

thoroughly entranced. "The name Whirlwind Rider, was it a family name?"

"No, not then. Whirlwind Rider never took a Christian name for himself," the old woman explained. "He was at Wounded Knee. Shot four times, but he lived. Marcus was there. Just a baby. So many died that day, but Marcus . . ." She nodded, recalling what she had been told. "My mother used to say that Marcus was too hot-blooded to freeze. And Toby—" She threw up her hands in mock exasperation. "*Ošti!* He was worse yet, that one."

"But he *did* freeze," Kiah reminded her, almost offhandedly. She looked at him as though she wasn't quite sure what he meant. "Isn't that right? He got drunk, passed out, and froze to death. End of story, as my mother used to say."

"She was a good woman, that Rebecca. It was hard for her. She was here with me when the BIA cop came with the white sheriff from over in Martin. They wanted her to identify the body. I watched you while she went with them. When she came back, she said she was going back to her people up at Standing Rock. We didn't see too much of her after that."

"She stayed around long enough to bury him, didn't she?"

"Oh, yes. Over at Wounded Knee, at the cemetery there. You've been there, haven't you?"

He studied the coffee he'd yet to taste. He knew it was probably cold. "I don't have much use for cemeteries."

"It's not a good thing to disturb the spirits too much. They like to be left alone." A quiet moment passed before the old woman said, "Moses Red Thunder was your father's friend. Did you know that?"

Kiah shrugged. "They never talked about my . . . about Toby Rider much."

"Toby had no brothers to look after his widow, and Moses was his friend. They were right not to talk about him. It's not a good thing to talk about the dead." Grandma Emma gave a dry chuckle. "But I'm too old to worry about ghosts. I'm close to being one myself."

"Jeez," Kiah scolded. "What a thing to say, Grandma."

"You should know these things about your Oglala relations, *takoja*. Pretty soon there will be no one left who can tell you." There was another long pause. "Nobody ever found out who beat him up," she said.

"My father?"

"He used to drink around and raise hell sometimes. In those days, Indians had to bootleg." She turned to Cecily to explain. "You know, they had to get someone to buy booze for them. Selling it to Indians was illegal back then. But those cowboys, they always found a way when they wanted to go on a party."

Emma shook her head sadly. "He was frozen stiff when they found him. They said he must have been in a fight because he was all beat up. So they said he got drunk, got in a fight, walked fifteen miles or so, sat down, and froze to death."

"How in the hell can anybody think—"

"He was dead," the old woman told Kiah. "It was no good asking too many questions."

"Why not?" Cecily asked, that old guileless outrage creeping into her voice.

"Because you're not likely to get the truth as long as the dead can't answer," Kiah reminded her. "We know that from experience, don't we?" And then to the old woman he explained, "Cecily was my sister's very close friend."

"It's not a good thing when they put Indians in the white men's jails." Grandma Emma wagged her gray head solemnly. "*Eces tuwale.* Not a good thing at all."

"One question, Grandma." Kiah slid Cecily a pointed glance as he again broke his own rule in her behalf. "Did old Whirlwind Rider have more than one wife?"

"I knew him only as an old man, but I think . . ." She took her time, then nodded. "I think he had two."

"Were there any children from the first wife?"

"I never heard of any."

It was early evening when they took the road back to the northern Black Hills, but the summer sun was still high. They were quiet at first, each thinking about the aspects of Grandma Emma's recollections that hit closest to home. Cecily had wanted to ask more questions about the distant past, but she'd respected Kiah's sudden need to know more about his father.

"All I ever heard was that my father got drunk and froze to death," Kiah said after a time, thinking out loud. "I never heard anything about any beating. I'm glad she didn't have to see Ellen end up that way, too."

He glanced at Cecily. "My mom," he clarified. But Cecily still had that look on her face, the one that voiced doubts without making a sound. Was that an accusation he saw in her eyes?

"I *did* ask questions," he averred. She didn't have to accuse him of just letting the whole thing go; he could see what she was thinking. "I asked questions until I was blue in the face. 'How did she get all those bruises? Was she sexually assaulted? Let me see the full report.' You don't know what it's like. You feel so—"

He wrapped both hands around the steering wheel and stared hard at the road ahead. She hadn't asked him how he'd felt, and he didn't know why he was telling her. "You feel impotent," he said, his voice toneless. "You feel like they're holding all the cards. You make your appeal, and you wonder if you're so small they can't even see you. And then you get angry because you're trying to make yourself heard, and they don't listen. They just—" He shook his head, bewildered. "They can't *hear*."

"Who can't?" Cecily asked softly.

"Cops, councilmen, congressmen, the whole damn bunch. When I didn't get any answers, I thought about . . . I wanted to kill somebody. The assholes who put her in jail, for starters." He squeezed the steering wheel until the veins stood out on the backs of his hands, and he spoke venomously. "Hell, I can kill people, too. I was trained for it, and I did it, and they gave me a shitload of medals for it. I coulda done a damn good job cuttin' up those pigs if I'd . . . wanted to." He gave his head a quick shake, as if to dismiss a bad dream. "But it's like Grandma Emma said, Indians don't do well in jail."

"We don't know for sure what happened. And even if

we *could* be sure . . ." Cecily drew a deep breath. She, too, shook her head. "There has to be another way."

"I just wanted you to know that I"—he slid her a quick glance—"I did ask questions." He barked a dry laugh. "Doesn't that sound lame? I can't do anything about my sister except ask a few questions, but I went halfway around the world to kill people I had no quarrel with."

"So did your grandfather. You had nothing to do with the politics. You were both fighting for your country."

"But my great-grandfather was a Tokala. He fought for his people." That said with pride, he added hesitantly, "You really think the lady of the locket was my grandfather's first wife?"

"How many Whirlwind Riders could there be?"

"Hard to say. 'Long about that time, people had to register at the agency for land allotments, and they started changing names, maybe using only part of a name. In Whirlwind Rider's day there weren't last names, but that soon changed." He shrugged. "So it's hard to say."

"I think that the Whirlwind Rider in the journal was your great-grandfather." She had not a trace of doubt.

"Well, if he was, then he ended up taking a second wife after all." A mean-spirited sense of satisfaction burned in his smile. "Kinda shot Priscilla's romantic illusions all to hell, didn't it?"

"I don't think he took another wife while she was alive. He loved her too much to do that. I wonder when she died." Cecily glanced out the side window, admiring Rapid City's modest skyline. "I wonder *how* she died."

"She died. That much we know. Grandma Emma's a full-blood, and so am I."

"She probably died in childbirth. She wanted a child so badly, and she was just so small." She turned to Kiah. He responded with a cool glance. "Well, I feel as though I *know* her. It's almost as though I went through it all right along with her."

"Two peas in a pod," he said lightly. "Two incurable romantics."

"You see," she said, elated. "Deep down you feel the same way. You're talking like you know us both, or you *think* you do." She cleared her throat and offered quietly, 'I think the journal rightfully belongs to you, Kiah."

"Finders keepers," he said with a smile. "No, you keep it. You're the one who's all sentimental about it. What interests me is where she talks about the way people started bickering over this whole treaty thing way back then. It's been going on ever since. When the first news of the Supreme Court decision came, some people started talking right away about per capita payments and who should get the money. Some people wanted to cut out anyone who wasn't at least half Indian. Some people started saying the Tribal Council didn't speak for them. The same damn arguments have been going on for a hundred years. And what it still boils down to is that the treaty wasn't worth shit. They took the land, and that's that."

"When the people understood that, most of them walked away," Cecily recalled. "I mean, back then. Only about seventy people actually signed the agreement to sell the Black Hills, and that was practically at gunpoint."

"So nothing's changed. People say we could use the money for programs, for economic development, education, jobs. Hell, we could even buy back some of the land." He shook his head at the irony of that prospect. "That's a hell of a deal. We've said all along, 'The Hills can't be sold, and they can't be bought.' So the government puts the money in the bank and says, 'Somebody come and take it."

"It's a lot of money."

"You remember Genghis Khan?" He quirked a brow in her direction. She nodded tentatively. "He used to attack a city, steal their treasure, and pile it up where everybody in town could see it, and then he'd back off and wait for some greedy bastard to commit suicide." He chuckled humorlessly. "It's a goddamn dare is what it is."

"I hardly think it could be that calculated."

"Maybe not. But it's an interesting idea, isn't it? Can't you just see ol' Genghis saying, 'Let's let the interest on the award build up, and we'll see just what their price is.'"

"Would it be political suicide to claim the money, from a tribal councilman's perspective?"

"Not if you were really good at counting coups." He smiled mischievously as he executed a horizontal karate chop in the air. "In and out. Snatch it right out of their hands and ride away. Crazy Horse could have done it, and ol' Genghis Khan would've been lookin' around." He scanned the horizon comically to demonstrate. " 'What th' hell was that?' he'd be sayin'." He snapped his fingers and grinned at her. "Whirlwind Rider! He could've done it, too."

"He counted coups on a train," Cecily was delighted to reminded him.

"Damn, wouldn't it be great to see one of those guys take on Genghis Khan?"

"I can't believe you're comparing the U.S. government to Genghis Khan. I can't believe I'm not telling you what a ridiculous analogy it is." She threw back her head and laughed. "I *really* can't believe Whirlwind Rider is actually your great-grandfather."

"Believe it or don't," he said with a chuckle, then quipped, "Don't make me no never mind."

"Will the council be voting on this soon?"

"If somebody has the guts to put it to a vote."

"So what about Kiah Red Thunder?" She challenged him with a winsome smile. "How good is he at counting coups?"

"*That,* newspaper lady, is the hundred-million-dollar question."

Chapter 21

The Latchhook Inn in Spearfish Canyon rented double cabins with two separate bedrooms, two bathrooms, and a shared porch nestled in pine woods. It was a good place for two friends to sit together and talk and share the supper they had collected at a Spearfish grocery store. It was a place where two former lovers might watch evening draw down on the canyon's granite "needles" formation, listen to the wind whispering in the tall pines, and wonder what kind of whispers the night would bring.

They had just visited Bear Butte together. It was the first time Kiah had been back, and it felt good to be able to tell Cecily that, and to look into her eyes and see that she understood why. There were so many feelings, so few words. Only Cecily would know that. She alone had been there with him, and he with her. The rush of emotion scared them both even now—the anger, the fear, the loss, the sense of obligation to something neither could name. High on the mountain they had stood together, hands clasped between them, and they'd said nothing as the wind dried their tears. They'd said nothing as they'd made their way back down the path. But over a picnic supper shared on the porch, the conversation flowed smoothly between them, from a discussion of the kinds of cheese they liked best with ham to the kinds of memories each of them had of Ellen.

"She wanted me to go down to Red Creek and see for myself what was going on," Cecily recalled. "She said she thought I would be in a position to tell the story someday." A look passed between them, acknowledging Ellen's foresight. "Now that I am, I keep telling myself I can't be sentimental about it. I have a job to do, and I have to be objective about it."

"So how's it going?" he asked, shifting a toothpick from one corner of his mouth to the other.

"You mean the story?"

"I mean the struggle. Your boss wants you to put a certain kind of slant on this story, right?"

"I decided today that sentimentality is no worse an obstacle to objectivity than greed." She raised a can of diet pop in toast. "How's that for justification?"

"Depends on what you need to justify." In the dim light his smile was wolflike. "Are you sentimental about me?"

"Yes, I'm afraid I am." She thought she deserved credit for her honesty, at the very least. "And if you're looking for advantages, I guess I just handed you one."

"You know I'll use it, too." He plucked the toothpick from his mouth as he leaned closer. "What you don't know is that I've missed you, Cecily. I've missed you a lot." His eyes glittered with the restoration of his lazy smile. "There. Now we're almost even."

"Almost?"

"Well, maybe I've given you a slight edge. I don't ever let myself get sentimental, and missing a woman is not my style. Especially not when I've been the occasional bonus during her vacations from school."

"My bonus?" She gave a brief laugh. "That's funny. I thought love on the run was just your style and that I was your R-and-R."

"Then why have I missed you so much?" he challenged. "And why do you get sentimental over me?"

"Because you were the first. Remember?" She plucked a green grape from the plate of leftovers and offered to feed it to him. "How did you phrase that? Rather crudely, as I recall. It had something to do with fruit."

"It must be hard to get sentimental over such a

oldhearted bastard." He managed to lick her fingertip as e took the grape into his mouth. "You should have held ut for a gentleman."

"I really should've," she agreed with a coy smile. "I hink I've learned my lesson, though."

"Damn." He caught the hand that fed him, trapped it oosely in his, and sneaked his thumb into the hollow of her palm. "I'm going to take you to Pine Ridge tomorrow, see if we can dig up some more of Whirlwind Rider's re- lations. Does that sound like a pretty decent plan?"

"Dig up?"

"Find." He bowed his head and nibbled her knuckle. "Funny girl. There's a celebration going on this weekend. They might not let you in to see the Sun Dance, but the powwow is always open to anyone."

"Have you ever participated in a Sun Dance?"

Kiah shook his head. "Looks pretty painful to me." He continued to hold her hand as he shifted in his chair. "Those days are over. We don't hunt buffalo. We don't live in tipis. I've done a few sweats, but not lately. They started giving me the creeps."

"The creeps?"

"I don't know what it was. Kinda like the feeling I got when I was reading that journal, like some kind of ghost was getting into my head."

"So you believe in ghosts."

"I grew up with the *wanaǧi*. The *gigis*. Ghosts," he ex- plained. "The Indian way, you know? You just wait. You start listening to the old people tell stories, you'll start hearing voices in the wind, too."

"I hope so." Impulsively she pulled their clasped hands onto her knees. "I'd love to hear voices from the past. Think of all they could tell us, Kiah. The world has changed so much in the last hundred years, but people haven't changed. For better or for worse, people haven't changed that much at all."

"You don't think so?" He laughed. "No wonder the *wanaǧi* can't rest in peace. They're watching us make the same damn mistakes over and over again."

"Maybe," she allowed. "Wounded Knee is at Pine Ridge, isn't it?"

"You're not getting me to go there."

"Why not?"

"I'll take you to meet some real live Indians, okay? No ghosts, no graveyards. But you'll hear stories. You go to an Indian doings, you can count on hearing stories."

They took a walk together in the woods, voiced their plans for the next day, and wordlessly spoke of wants and wishes for the intervening hours. An innocent touch became intimate in its lingering. A moment of quiet was made more engaging by a night bird's call. The near approach of the kiss they had yet to share was deliciously enticing.

But they went to their separate rooms. When she heard him shut the shower off, she turned hers on. She'd brought some scented soap. For the first time she would be wearing a feminine nightgown—thin white summer cotton—when he came to her. When he did—if he did—it would be a sign of nothing more than the desire they had always shared. Take it for what it was, she told herself. It had always been glorious.

He didn't come right away, so she went to bed. She felt like a spring-green girl when she heard the doorknob turn. She sat up. The light shone from the window of his room, illuminating the porch behind him. He was a dark silhouette in her doorway.

"Kiah?"

"You left your door open."

"I know."

He came in, closed the door, and locked it. "You take a lot of chances for a sensible woman."

"I don't, really." He came to the foot of the bed, and she met him there, kneeling at the edge of the mattress. "I mean, I seldom do," she amended, aligning the heels of her hands with the waistband of his low-riding jeans, spreading her finger over his lean abdomen. "Except when I'm around you."

"I've driven myself nearly crazy trying to stay cool tonight." He slipped the straps of her nightgown off her shoulders. "I'm nearly crazy now, just so you know."

"Your skin is hot," she whispered as she moved her hands slowly upward, thrilling to the feel of hard, masculine muscle. "You can't be cool on a night like this."

"It's stupid to try." He pushed the straps down.

She lowered her arms and let the loose gown fall.

"I wanted to be sensible about you this time," she confessed in a small voice as his hands reversed their motion, trailing back up her arms. His thumbs brushed the sides of her breasts. She inhaled sharply, and her nipples touched his stomach.

"Why?"

She groaned. "For the same reason you were trying hard to stay cool, I suppose."

"Let's give it up for each other, should we?" He brought his hands up under her breasts, cupped them, lifted them. "I'll do it for you if you'll do it for me."

"Oh, Kiah." She closed her eyes. Her hands went to his waist, but one slipped and found the turgid bulge in his pants. "Oh, Kiah, you're so . . ."

"You bet I am." He caressed her nipples with his thumbs until he had made them just as hard as he was. "I have been since I first laid eyes on you," he said, toppling her back on the bed, unzipping his pants just to ease himself as he followed her down. "Before that. Since I first heard your voice on the phone. God, what a sweet voice." Their hips joined, he pressed himself against her tight, rubbing hardness against hardness, need against need, making it feel both better and worse. "Oh, God, what a sweet, sweet"—he went slowly, nuzzling, licking her nipples, suckling, tasting—"woman. Woman, woman, I've missed you . . ."

He kissed her—breasts, lips, belly, her soft inner thighs and the succulent bud she harbored in the feminine folds between them. He touched her and teased her until he could feel her sizzling at every point of contact. He suckled her until she crooned his name so lovingly that he could not resist the invitation to come down inside and be one with her, to come down, come down, come down until there was nowhere to go but up very, very high.

Much later, after they had lain together, trembling softly, nuzzling languidly, she whispered his name again. He responded with a gentle caress.

"Kiah, there's something I want to tell you. I want to tell you why—"

"I don't want to hear it." He was content, and he was afraid she'd try to explain his contentment away, so he touched a finger to her lips.

But he hadn't meant to sound so brusque, and he told her so with a brush of his lips against hers. Then he whispered, "Not now. We made love. I don't know why. I don't *want* to know why. I just know we made love."

The powwow was the highlight of summer in Indian country. Every community had one, and generally the bigger the town, the bigger the event. Indian dancing had become more competitive than Cecily remembered, with cash prizes offered for the best dancers sporting the most elaborate costumes. Bright colors and synthetic fabrics added a twentieth-century twist to nineteenth-century Native American traditions, as did a traveling carnival show and the local rodeo. Kiah saw many familiar faces, and he was reintroduced to others he hadn't seen since childhood.

The last time he'd seen his cousin Lawrence Crow Foot they'd both been missing their two front teeth. Lawrence was still missing one. As he herded them into line for the traditional "feed," he delighted Cecily with his description of a toothless young Kiah with an unruly cowlick and legs like a Thoroughbred foal.

"You had to think twice about teasin' him 'cause you could never outrun him," Lawrence said with a chuckle as he slapped Kiah on the back. "Your Oglala blood calling on you to powwow with us, cousin?"

"I smelled that *papa* soup from way the hell up on the Grand River." Kiah took two cups of it from the serving table. "Smell the wild onions and turnips," he told Cecily as he passed a cup under her nose. She was juggling a plate of frybread and cups of *wōjapi*, but she acknowledged the pungent scent with an appreciative nod.

"*Papa* is the dried meat," Kiah explained. "Used to be buffalo."

"Still is," Lawrence said. He led the way to an open spot on the bowery bleachers. "We butchered a couple from the tribe's herd. We're eatin' real traditional this weekend." He glanced at Cecily, eyes twinkling. "Puppy soup tonight."

She looked to Kiah, hoping for some assurance to the contrary.

Kiah laughed. "Hey, this is the real thing. This is the way Whirlwind Rider used to eat."

Cecily sat down to her meal, thinking she'd better fill up on the buffalo this afternoon, for there was no way she could choke down any puppy soup later on.

"You didn't know ol' man Whirlwind Rider, did you?" Lawrence asked Kiah.

Kiah shook his head as he tore into a piece of frybread. "He died a little before our time."

"He would have been some relation to you, being related through my mom's side," Lawrence said. "I know I've heard a lot about him. World War I hero. Every year they give a track award that's named for him. They say he could *really* run, that guy."

"You're talking about Marcus, right? He was my grandfather. I never knew Toby Rider, you know"—Kiah gestured, frybread in hand—"my dad. Kind of a flash in the pan, that guy."

"Yeah, he kicked pretty young. I didn't realize it was that kind of a connection—Rider, Whirlwind Rider. You know, you have to listen to the old people to get these things straight." Lawrence pondered for a moment while he dunked a slice of white bread in his soup. "You know who could tell you about Marcus Whirlwind Rider? Ol' Ezra Hairy Chin. He's eighty years old, maybe more." He scanned the bleachers. "I know I saw him here somewhere, kinda coolin' his heels. He don't much like talking English, but he'll do it if he's in the right mood."

Ezra was in the right mood. His granddaughter had

plunked him in a lawn chair in the shade behind her Indian taco stand where he could listen to the powwow drums and sip from a plastic liter bottle of root beer. He enjoyed the elder's role. He graciously offered chairs all around.

"If you want some pop, you have to buy it from my granddaughter," he said, dangling his root beer by the neck from two gnarled fingers. "Talk's cheap, she says. Pop's sixty cents a can. That's why I brought my own."

Kiah shook off the suggestion. "My father's name was Toby Rider. Did you know him at all, Tunkaśila?"

"Not good. He didn't live long enough." The old man eyed him carefully. "You drink heavy like that, too?"

"Not anymore."

"You smoke?"

"Gave that up, too, pretty much."

"Damn, I could use a cigarette," Ezra said, disgusted. "If you decide to give up women, too, send this one over to my place. I'm old, but I ain't cold." He slapped his bony, denim-clad knee, then wagged a finger at Cecily. "Heh heh heh, just kidding. I had you worried, though, didn't I?"

"You had *me* worried," Kiah said with a smile. "Grandma Emma says my father was a good kidder, too."

"Not so's you'd notice. Too busy tryin' to be a cowboy." Ezra propped the big pop bottle on the aluminum arm of his chair and studied Kiah's face as though he were committing it to memory. "I knew your grandfather."

"Marcus Whirlwind Rider?"

"To boot, I remember *his* father." The old man nodded imperiously, as though that fact alone gave him special status. "I remember Whirlwind Rider. He was a proud man. He took four bullets that day at Wounded Knee." He pointed to his own thigh, hip, and shoulder, and finally to his side. "But he didn't die. His wounds gave him trouble for the rest of his life, but he limped only when he was tired. In the end, of course, he was very tired. And the day he died, the women raised such a keening we thought the hills themselves would weep. I was still a young man. I remember that day well."

"I always thought that Grandma Emma was my grand-ther's sister," Kiah said.

"The Indian way, she was. Whirlwind Rider's sister arah and her kids helped raise his boy, Marcus. Emma as one of Sarah's kids. So was Marcus. The Indian way." he old man paused to take a drink from the bottle. It was alf empty, but still it seemed a burden for him to carry it ll the way to his mouth. Kiah had half a notion to do it r him so he'd get on with the story, but he knew that a an like Ezra would let him know if he wanted his help.

Ezra wiped his mouth with the back of his hand, inced, and shook his head. "Damn diet pop. They don't ant me to have sugar." His head kept wagging as he arked back to the past in the next breath. "Marcus was lso there at Wounded Knee. He was a baby. They found im alive, too. Only a few who were there lived through hat day. Only a few survived it."

"What about"—both men turned to Cecily as she fin-shed quietly—"Marcus's mother?"

"She died that day," Ezra said. "After that, the father ved for his boy. He taught him the old ways, but Whirl-vind Rider permitted him to learn the new ways, too. It vas bad to take the children away from their parents, he aid. There must be teachers for them here." Ezra paused) collect his thoughts. "Marcus was a teacher," he said. Did you know that, son? Your grandfather became a eacher."

"I didn't know much about either of them," Kiah said. I guess I never asked."

"Then here is a thing you should know. There was a me, long time ago when Whirlwind Rider still lived, that ome people appealed to Washington for a payment to be ade to the Wounded Knee survivors. In those days every-ne was poor here. Some people said, 'They never paid us r our land. They promised to pay for Paha Sapa, and ey never did. Maybe we can get the money now.' Yes, at long ago, all this started.

"And there were soldiers, like General Miles, who said at the army did a terrible wrong that day at Wounded nee. Some of the soldiers had been decorated for brav-

ery. The general told that it was a shameful thing. And
there were congressmen who said that money should be
paid. They wanted some of those survivors to ride the train
to Washington and tell about what happened that day, how
Big Foot's Minneconjou people and some of the Hunkpapa
who had been with Sitting Bull had surrendered, and how
their guns had been taken, and still the soldiers turned
their guns on them.

"But Whirlwind Rider would not go to Washington. He
was never an agency Indian. He would not ask for money,
and he said that if they gave him money, he would throw
it away. 'An award,' they said, 'to compensate you for
your pain and loss.' " Ezra shook his head slowly. "Whirlwind Rider said no. They could not pay him for what he
lost at Wounded Knee."

"His wife," Kiah said quietly.

"Do you know who she was?" Cecily asked.

"She was not named among the dead except as Mrs.
Whirlwind Rider. That was the way many of the women
were identified. Those who were identified at all. Whirlwind Rider was a spiritual man. None of us ever heard
him speak his wife's name. But like a few of the mothers
who died that day, she was able to save her baby's life."

After a long silence, Ezra asked, "Did you pledge yourself?"

"You mean, for the Sun Dance? I'm not much for . . ."
Kiah glanced away, embarrassed to confess to this particular old man a deficiency that, before this moment, he had
never counted among his worst shortcomings. "I guess I'm
not a very spiritual man."

"You can change that whenever you want to." Ezra
pointed to a small hut nestled by itself in a copse of cottonwoods a short distance away. Compared with the array
of canvas and nylon tents in the camping area, the hide-
covered hut looked like an anachronism. "Come to that
lodge tonight. We're gonna be having a sweat."

Kiah slid Cecily a reassuring glance. She was his guest.
He knew his responsibilities. "We've rented a cabin up by
Spearfish."

"That's a long drive," Ezra said. "You should stay here tonight. Someone will find you a tent to sleep in."

"I don't think we can—"

"We can if you want to, Kiah," Cecily offered, blithely canceling his excuse. "I'd like to stay."

So they did. Cecily passed on the soup at the evening feed in favor of trying one of Ezra's granddaughter's Indian tacos. They watched some of the dance competitions, interspersed with "intertribal" periods when anyone might dance. Not everyone did. Most people were there to watch and listen, visit with friends, or chase them around the grounds, depending upon their age. Everyone came to eat, except the young lovers, who strolled together around the perimeter of the bowery, needing little sustenance besides the look in each other's eyes.

Kiah wasn't a young lover anymore, but he identified with that look. He slid one Cecily's way every now and then, and she rewarded him with a pretty smile. She seemed to be enjoying the festivities. He resolved to see that she continued to do so. He did take notice when Ezra and several other men took their leave. Ezra raised his chin and turned his head as though he were waiting for one more person. Kiah knew he was being summoned, but he kept his seat on the plank bleachers. The others led the old man away.

Lawrence Crow Foot invited Kiah and Cecily to join his family around the campfire near their tent. Several of the children—Kiah knew they couldn't *all* have been Lawrence and Rita's—divided up the last of Lawrence's change for the carnival, which had been set up a couple of miles from the powwow grounds, close to the highway. They'd found a ride, the kids said. Kiah contributed a few dollars to their booty, and off the younger ones went. Some of the older kids stayed around. A trio of girls had a card game going by lamplight inside the tent, and a couple of the boys passed a bag of sunflower seeds between them and listened to the campfire talk.

"We've got a vacancy for you," Lawrence told Kiah. "Mousie and Jim have a spare pup tent. Their boys are up to Fort Yates for a track meet. You know Mousie? What's her real name?" he asked over his shoulder.

Someone in the campfire circle supplied, "Madeline, isn't it?"

Kiah shrugged and shook his head.

"Anyway, she's a LaPointe. I guess she'd be related to you somehow," Lawrence said. Kiah's Pine Ridge relations seemed to be mushrooming at every turn, but that didn't surprise him. It was the way of Indian relations. If you established one, you were soon related to everyone within a fifty mile radius and then some.

"Did you hear about how Mousie really told Tinsley off?" The opening came from Lawrence's wife, Rita, who was pitching sprigs of sage into the fire to chase mosquitoes away. "Tinsley's the one who runs the store over in Kyle."

"The gas station, too," one of the older boys put in. "White guy with big frybread ears."

"So, anyway, Mousie's in the store, and Tinsley's coming along behind her, kinda watchin' her like, and Mousie picks up this can of chili." Rita made a polishing motion with a flat hand. "Kinda rubs the dust off the top of it, and she says, '*Ťuwale!* This is less than what I paid in Rapid City last week. Same kind.' And Tinsley, he says, 'Same size can?' Mousie says, 'Same exact can.' "

With a chuckle Lawrence chimed in. "So next time she goes in—he's kinda following along behind her again—she picks up the same damn can of chili—"

"Been on the shelf since he bought the store," Rita said.

"No shit." Lawrence cackled a little more. "So now Mousie looks at the can, she goes, '*Ťuwale!* Is this a collector's item now? It's gone up a whole dollar.' Tinsley says, 'It's been that price for a week now. Inflation.' " Lawrence had to stop and laugh at what was to come, reducing his eyes to small slits as the firelight gleamed in his cheeks. " 'Inflation's *really* bad these days,' Mousie says, just serious," he sputtered. Then he jabbed a finger in the air to dramatize Mousie's punch line. " 'Eeez, just look what it's doing to your ears, Tinsley!' "

The night exploded with laughter, detonated around the

campfire first by that story, then by several more. But the first time Kiah yawned, Lawrence took the cue to show them to their accommodations. "Mousie said they cleaned up after the boys," he said. "Hope it's okay."

"I'm looking forward to meeting Mousie so I can thank her." Cecily paused, then took a brave chance, just to see if she'd really gotten it. "I'm guessing she has tiny ears? Mousie?"

Lawrence shrugged, glancing at Kiah for help making the connection.

"She's looking for hidden meaning." He put his arm around her shoulders and gave her a fond squeeze. "Teaching her about Indian humor. She's getting there, but sometimes she tries too hard."

"Yeah, well, we just like to laugh." Lawrence offered Cecily a handshake. "It's good to try hard. I'll have to remember to notice Mousie's ears next time. Maybe she shouldn't talk. Maybe she's got frybreads, too."

With a chuckle, Lawrence shook Kiah's hand and went on his way, leaving the two alone to cocoon together in their pup tent. "Pretty close quarters," Kiah said as he set his boots aside and started shucking his jeans. "We'll just have to hold each other pretty close."

"We're good at that, aren't we?"

"We sure are."

Her hands went to the top button on her shirt, but on second thought she abandoned it in favor of helping him with his. "Are my earlobes kind of big, too, do you think?" she asked tentatively.

"You mean, do you have frybreads?" He chuckled as he swept her hair back. "All I've got to say is, let's have a nibble."

He'd experienced few pleasures more satisfying than making love surrounded by the rolling thunder of the dance drums. They started slow, building the cadence in his blood. Then they picked up the pace as the urgent wail of the singers called him to take his woman to new heights. And she, her body enveloping his very essence, returned the blessed favor. He could have sworn they'd run a two-person relay together, and that the victory drums pounded as euphorically as their heartbeats.

But when he tried to sleep in her arms, sleep wouldn't come. He was hot and restive. His mind wouldn't shut down. They should've gone back to the cabin, he told himself as he recalled the deep serenity he'd enjoyed the previous night, lying beside the woman who'd returned to his life like a recurring dream. They'd shared much more than their bodies, and he had made up his mind not to let her go this time. This time he would say the things that needed saying, the love words a woman needed to hear—if he could just find the right ones.

She stirred closer to him and whispered against his neck. "What are you thinking about?"

He couldn't tell her. He didn't know the words yet, and he didn't want to screw anything up by saying something stupid. So he clamped his jaw tight and stared at the overhead curve of the tent that was closing in around him.

Cecily kissed his shoulder tenderly. "I think you should go to the sweat."

"I'm in a fine sweat right now," he said. He lay there buck-naked on top of the pallet they'd made of borrowed blankets. The breeze through the side vents didn't seem to cool him any. "I'd kill for a cigarette right about now."

"Please spare me, kind sir, for I have no cigarettes."

" 'Spear me'?" He gave a husky chuckle. "Is that what you said?"

"I said . . ." She propped herself up on one elbow, modestly tucking a blanket around the breasts he'd kissed and caressed lavishly a short while ago. "I think those drums are calling you, and you ought to put aside your fears and heed the call. Don't they pass the pipe in the sweat lodge?"

"Mmm, they do, but it doesn't taste much like a Marlboro. And I'm not afraid to go in there. I just don't believe in it the way they do, you know? I'm not . . ." Why was it so hard to say? He was just being honest. He lived in the present, in the real world. "I'm not a spiritual man," he said firmly. "What's done is done. The Black Hills are full of billboards and tourist traps, not ghosts. We

n crawl into a hole and sweat blood if we want to, but
hen we come out, Mount Rushmore will still be there.
hose four big white faces with frybread ears will still be
ttin' up there, stakin' out their claim."

"They were just men, too. They did some bad things,
m sure, but they also did some good things." She
uched his arm, assuring him in the timeless way of a
oman. "Just like you."

"Yeah, well ... I'll tell you one thing, my great-
randmother was no white woman. There were no white
omen killed at Wounded Knee," he claimed fiercely.
They were all Indian women. And children. There were
ome young men, and there were old men, like Ezra."

"I'm ... sorry." She sighed and spoke with genuine sad-
ess. "I don't know what else to say."

"You can say something like ... You could tell me we
hould take the money. Remind me that the land belongs
o someone else now."

"I don't know if I believe that. The people who actually
ook the land are all dead now."

"So are the people who actually lost it."

"But the Hills are still there." She adjusted the blanket
gain, and he wondered how she could stand to cover her-
elf with anything, hot as it was. She didn't seem to no-
ice. "The billboards have to be replaced from time to
ime, and they've had to repair Lincoln's nose. But the
Hills are eternal, and the Lakota people have survived."

"Barely." He tucked his arm behind his head. "Trying to
ind some way to stand on our own feet, feed our kids our-
elves. A hundred million dollars might be the answer."
He was thinking out loud, and he appreciated the fact that
e could do it so readily in her presence. "The only reason
Crazy Horse came in at the end was because the children
vere starving. The reason the old chiefs signed papers
hey didn't understand was because they understood the
vords, 'Take the deal, or your children will starve.' "

"Has anyone said that to you?"

"No." He rolled to his side, facing her, smiling. "They
ay, 'Crazy Indian, take the money!' I say, 'Keep the
noney. Send me a good-lookin' newspaper lady.' "

"You're incorrigible." She smiled back and touched hi
cheek. "You know that, don't you?"

"Does that mean horny?"

"Uh-uh. It means you're just trying to avoid tha
sweat."

He flopped over on his back again and sighed. "You'r
right. Jesus, how come my great-grandfather had to be s
damned ... *idealistic?*" He turned his head. "Just lik
somebody else I know."

"Me? Idealistic?"

"You, idealistic. Me, all I ever wanted to do was ride
broncs and raise hell, like my dad."

"Who didn't live very long, as Ezra said." She leaned
over him—past the proof that *incorrigible* could, indeed,
have meant horny—and located his jeans. "Go on, cowboy. Listen to the drums. Go to the sweat. And if a
friendly spirit gets into your head, I think maybe you
should see what it wants."

Chapter 22

Cecily was alone in the small tent when the sun rose and brightened its yellow walls the following morning. Kiah was still doing his man-thing. She decided that she had some time to do a woman-thing. She took the journal and the keys to Kiah's pickup and found her way back to Grandma Emma's house.

Cecily welcomed a cup of coffee, but, tugging absently at her earlobe, she turned down the offer of more frybread. She waited until she was again sitting across from Grandma Emma before she announced that she had something to show her and solicitously placed the book on the table.

"I can't read much anymore with my eyesight the way it is. It has to be in big print." Sighting down her nose, the old woman peered through the glasses balanced near the hawk's-beak tip. "What's it about?"

"It's a diary, written by a woman named Priscilla Twiss." The name brought Grandma Emma's chin up quickly. "You've heard of her?"

"Yes. She was my grandmother's friend."

"In her diary she claims to be Whirlwind Rider's wife. He would have been your uncle, right? Your *great* uncle."

"My uncle. We don't get fussy. His son, Marcus, wasn't too much older than me. My mother was only about fourteen or fifteen when Marcus was born."

Cecily nodded. She waited for a moment, hoping the

woman would just spill it all out so she wouldn't have to grill her with the myriad questions she could barely contain. No such luck. She cleared her throat and wished in vain for a tape recorder. "Did your mother ever talk about what happened at Wounded Knee?"

"She wasn't there, but she heard a lot about it. They took Marcus in after that time. His father was hurt bad."

Again, Cecily nodded. She decided to try to share rather than interrogate. "Ezra Hairy Chin told us that Marcus's mother was killed at Wounded Knee. She must have been Whirlwind Rider's wife after Priscilla, but I'm wondering . . . You said you *thought* he had two wives.

"I think his first wife was Hunkpapa, like Kiah's mother," the old woman said, avoiding Cecily's eyes. "But, you know, it was so long ago. I think she died very young."

"The journal ends just after Crazy Horse surrendered in 1877. Priscilla sent it to her father in a trunk, which I bought at an auction."

The old woman listened intently, her interest nearly a match for Cecily's own, but still she avoided looking into Cecily's eyes.

"I found the journal only recently," Cecily said, persisting carefully. "It's a remarkable coincidence that I've known Kiah all this time, and I've had this trunk with the journal hidden inside." She gestured effusively. "It has to be a coincidence. I mean, these things don't just come full circle like this after a hundred years, back to where they started."

"How long have you known Kiah?"

"I first met him when I spent a summer here nine years ago." She added, suddenly contemplative, "And I seem to keep coming back."

"Coming full circle? With this book, this story," Grandma Emma said, touching a weathered finger to the journal. "Or maybe with this man?"

"I've gone in circles with Kiah," Cecily admitted. "That's for sure."

"A woman's life is a circle. Her breast is a circle. The door to her womb is a circle, just like the door to her lodge, and like the lodge itself. All circles. We have all these corners now. That door, this house. We've gotten to be just square." She nodded toward the door and gave a dry chuckle. "One of my grandsons—he was just a little bitty guy that time—I told him to turn that radio down, and he said, 'Oh, Unci, you're just a square.' "

"I'll bet he's changed his mind about that since."

"He died, that one. He got to boozing and got in a car wreck."

"Oh." It took Cecily a moment to switch gears emotionally. "I'm sorry."

The old woman nodded.

"Grandma Emma, in the journal, Priscilla calls Whirlwind Rider her husband. I don't know whether they were formally or ... or legally married or whether he took a wife after he lived with Priscilla. Priscilla had a child, but he was stillborn. When you said his first wife died very young ..."

Emma's voice drifted with her focus, to another time, another talk between women.

"They lost three, my grandmother said."

"Three babies? You mean ... Whirlwind Rider and Priscilla," Cecily insisted.

"The fourth time they thought she might be too old, and everyone was worried, but that time it finally went okay. They had a son." She smiled wistfully. "He was a big one, my grandmother used to tell him. He was almost too much for his small, little mother, but her husband got her a doctor that time—Dr. Charles Eastman, who was at Pine Ridge, and he was a Santee Sioux," she claimed with pride. "And they finally had their baby after trying so hard."

"Priscilla *was* Marcus's mother." Cecily concluded quietly. She was filled suddenly with a sense of light and warmth, an inexplicable sense of fulfillment.

The old woman nodded. "She used to teach the children in the camps of the Oglala and the Minneconjou. But they never went to the agency. No one ever spoke of her as white. They called her Glass Eyes Woman because her eyes were blue. No one ever spoke of Marcus as a mixed-blood. He was not a trader's son. He was the son of a Tokala, a warrior." The old eyes met Cecily's at last. "She belonged to the Lakota. They guarded her. They guarded her spirit. Certain things were never said. You understand this?"

Cecily nodded. "How did they come to be with Big Foot's band?"

"The Minneconjou were his mother's people. Whirlwind Rider and his wife and son were camped on the Cheyenne River with Big Foot's Minneconjou that winter. There was no game left and no rations to be had unless they would join Red Cloud at Pine Ridge. They were talking about doing this, but some of them remembered how Crazy Horse had been murdered after he surrendered. Then a few of the Hunkpapa people came from Standing Rock and told how Sitting Bull had just been murdered in his own camp by Indian police. And now the soldiers were coming for Big Foot's little band of about four hundred people. The soldiers said that the dance some of the people were doing was like a war dance, but it was called the Ghost Dance, and it was just a dance to make a vision. That was all it was.

"They decided to try to make a run for it, to try to reach Pine Ridge, where their Oglala relations were waiting for them. There would be food there, and Red Cloud might be able to reason with the army. Big Foot had a coughing sickness, but the plan was to make the journey at night, under cover of darkness. They were headed south."

Grandma Emma's voice grew distant as the story came alive in Cecily's head. She felt the icy wind in her face, and her feet were numb. It had been an open winter, but one of the old men who was known for his ability to forecast weather changes had said that there would be a blizzard in three days' time . . .

Priscilla knew full well that Whirlwind Rider regretted coming north in the first place. Marcus had been born at his sister's place nearly a year ago, and they could have stayed there. But it was too close to the agency, and Whirlwind Rider wasn't sure he trusted Eastman or Red

Cloud or anyone else who was in the habit of feeding on agency beef all year round. He talked about taking his wife and child and camping on Cherry Creek for the rest of the winter, but Priscilla assured him that she was strong enough to make the journey with the people. She knew they needed him as much as she did, for he was a Tokala, and it was his duty to protect the helpless ones.

On this journey, the helpless ones were many, indeed. Big Foot made sure that the last of the food went to the nursing mothers. For Marcus's sake, Priscilla accepted her share. The baby hadn't cried once. She hadn't told Whirlwind Rider that her milk had gone dry, but he knew.

Big Foot's strength was deteriorating, but he was not to be left out when plans were made. While the people rested, hunters were dispatched to find food. Whirlwind Rider knew that there was not time to find enough game to feed the people, so his party of four took the risk of heading north, where an encounter with soldiers seemed most likely, to a place where they had seen a herd of cattle grazing on the brown hillsides.

They didn't dare fire a shot, nor did they speak. One man was left to hold the horses while the other three stalked the quiet herd with the skill they'd once used in hunting buffalo in these same coulees. Whirlwind Rider prepared his rope while he signaled the other two to be ready with their knives. Then he swung a loop and dropped it neatly over the cow's horns. Within moments they had slit the animal's throat, gutted and butchered it into four quarters.

That night the *ak̇icita* saw that the meat was divided so that everyone was fed. The small game brought in by other hunting parties was saved to give the nursing mothers the next day. After another day's march they reached Medicine Creek, and since they were exhausted and had no more food, they were forced to slaughter a few young horses for meat. Priscilla understood her husband's utter despondency that night, for she knew well that only in times of terrible hunger had Lakota people ever eaten horseflesh. The horse was called *wakan*, that which was holy.

But with morning prayers there was always a return of hope. If all went well the people would be in Pine Ridge by nightfall, where they would find refuge with the Oglala, Whirlwind Rider's father's band. As the cold winter sun eased its way toward the western hills, a column of soldiers was spotted in the south. Big Foot's voice was almost gone, but he instructed the *aḱicita* to raise a white flag over his wagon. Among the younger men there was some talk of making a stand, but they were sternly reminded that the safety of the helpless ones was paramount. They had taken a gamble and lost. The men of the *aḱicita* took their places in the forefront as the only protection the helpless ones had on the open prairie. But they displayed a number of white flags so that there could be no doubt of their intent to surrender.

After the army major deployed his Hotchkiss guns and his detachment of mounted troops, he approached the line of Lakota men and announced that he required an unconditional surrender from their leader. The Lakota men deferred to Big Foot, who agreed to every demand the major made. The people were told that they would camp on Wounded Knee Creek, where more soldiers waited.

Neither Whirlwind Rider nor his wife let it be known that they understood the soldiers' English. Priscilla kept her head covered and her child tucked beneath her robe as she proceeded among the women. At the order to set up camp, Whirlwind Rider helped her pitch their tipi. They shared the bit of bacon and hardtack the army had provided. He insisted that she take most of his portion, but he ate enough to curb his hunger and give him strength for his visit to Big Foot's lodge. The old man was too sick to counsel with the *aḱicita* that night, but he told the warriors that in their plans for the next day they must keep the safety of their families foremost, as always. They were outmanned and overwhelmingly outgunned, and they had no choice but to obey the soldiers' demands.

Whirlwind Rider smoked and prayed and counseled with his Tokala brothers late into the night, but when he finally joined his wife in their bed, he knew that only little Marcus had been able to rest. Priscilla had lain awake, keeping a woman's vigil, planning the reassuring words she whispered to him now.

They were on Sioux land, she said. They had done nothing wrong. They were only traveling to join their relatives, as was the custom. Many times in the past the roaming bands had brought food to the agency Indians when there were no rations. Now the tables were turned, she acknowledged, but it was all part of the circle. Tomorrow they would find refuge with Sarah and Henry. They would warm themselves by the fire and share whatever food there was. They would regain their strength and soon laugh again.

Whirlwind Rider nodded. He said nothing of the thing that most troubled him—the Seventh Cavalry guidon he'd noticed fluttering above the heads of the soldiers to whom they had surrendered. He had seen the same flag many years ago when his people had been attacked on the Little Big Horn. The Lakota had been victorious then. The warriors had defended the helpless ones from harm. But those days were gone. Crazy Horse, Sitting Bull, even Spotted Tail had been murdered, and now there was only Red Cloud, who had sold out . . . and Big Foot, who was dying.

Whirlwind Rider took Priscilla in his arms, reminded her of his love, and promised her his protection. There had been many times over the years when love and protection were all he had to give, and in those times she'd asked no more of him. But this was the first time he had ever agreed to surrender unconditionally. It had not even been this bad when he had followed Crazy Horse in surrender. Tomorrow he would have to lay down his weapons. His gaunt body would be his family's only protection. Once the soldiers disarmed him, the second part of his promise would become an echo in the wind.

But not the first. Never the first. His promise to love her burned like a torch in the night, and the white soldiers could never extinguish it, no matter what they did to him tomorrow.

"I will speak to them," he told her. "I will tell them who you are."

"I am your wife. I am the mother of your son." She laid

her hand on his concave belly. "And you are the love of my life. Your son and I will have it no other way."

She had chosen for herself, as was the undisputed right of a woman among the Lakota. If the soldiers knew of this choice, they would scorn her, and she was not a woman to be scorned.

When morning broke over the frozen hilltops, the Lakota greeted the sun as they always did, by giving thanks to Tunkašila. The soldiers greeted it with a resonant reveille, as was their practice. More rations were distributed and traditional details were performed in both camps. Then all the Indian men were summoned to assemble in front of the heated army tent to which Big Foot had been moved the night before. There they were told that they must surrender their guns. As they stood between their women and children and the heavily armed soldiers, the Lakota could see the four Hotchkiss guns that had been placed on the hillsides and trained at their camp. They knew that additional troops from the Seventh Regiment had arrived during the night. Reluctantly they began giving up what few guns they had.

The officers moved their troops to surround the camp and also to cut off the warriors from their families. Troopers were detailed to search the camp for weapons. They took every gun they could find, along with every instrument, be it sharp or blunt, while Lakota eyes watched in horror. It would not be easy to replace so many knives, awls, crowbars, and grinding stones.

Priscilla quietly surrendered the stone fleshing knife her husband had once handed her through the window of a moving train. The trooper, who had been in a hurry, paused for a moment. She kept her eyes downcast, her shawl pulled tightly over her head, and she prayed he had not noted the difference in color between her hand and those of the other women. Little Marcus squirmed in her arms.

The soldier grunted and moved on.

When the troopers dismounted, Whirlwind Rider instinctively tried to break through their ranks, to somehow maneuver himself into a position to defend the helpless ones. But the soldiers pushed him back. Across the line of troops he saw the soldier take Priscilla's fleshing blade. She turned her face away from the man as he moved on, and her light eyes met her husband's dark ones. Neither of them attended to the death song raised by one of the old men, or to the scuffle over the rifle that one of the younger men vociferously demanded the right to keep since he had paid for it. Neither of them saw who fired the first shot. In that instant, each saw the face of the other, and for that cherished moment, nothing else mattered.

But Whirlwind Rider was a Tokala. He lunged for the nearest rifle and managed to fire several rounds, even after the first bullet struck his hip and the second his thigh. The third bullet silenced his rifle. The fourth stole his consciousness. The cold kept him from bleeding to death, and Tunkaśila guarded the scant breath in his body.

Priscilla tried to run to her husband, but she lost sight of him in the thundering, smoking chaos. People were running toward a ravine, screaming, shouting, falling, and crawling through a hailstorm of bullets. She ran, too, clutching her son to her breast, head bowed, shoulders hunched to give the baby all the protection her small body would afford. She went down on one knee, and at first she thought she had tripped. The white-hot pain in her back told her otherwise. She tried to get up, but there was no feeling in her legs. Another bullet struck her hand. It hurt more than the first.

Black boots stormed past her. She started to call out to the blue legs, to beg them to come back and take her baby, but they stopped running. Priscilla lifted her eyes and watched the soldier take aim and fire. A small boy fell to the ground.

Marcus whimpered. "Shhh," his mother whispered as she used her good hand to wrap her shawl around her child and tuck him beneath her. "You must speak out, little one, but not today."

As the life ebbed from her body she heard the distant crying of a newborn child. The echo mingled with a woman's mourning song.

The echo faded. Cecily covered her face with her hands. Her cheeks flamed feverishly as her icy fingertips slid over them. She drew a deep, cleansing breath and realized that Grandma Emma was staring at her curiously.

"You look whiter than you did when you first came in," the old woman told her. "It was a bad time, but it happened a long time ago."

Cecily brought her hands down slowly. Feeling a little light-headed, she thought she probably needed some breakfast. She swallowed hard. "Who found the baby?" she asked.

"My grandfather, Henry LaPointe. He came along way after it was all over, him and some other Indians. They quick got a wagon and took some of the wounded away. He found Marcus when the baby raised up a big shriek. He saw that my grandmother's good friend was dead, so he went looking for her husband. The wounded were taken to a church. My grandfather said that his wife's brother would not want to die in that place, and so he took Whirlwind Rider and his son home to my grandmother.

"That night Tunkaśila put a blanket of snow over the bodies, and after three days the soldiers made a big grave on the hill where the big guns had been, and they put all the frozen bodies in there together.

"I can't say whether they ever saw that she was white. If they did, they never told no one. But I can say that Marcus knew. He said that his mother was sure proof that there were some good white people back then." She laid her hand on the journal and gave Cecily a warm smile. "I always remember him saying that."

"I'm glad."

"And I remember when Marcus returned from the war. His father gave a feed and told of the coups his son had counted against the enemy. 'My son brings honor to his people, and he is the image of his mother's courage,' he said. Whirlwind Rider was a proud man that day."

"Ezra said that Marcus became a teacher?"

"That was later. He married an Oglala woman who had gone away to boarding school. They were both teachers. Not many Indian teachers back then. I remember wishing old Whirlwind Rider could have lived to see his son become a teacher, like his mother was."

"It sounds as though Marcus took after both of them." And in many ways, Kiah did, too. "Kiah believes that he's a full-blood."

"His mother enrolled him at Standing Rock as a full-blood—half Oglala, half Hunkpapa. They make rules; they change rules. Nowadays he could only be enrolled as half Standing Rock Sioux, but he is more than half Indian." When she lifted her chin, the old woman had the look of teacher, mother, matriarch. "Who is he in his heart?" she asked instructively.

"He's Kiah Red Thunder. He's the son of many people— Toby and Rebecca, Whirlwind Rider and Priscilla, Marcus, Moses . . ." Cecily's eyes were soft with the tenderness she felt for the man he was. "Who else could claim a piece of him, Grandma?"

"You, maybe. How long have you loved him?"

"I've loved him"—she, too, lifted her chin and gave a nod—"for a very long time."

"Have you told him this?"

"No." Not lately, anyway. "I'm afraid . . . I don't know how he feels about . . . me."

"I think my grandmother's friend brought you here." She patted the journal. "Through this book, maybe."

"I'm not sure I believe in ghosts," Cecily said quietly. "And, anyway, I came here before I read the journal. Twice I came here, and twice I left thinking, He cares about me, but not enough." She pressed her lips together tightly and shook her head. "Not enough to ask me to be part of his life."

"But now you have read this book, and you have come to him a third time, granddaughter. We have many circles in our lives, but the one that is most sacred is too big for us to see with our small eyes and too old for us to know in our short lives.

"I don't speak to you of ghosts," the old woman said, tapping a finger on the journal's leather cover. "You are a reader of books, and this book is speaking to you from another part of the circle. Maybe you should read it once more."

Chapter 23

Kiah figured Cecily hadn't gone far, but she'd been gone too long for his comfort. It occurred to him that she might have gone exploring and gotten lost. He had one or two ideas about where he might find her, but he had to break down and ask Lawrence Crow Foot for a ride. Then, of course, he had to take some teasing when Lawrence announced that Kiah's woman had run off on him and taken his pickup. Kiah found that he didn't mind it much. Being teased about a woman could be damn embarrassing, unless it was the right woman. Then it seemed to feel okay.

He wasn't surprised when he spotted his vehicle on the hill at Wounded Knee. He wasn't surprised to find her leaning against the chain-link fence surrounding the long, narrow grave that was outlined with a neat white concrete border. She held the leather-bound journal to her breast, and he wasn't at all surprised to see that her eyes were red or that bits of her hair, tossed by the warm summer breeze, stuck to her damp cheeks.

What surprised him was that she'd never looked more beautiful to him. He liked the idea, even though it scared him almost as much as the earthy smell of this place and the hollow sound of the wind in his ears.

The tall prairie grass rustled against his boots as he trudged up the slope and took up the vigil by her side. They stood together in silence for a time, listening to the

354

double-noted flute song of the meadowlark as they gazed across the fence at the motley array of little stone markers on the far side. Those were the graves of some who had survived to walk the earth awhile longer.

Cecily turned her face into the wind, vaguely directing Kiah's attention just past a scrap of red cloth that had been tied to the chain-link fence by an anonymous prayer-giver in the traditional way. "There's a small white headstone over there that says Whirlwind Rider," she said. "It appears to mark several graves."

He nodded. The wind burned his face and made his eyes sting. He'd driven the road past this place many times, but he hadn't stopped. He thought about the time he had just spent in the sweat lodge and how hard it had been to perform the simple act of opening his mind to whatever was there for him, outside or inside. It had taken him a while. The effort had consumed him, left him breathless. He wasn't even sure he had made a good job of it, but he knew he had at least made a start.

"She's here, though," Cecily said, indicating the elongated plot. "They put her in this trench with the others who were murdered here."

"My great-grandmother?" Awareness seemed to be pummeling him from all sides lately. Just when he got his wind back, he got hit again.

Cecily nodded toward the tall monument that marked the mass grave. "Mrs. Whirlwind Rider is the way she's listed there. The survivors themselves raised the money to put up this memorial in 1903. Her husband was still alive then, a survivor also."

"The woman who wrote the journal was my great-grandmother," Kiah acknowledged at last. "Which makes me part . . . white."

"Do you mind?"

"I don't know." He extended his hand slowly, touching the journal like a tentative suitor. "I really like the woman who wrote this. I mean, when I read it, I thought, This lady was one hell of a beautiful woman."

"Your great-grandfather thought so, too."

"I guess it doesn't matter about her being white,

except . . ." He shrugged. "I always thought I was a full-blood." He turned the term over in his mind, then chuckled at the irony. "Although I can remember a time when I wished I wasn't."

"I hope that time didn't have anything to do with me."

"No." With the back of one finger he traced the soft curve of her chin. "It never seemed to matter to you, but in the back of my mind I had this idea that it might be a problem."

"For me?"

"For us." He turned back to the fence, gripping sun-warmed steel pipe in both hands. "If we ever . . ."

"If we ever *really* got together?"

He glanced at her and nodded sheepishly.

"I went to see Grandma Emma this morning. She told me how Priscilla came to be here in this grave with all those who were shot down that day." She tucked her hand in the crook of his elbow, as if to comfort him for a loss he had just sustained. "You have to let her tell you the story, Kiah."

"I'd rather hear it from you," he said in a husky voice. "I have a feeling you know this great-grandmother of mine pretty well."

"She asked me if I loved you." His arm stiffened beneath her hand, but she pressed on. "Grandma Emma did, straight out. And I told her straight out"—she waited until his eyes met hers—"that I do. I wanted to tell you, but you said you didn't want to hear it. I should have told you anyway, straight out."

"I didn't know what you were going to say."

"You can't know unless you let a person *say* it. You let other people tell you all kinds of stuff. So I'm telling you here and now, right in front of all your ghosts—"

"Jesus," he muttered as he pulled her against his chest, trapping her arm and the precious journal between them. "Jesus, honey, be careful how you talk."

"Do they scare you?"

"Not as much as you do."

"Why? Because I love you?" Silence. She took a deep breath. "You're a big boy now. You can handle it."

Not if she left again, he couldn't. Not if he asked her to stay, and she turned him down.

"I'm sorry I was gone so long," he told her, holding her close. "When I came back and found you gone, I felt kind of funny. I knew you wouldn't just run off, but . . . well, you weren't there." He laid his cheek against her wind-tossed hair and closed his eyes for a moment. "Kinda scared me a little bit."

"You said you didn't want to come up here, so I decided to come by myself," she explained. "How was the sweat?"

"Good," he said lightly, but he could tell she wasn't going to let him off that easily. "You don't talk about the things that were said inside."

"I just wondered if it helped."

"Yeah, it did. It was hard to be there at first. I was half hoping for some kind of revelation, half afraid I'd hear Ellen's voice, or maybe some guy's . . . like maybe Whirlwind Rider's." He tried to laugh, but he couldn't quite pull it off. "Anyway, nothing that dramatic happened."

"But it helped," she reflected.

"I felt clean when I came out. I felt like I really had a clear head. My brain wasn't all cluttered up with ifs, ands, and buts."

She leaned back and offered a sympathetic smile. "Now I suppose I've cluttered it up again."

He feigned a little self-scrutiny with an exaggerated furrowing of his brow. "Nope. Still pretty clear." Again he pressed her head to his chest. "My heart's thumpin' pretty hard, though. Can you hear it?"

She nodded, her ear rubbing against his shirt buttons.

"Let's go back to the Hills this afternoon," he suggested eagerly. "I feel like spending another night up there. How about you?"

They spent the rest of the morning at the powwow, then took their leave in the heat of the afternoon and drove back to the cabin. It was cooler there, and quieter. Without discussion they undressed each other, went to bed together, and made love. Then she told him about her talk with Grandma Emma. He envied her the experience she'd had listening, envisioning, all the blanks somehow filling in with amazing images that would not, need not be explained.

"I sent in the first part of my story," she told him after they'd shared a long silence. "They don't like the way it's going. There are certain words they expect me to include."

"Like what? Plight? Poverty? Pitiful people, those Sioux." He sighed. "Am I leaving anything out?"

"Pathos," she added to his list of *P*'s, but then, more soberly, "Mismanagement."

"Ah," he said as he turned on his side, facing her. "They want you to uncover a little corruption, maybe."

"I think just plain ineptitude would do." She stared at the rustic rafters. "I think I'm supposed to come to the conclusion that all the good Indian leaders died out with Red Cloud and Spotted Tail."

"And there's not a single noble savage left, huh?" He pulled her into his arms, turning her back to him and fitting his knees into the hollows of hers as he lamented, "What a shame. No wonder even God can't help the poor bastards. He only helps those who help themselves." He took a breast in each hand. "To whatever they can grab."

"Ummm, dare I mention . . ."

"Did I forget to say grace? I'm sorry. *God help me. I'm about to help myself.*" He nuzzled the side of her neck and gently squeezed his prize catches. "I'm pretty picky about what I grab, but I really like these."

"Do I get to grab, too?" Twisting a little to reach back, she slipped her hand between his thighs and cupped his velvety sac in her palm. "I like these."

"As long as we're gentle, huh?" He groaned, gratified. Ordinarily he would have found some casual way to deflect such free and intimate access, but this was a woman he was learning to trust. And admire. And cherish.

"Damn, you've always been full of surprises, you know that? The first time I met you, I thought, This girl's too good to be true. She's too sweet. Too innocent. Her eyes are too damn pretty. I wonder how far she'll let me go before she backs out."

"I surprised us both," she recalled.

"Like Christmas morning, only I never got much at Christmas, so I didn't quite know what to make of a gift like"—behind her back he christened her sweet favor with a wistful smile—"what you gave me."

"And you found out I wasn't all that good." Petulantly she slid away.

"You were still just as good, college girl, but you weren't all that smart. A smart girl knows better than to trust a smart-ass cowboy."

"They don't teach that in college."

"They should." He pulled her back into his arms, face to face this time. "I'm lucky they don't. When you came back the second time, you were like some kind of an angel. I didn't have anything much to offer you. It was like I had this godawful ulcer festering in my gut, and all I knew was that you made it hurt less. I wanted you to stay and heal me."

"You didn't ask me to."

"I've never been one to interfere with a person's education. In fact, I like to think I contributed a little to yours."

She smiled, but only a little. "Do all smart-ass cowboys have such colossal egos?"

"Only on the outside. Very fragile on the inside. Want me to show you how to really get the best of one of my fragile places?"

Her smile turned lascivious as she reached between his legs again and found it for herself.

"Mmm, that's right, you've had that lesson already." He guided her hand from the root of his shaft to the tip. "But now come up to the head of the class like this and get me ready to duck inside the coatroom again."

"You're so much fun to play with," she teased unmercifully, and her touch rendered him happily helpless.

Much later they went out for supper, and when they came back, they took their evening walk. Early in the morning they would have to leave. Neither of them relished the thought. Arms behind each other's backs, thumbs tucked in the waistbands of each other's jeans, they strolled along a wide tree-lined path as the light of sunset turned to dusk.

"Having you with me is like trapping a firefly," Kiah mused, waxing frankly poetic. "You fill me with a warm glow, but when I open my hand, you fly away. Off to school. 'One can never have too much education,' " he said, echoing her with gentle sarcasm.

She responded with a challenge. "Do you want me to stay, Kiah? It would help if you would tell me. *Something.*"

"I'll tell you a big secret," he parried cleverly. "Something I never tell anyone. I'll tell you my name."

"Your secret name that ensures long life if you *don't tell anyone?*"

"You've been studying up on the old ways?" He chuckled and shook his head. "No, this is my *real* name. The one that isn't in print anywhere except my birth certificate and the papers Moses Red Thunder signed when he adopted me."

"You mean Hezekiah?"

He looked down at her, scowling. "Who told you?"

"I figured it out. You said it was from the Bible." She offered a smug smile. "That is one of your fragile parts, isn't it?" And then she leaned closer and whispered, "Like holding your balls in my hand."

"Exactly. Very touchy."

"So these are the two very sacred trusts you've chosen to bestow upon me."

"Three, counting my name."

"You're still holding out on me." They bumped hips as she tightened her arm around his waist. "And, as you've already so eloquently recounted, I didn't hold out on you."

"You want me to ask you to stay," he reflected carefully. "And I want you to choose. Not in bed, where we're good together because I'm a man and you're a woman. And not now, when it's just you and me and the differences between us don't mean a damn."

"What differences?"

"The differences the rest of the world thinks about when

hey see us together. And maybe some they don't think
about. Some we don't even know about yet."

"I don't care about—"

"I care." He stopped, turned her to him, took her face in
his hands, and made her look at him. "I care because if we
ever *really* get together, as you put it, I think it would be
nice to *stay* together. Like . . . like *they* did."

With a sigh, he scanned the evening sky. An early star
had appeared. "My great-grandmother made a choice that
cut her off from much of what was familiar to her. It
wasn't going to be easy, and she wasn't going to be safe,
so Whirlwind Rider didn't ask her to stay. He asked her to
choose." He looked down at her, plumbing the depths of
her soul through her eyes. "You think about it."

"I want to know what you think. Do you think she made
a mistake?"

"She made at least one mistake," he said. "She sent her
journal to the wrong man, and it never saw the light of day
until you found it. I'd hate to see you make the same mistake."

"Nobody's going to bury my story." It was her turn to
turn fierce eyes on him. "Nobody's going to tell me what
to write, either. Not even you. *Especially* not you."

"That's good. That's the way it should be. Tell it
straight out."

"Right. Like you ever would." She glanced away. "So
do you think Priscilla was another college girl who didn't
make very *smart* choices?" Then in a rush she added,
'You're talking about making choices, and I don't want to
make a fool of myself a third time."

"I never thought you were a fool. Never."

"You thought I was too good to be true."

"Yeah. But, see, that's *my* problem, not yours." He put
his arm around her, sheltering her from the cool evening
breeze. Softly he slid his hand underneath her hair and
rested it at the base of her neck. "And the other problem
is, I know it's true that I'm not all that good."

"Good in what sense?"

"Any sense." He laughed. "Here I've just found out I'm
not all Indian. I've got some soft spots, kind of a senti-

mental streak. Scared of ghosts. I'm not even sure I was ever such a goddamn kick-ass cowboy."

"That sounds like one hell of a plight."

"Yeah, well, don't quote me. That's strictly off the record." His fingers stirred against her nape. "And I'll tell you something else that's just between us." With a warm smile he confided, "I love you, too."

Chapter 24

After Cecily filed her second story she had another phone conversation with Harold Severson. When he told her she still needed to do some digging, she took a deep breath and shifted the receiver to the other ear.

"Just what do you think you know about all this, Harold?"

"I know there's a bill before a congressional committee right now that would return the federal lands in the Black Hills to the Indians, and some people think there might be enough bleeding hearts in Congress to get it passed. Obviously they're not from around here."

"Not from any of the states where the constituencies feel threatened by treaty rights."

"That's right," Harold barked, then shifted into more of an unctuous whine. "I mean, it's a shame the way things worked out for the Indians, but what's done is done. Imagine giving them even part of the Black Hills back. What a mess that would be."

"A mess? You mean they'd mess up the landscape somehow?"

"I mean, it would be a mess. That's a national treasure, for crissake. We're not interested in any sentimental story about the passing of the old ways. We're interested in the truth about tribal politics. We know there's a lack of good leadership. Remember all that stuff back in the seventies?

Trouble from here to Texas. Protests. Shootings. Hell, you said you were there. And who got hurt? The Indian people themselves."

"I guess you should know."

"Me? Hell, I didn't have anything to do with it, but I read, and I saw all that stuff on TV. We need to show why, you know, *why* all the statistics on these people are so depressing."

"You want depressing," she repeated.

"You know, suicide, alcoholism, all that stuff. They're always arguing among themselves."

"That can be a problem, yes, but they don't like to make decisions for each other. They generally take the time to let everyone have a say."

"Yeah, meanwhile what happens? Time marches on, right?"

"Or what goes around comes around, depending on your philosophy."

"I'm not talking philosophy, I'm talking the way things are. We tell our readers the way things really are." There was a brief pause. "Are they gonna take the money or what?"

"That might be considered at today's council meeting."

"Considered or decided? When will they *decide?*" He paused, not so much to allow for an answer as to light up another cigarette.

Cecily had no answer, and even if she did, she decided then and there that she wouldn't have entrusted it to Harold. Like her story, it would have been wasted on him.

"What do you think they'll do with the money?" he asked finally. "Piss it away? Any chance they'll put it to good use? They're getting a lot of suggestions, right?"

"There seems to be no shortage of suggestions."

"Well, look, in your next version of this thing, let's get some local color. You know, you can't leave out the drunks. You can't leave out the poor little kids. You've gotta *show* that stuff because that's what people—"

"That's what people expect," she finished for him. "*You* give them what they expect, Harold. I'd rather give them surprises."

"What kind of surprises?"

"Anything that's not a stereotype is usually a surprise. Sometimes it's even a *pleasant* surprise. You think the readers could stand that, Harold?"

"Oh, come on, Cecily, you know I don't promote stereotypes, and I don't have any biases. I just—"

"I've decided not to let you publish my story, Harold. Send it back."

"What?"

"I still have some work to do on it, and it might take me a while to do it right. Send it back, Harold. It's my story."

Cecily was laughing when she hung up the phone. It was so much fun to be full of surprises.

The Tribal Council chambers were packed. The councilmen sat at a U-shaped arrangement of wooden tables, facing a gallery of their constituents who were seated on folding chairs or standing against the walls. There were a couple of clutches of people who could easily be identified as visitors to the reservation, partly because they were non-Indians and partly because they were dressed like dudes—either in white shirts and ties, pantyhose and high heels, or brand-spanking-new urban cowboy outfits.

For her own part, Cecily had put on a pair of slacks and a blouse and staked out a corner with a view.

The meeting began with a discussion of a feasibility study for a gambling operation, done by the non-Indian management company proposing to run the business. After that came the plan for a restaurant, culture and art center to be built at the edge of the reservation, across the river from nowhere. It would, some believed, *become* somewhere once the enterprise took hold.

Cecily took copious notes, even as the more mundane community concerns were discussed. With each order of business, the Black Hills award was mentioned as a corollary, but not as a focus of discussion. It simply hovered in the air like a hot-air balloon. Eventually someone would have to climb into the basket to test it out.

Finally Kiah rose to speak.

"These are interesting proposals," he said as he pushed

his chair under the table. "It's good to hear about these things, good of you people to take the time to put these ideas together and present them to us. I've heard all kinds of interesting ideas over the last few months, and it's given me a lot to think about." He gestured inclusively. "All of us, we've been hearing ideas and concerns, requests—even some accusations, but I think those are a little premature. We haven't squandered anything yet, have we?"

He paused for a round of chuckles. Here and there among the spectators, one head merged with another for quick, whispered commentary.

"What I have to say is this. I've never been a traditional man myself, but I was raised by traditional people. I never tried to speak up for Indian civil rights, but my sister gave her life as an activist for her people. I carried a weapon as a warrior, but that doesn't make me a leader. An Indian leader is a spiritual man who understands what it is that makes us who we are—what's important to us, what we value most.

"For one thing, we value listening to people," he said, addressing the group of enterprising non-Indians. "People like you, who come to us with these good ideas." He nodded toward another part of the room, where a small group had pulled their chairs into a semicircle. "People like John Iron Road, who says he doesn't like the way they're running the detox center. People like Mavis Charger, who says we need more aides in the Head Start program so the kids get more individual attention. And people like Ezra Hairy Chin and one of my grandmas down at Pine Ridge—the ones who remember. The memories of the old ones connect us to the time when it seemed easier to define ourselves as a people by what we believed. We must always take time to listen to our elders. They can help us clear our minds.

"I am seeing now that there are some things that money does not change. I understand that the money is supposed to be 'just compensation' for the taking of the Hills. But I also understand that there is no such thing. No earthly thing—no bullets, no congress, no court—can change what has always been true. We don't own the land. We are *one with it.* It is not so much that the Black Hills belong to the Lakota people as that the Lakota belong to Paha Sapa.

"I believe we must walk away from this so-called award because it makes no sense in the context of our life as Lakota people. More and more we are seeking direction for our lives in the old way because so many of the new ways have proven unsatisfying. More and more we remember that the things we value cannot be bought and sold. The non-Indian world wants something from us. They're not sure what it is, and we've almost forgotten. The truth is, it's something no one can buy or steal from us. It lives as long as we survive. And we've always been willing to share.

"The court says that what was done was wrong. This is not a purchase or a settlement; it is an award for damages. It is guilt money. But it can't make things right. Treating people honorably and with respect is what makes things right. Maybe in time the government will do what's right, but since Paha Sapa and the Lakota have been around for a long time, I guess there's no hurry.

"In the meantime, let's see if any of these people with good ideas will still be willing to work with us if we tell them that we have no hundred million dollars, but we've got other things going for us. We've got the Indian Self-Determination Act, so they're not trying to terminate us anymore."

There was a round of chuckles over Kiah's sardonic reference to the government's aborted attempt to terminate Indian reservations.

"We're building houses, roads, putting in water and sewers. We've started our own community college." He smiled and offered the visitors an openhanded gesture. "And we *do* have a treaty with the United States government. That should be worth something, don't you think?"

"That is all I have to say. *Mitakuye oyasin,*" he said, closing traditionally by paying respect to "all my relatives."

His speech was well-received, with some symbolic drumming around the table and a chorus of *"hau hau."* Kiah moved that the council draft a resolution to refuse the monetary award for damages and to assert the Lakota' long-standing claim to the Black Hills by right of the 186 treaty. His motion was unanimously approved.

Before he'd made the break for the great outdoors Kiah had managed to mooch a cigarette from one of the glad handers. Cecily seemed to be engrossed in a conversation with the council chairman, and Kiah needed some space. He caught her attention across the room, pointed to the back door, got a quick nod from her, and left. Then he strolled down to the river bluff and plunked himself in the grass a few feet away from the Standing Rock monument.

He'd just struck a match when he heard footsteps at his back. He lit up quickly. He was already acting like a husband, and he didn't even know whether he was going to ask her yet. He wanted to see what she had to say first.

"That was a kick-ass speech you gave in there," she said proudly as she sat down next to him. "I have a feeling it doesn't have anything to do with being a cowboy."

"It has to do with being an Indian." He blew a quick stream of smoke—the first he'd had in months—then turned, squinting into the sun. "We love to speechify. Bet you didn't know that."

"I'm learning." She gazed across the river at the bluffs on the opposite side. "What do you really think your chances are of getting the Black Hills back?"

"If we ever open a casino, the odds on that bet will be the longest of the long shots. It's a grand and noble pipe dream." He chuckled and added, "For hopeful romantics."

He draped his arms atop his knees, looked out over the river, and indulged himself in another puff of smoke and some wishful thinking. "The Lakota have always respected the pipe, which explains the beauty of pipe dreams. They seem to keep us going."

She plucked a tuft of gama grass. "I've quit my job."

"Really? I saw you taking notes. What's going to happen to your story?"

"One way or another, I'll see that it gets told." She rubbed the stem between her thumb and forefinger as she spoke. "I've applied for a teaching job at the Indian community college. Maybe one of my students will tell the story better than I could." She risked a glance at him. "Or maybe I'll tell it myself some other way. I'll keep writing. I'd like to help with the newspaper here." She shrugged. "A person doesn't have to be a cowboy to be a jack-of-all-trades."

"Be careful you don't end up a master of none," he warned as he ground his cigarette out on the bottom of his boot and flicked it away.

"Who wants to be a master? I'll be the master of myself, huh? That's enough. Oh, Kiah, look." She shoved the prairie grass under his nose, twirling it to make the grainy heads dance. "It has four heads."

He tipped his hat back and examined her find, sliding his hand firmly over hers. "So it has. Good lovin' guaranteed to the woman who finds one of these."

"That settles it. Job or no job, I've decided to stay."

"With me?" He squeezed her hand. "I mean, let me rephrase that, as long as you've decided. If you choose to stay here, then will you be with me?"

"In the man and woman sense, for all the world to see?" she asked, dazzling him with her wide-eyed smile.

His smile was in his eyes. "In the husband and wife sense, for the world to just go figure."

Author's Note

Although *Fire and Rain* is a work of fiction, I have made every attempt to portray historical people and events accurately. To my knowledge, no white woman died at Wounded Knee, but I do believe that a piece of the American dream of freedom and justice for all was martyred there. I hope we will resurrect it somehow, someday. All contemporary characters are fictitious, but that aspect of the story was inspired in part by real events and circumstances as I observed them when I lived and worked at Standing Rock in the 1970s and 1980s. The Black Hills claim remains a controversial issue. To this day, none of the Lakota Sioux tribes has accepted any part of the Court of Claims monetary award, and the judgment fund continues to accumulate interest. Should the reader wish to learn more about the background of *Fire and Rain,* here are a few of the many sources I found useful in my research: *The Sioux: Life and Customs of a Warrior Society* by Royal B. Hassrick; *Crazy Horse: The Strange Man of the Oglalas,* a biography by Mari Sandoz; *The Mystic Warriors of the Plains* by Thomas E. Mails; *Wounded Knee: Lest We Forget,* edited by Alvin M. Josephy, Jr., Trudy Thomas, and Jeanne Eder; *The Wounded Knee Massacre From the Viewpoint of the Sioux* by James H. McGregor; *Black Hills/White Justice: The Sioux Nation Versus the United States 1775 to the Present* by Edward Lazarus; *Lakota-English Dictionary* by Eugene Buechel.

Lakota Words Used
in Fire and Rain

akicita - warrior society (each society had its special function in policing within the society as well as defending the group)

ate - father

cinca - baby

cinks - my son

ciyotanka - flute

eceś ŧuwale! - no way! (traditionally used only by women, it has become a catch-all expression)

gigi - ghost

hi ye - much like *amen*

hoka hey, heya hey - listen up, hear me; also indicates approval

hopo! - all right! (a man's interjection)

hau - greeting; also agreement

hau hau - expression of agreement, confirmation

inipi - purification ceremony performed in sweat lodge; often called "the sweat" in contemporary language

kinnikinnik - tobacco; traditionally it was a mixture of bark shavings

kola - friend

lila wašte - very good

mahn! - look here! (a woman's interjection)

misunka - my younger brother

mitakuye oyasin - all my relatives

mitawin - my woman, my wife

nimitawa ktelo - now you will be mine

ŏhan! - yes! (a man's interjection)

ohinniyan - always, forever

ošti! - oh, alas!

Paha Sapa - Black Hills

p̌apa - jerked meat

pejuta wicaša - herbal healer ("medicine man")

pilamaye - thank you

takoja - grandchild

tanke - a man's older sister

tankši - a man's little sister

tiošpaye - extended family, clan

tokala - kit fox; also one of the Lakota warrior societies

ı̆ōkša - pretty soon (pronounced doke-sha)

ı̆ona - how many? (pronounced dona, contemporary adverb meaning much or many, as in "*Tona* people came")

tonška - a man's nephew

tuki! - is that so! (a woman's interjection)

Tunkašila - God; grandfather

wale - expression of disbelief

ci - grandmother

śica - pathetic

akan - holy

akan Tanka - God

amniomni Akanyanka - Whirlwind Rider

anaǧi - ghosts, spirits (*gigi* or *gigi-man* is a more contemporary expression for bogeyman)

aśicun - white man

aśte - good

icaśa - man

iǧopa - pretty woman

inyan - woman

ōjapi - a fruit soup or pudding